Praise for
The Tamir Triad

"Some of the most inventive and emotionally gripping fantasy to come down the pike in years...Flewelling's writing is both intelligent and visceral, with unflinching detail that compels readers to turn pages in wide-eyed fascination....Flewelling takes the stock trappings of the sword-and-sorcery genre and turns them into a riveting epic story that is unique, disturbing, and enthralling."

—*Mythprint*

Praise for
The Oracle's Queen

"A splendidly stirring coming-of-age tale."
—*Romantic Times* (4½ stars)

"A terrific ending to a great fantasy trilogy."
—AlternativeWorlds.com

"It is a great book!"

—*Affaire de Coeur* (4½ stars)

"I've been looking forward to *The Oracle's Queen,* the third volume in the Tamir Triad, with eager anticipation, and it doesn't disappoint....I can recommend it and indeed the whole series to lovers of intelligent contemporary fantasy that nevertheless keeps faith with all the strongest traditions of the genre."
—JULIET E. McKENNA, Emerald City

"This novel delves deeply into the psychological effects of razzle-dazzle magic, thrones, swords, and the rest, and makes for a terrific read....There is never an easy answer in *The Oracle's Queen:* the characters gain so much dimension that they linger in the mind long after one reads the last page. This trilogy is a must for those who love fantasy with all the Good Stuff stitched together by intelligent world-building and a wise eye for the frailties, and the greatnesses, of the human spirit."
—SFsite.com

"A fine conclusion to an above-average series...Flewelling does an excellent job of adding depth and texture to the story of a young person thrust onto the throne of Skala."

—*Contra Costa Times*

"Lynn Flewelling's *The Bone Doll's Twin, Hidden Warrior,* and *The Oracle's Queen* are brilliantly original and moving. This story still haunts me, months after reading the books. There's plenty of gritty realism to make this a book for adults and mature teenagers, but what it definitely is not is 'escapist.' This book drags you through so much emotionally painful territory that you're almost relieved when it's done and you can escape to your safe regular life."

—ORSON SCOTT CARD

Praise for
hidden Warrior

"Stellar high-concept fantasy."

—*Mysterious Galaxy*

"A rousing prince-in-hiding adventure, with some unexpectedly satisfying developments for a middle volume in a series."

—*Locus*

"A beautiful, compelling, dark tale."

—*Booklist*

"A superlative job...the world she has built is complex, and the action nonstop....Flewelling handles the gender questions with such skill that the reader really feels Tobin's ambivalence, and gradual change....Recommended highly for anyone seeking a rollicking good read."

—*SFsite.com*

"Satisfying...intriguing...exploring not merely issues of gender and power but questions of honor as well."

—*Lambda Book Report*

"Lynn Flewelling doesn't disappoint.... Questions of obligation and independence have no easy answers for anyone in this maze, adding a welcome depth to the tale."

—Alien Online

Praise for
The Bone Doll's Twin

"*The Bone Doll's Twin* is a thoroughly engrossing new fantasy. It got its hooks into me on the first page, and didn't let loose until the last. I am already looking forward to the next installment."

—GEORGE R. R. MARTIN

"Lynn Flewelling's *The Bone Doll's Twin* outshines even the gleaming promise shown in her earlier three books. The story pulled me under and carried me off with it in a relentless tale that examines whether the ends can ever completely justify the means."

—ROBIN HOBB

"Fresh and original—and unlike most fantasies that try to put women in traditionally male roles, hers works. I found the world exceptionally well realized and coherent. I think you have a winner here! My congratulations to Lynn. Books like this are too good not to share."

—KATHERINE KURTZ

"[This is] how good books are supposed to make you feel: like you're living in another world, with people you really care about, and you don't want to close the book and go home. If these books hadn't turned out to be excellent, I wouldn't be reviewing them, of course—because I rarely review books I didn't finish, and I rarely finish books that I don't enjoy. I loved these."

—ORSON SCOTT CARD

"*The Bone Doll's Twin* is a great read. Lynn Flewelling has outdone herself with this vibrant tale of dark magic, a hidden child, and the demon ghost that haunts it. She builds a convincing, colorful world with carefully chosen details, and her characters are memorable because their dilemmas are vividly drawn and heartbreakingly believable. This is exactly the kind of fantasy novel that will keep you up long past your bedtime."

—KATE ELLIOTT

"A fascinating read, both intellectual and haunting."

—BARBARA HAMBLY

"A dark and twisting enchantment of a book, a story of deception and loyalty and heroism that will magick its readers along with its characters."

—LOUISE MARLEY

"Flewelling accompanies her skill at storytelling with an exquisite level of detail that brings her entire world to life. A most satisfying tale for readers already familiar with her Nightrunner series—for others, an excellent introduction to the joys of a Flewelling fantasy."

—SHARON SHINN

"You liked Lynn Flewelling's Nightrunner series? This novel is even better. *The Bone Doll's Twin* is a sharply honed, powerful story where good and evil are as entwined as two children's lives, and salvation carries a very high price. Highly recommended."

—ANNE BISHOP

"An intriguing prequel to Flewelling's splendid Nightrunner series and a solid beginning to a new triad of fantasy from a most generous and skilled fantasist, *The Bone Doll's Twin* will satisfy old fans and capture many new."

—PATRICK O'LEARY

"Masterful . . . readers will be hooked."

—*Bangor Daily News*

"Magnificent, impressive . . . capture[s] some of the same flavor found in T. H. White's classic, *The Once and Future King*, as well as in Ursula Le Guin's Earthsea books. Factor in some essence of Mervyn Peake, and you have a winning combination."

—*Realms of Fantasy*

"Flewelling's Nightrunner books are popular among fantasy fans for a very simple reason—they're good. *The Bone Doll's Twin* continues that trend, and I look for her to be a major force in the future of fantasy."

—*Monroe (LA) News-Star*

Praise for the Nightrunner Series
Luck in the Shadows

"Memorable characters, an enthralling plot, and truly daunting evil...The characters spring forth from the page not as well-crafted creations but as people....The magic is refreshingly difficult, mysterious, and unpredictable. Lynn Flewelling has eschewed the easy shortcuts of clichéd minor characters and cookie-cutter backdrops to present a unique world....I commend this one to your attention."

—ROBIN HOBB

"Part high fantasy and part political intrigue, *Luck in the Shadows* makes a nice change from the usual ruck of contemporary sword-and-sorcery. I especially enjoyed Lynn Flewelling's obvious affection for her characters. At unexpected moments she reveals a well-honed gift for the macabre."

—STEPHEN R. DONALDSON

"A new star is rising in the fantasy firmament....I am awed by the scope of the intricate world....It teems with magic and bustles with realistic people and spine-chilling amounts of skullduggery."

—DAVE DUNCAN

"A splendid read, filled with magic, mystery, adventure, and taut suspense. Lynn Flewelling, bravo! Nicely done."

—DENNIS L. McKIERNAN

"An engrossing and entertaining debut...full of magic, intrigues, and fascinating characters. Witty and charming, it's the kind of book you settle down with when you want a long, satisfying read."

—MICHAEL A. STACKPOLE

"Exceptionally well done and entertaining."

—*Locus*

"Lynn Flewelling has written a terrific first novel, a thrilling introduction to this series....Highly recommended."

—*Starlog*

Stalking Darkness

"Flewelling is...bringing vigor back to the traditional fantasy form. In this highly engaging adventure novel, the most powerful magic is conjured out of friendship and loyalty. The author has a gift for creating characters you genuinely care about."

—TERRI WINDLING, *The Year's Best Fantasy and Horror,*
Eleventh Annual Collection

"Events move forward in this second adventure....It's up to four companions to stop Mardus's schemes. Things get very violent and there's also a strong emotional undercurrent...an amusing twist on the old 'damsel in distress' scenario."

—*Locus*

"While fans...will find enough wizardry, necromancy, swords, daggers, and devilishly clever traps here to satisfy the most avid, this book also provides entry to a complete and richly realized world that will please more mainstream readers."

—*Bangor Daily News*

Traitor's Moon

"What most fantasy aspires to *Traitor's Moon* achieves, with fierce craft, wit and heart. It is a fantasy feast—richly imagined, gracefully wrought and thrilling to behold. An intoxicating brew of strange and homely, horror and whimsy, lust and blood, intrigue and honor, great battles and greater loves. It is a journey through a world so strange and real you can taste it, with companions so mysterious and memorable you won't forget it. Lynn Flewelling is a fine teller of tales who delivers all she promises, cuts no corners and leaves us dazzled, moved and hungry for more. *Traitor's Moon* is a wonderful book."

—PATRICK O'LEARY

"While fans of Dungeons and Dragons–style lore will find enough wizardry, necromancy, swords, daggers, and devilishly clever traps here to satisfy the most avid, this book also provides entry to a complete and richly realized world that will please more mainstream readers."

—*Bangor Daily News*

Shadows Return

LYNN FLEWELLING

BANTAM SPECTRA

SHADOWS RETURN
A Bantam Spectra Book / July 2008

Published by
Bantam Dell
A Division of Random House, Inc.
New York, New York

This is a work of fiction. Names, characters, places, and incidents
either are the product of the author's imagination or are used
fictitiously. Any resemblance to actual persons, living or dead,
events, or locales is entirely coincidental.

Bantam Books and the rooster colophon are registered trademarks
and Spectra and the portrayal of a boxed "s" are trademarks of
Random House, Inc.

ISBN 978-0-553-59008-1

Printed in the United States of America
Published simultaneously in Canada

www.bantamdell.com

OPM 10 9 8 7 6 5 4 3 2 1

This book is dedicated to
Doug, Matt, and Tim, with love, for everything.
And to Nancy Jeffers, my friend, guide, head
cheerleader, and all-around goddess. Long overdue,
babe! Thanks for all your enthusiasm for this
project, and all the others.

Acknowledgments

Special thanks, as always, to all my family and friends, without whom I'd be very lonely. To my tireless agent, Lucienne Diver; my wise editor, Anne Lesley Groell; to the wonderful artist Michael Komarck, and the good folks at Bantam. To my readers, who keep me going. To the amazing folks at the Flewelling Yahoo! Group and my Live Journal who, as always, know far more about my work than I do, and are always there to help and cheer me on. Much appreciated. And a special shout-out to fan artist Mathia, whose rendition of Korathan inspired a nice bit of business.

Map by James Sinclair

City Of Rhíminee

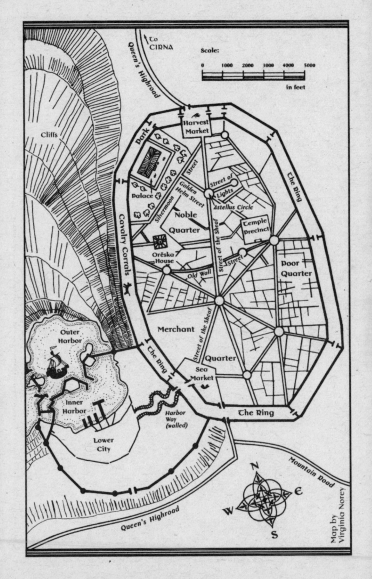

You are the wanderer who carries his home in his heart. You are the bird who makes its nest on the waves. You will father a child of no woman.
　　　　　—words of the Dragon Oracle at Sarikali,
　　　　　　　　to Alec í Amasa of Kerry

CHAPTER 1

The Stag and Otter

SEREGIL BALANCED PRECARIOUSLY atop the shard-lined wall, impatiently scanning the shadowy garden below for his misplaced partner. Alec had been right behind him when he'd shimmied out the library window, or so he'd thought.

Everything about this job had taken too long: finding a way in, finding the right room (for which they'd been given the wrong directions), then finding the stolen brooch in question, the possessor of which—one of the most vicious new blackmailers in Rhíminee—had very wisely kept in a casket with several dozen others. Seregil had to scrutinize each one by a lightstone's glow. If he hadn't been so fond of the young lady whose reputation hung on the success of this night's work, he'd have given up the whole damned mess hours ago.

Dawn was a faint smudge above the rooftops now. A weak but welcome breeze whispered through the yellowing leaves of the garden below. It tugged at the long, stray strands of dark hair clinging, sweat-plastered, to Seregil's forehead. Summer's heat was lingering into early autumn this year. His thin linen shirt was soaked through and rank under the arms. The swath of black silk across his lower face was sticking to his lips. He just wanted to go home to a bath and clean cool sheets...

Yet there was still no sign of Alec.

"Hey! Where are you?" he called softly. He was about to risk calling out again when he heard a muttered curse from the shadow of a pear tree near the house.

"I dropped it," Alec hissed, still out of sight.

"Oh, please tell me you're joking!" Seregil whispered back.

"Shh! They'll hear you."

The telltale scrape of iron against stone came from the nearby kitchen as some early-rising servant stirred up banked coals on a hearth.

Seregil climbed down the lime tree they'd used for a ladder, with every intention of collaring Alec and dragging him away—by force if need be.

The younger man's dark clothing made him all but invisible in the shadows, except for his blond braid. He'd pulled off his head scarf somewhere along the way and his hair gleamed tellingly over one shoulder as he scrabbled about on hands and knees, searching frantically in the grass.

"Leave it!"

Stubborn as always, Alec crawled back toward the house instead, frantically brushing his hands over the clipped turf. Seregil was reaching for Alec's braid when the sound of a door opening sent them both flat on their bellies. Neither breathed as a young servant trudged by with reeking pails of night soil, passing within a few feet of where they lay.

As soon as he was gone, Alec was on his feet, pulling Seregil up. "Found it! Come on."

"*Now* you're in a hurry?"

They ran for the tree. Seregil, the better climber, laced his fingers together and gave Alec a one-footed boost up into the lowest branches. Before he could follow, however, he heard a startled gasp behind him. Turning, he found the servant staring straight at him, empty pails on the ground at his feet. They stood eye-locked for an instant, then the child found his voice and shrieked, "Robbers! Mistress Hobb, loose the dogs!"

Seregil scarcely felt the rough bark of the tree as he launched himself up. He hadn't once been known as the Rhíminee Cat for nothing. In his haste, he was careless, though, and sliced his hand open on one of the pottery shards set into the top of the wall. Ignoring the pain, he vaulted over and landed in a crouch on the pavement beside Alec. As they sprinted away, two enormous mastiffs came pelting out through a side gate, and several men with them, armed with cudgels.

"Do it!" Alec hissed, eyes wide above his mask. "Do the dog thing!"

"I'd have to *stop* first, wouldn't I?" Seregil panted, trying to staunch his bloody hand in his shirttail as he ran. "Follow me."

The Temple District was not the sort of

neighborhood in which masked men being pursued by large dogs went unremarked upon, even at this hour. The Scavenger crews were already at work, and Seregil collided with one of them as he rounded the corner into Long Yew Street. He kept his feet but had to roll awkwardly across the top of her stinking barrow, coming eye to eye with a rotting dog in the process.

"I'll have the Watch on you, you bastards!" she screeched after them as they pelted on.

And all the while, their enemy the sun was rising, and the dogs were gaining.

Seregil caught Alec's arm and steered him down a side street lined with shops. Alec pulled away hastily.

"Bilairy's Balls, you stink!"

Seregil thought that certainly summed up their night's work.

At the far end of this street, a wall screened the sacred grove behind the temple of Dalna.

"Up," he ordered, making a stirrup of his hands again.

He winced as Alec thrust a dirty boot against his wounded palm and jumped. Making the top of the wall, Alec reached down to Seregil, but once again, it was too late. The dogs came boiling up, snarling and slavering.

Cornered, Seregil thrust out his bloody left hand, first and little finger extended and turned it like a key in a lock. "Soora thalassi!"

It was a minor spell, and one of the very few he'd ever been able to reliably accomplish. But this one always worked, and he'd probably done it thousands of times over the years. All the same, he held his breath as the dogs skidded to a halt. The larger of the two sniffed at him curiously, then wagged her tail. Seregil gave them both a pat on the head and waved them off.

Judging by the outcry close behind, though, their masters hadn't given up yet. With Alec's help, Seregil scrambled quickly up the rough stonework. They dropped over the other side and collapsed, panting, with their heads between their knees. It was still dark and cool in the beech grove. Overhead, the fading leaves rattled soothingly in the breeze. A small shrine stood nearby, and a broad path led in the direction of the temple.

Seregil breathed the fragrant, herb-scented air and willed his heart to stop pounding. A few of the brown temple doves fluttered down to join them, cooing eagerly for a handout. On the other side of the wall, he heard their pursuers pound by, cursing the dogs and still thinking their quarry somewhere ahead.

"Cut that a bit close, didn't we?" Alec pulled off his sweat-soaked mask and used it to bind Seregil's hand.

The salt stung the raw skin and Seregil winced. "We're going soft. Too much larking about. So, how the hell did you drop the thing?"

Alec pulled the brooch from inside his shirt. It was a delicate piece; a tiny crescent set with pearls. "It's so small. I was trying to put it somewhere safe, so I wouldn't—"

"Drop it?"

Before Alec could defend himself, a high-pitched voice called out, "You there! What do you think you're doing? This is sacred ground!"

Seregil stood up, scattering the doves. A half-grown acolyte came hurrying toward them, his short brown robe whipping around his skinny legs.

It was force of habit, more than anything, that made Alec and Seregil both head for the wall. Before he could find purchase, however, Seregil felt something like an attack of bees shoot through the backs of his legs, cramping his muscles and halting him in his tracks. Alec let out a yelp and whirled around, slapping at his thighs and buttocks.

"Peace, brother," Seregil gritted out as he faced down the outraged Dalnan. "We mean no harm."

"Lord Seregil? Lord Alec?" The boy made them a hasty bow. "Forgive me! I didn't realize you were here. There was an outcry just now and I took you for the thieves."

"I guess you startled us as much as we did you," Alec replied, with the full force of the country-bred guilelessness "Lord Alec" was known for.

Seregil smothered a grin as the acolyte laughed. Being a *ya'shel*—a half-breed—Alec still looked deceptively boyish at twenty. Somehow, all the evil and hardship he'd seen in his short life, most of it since meeting Seregil, had not dimmed his innocent glow. With those dark blue eyes and that golden hair, he could charm man or woman, old or young, with no more than a smile and few well-chosen words.

"I'm afraid we came straight on from the Lower City," Seregil said, feigning chagrin as he brushed a hand over his questionable attire. "My friend here is in need of some spiritual solace, after the drubbing we took at the gaming houses. Lost the coats off our backs, as you can see, and saw a bit of fighting."

"But what are you doing way back here?" asked the boy.

"Praying," Alec replied quickly. "I wanted to see Valerius, but it's so early I thought I'd meditate a bit until he was up."

"Of course, my lord. I hope you'll pardon my interruption. I'll tell him you're here."

Seregil watched him go, then raised an eyebrow at Alec. "You just lied to a priest."

"So did you."

"*I* lie to everyone. You're the good Dalnan boy."

"I haven't been a good Dalnan boy since I met you. All the same . . ." Alec went to the shrine and softly sang some prayer, the picture of piety.

Seregil left him to it, steeling himself to face Valerius. He and the priest had both been Watchers, and had worked together many times over the years, but Seregil's gut still tightened as he caught sight of the man striding toward them, his black beard and eyebrows noticeably bristling.

Valerius had been the high priest of Dalna in Rhíminee for four years now, but it hadn't smoothed his temper. He went straight for Alec and gave him a sharp cuff on the ear.

"That's for lying inside the precinct, you whelp!"

"Ow! Sorry," Alec said humbly, clasping the side of his head.

Valerius knew better than to raise a hand to

Seregil, but his expression was enough to make the smaller man take a step back. "All the barking and yelling that just disturbed my morning meditation would be your doing, I take it?"

"All in a good cause."

Valerius snorted and folded his arms across his broad chest. A northerner like Alec, he was half a head taller than either of them and built like a mountain bear.

And just as ill-tempered, Seregil reflected sourly. *Considerably more dangerous, too, even in a good mood.*

"Well, I suppose that's better than what Brother Myus thought he caught you two at."

"I wouldn't!" Alec gasped, going red to the ears. "Not here."

Valerius gave him another disapproving look. The truth was he liked Alec and had always blamed Seregil for what he deemed the young man's fall into bad ways. In the eyes of most of Rhíminee society, Alec was a minor noble of no consequence beyond his somewhat scandalous association with the dissolute and clever Lord Seregil. The fact that he'd first been introduced to society as Seregil's ward only added to the gossip. But in Rhíminee, of course, that was generally a plus.

"So you're still up to your old tricks?" Valerius rumbled as they walked back toward the temple.

"Not much else to do, these days," Seregil replied. "With Thero still in Aurënen, there's been no—" He waved a hand casually, thumb hooked over the top of his third finger: the sign for *Watcher business.*

Valerius paused near the portico and lowered his voice. "And Phoria still hasn't summoned you? It's been well over a year now, hasn't it? After what the two of you accomplished for Skala in Aurënen, I should think she'd want you with her spies."

"Then you don't know Phoria," Seregil muttered.

"We hope to see her when she returns from the front," Alec told him, anxious to change the subject. "Duke Tornus wrote to her on our behalf, offering our services again."

"Ah, yes. Will you be sitting with the Royal Kin for the Progress?"

Seregil gave him a wry look. "We haven't received our invitation yet."

Acolytes were spreading the morning crumbs for the doves in the temple courtyard. A few birds fluttered up at their approach, and one landed on Alec's shoulder. He offered it a finger and it perched there, preening.

Seregil grinned at Valerius. "See? Your Maker still loves him, even with me around."

"Perhaps," Valerius muttered.

Seregil regretted his choice of hiding place. Valerius's jibes about Alec still struck more deeply than Seregil liked to admit.

Friend, partner in their precarious secret business, and *talimenios*—there was no proper translation for all that encompassed, or the deep bond of heart and body he and Alec shared. Seregil had taught him guile and all the tricks of the nightrunner trade, but at heart Alec was still the honest woodsman he'd found in that northern cell, and for that Seregil would always be grateful. Loving Alec made him feel almost clean again, himself.

Valerius lent them light cloaks and they set off for the Stag and Otter to change clothes.

"Well, that could have gone better, but at least we got what we went for. That's the most fun we've had in ages!" Alec flipped the brooch up in the air.

Seregil snatched it in midair and shoved it into his purse. "Are you trying to drop it again?"

"I found it, didn't I?" Alec teased, determined not to let Seregil sink into one of his moods. "Admit it. That was fun!"

"Fun?"

"Well, more fun than moping around Wheel Street, or at some noble's salon."

"And when have we been doing that? I'm quite out of fashion at court these days, along with most things Aurënfaie."

"Ingrates," muttered Alec.

There had been a number of notable shifts at court, following the death of Queen Idrilain two winters earlier—even with her successor, Queen Phoria, away most of the year, fighting in Mycena. Despite the obvious benefits of reopened trade with Aurënen, she had issued a royal decree: the Aurënfaie style of naming, popular since the time of the first Idrilain, was no longer used at court. Southern styles in dress, jewelry, and music were also out of fashion. Young men were letting their beards grow and wearing their hair cropped short about the ears.

Seregil's response had, of course, been to refuse to cut his hair at all. It was well past his shoulders now. Alec did the same, but braided his to keep it out of his face.

Among the general populace, however, Aurënfaie goods were in great demand. Whatever the nobles might do in public to please the new queen, the people hadn't lost their taste for luxuries and novelty.

The Harvest Market was bustling by the time they reached it, the huge square filled with the colored awnings and ranks of booths selling everything from cheap jewels and knit goods to live poultry and cheese. A Queen's Herald stood on the platform near the central fountain, announcing some victory on the Folcwine.

The war against Plenimar was still grinding on, and brought home to Rhíminee in the form of the criers' daily reports, cartloads of funeral urns and crippled soldiers, and the growing shortages of metal, horses, and meat. Seregil kept a large map on the dining room wall at Wheel Street, stuck with brass pins to mark the surging tide of battle. After this summer's bloody fighting, Phoria and her Mycenian and Aurënfaie allies had finally pushed the enemy back halfway across Mycena, and held a line past the eastern bank of the Folcwine. Northern gold and wool were trickling south again, along the recaptured Gold Road, but supplies still had to flow north.

Famished and exhausted, Alec and Seregil paused long enough to get the gist, then ambled on to the booth of their favorite baker for slices of warm bread slathered thickly with fresh butter and honey.

As they turned the corner into Blue Fish Street, Alec looked up at the cloudless sky. "Another hot day."

"Not for much longer, I hope." Seregil pulled his damp hair over one shoulder, trying to get the breeze on his neck.

Even after all this time, it still felt odd to Alec, walking down this familiar street and not finding the Cockerel Inn there. They'd had a new inn built in its place. The Stag and Otter—a tongue-in-cheek reference to the animal forms they'd each taken during Nysander's intrinsic nature spell— had been open for business for three months, and had already established a good name for its beer, if not the food. The Cockerel's cook, old Thryis, had been well-known on this side of the city for her excellent fare.

To rebuild on the same spot had seemed like a good idea when they'd come back to Rhíminee a year and a half ago. Now Alec thought it had been a mistake. Some of the foundation stones were still blackened—a stark reminder of the night Seregil had burned the old inn as a funeral pyre for their murdered friends.

"You two are up and about early today," Ema called as they passed the open kitchen door. Broadly pregnant, she held her apron hem carefully under the bulge of her belly as she bent to check on the contents of a kettle bubbling on its hook over the kitchen hearth.

"Never came home last night at all," Alec said

with a wink. Mistress Ema was blond and pretty and cheerful, and Alec had warmed to her at once, even though her cooking skills left much to be desired.

"You wicked things! But you'll be hungry, I bet. I've got some cakes rising for breakfast, and some salt cod and onions on the boil."

"Don't trouble yourself. Just tea," Seregil replied curtly, striding on. He hated salt cod and onions and had told her that a dozen times or more. The kitchen reeked of it.

"I'll come down for some cakes later," Alec put in quickly as he took the tea tray. He'd have taken the fish, too, but Seregil wouldn't allow the smelly stuff in their rooms.

Magyana—the last remaining wizard at the Orëska House who called Seregil friend—had found the couple who ran the place. The husband, Tomin, was some kin of hers, from a town south of Ardinlee. Alec liked them well enough, but Seregil was still keeping his distance, and not just because of the food. Even with everything new right down to the pot hooks, neither of them could set foot in the place without expecting to hear Thryis snapping out orders to Cilla in the kitchen, or Diomis's laughter as he bounced his grandson Luthas on his knee by the hearth. The child was the only survivor of that night, aside from Seregil's cat, and was now safely fostered with the Cavishes at Watermead. Alec still caught a glimpse of Seregil's guilt every time they saw the child; he'd never stopped blaming himself for the massacre.

•   •   •

The stink of the fish gave way to the sweetly cloying smell of fresh wood and plaster as Alec followed Seregil upstairs. The Cockerel had been as settled as an old ship, steeped with years of cook smoke and soap boiling and lives lived. This place would smell new for years.

The third-floor rooms they shared were well hidden, just as they had been at the Cockerel. Magyana had obscured the door that led to the secret stair, and warded those stairs just as they had been at the Cockerel. As with the old place, the wards on the stairs were keyed not to incinerate cats.

Seregil whispered the passwords for the current wards as he reached each one. He still insisted on changing them frequently, though it was unlikely anyone would come hunting them now. Fortunately, Alec had a good memory. This month they were the Aurënfaie words for the phases of the moon.

"Aurathra."

"Morinth."

"Selethrir."

"Tilentha."

Ruetha was sitting at the top of the stairs, busy cleaning her white ruff and paws. She ignored them until Seregil opened the door, then bounded through with her plumed tail held high.

These new rooms were pleasant enough. The windows were clean enough to see through, the newly purchased furniture didn't smell of must and smoke, and the new white marble fireplace certainly drew better. All the same, the whitewashed walls lacked the patina gained from years of smoke and candles, and they weren't yet covered with trophies of past jobs and adventures. Those had all been lost. The only object that had survived the fire was the mermaid statue, now back in her place by the front door. Her marble skin was soot-stained and her upraised hand had broken off, but Alec had insisted on keeping her. Seregil pulled off his borrowed cloak and tossed it over her head.

A door on the far side of the room led into the bedroom, where a broad, curtained bed and their clothes chests took up most of the floor space. Both rooms were still neat and orderly.

At least for now, Alec thought with a tinge of regret.

Gone were Seregil's carefully hoarded books and scrolls, and the dusty store of maps he'd collected over the years and stored under the couch. All lost. The new worktables were well stocked with tools and a small forge, but lacked the comforting clutter of old locks and odd bits of metal, string, weapons, and wood. Though he'd often counseled Alec against burdening himself down with possessions, Seregil was a raven at heart, unable to resist picking up anything useful or shiny.

Despite all the changes, they were both glad to finally have a place to escape to again when playing the dissolute nobles at the Wheel Street villa became too much of a bother.

They washed the night's dirt from their bodies and faces with water from the rain barrel on the roof and drank their tea as they dressed in light summer surcoats, doeskin breeches, and tall polished boots. Seregil went to a small casket on the mantelpiece and took out a heavy gold ring. It was set with a ruby carved with Klia's profile. She'd given it to him in Aurënen, ostensibly in gratitude for his help there. Seregil wore it often—out of pride, certainly, and as remembrance of his absent friend—but also, Alec suspected, to spite Phoria and her lapdogs.

Ostracized and unwanted, they'd spent the past year alternating between the bright salons of the nobles who would still associate with them, and carrying out minor intrigues like tonight's job—often for the same people. Seregil was growing increasingly restless with the situation and had taken to slipping out alone at night again, as he used to before they were lovers.

So far, Alec had resisted the temptation to follow him. Seregil seldom stayed away long, and usually returned in a better mood and eager to make up for his absence. Reluctant as always to admit whatever might be troubling him, Seregil was more than generous with the silent language of the body. It was a language Alec had learned well and easily.

Perhaps it spoke now, carrying Alec's irritation, for as he braided his hair into a neater plait, Seregil caught him by the wrist and pulled him close. Wrapping his arms loosely around Alec's waist, he nipped him on the side of the neck and chuckled. "I'm sorry. I've been a bastard. So you really still like it so much, doing silly little jobs like that?"

"Yes. I mean, it wasn't much of a challenge, but at least we were working."

Seregil lifted Alec's left hand, tracing his thumb over the round, faded scar on the palm. It was a reminder of the first job they'd shared, one that had nearly killed them both. Seregil bore a similar mark on his chest, just above his heart.

"Maybe that's the problem, talí. Too much risk for too little purpose these days."

Alec stroked his lover's smooth, beardless cheek. "It's not the same here, anymore, is it? I hoped getting back to work would help."

Seregil gave him a sad little smile. "I thought so, too, but it hasn't."

When Alec had first come to Rhíminee, Seregil was still the Rhíminee Cat, the city's faceless and most fearless thief for hire. When they'd abandoned the city after Nysander's death, the Cat had died, too, or so rumor had it. There'd been no way to resurrect him without giving rise to unwelcome speculation. Seregil had been known in some circles as a man who could find the thief when he was needed, and he'd let it be known that he'd found a new nightrunner, but these little clandestine jobs were harder to come by lately.

Alec tightened his arms around Seregil and leaned his forehead against his lover's. He had to stoop just a little. He was slightly taller than Seregil now, with a trace of colorless down on his cheeks; both signs of his human blood, just like his yellow hair.

"When we were running from those dogs, all I could think of was what it would be like if they caught us," Seregil murmured. "Imagine—Lord Seregil and Lord Alec slapped up in the Red Tower for common housebreaking? No one knows what we really are, or what we've done for Skala. It would just be shame and dishonor, and for what?

Because some titled slip of a girl couldn't keep her skirts down on Mourning Night, then decided she wanted a proper marriage? For that, I risk losing you?"

"Is that why you turned down so many jobs?"

"You knew?"

"Of course I knew. So you're getting scared, after all this time?"

"It's not fear." Seregil gave Alec's braid an annoyed tug. "It's the sheer pointlessness of it all!" Pulling away, he threw himself down on the couch. "Is this what we came back for? Errand boys for bored nobles? I wish we'd stayed up in the mountains, hunting wolves and screwing in the tall grass."

Alec settled down next to him with a resigned sigh. Seregil was always at his worst when he was bored. "Maybe Magyana—?"

"She's never needed our kind of help. She's a scholar, not a Watcher. If Phoria would just swallow her pride and bring Klia and Thero back from Gedre, maybe things would pick up. Otherwise?" He pulled out the brooch and eyed it with distaste. "Well, at least there's no shortage of this sort of thing."

CHAPTER 2

Too Much, and Not Enough

PHORIA AND HER army sailed back to Rhíminee at
the end of Rhysin, and rode up to the city through
the Harbor Way, through the cold autumn rain
and the last of the falling red and gold leaves. The
official Progress would be held the next day, but
this entrance was carried out with as much pomp
and ceremony as if the war had ended, rather than
trailed off in yet another season of stalemate.

Peace still seemed beyond anyone's grasp, but
Phoria had decreed that there be a new holiday in the
calendar—the Celebration of Returning Heroes—
nonetheless. The stated purpose was to commemo-
rate the year's victories—without mention of the
defeats, of course—and to honor the fallen. She'd
done the same last year, when hopes had been higher.

The rain-soaked banners and golden shields
hung along the streets looked a little forlorn this
year, thought Alec, as he and Seregil stood with the
common masses along the walls of the Sea Market,

well bundled against the damp chill off the sea. From here they had a good view of the queen as she rode by, brilliant even in this watery light in her gold-chased war helm and breastplate, holding the great Sword of Gherilain upright before her. Even more than the crown, the ancient blade was the most potent symbol of her reign, both as ruler and the country's supreme war commander. The first time Alec had seen Phoria's mother, Idrilain had been wearing that same armor, and that sword had been hers.

Phoria's twin brother, Prince Korathan, rode on her right. He was the Vicegerent now, and it was odd to see him, her equal as a warrior, dressed in robes of state and the flat velvet hat instead of a commander's uniform. His greying blond hair was still long, in contrast to most of the court. Sitting his huge black charger with the ease of a born warrior, he cut an elegant and regal figure. Unlike Phoria and their younger sister Aralain, he had always been friendly with Seregil, and with his half sister Klia, too. Alec liked him for that.

The rain pelted down harder, but they lingered on, counting regiments and banners. By the time the last men-at-arms marched past, Alec estimated she'd lost nearly five hundred soldiers, and this was only the Rhíminee force they were seeing. The cartloads of funeral urns were never part of the official proceedings.

"Come on," Seregil said at last through chattering teeth. "The Cavishes will have arrived by now."

They stole a ride on the back of a passing wagon and arrived back at Wheel Street to find Micum and his family waiting for them in the painted salon.

Kari hurried over to embrace Alec, balancing three-year-old, red-haired Gherin on one hip. The child reached out and grabbed at Alec's braid. "Muncle Arek!"

"There you are, my sweet boy!" Kari cried, kissing Alec soundly on both cheeks. "A whole lovely summer gone and you only came out to Watermead twice? What has Seregil had you doing?"

"You know better than to ask that, my love." Micum chuckled, limping over to clasp hands with Seregil. He was dressed for town today in a fine embroidered coat and his best sword belt, and leaning on a polished walking stick with an ivory head carved in the shape of a fish—a gift from Seregil.

It still hurt to see him like this, his stiff leg a constant reminder of that awful day four years ago. They all carried wounds; Micum's was the most visible, but Seregil's by far the deepest. The closest he ever came to speaking of it these days were the nights when he woke up yelling or crying, drenched in cold sweat. But none of that showed when he was awake and in command of himself.

Seregil embraced his old friend, then looked around. "And where's my little bird?"

"Here, Uncle!" Illia came tripping lightly down the staircase, flanked by Seregil's two huge white Zengati hounds, Mârag and Zir, and carrying her foster brother piggyback. Ten now, Illia was dark and pretty like her mother and middle sister, Elsbet, and trying to act very grown-up. "Luthas wanted to see the picture books in the library again. He remembered them from our last visit. Just a minute, though. I brought you presents!" She let Luthas down and ran back upstairs.

"Uncle!" Luthas ran to throw his arms around Seregil's knees. Seregil ruffled the child's hair, but Alec didn't miss the fleeting look of sadness in his friend's eyes.

Mercifully, Luthas was too young to remember his mother and grandparents, or how Seregil had saved him from the burning inn. He'd always had a special affection for Seregil, though, and Seregil was always kind to the child, even though Alec knew how he dreaded the day that the boy learned the truth of his past.

Illia clattered back downstairs with two bulky brown bundles under her arms. "I made these for you. It took me all summer!"

Alec unfolded his and shook out a well-made woolen sweater. Seregil's was the same, in darker wool.

"Well now, look at that." Seregil gave Alec a wink. "The arms are the same length and everything."

"I'll take it back!" Illia warned, grinning too broadly to look very insulted.

Seregil hugged her. "Oh no you won't! The first flake of snow I see, I'm putting this on until spring."

"It's because of all those stories you told me, how cold it was at that cabin you lived in. If you ever go off like that again, you can take these!"

Alec kissed her. "Thank you. And as it happens, we have some surprises, too."

He went into the dining room and retrieved two

little silk-wrapped parcels from the top of the painted plate chest. Returning, he knelt down in front of the boys. "You first!"

Two pairs of eyes widened—Luthas's the same blue as Cilla's had been, Gherin's the same hazel as Micum's.

"Presents?" lisped Gherin. The shyer of the two, he hung back while Luthas boldly reached for the parcels.

The coverings were loose and quickly cast aside, and both boys crowed happily over the brightly painted toy dragons. Alec had tried to give them toy bows on their last visit, but Kari had put her foot down firmly.

"Give me a few years before you go putting weapons in their hands!" she'd scolded. "Besides, they'll only put out each other's eyes with the damn things."

Alec had had a bow in his hands for as long as he could remember, but he honored her wishes.

"I see you over there, pretending you don't care for presents," Seregil said to Illia. "Or are you too old for such things, now?" It was a long-standing game between them.

"Oh, I don't care!" she replied with a coy smile, twisting this way and that to make her striped skirt twirl.

"Well, then, what am I to do with this?" Seregil wondered, pulling a small box from the air with practiced sleight of hand.

Illia's dark eyes lit up. "Is it something magic?"

"Not this time, I'm afraid. But if you give me a kiss, I'll show it to you."

Illia skipped over to Seregil and sat on his knee to kiss him.

"Alec and I used to promise you necklaces of dragons' tongues and eyeballs. Do you remember?"

"You didn't bring me any of those!" She wrinkled her nose comically eyeing the box with distrust. "Did you?"

"You'll have to look to find out."

Illia opened the box and lifted out a pair of tiny, tear-shaped pearl earrings. "Oh, Uncle!" she cried, throttling him with an excited hug.

"A young lady old enough to attend a Royal Progress ought to have suitable jewels, don't you think?" Seregil asked, chuckling. "And I did notice on our last visit that you had your ears pierced. Alec has a gift for you, too."

"My lady." Alec presented her with the necklace to match—three matching pearls on a little gold chain.

"You spoil my children," Micum said, laughing. "Proper uncles, both of you."

Alec bent to fasten on the necklace. "Stop squirming."

"I'm too excited!" Illia exclaimed. "We're going to see the queen, and Beka's coming home for Mourning Night!"

The chain slipped from Alec's fingers, and the necklace slithered into the girl's lap. "She's coming back from Aurënen?"

"You mean you haven't heard?" asked Micum. "We had a letter from her last month. Her Urghazi Turma is on border duty above Cirna right now."

"And Thero?"

"On his way back to the city, last I heard."

"But not Klia?" asked Alec.

"Not yet. She's with your sister in Bôkthersa for the winter. A new guard was sent to replace Urghazi Turma."

"Under whose command?"

"That I don't know. You mean you haven't had any word of this?"

Alec shared a worried look with Seregil.

"Maybe they wanted to surprise you," Illia offered. "Oh dear, and now I've spoiled it, haven't I? But I didn't tell the other part, did I, Mother?"

"Other part?" asked Alec.

"Beka's married," Micum told him. "I believe you know the fellow. A 'faie she met down there, name of Nyal."

"Our interpreter." Alec shook his head, smiling. "Well, that's not much of a surprise. I think you'll like him."

"I know I will," said Illia. "Beka says he's *very* handsome!"

Seregil gave her a wink. "He is, indeed."

"But you mustn't let on that we told you."

Seregil fastened the necklace, then swung her around until she giggled. "Don't you fret, little bird. The joke will be on them when we meet again. Come, let's go see what Cook's got for supper.

Seregil kept up a cheerful façade through dinner, but his mind was already turning over possibilities suggested by this new development. This sudden change of bodyguard boded ill for Klia, and Thero would certainly be concerned about it. Why hadn't he sent word? Phoria had left her popular half sister in unofficial exile all this time, when every good commander was needed in the field. Now she'd stripped her of her trusted entourage and wizard? He began to suspect that Klia's "visit" with his sister was a strategic withdrawal into friendlier territory.

After dinner they gathered around the hearth in the salon again, Kari and Illia with their knitting, Micum with his pipe.

"Uncle Seregil, why doesn't the queen like her sister?" Illia asked, looking up from the stocking she was working on.

"Well, they are only half sisters, you know. Klia and her two late brothers were the children of Queen Idrilain's second consort. And besides, not all sisters get along as well as you and Beka and Elsbet."

"But why?" Illia persisted.

"It's not polite to talk about the royal family's business," her mother told her. "Tend to your stitches now, and count for the slips. If you don't turn that heel properly, you'll give poor Beka blisters." Kari had been around Watcher business for most of her life and had a good sense of when a conversation wasn't for young ears.

Alec had somehow ended up on the floor and provided a welcome distraction as he let the two little boys crawl delightedly over him, pulling his hair and wrestling him down onto the rushes. He let them win for a while, then tickled them until they shrieked with laughter and Illia forgot her newfound dignity and joined the fray in their defense. The dogs watched from a safe distance, heads on paws, following the tussle with alert yellow eyes.

Alec had a soft heart for children, and it was never more apparent than around the Cavishes. Seregil had often wondered at that, since Alec had no brothers or sisters of his own, and his father had been a wanderer, never settling anywhere long enough for Alec to make any real friends. Gherin was sitting on Alec's back now, taking his braid to pieces and Alec laughingly submitted, like an indulgent older brother.

Or a father, thought Seregil. An ordinary, full-blood human of Alec's age, especially a Dalnan, would have married and fathered a child or two by now.

Seregil was generally very good at not thinking about things that displeased or discomforted him; he'd had a lifetime of practice at that. But when those discomforting things involved Alec, they were harder to put out of his mind.

It was baffling, and not a little annoying, this breach of control.

A touch on his shoulder pulled him from his uneasy thoughts. Micum stood over him, with a look of understanding Seregil wanted no part of. But all he said, with his usual tact, was, "What do you say to a few games of cards? It's been a while since I've taken your money. My purse is feeling a bit light."

"It'll be lighter when I'm done with you," Seregil warned.

"Aren't we cocky tonight?"

Alec joined them, then Kari, when she'd put the children to bed.

Grateful for the distraction, Seregil threw himself wholeheartedly into the game, and managed to win without cheating much at all.

• • •

"I can't believe no one wrote to us!" Alec grumbled as he and Seregil readied for bed that night.

"Who says they didn't?" Seregil countered as he sat naked on their wide bed, combing the day's snarls from his hair.

This room was fitted out with Aurënfaie furnishing, airy and colorful. The gauzy bed curtains rippled lazily as Alec pulled off his shirt and tossed it onto the clothes chest across the room. "You think someone has been stealing letters from us?"

"More likely intercepting them from Klia and Thero."

"But Beka's got through."

"To her parents, outside Rhíminee," Seregil reminded him. "Not to us. If the Watchers were still active . . ." He worked at another tangle, leaving the rest unsaid. Again.

Alec shucked off his breeches and flopped down beside him. "So what does it mean? I thought Phoria had forgotten all about us. It's not like we're any threat to her."

"We're friends with Klia, and helped her succeed in Aurënen, when Phoria was against it."

"Klia's always been loyal to the throne, *and* she's one of the best commanders!"

"Phoria's a childless queen, Alec, and she's not young." Seregil gave up on his hair and tossed the comb aside. "There's nothing to secure her throne but her own will. Klia *could* make a claim for it, as Idrilain's daughter, even if she is the youngest. Hers would be a stronger claim in some minds than

Princess Ariani's, with her war skills, and certainly better than Ariani's daughter's." Of all Idrilain's children, Ariani, who shared a father with Phoria and Korathan, was the only one with children. The eldest girl, Elani, was supposed by most to be the heir apparent.

"Klia's always been popular with the people," he went on. "Why do you think Phoria's kept her out of sight since their mother's death? Phoria's never been one to think the best of others—particularly those she sees as potential rivals. It's a good trait in a general, but not so good between sisters. The nobility are different, Alec. Don't ever forget that."

"You're a noble," Alec teased.

"Only a very minor one, and only in the minds of Skalans. I think my people have the right idea when it comes to that. But here it comes down to heirs, and Phoria means to control that and keep it to her own father's line."

"Makes them sound like horse breeders," Alec snorted, climbing under the covers.

Seregil blew out the lamp and joined him.

Alec settled his head on Seregil's shoulder. "Still, it makes you wonder, doesn't it, Phoria being barren and all? Why would the gods curse her?"

"A bit of bad luck for her, that's all. And I'm sure she wouldn't care, if she wasn't queen."

"Mmm. Can't picture her as much of a mother," Alec agreed with a yawn.

"Some are better suited than others." Seregil idly stroked Alec's bare shoulder, enjoying the length of warm body pressed to his. This was one of his favorite moments of the day. Comfortable and sleepy, he spoke without thinking, as images of Alec rolling around with the children came back to him. "Do you still think about it? What the oracle told you at Sarikali?"

He regretted his careless words the instant he felt Alec go tense beside him.

"Why bring that up again?"

"They aren't always clear in their prophecies, you know. And I still think maybe you got some of it wrong."

Seregil's heart sank further when Alec pulled away and settled on his back. "I'm 'the wanderer who carries his home in his heart.' I'm 'the bird who makes its nest on the waves.' I will father a child of no woman. And it's a blessing. What part of that didn't I understand?"

"I'm sorry. Forget I said anything."

"Until you bring it up again."

"I won't!"

"Yes, you will. Just like you did last time we were at Watermead. Sometimes I think it bothers you more than it does me."

"I just want you to be happy."

He couldn't see Alec in the dark, but the sigh that answered spoke volumes. "I am. Let it be."

Easier said than done. Those uncontrolled feelings were threatening again, chasing away any hope of sleep. "You know, Alec, there's no reason you couldn't find some willing girl . . ."

"Don't!"

Despite the dangerous edge in Alec's tone, Seregil pressed on. "I'm just saying that it wouldn't matter to me if you wanted to get a child on someone."

There was a moment of truly ominous silence, then the bed lurched as Alec left it. He snatched the robe from the end of the bed and stormed out. A moment later the door of the library down the hall slammed decisively shut.

Seregil sat up, stunned. Nothing like this had ever happened between them. They'd had disagreements, certainly, and even come to blows a couple of times during the long winter days in that cabin, but Alec had never just walked away.

Seregil pulled on his own robe and went out into the corridor. No light showed under the guest chamber doors, but he suspected Micum and Kari had heard.

He found the library door locked against him. It would have been an easy matter to pick it open, but he knew better than to do such a thing. Baffled and more than a bit guilty, he slunk back to his own bed, hoping things would be better in the morning.

They weren't. Alec came down late to breakfast, and when he did speak to Seregil, it was no more than absolutely necessary. Micum gave them both questioning looks, but it was Kari who cornered Seregil in the garden as soon as the meal was over.

"What did you do to him?" she demanded, already laying the blame at Seregil's feet.

"Nothing!"

She fixed him with a dark look. "I love that boy as one of my own, and any fool can see he's hurting. What did you do?"

"It was just a disagreement," Alec informed her

from the kitchen doorway. Coming over, he slipped his arm through Seregil's. "Nothing to worry about. Right, talí?"

Seregil's relief was short-lived. As soon as Kari was gone, Alec pulled him to the back of the garden, behind a screen of tall rosebushes. The false smile was gone. He was still fuming.

"If you *ever* suggest such a thing to me again, you'll be sleeping alone a lot longer than one night!"

"I thought I was being helpful!"

"Helpful!" Alec's eyes narrowed dangerously for a moment, but the look quickly changed to one of defeat. "You really don't see anything wrong with telling me to bed someone else, do you? Is that what you do when you go off by yourself at night? Are you back to your old haunts on the Street of Lights?"

"Well, yes, I went there, but—"

"You didn't!" Alec gasped.

"What? No! Just to visit, with Eirual and some friends, but not to bed them!" Seregil quickly assured him, and it was the truth. He'd hardly even been tempted.

"And that green-eyed one? Tyrien, isn't it?"

"Well . . . yes. I'm sorry I didn't say anything. I just didn't think—"

"*You?* You didn't think something as important as that through?"

"I'd never hurt you, talí. I haven't touched anyone else, and I won't!" Seregil whispered, hoping to calm him down before he was heard in the house. "You know I've never been with anyone I really cared for before."

"Not with all the lovers you had?"

"Lovers in name only, Alec. A bit of fun on both sides, and nothing more."

Alec looked sad. "I don't see how you could have so many and not love any of them."

Seregil hesitated, still very much on uncertain ground. Finally, he just shrugged and spoke the truth, stupid as it sounded. "I didn't know the difference."

Sometimes Alec's ability to see through him was a blessing. The last of his anger faded, leaving only a trace of sadness behind. "Do you mind it very much, not being free anymore?"

"I am free, Alec. I'm with you by choice. And I promise you, this is the last time we'll speak of any of this. I swear it, by the Light, and by my love." Raising their joined hands to his lips, he kissed Alec's fingers. Alec pulled him in for a real kiss, then let go and headed back to the house and their guests.

Seregil followed, his relief marred by the knowledge that nothing had really changed. Not for Alec, at least.

CHAPTER 3

Movement

THE RAIN BLEW back out overnight, and the sun shone brightly for the queen's official Progress.

"That seems like a lucky sign," Alec noted, looking up at the cloud-torn blue of the sky as he rode to the Temple Square with Seregil and the others.

"Yes, but for whom?" Seregil replied with a wry smile. "The same sun shines on everyone, you know."

"Hush, someone will hear you!" Micum admonished as they passed a line of White Hawk Cavalry, known to be some of the queen's favorites.

Seregil gave him a maddening wink, but did shut up.

They left their horses at a crowded ostler's yard set aside for nobles and entered Temple Square on foot. Alec and his friends made their way up to the parapet of the Temple of Astellus, bundled in their embroidered cloaks. From up here the crowd gathered below looked like a colorful mosaic. The temples of the Four each gleamed against the autumn sky, squat and tall, dark and light.

The little boys were back at the house, but Illia, proudly decked out in her new pearls, was bouncing with excitement between Alec and her sister, Elsbet. The older girl was more composed, conscious of her dark initiate's robes.

"It's so beautiful!" Illia exclaimed, overwhelmed by the scene before them. "Elsbet, do you really live in that white temple now?"

"The initiates' dormitories are nearby, but I study there every day," Elsbet replied serenely.

Banners of blue and gold silk lined the square, embroidered with the silver crescent moon and flame device of Skala. The highest-ranking nobles stood in the portico of the Temple of Illior, dressed in jewels and furs, while those of lesser ranks fanned out from there. Guildsmen and merchants filled the square to capacity, held back from the steps of the Illior temple by a line of the Queen's Household Guard.

Alec rested his elbows on the parapet, taking in the scene. "I wonder what a real triumph would look like?"

"The soldiers deserve a welcome," Micum told him. "And the rest are just glad to get their people home for the winter."

Lady Kylith waved to them over the heads of the crowd and made her way through to join them, arm in arm with her current love, Captain Lillia of the Golden Lion Guard. Kylith, as usual, was clad in the height of fashion. Necklines were a bit higher this year, but her blue silk gown still managed to show off a generous expanse of pale bosom below the heavy netting of jewels that adorned her throat. More jewels sparkled brightly in her silver-streaked hair.

"Lady, how lovely you look!" Kari greeted her warmly. She wore jewels, too, but kept to the more modest fashions of the north, even after all her years in Skala. Illia excitedly showed off her new pearls.

"Sakor shows his favor for our queen, wouldn't you agree, my lords?" Kylith remarked as she kissed Seregil and Alec in greeting.

"Lucky for her, and all of us, in these times of war, my lady." Alec had always liked Kylith, even given her past with Seregil. Perhaps because it was hard to imagine; she looked old enough to be Seregil's mother, while Seregil, a full-blood 'faie, probably looked as young as he had when they were lovers years ago. Whatever the case, she'd been among the first in noble society to make Alec feel welcome.

As they waited, he caught snatches of conversation on all sides as the crowd grew restless. Apparently the war was slowly turning in the Skalans' favor as the early onset of a northern winter brought down the curtain for another year.

At last priests emerged from the four temples and processed to the center of the square. The Illiorans wore their silver masks and swung huge censers, filing the square with billows of sacred incense. The priests of Astellus carried on their shoulders a miniature ship decked with harvest bounty. Valerius, at the head of the Dalnans, led a black bull decked with wheat and pomegranates, its horns gilded silver and gold.

The priests of Sakor were the last to emerge, bearing the huge golden Aegis of Sakor on a stand. Phoria followed them, resplendent in a long-trained gown of silver and white, and a war helm and breastplate of burnished gold that gave back the sun like a mirror.

Korathan escorted her, carrying the crown of Skala on a velvet cushion. Princess Aralain walked behind him with her eldest daughter, Princess Elani. Aralain should have been the successor, in the event of Phoria's death, but she was too soft to wield the Sword in battle.

Alec squinted in the slanting afternoon light as he tried to make out Elani's features. At this distance he had no more than an impression of a solemn young face under a coronet and a long fall of pale hair. Leaning over to Seregil, he asked softly, "What do you know about her?"

"Not much," Seregil replied. "Phoria has been grooming her for battle. A hard education that will have been, too, with her in charge of it."

Surrounded by the symbols of the Four and her powerful family, Phoria held up the Sword as she approached the bull to perform this year's sacrifice.

"Phoria looks just like her mother from here," Micum noted softly as the priests began the chants and prayers. "I still miss her."

The words of the ceremony, or at least what Alec could make out at this distance, were similar to the investiture oath the queen gave each year on

Mourning Night. She pledged to defend the land and uphold the will of the Four. When she was done, the priests pulled the docile bull's head back and Phoria made the fatal swing. The animal did not struggle as the bright blood sprayed out across Phoria's golden armor and the pavement in auspicious patterns.

More prayers followed.

Bored, Alec leaned on the railing, fretting with the gold rings he'd worn for the occasion. He hated jewelry; hated having to the play the role of a noble of no account like this. And as the ceremony dragged on, his mind wandered again to the simple life they'd so briefly shared, exiled up in the northern hills. At moments like this he wondered why he'd been so insistent on coming back.

Distracted, he didn't see what caused the sudden commotion among the queen's party. Korathan had an arm around his sister, supporting Phoria as she pressed one hand to her brow.

"What happened?"

"A hawk came out of nowhere and struck her head," Micum told him, frowning.

"An omen," Captain Lillia muttered, crossing her fingers against ill luck.

"I'm no bird reader, but it doesn't seem a good thing," Kari murmured behind an upraised hand.

Seregil said nothing.

Order was soon restored, but an air of unrest hung over the crowd as Phoria continued the ceremony, exchanging her war helm for the crown.

When the ceremony was finally over, Phoria faced the people and raised the bloody Sword. In a voice trained to carry across battlefields, she declared, "By the Four, by the Flame and by the Light, I will defend Skala!"

The royal party moved on into the Temple of Illior, signaling the distribution of free ale and food to begin. Signs and omens were quickly forgotten as the festivities commenced.

Alec and the others went to Kylith's for a feast. Micum and his family left early, but Seregil and Alec stayed, singing and drinking, and returned to Wheel Street late and drunk.

It was well past midnight, but they found the steward, Runcer, waiting for them in the salon with a royal herald.

"This man arrived for you at sundown, my lord," he announced, and withdrew.

Seregil collapsed into an armchair and looked blearily up at the blue-clad messenger. "Well, well. What can she want with me at this hour?"

"I was sent by his Highness, the Vicegerent, with a message for you and Lord Alec of Ivywell," the man replied. "You are commanded to attend the queen first thing tomorrow morning, in the Chamber of Judgment."

Drunk as he was, Alec's gut tightened at those words. "Are we being arrested?"

"If past experience is anything to go by, he wouldn't send us a warning first." Seregil chuckled. "Please, good sir herald, give my regards to his Highness, and assure him that we are honored by this invitation, and will do our best to be there."

The herald arched a brow at the flippant reply. "Go on, tell him. He won't mind."

"As you wish, my lord. From your lips to the Vicegerent's ear."

"You're drunker than I thought," Alec muttered, helping Seregil up to their room. "What were you thinking, sending a message like that?"

Seregil let out an inelegant snort and leaned on the wall while Alec fumbled with the bedroom latch. "Kor? He won't care. And serves 'im right, calling us out at such a wretched hour, after a festival night. Mark my words; it's *her* doing."

He staggered inside and collapsed facedown on the bed. Before Alec could draw him out further on the matter, Seregil was snoring.

"Fine then. Sleep in your clothes," Alec muttered, letting his own fall where they would as he followed.

If he'd been more sober himself, he'd probably have been more worried.

CHAPTER 4

Those Who Serve at the Queen's Displeasure

BY THE TIME they rode to the Palace the next morning, Alec was sober enough to be worried and wine sick in equal measure. Even the weak early light made his head throb. Seregil, as usual, was feeling fine and didn't seem particularly perturbed about the summons. They'd left Micum pacing the courtyard, clearly worried whether or not he would see them again.

"Bilairy's Balls, Seregil, why did you let me drink so much?" Alec grumbled.

Seregil snickered. "*Let* you? I seem to recall being told to 'hand over the bottle or piss off' at several points during the evening."

"So you're as immune to drink as you are to magic?"

"Hardly. I've just had better luck with drink. You've seen what magic does to me." He raised a hand unconsciously to the faded scar hidden beneath his fine surcoat. "I'll take a bad wine head any day."

Alec's horse missed a step on the worn cobbles and lurched. Alec's belly did the same. "Easy for you to say." He kept his real worries to himself as the dark bulk of the Palace loomed before them.

Built of black and grey stone and buttressed by the western wall that surrounded the city, with square towers overlooking the harbor below, it was as much fortress as castle, and one that had never been successfully taken. Alec had read the histories of how Queen Tamír the Great had built Rhíminee, guided by visions and the best builders in the land, after Plenimar had destroyed the original capital at Ero. The Orëska House had been built at the same time, but where it was airy and open, the Palace had a closed, oppressive feel.

At least we came in through the front door this time, thought Alec as a liveried servant led them through the large receiving hall and down a twisting series of corridors to a smaller, but no less imposing chamber.

This one was long and rather narrow, with a row of stained-glass slit windows set high up under the vaulted ceiling. These left the room in semi-darkness at this hour, and it was cold. At the far end, several rows of long oak benches faced a large throne on a raised dais. The queen's banner hung behind it, glimmering in the lamplight.

"Please have a seat, my lords," the servant said, directing them to the front bench. "Her Majesty left orders for you to attend her here."

Seregil sat down on one of the front benches and stretched his legs out, still looking more bored than worried. Alec tried to do the same but was soon up and pacing the polished stone floor. His footsteps echoed hollowly in the cavernous room, drawing attention to the fact that they were the only people here.

"There are better ways to pass the time, you know." Seregil took a bag of gaming stones from his purse, and a lump of chalk.

Alec caught his arm as he bent to mark a bakshi board on the floor. "Stop that! How is that going to look, when she comes in?"

Seregil rolled his eyes, but sat back and put the chalk away. "How will it look, with you wearing a trench in the floor?"

The sun clocked nearly an hour down the wall before the great doors at the far end of the room opened and Phoria swept in with Prince Korathan and Thero.

Alec elbowed Seregil, then tried to catch the young wizard's eye, but Thero gave him only a slight nod as he came to stand with them. This didn't seem a sign of good things to come.

He looked well, otherwise. He'd put on a formal robe for the occasion, and his belt and purse were finely worked with Aurënfaie patterns. He was clean-shaven these days, and a smooth dark blue gem set in silver dangled, 'faie style, from his left ear. His black curly hair was much longer, and tied back with a black ribbon.

Phoria took the throne and waited as Seregil and Alec came forward and bowed.

"Welcome home, Majesty," Seregil said, suddenly very formal and respectful.

Phoria acknowledged the greeting but did not

smile. Alec stole a glance at her brother; how could womb mates be of such different dispositions?

"I suppose you're wondering why I've called you here?" the queen asked.

Seregil made her another small bow. "We are at your service, Majesty."

"You three are Watchers, are you not?"

"Yes, Majesty," Thero answered for them all. "Under the guidance of my master, and Lord Arkoniel before him, the Watchers have served the Crown since the city was founded."

"So you say. Yet I believe you Watchers have also served your own interests, under this guise of self-appointed protectors. And always in secret."

Thero looked genuinely taken aback. "The interests of the Watchers have always been Skala's, Majesty."

Phoria turned to Seregil. "And are your interests those of Skala, Lord Seregil?"

Seregil drew himself up a little taller; Alec sensed his friend's sudden flash of anger and prayed Phoria wouldn't notice. "Yes, Majesty."

Phoria waited for him to elaborate but he let his answer hang in the air between them.

"But you are not Skalan, and neither is your companion." Phoria spared Alec a glance. "Your loyalty to Nysander is not in question, only your loyalty to me. You served him, not my mother."

"Through him we served her, and Skala," Seregil replied evenly. "I was accused of treason once, and my name was cleared. Your mother didn't doubt me."

"Careful," Korathan murmured.

"And you, Lord Alec," Phoria turned the full force of that pale-eyed gaze on him. "Whom do you serve?"

"I would never betray Skala, your Majesty!"

The queen looked less than impressed by his answer, but Alec thought he caught the hint of an encouraging smile from Korathan.

"My brother the prince tells me that you have lost your name in your own land, Seregil," Phoria continued. "That instead of exile, you have been completely cut off from your own people."

"That's correct—and I trust he explained that it was because Alec and I chose Skala and the kinship I have with your family over our duty to Aurënfaie law."

A moment of ominous silence followed, as Seregil and Phoria stared each other down. Alec held his breath, certain now of a quick journey to a Red Tower cell.

"Is it Skala you are loyal to, Seregil, or my sister?" Phoria asked at last.

"Majesty, if you please, I've known Seregil most of my life," Thero interjected quickly. "I vouch for his loyalty with my own oath. He's risked his life for Skala's sake more times than you can imagine, and Alec with him. You have nothing to fear from them, or me. We all serve at your pleasure."

Phoria chuckled darkly. "Be assured I fear none of you. Does he speak for you, Lord Seregil?"

"He does."

"And you, Lord Alec?"

"Yes, Majesty!"

"Then let us leave it at that for the moment.

Thero, you have taken your master's place as the head of the Watchers?"

"Yes, Majesty. But while in Aurënen these past months there's been little I could do on your behalf, other than help oversee the trade agreements at the behest of the princess. I hope I have served you well in that capacity."

"Your efforts are noted. However, it is my command that you disband the Watchers. No more secrets. If I require your aid in any fashion, I will order it, and you will answer to no one except me. Is that understood?"

"Yes, but—"

"I have spoken!"

Thero pressed a hand to his heart and bowed deeply. "You have my oath, by my hands, heart, eyes, and voice."

"Good." Phoria sat back, regarding Alec and Seregil again. "As for you two, I am satisfied for now. In fact, I have a task for you—one you're well suited to."

"We are yours to command, Majesty," replied Seregil.

"You most certainly are. You're going to Aurënen as my emissaries to Princess Klia. My half sister is to return at once and resume her duties as my field commander. Her swift obedience is imperative, as proof of her love. You are to return with her as quickly as possible. Is that clear?"

"As spring water, Majesty. But crossing the Osiat this time of year—it's already late enough that there could be problems."

"I'll give you a decent ship."

"Am I to go with them, Majesty?" asked Thero.

"What use would you be? There's work enough for you here. You're dismissed."

Thero bowed and made a hasty retreat. He didn't look at the others, but Alec saw the angry flush suffusing his thin cheeks.

"I'm sending an escort for you under the command of Lord Traneus. And I've had these prepared." She gestured to Korathan, who stepped down and handed Seregil three small, painted sticks.

Alec recognized them; they were message wands. These talismans were infused with a simple magic, usually a message of some sort, which would be released when the wand was broken in two. Such devices required no magic from the user; even Seregil could make them work.

"Use the red one when you arrive at Gedre, to signal that you arrived safely," the prince explained. "The blue is for Bôkthersa. The last is for Klia. She's to break it on the morning she sets out to return. The messages will come to me directly."

"I trust your sister will have no objection to the princess cutting short her visit there?" asked Phoria.

Seregil's expression betrayed nothing but mild surprise. "I'm certain she won't, Majesty. She understands the gravity of the situation."

Phoria rose. "I'm sure I don't need to stress the importance of your task. Korathan, I'll leave the rest to you. Farewell, my lords, and may your voyage be a swift one."

Alec stood at stiff attention as she took her leave, then let out a shaky breath.

Korathan grinned at him. "You look like you've just escaped the block, Lord Alec."

"I think maybe we just did." Seregil strolled over and hitched himself up on the edge of the dais. "So, how long did it take you to talk her out of having us executed?"

"Oh, not quite so bad as all that. There was talk of exiling you, though."

This was too much for Alec. "For what? What did we ever do to her?"

"She knows of your role exposing her indiscretion in the Leran affair and the 'misplaced' gold shipment she and Vicegerent Barieus were embroiled in."

"Completely by accident!" Seregil reminded him. "We didn't know anything about it when we started, and we've never said anything about it since."

"True, but you know how she is. She was embarrassed, politically and personally, and not likely to forgive you for that. But that's not all. There's also your close friendship with Klia. And now Klia is fast friends with your sister, the khirnari of a powerful clan."

"Ah, so that's why she was even colder to me than usual," Seregil said with a wry smirk. "Now my whole clan is conspiring against her, too? This little jaunt is really a loyalty test all around."

"But Klia has served Phoria well in Aurënen," Alec pointed out. "The agreements she got securing stores and trade, and wizards to fight for her—surely that's been to Skala's benefit?"

"Of course it has, but Phoria would bite off her own tongue rather than admit it."

"Why?"

"Because the plan was our mother's, not hers, and Klia was the one to support it."

"So Phoria's still putting her trust in swords over magic," added Seregil.

"Always, and Skalan swords in particular."

"And Phoria can't see past her own jealousy," Alec muttered.

Korathan gave him a warning look. "Remember where you are and whom you're speaking of! She's the queen, and my sister."

Alec made him a hasty bow. "I beg your pardon, Highness."

"So, what's the plan?" asked Seregil, shooting Alec a warning look of his own.

"Your ship, the *Lark,* is berthed at the Lantern Street quay. You sail with the tide at first light."

"The queen seems in a hurry to get us out of town."

"More anxious to settle the matter, I think." Korathan took a thick packet sealed with the Royal Signet from his coat and gave it to Seregil. "Here are letters of passage to the khirnaris of Gedre and Bôkthersa, and Phoria's orders to Klia. Come back swiftly, and you may just buy yourself some favor."

Seregil hopped down and made Korathan an exaggerated bow. "Your royal errand boys hear and obey, Highness."

"Seregil—"

"Don't worry, I understand how important this is. There's just one thing I'd like to ask you before we go. As a friend?"

Korathan softened noticeably at that. "Go on."

"Will you give me your word that Phoria means no harm to her sister?"

Korathan thought a moment, then put his hand to his heart. "I give you my word that I believe her when she says so."

"Hmm. Very well. I'll bring Klia home safely, and trust you to keep her that way once she's here."

"One of these days, that mouth of yours is going to get you into serious trouble."

"Has before. Will again, I expect. Take care, Highness. I'm glad it's you standing beside the throne."

They took their leave, but it wasn't until they were free of the Palace that Alec could finally breathe freely. "Phoria must have been satisfied with our answers, or she wouldn't have given us a commission, right?"

Seregil shrugged, looking more upset now than he had when Phoria was insulting them. "It could have been worse. At least we have something worthwhile to do."

Alec waited for him to say more, but Seregil was uncharacteristically quiet as they rode to the Orëska to catch up with Thero.

We lied, Alec realized. Given the choice between following Klia or Phoria, there would be no question. He prayed it never came to that.

Perpetual summer reigned in the walled gardens that surrounded the Orëska House. The shining white palace, with its four domed towers, gleamed against the faultless blue sky. Here were beds of flowers and herbs, and groves of trees covered in every sort of fruit. Magyana had brought back many of the most exotic ones, found in her long years of traveling.

Red-liveried servants bowed to them as they entered the echoing atrium. Sunlight streamed down through the central dome, making the brilliant mosaic that paved the entrance chamber glow. The great Dragon of Illior was whole again. Looking around at the graceful archways and the scores of robed wizards and apprentices going peacefully about their business, it was as if the devastation of the Plenimaran attack had never happened. Nysander was gone, but, Alec reminded himself, so were Mardus and his followers. The Orëska remained, strong and powerful. Why was Phoria so bent on alienating them?

"You're gaping," Seregil chuckled as they crossed to the staircase leading up to what was now Thero's tower. As they reached the top, however, he was no longer smiling. They'd been in to visit Magyana several times since their return, but had avoided these rooms until now.

Wethis answered Alec's knock. The young servant had grown up since Alec had seen him last and was sporting the beginnings of a passable beard. "My lords! It's good to see you. Master Thero and Mistress Magyana are waiting in the parlor downstairs."

Gone were the precipitous stacks of dusty manuscripts in the entry, and the jumbled wonders covering every flat surface. Everything was orderly and clean now, though evidence of Thero's own work was everywhere visible in the neatly arranged books and papers, and the various crucibles simmering over little braziers. The freshly polished steel and brass astronomical instruments arranged on the walkway below the leaded glass dome gleamed. It was at once pleasant and sad, and Alec saw the same emotions warring in Seregil's grey eyes as he looked around, taking it in for the first time.

The painted parlor was less changed, if neater. The fine mural painted with monsters and marvels still ringed the room, and its innate magic still tugged at the eye, even though Alec knew what it was up to now. The overstuffed furnishings were the same, well-worn and comfortable.

The wizards rose from their chairs by the fire as Wethis ushered them in. Magyana embraced them, her smile making the wrinkles around her eyes and mouth deepen and tilt. "So she's finally found something for you to do, has she? Did she give you my message sticks?"

Seregil took them from his coat and handed them to her. "You think she's tampered with them?"

"That would be very difficult." Nonetheless, she examined each one closely. "Yes, these are mine, and still properly magicked. You should have no difficulty using them."

"Phoria must trust you to have you make these," Alec remarked. "She doesn't seem very fond of any wizards these days, especially those who knew Nysander."

"It was her brother who came to me."

"We thought you might like to have these, as well." Thero reached into his sleeve and handed Seregil another set of sticks, similar in design, but painted different colors. "The yellow is for Gedre, and the green for Bôkthersa. The brown one is in case Klia does decide to defy her sister. The messages will come to me."

"Thank you. Alec, you hang on to these so we don't get them mixed up. And I don't think we want Captain Traneus to see us use them."

Magyana's grey brows shot up. "That reptile? Watch out for him."

"That's going to be difficult, seeing as how Phoria's put him in charge of our escort."

"What the hell is going on, Thero?" asked Alec. "Why did Phoria call you and the turma back first, if she was going to call Klia back anyway? Does she really think Klia would betray her?"

Thero waved them to seats by the hearth and poured the wine into the ornate crystal goblets. "I can't say what was in the queen's mind, of course, but it can't have been lost on her that Klia has made a great many friends in Aurënen."

"Friends Phoria fears could turn to allies?" Seregil scoffed. "That's an insult to Klia *and* the 'faie."

"It could be construed that way," the wizard replied. "However, Prince Korathan indicated in his letters that Phoria is merely being cautious."

"Or the family mad streak is coming out," Alec muttered.

"Queen Phoria is not mad," Magyana assured him. "She is a canny ruler, though, and a cautious one. I suspect that until Princess Klia bends her knee before her, that caution will prevail."

"How did Klia react to Urghazi Turma being taken from her?"

"Phoria's order indicated that Captain Beka Cavish is to prepare the rest of the regiment to receive their commander," Thero replied.

Seregil gave him a crooked grin. "Sounds like you became her close adviser, down there together for so long." The grin widened a bit as a faint blush rose to color the young wizard's cheeks.

Klia—and Thero? Alec tried not to laugh, picturing those two as a couple.

"So, what happened at the Palace after Phoria sent me out?" Thero asked, quickly composing himself. "I see you both have your heads on your shoulders."

Seregil quickly sketched out the situation, then turned to Magyana. "What can you tell me about this Traneus fellow?"

"I'd never heard of him until Idrilain lay dying that terrible winter in Mycena, just before you two were sent off to Sarikali. After that, Phoria never seemed to be without him. He had been a corporal in her guard, then suddenly he was a captain, and a lord. He has a nasty habit of turning up like a stray cat anywhere someone voices support for anyone but her. He certainly had his eye on me then."

Alec sighed. "So much for her trusting us."

"It's probably Klia he's being sent to spy on, rather than us," said Seregil. "And besides, we've nothing to worry about. We're doing exactly what Phoria wants."

"The queen leaves nothing to chance, and she likes to hold all the cards," Thero warned. "I'd have given you more warning, but she's had me under watch since my ship came in yesterday. Did you get any of my letters?"

"So you did write? No, not one," Seregil replied. "Is Klia well?"

"Oh yes, and well loved by your clan, and their allies."

"Do you think she'll come back?" asked Magyana.

Thero nodded. "Of course she will. She's wanted nothing else since the Aurënfaie signed the accord. It's been very difficult for her, getting news of the war but not being able to do anything."

The older wizard sighed. "Phoria has been very foolish, keeping such an able commander from the field."

"It looks like she finally figured that out," said Seregil.

"How's Klia's hand, Thero?" asked Alec.

"It healed well." During their diplomatic visit to Sarikali, an assassin's poison had cost her two fingers on her right hand. "The poison caused no lasting damage but she has only limited use of it now."

"Did Phoria give you any idea what she has planned for you after you've done this?" asked Magyana.

"No. I imagine she's waiting to see if we actually obey."

"And?"

"We will, of course. We've only just gotten settled in the new place. I'm not ready to be run out of town just yet. Not on her say-so, anyway. What about you, Thero? What will you do, without the Watchers to oversee?"

"I have my own work. To be honest, I'm almost relieved. I wasn't sure what I was supposed to do. Nysander kept me out of most of his Watcher business until those last few months." He paused, one corner of his mouth tightening with a hint of lingering bitterness. "It was always you and Micum, coming and going mysteriously, and whispers behind closed doors."

"He did trust you," Seregil assured him. "He wouldn't have kept you with him if he didn't. You were the best student he ever had."

"Perhaps."

Seregil reached over and squeezed his hand. "He told me so himself, many times. Don't ever doubt it."

Thero managed a sad smile, then changed the subject, telling them of his time at Bôkthersa, and giving Seregil news of his family and friends.

"Well, we should be getting back before Micum storms the prison looking for us," Seregil said when Thero finished, rising to go.

"Please give him my regards, and ask him to visit me here soon," said Thero.

"A safe journey to you," Magyana said, pressing travelers' charms into their hands.

"And Watchers or no Watchers, I will keep a close eye on Rhíminee, and on Klia when you bring her back," Thero promised.

Seregil clapped him on the shoulder. "I hope we live to see such services welcome again."

CHAPTER 5

Lovers and Enemies

AS THEY RODE back to Wheel Street, Alec finally asked the question that had been niggling at him for days now. "Why *does* the queen dislike you so much?"

Seregil gave him a smile that was patently false and shrugged. "Who knows why Phoria does anything?"

Alec sensed the evasion but guessed this was something Seregil didn't want to talk about in public, so he let it go until they reached the house. Micum and Kari were waiting anxiously for them, as expected, and Seregil soon put their minds at rest. He waited until Kari and the girls went off to the kitchen to see about the midday meal before telling Micum of Phoria's orders regarding the Watchers.

"That vindictive woman!"

"What are you complaining about? I thought you were well out of all that, sitting by the hearth with your babes playing around your feet."

"I don't know," Micum mused sadly. "I've always thought I might have another journey or two in me. To be honest, I get a bit restless sometimes, missing the old days. With you two back, and now Thero, I thought maybe..." He tapped his boot with the tip of his cane. "I might not be able to cover so much ground on foot anymore, but I can ride as well as ever, and there's nothing wrong with my sword arm."

"I'll keep that in mind," said Seregil. "We'll miss you, you know, but I don't think I dare go back and ask Phoria if you can go with us."

Micum laughed and clapped him on the shoulder. "I wouldn't ask you to put your head in the bear's mouth again so soon, anyway. There's all the winter planting and work to be done, and I wouldn't feel right, leaving it all to Kari."

"It never used to stop you," Seregil pointed out.

Micum glanced over at Kari, who'd come back with Gherin in her arms and Luthas swinging from her skirts. "Well, maybe it should have."

The morning ride had cleared Alec's head, but the night's rest had been too short. They shared a late breakfast with the Cavishes, then retired upstairs to sleep a little while Runcer began packing for their journey.

Seregil kicked off his boots and stretched out on top of the coverlet with his arms behind his head, and closed his eyes.

Alec lay down beside him, head propped on one hand, and shook him by the shoulder. "So are you going to tell me the real reason you and Phoria don't like each other or not? I've hardly seen you two together, but when you are, it's like two tom-cats in an alley. I think it's more than just the Leran business."

Seregil threw an arm across his eyes. "Later, talí. I'm exhausted!"

"No. Now."

Seregil said nothing, and just when Alec began to suspect that he was pretending to be asleep, Seregil sighed deeply. "It goes back long before your time, or Thero's. And it's more a matter of her hating me. I don't care much about her at all."

"But why?" Alec pressed. "Klia likes you, and Prince Korathan, too."

Seregil let out a wry little snort. "Ah, well, you've hit on it, haven't you?"

"Korathan? Why would Phoria care if her brother likes you? Is she jealous?"

"Mmm."

Alec recognized another evasion. He poked Seregil in the shoulder again. "So?"

"Let it go, Alec. It's long past."

Once upon a time, Alec would have obeyed. "Tell me!"

"You're not going to like it."

"Obviously."

Seregil dropped his arm and rubbed a hand over his face. "All right then. Korathan and I? We were lovers."

Alec gaped at him. This was the last thing he'd expected to hear. "Really?"

"We were both very young and it didn't last

long. Phoria caught us together and that was the end of it. But she's never forgiven me."

Alec was still trying to take it in. "You? And Korathan?"

"I warned you that you wouldn't like it."

Alec stretched out beside Seregil, leaving a little more space between them than usual. It had always been difficult, knowing that Seregil had bedded hundreds of men and women before he'd come along—and more after, too, for that matter. It was harder still when he learned their names and faces, and that so many of them, like Lady Kylith or the courtesan Eirual, were still good friends. And now it was Prince Korathan, whom Alec had always admired.

"When was this?"

Seregil stared up at the gauzy silk canopy. "Not long after I came to court. Korathan was always very kind and I was still reeling from—well, you know."

Ilar í Sontir, thought Alec. Seregil always had a hard time speaking of the seducer who'd cost him his family, his name, and his homeland. Alec had stored the name and the story in his heart, the one time Seregil had told him the sordid tale. He looked over at Seregil, gauging the worry in his lover's grey eyes.

"Why did Phoria care if you two were—together?" he asked at last.

"Because she's owned her brother from the womb. Twins often have a strong bond. And some a bit too strong, if you take my meaning?"

"You're not serious!"

Seregil shrugged. "Rumors have been floating

around for years. And neither of them have ever married, have they?"

"But she had Lord Barieus as a lover. She mourned him like a husband when he died."

"True, but he's the only one I know of. Korathan doesn't always sleep alone, but from what I've heard, never with anyone who matters. No, he's devoted his whole life to Phoria and will until he dies."

"So she hates you for something that happened, what, almost forty years ago?"

"If there's one thing Phoria excels at, talí, it's holding a grudge."

Seregil was relieved when Alec finally let the subject drop, but it was some time before he could get to sleep. He hated that singular sort of silence Alec pulled around himself when the subject of Seregil's previous liaisons came up. Alec was normally the most reasonable and easygoing of men; but on this one topic he always grew troubled, though he wouldn't say much about it. All Seregil could do was avoid the subject. He made no apologies for his past, but he hated causing Alec pain. He wanted nothing more right now than to pull the stubborn young man into his arms and apologize, but Alec had turned his back and seemed to be asleep.

Seregil lay awake a long time, watching the sun slowly pass across the window.

Far across the Osiat, the khirnari of Virésse sat on his balcony, enjoying a late breakfast with his eldest daughter as he watched that same sunlight dance on the waves in the harbor below. There were fewer ships there these days, and fewer still that hailed from Skala. The three great merchantmen at anchor near the harbor mouth flew the standards of Plenimaran houses; that land had always been a good friend to Virésse.

Ulan í Sathil was an old man and not easily startled. He didn't flinch when a tiny, pale green orb of light suddenly winked into existence inches from his face. He recognized the bit of Orëska magic, but not the sender's color.

"Would you excuse me, my dear?" he said.

"Of course, Father." Saliana withdrew, used to her father's ways. She could be trusted to say nothing of the odd messenger.

Ulan reached out one long finger and touched the spark, marveling as always that it had neither heat nor any form. He might not know the sender, but he knew the voice that spoke the message as the light disappeared.

"I have watched and waited as you instructed, Uncle. I have it from the lips of one in the great palace that the golden prize flies south to Gedre tomorrow, on lark's wings, and with him the nameless one."

"Ah, I knew you could not long keep away," Ulan murmured. He went to the balcony door and shook awake the young page dozing on his stool.

"Wake up, Mikiel, I have a task for you. Go to the house of Kiran Ashnazai and tell him to come to me at once."

"What shall I say, Khirnari?" the boy asked, rubbing the sleep from his eyes.

"Tell him that our wait is at an end."

He returned to the balcony, and the view of his half-deserted harbor, smiling to himself. "Two birds with one arrow. This will be most satisfying."

Supper was a subdued affair that night. After the dishes were cleared away Seregil brought out his harp and he and Alec sang for their friends. He watched Micum and Kari from the corner of his eye as he played a favorite love ballad. They sat close together on the settle, hands clasped, Kari leaning her head on her husband's shoulder. The firelight caught the glints of silver in their hair and shadowed the lines on their faces, but Seregil could still see in them the young lovers he'd known.

The price of exile, he thought. They'd all be dust before he grew old, if he lived out his span. He wondered how Nyal was going to cope, watching Beka age so quickly. He played on until the two little ones were asleep in their parents' laps and Illia was dozing against Alec's knee.

"That's enough for now," he whispered, setting the harp aside. "We've packing to finish and we'll be off before any of you are up."

"Luck in the shadows to you," Micum murmured.

Seregil managed a smile though his heart suddenly felt heavy. "And in the Light."

As they pottered about their room, deciding what to take and what to leave, Alec glanced up at his black bow on its peg on the wall and his battered old quiver beside it. The latter was still decorated with dozens of small, oddly carved charms hanging from long rawhide laces and made of everything from wood to chalcedony. They were *shatta*—betting prizes he'd won from Aurënfaie archers during their last visit.

"Planning to add to your collection?" Seregil asked.

Alec took down the bow and ran his hands over the dark limbs. "I doubt I'll have much time for that, this trip."

"True. Still, you might get in a challenge or two, at Bôkthersa." He gave Alec a wink. "Besides, I always feel safer when you have that along."

They rose before dawn and came down by candle-light to find Micum dressed and waiting.

"Having second thoughts about coming with us?" Seregil asked.

"Perhaps just a little." Micum chuckled, but there was no missing the longing in his eyes. "I'll ride with you to the quay. I figured you'd need someone to take your horses back for you."

"It won't be a very exciting jaunt, compared to what we're used to," Alec said.

"Well, there's something to be said for peaceful journeys, too."

The city slept around them as they rode through the Sea Market, and down the walled Harbor Way to the docks of the Lower City.

The first glow of dawn was just visible above the city now, but the western sky was still rich with stars. The tide was high, waves lapping at the stone pilings. A land breeze ruffled the calm water of the inner harbor.

People were stirring here: fishermen returning with their lantern boats, fishmongers opening their markets, and wastrels of all descriptions staggering out of taverns and brothels.

The *Lark*'s crew was busy, as well. She was a solid, well-trimmed carrack, with a complement of archers aboard, as well as the crew and their escort. The captain met them on the quay, impatient not to lose the turning tide.

"I can't promise you a smooth crossing this time of year, my lords," he warned.

Seregil laughed. "Get us across alive and I'll be satisfied."

Micum clasped hands with them as their meager baggage was carried aboard. "Well, I'll see you in a month or two, then?"

"We'll come out to Watermead for a hunt," Seregil promised, reluctantly releasing his friend's hand.

Micum remained there, a lone, still figure leaning on his stick as the ship got under weigh and headed out. Seregil stood at the rail, watching to see if he'd leave, but they were out of sight before he had his answer.

Alec joined him and rested his elbows on the rail as they passed through the stone moles and lost sight of the shore. "Funny, but I seem to miss him more now than I did when we were up north all those months."

"So do I."

Alec ran a finger across the back of Seregil's left hand, tracing the double line of blue spots there, a souvenir of their first trip to Aurënen together. A bite from a dragon of that size was always a dangerous thing. Such marks, stained blue with lissik, were considered lucky. The ones you survived, at least; Seregil had been damn lucky not to lose his hand to all that venom. Alec had gotten off lightly; it was only a tiny fingerling that had nipped his left earlobe. The blue marks were tiny but quite visible when he pulled his hair back.

Another paired set of wounds, he thought, smiling to himself. They shared an identical round scar from their first journey together, Alec's on the palm of his hand, Seregil's on his breast.

The melancholy feeling persisted until they were well out at sea, but then, with a new day dawning and cold spray on their faces, the old excitement took over.

"Who knows?" Alec said presently. "Maybe Klia will take us on as scouts when she's a general again. We'd be good at that."

"Still envying Beka that uniform?"

"No, I was just thinking that anything would be better than listening to you complaining about how bored you are!"

Seregil gave Alec's braid a sharp tug, then turned his face to wind, inhaling the sweet salt breeze, heart beating a little faster. Alec was right, though he wasn't about to give him the satisfaction of admitting it.

CHAPTER 6

A Welcoming Port

THE OSIAT WAS mercifully calm for this time of year, and their voyage was an uneventful one, though cold. Seregil and Alec passed the time gaming and singing with the crew. The escort Phoria had given them was small—just ten men. They were a good enough lot, except their captain, Lord Traneus.

A sharp-eyed young man, prideful and clearly ambitious, Captain Traneus was well liked by his men but no one else. He was obsequiously polite to Seregil and Alec, but now and then his gaze seemed to rest on them just a little too long for comfort. Keeping Magyana's warning in mind, Seregil was chilly in return, having the advantage of blood. Alec just did his best to keep away from the man.

Apart from that, Alec was glad to be on the water again and passed the time helping the sailors and watching for dolphins and spouting whales. At night, he and Seregil bundled up in warm cloaks and stretched out on a hatch cover to watch the stars wheeling through the rigging.

So far, Seregil had said little about returning to his clan, even though this was the first time since their mission to Sarikali with Princess Klia.

"Are you glad to be going home again?" Alec asked, their second night at sea.

Seregil smiled. "Yes. It's a bit simpler this time, isn't it?"

"Think I'll meet the rest of your sisters?"

"Maybe." But his tone was neither hopeful nor particularly enthusiastic.

Of Seregil's four sisters, only two of them had forgiven him for the crimes of his youth. Adzriel, who'd raised Seregil after their mother's death, was khirnari of Bôkthersa now, and Alec had been glad to become acquainted with her during their time in Sarikali. Mydri, the second oldest, was not as warm as Adzriel, but she'd been kind to Alec and at least tolerant of her wayward brother. Shalar and Ilina were another matter. They had cut all ties with Seregil when he was exiled.

"Do you ever get angry with them? Your sisters?" asked Alec, keeping his gaze on the stars. He never knew how Seregil was going to react when asked about his past, especially his family.

"How could I be? I committed the crime."

"But you were duped by that Ilar fellow."

Seregil was quiet for a moment, then said softly, "I should have known better."

"I don't understand. You were hardly more than a child."

"Well, you didn't grow up in Aurënen."

"Hmm. I guess neither of us has had the best experience when it comes to family."

Alec had known only his human father, and together they'd lived in virtual hiding from his mother's people, the Hâzadriëlfaie. Her own kin had killed her for loving an outsider, and had tried to hunt down Alec and his father to finish the job. Alec grew up believing himself to be human, until Seregil and Nysander had convinced him of the truth. The most frustrating part was not knowing why the Hâzadriëlfaie were the way they were, or why they would care that his father wasn't one of them. Even the oracles in Sarikali hadn't been able to tell him that.

Seregil reached over and smoothed his palm across Alec's forehead. "You're going to give yourself wrinkles, frowning like that. What's wrong, talí?"

"Nothing you haven't heard before."

"Going back to Aurënen makes you think about it, eh?"

"Yes. And you?"

Seregil grimaced. "Oh yes. I'm absolved, but not forgiven. But there's no shadow on you."

"Because they're not really my people."

"Let them know you as I do, and they will be. My sisters love you, and the clan will embrace you. Not because of me, or in spite of me, but for who you are."

Alec sighed and took his hand. There were some things even Seregil couldn't understand.

The weather blew fair and foul by turns, but the captain took full advantage of the winds and the *Lark* pounded swiftly on. They passed the Eamalie Islands

on the fourth day and glided into Gedre harbor just
as the sun was touching the jagged mountaintops beyond.

There was no jubilant welcome this time; Skalan
vessels had become a common sight here since the
pact was signed. Alec felt a certain degree of pride as
he counted the ships riding at anchor and the line of
newly built storehouses along the shore. The town
climbing the gentle rise beyond still looked the same,
with its domed, whitewashed houses and flowering
trees. Firelight glimmered warmly through hundreds of windows, formed a sparkling crescent
around the harbor. The iron firepots on the quays
cast wavering shafts of light across the water to meet
them. A thin new moon—called Aura's Bow here—
had already risen above the eastern horizon.

"I wonder if Ulan í Sathil has been here since
the change?"

"I hope so," Seregil replied with a crooked
smile. There was no love lost between him and the
khirnari of Virésse. The easternmost clan and their
allies had vigorously opposed the opening of another trade port, having enjoyed a monopoly on
trade during the time of the Edict of Separation. In
Gedre, however, the smugglers had been more than
happy to trade openly once more.

The surprised harbormaster met them at the
quay and quickly sent word up to the clan house. A
mounted messenger soon returned, leading a string
of horses for them and carrying the khirnari's warm
welcome.

Seregil took the red-painted message wand from

his coat and snapped it in half. A tiny flash of light sizzled out and whipped away toward Skala.

He smiled at Traneus. "That's one."

Korathan was walking along the castle battlements, enjoying the night air, when the tiny blue orb appeared before him, hovering like a hummingbird. He touched it and a tiny voice—Magyana's—said, "They have arrived at Gedre."

Pleased, he strode off to tell his sister.

He found Phoria at sword practice with Elani in the queen's private garden. He paused at the gate, admiring the skill on display. Dressed in plain practice leathers, Phoria and Elani struck at each other with blunted swords, catching each other's blades on spiked bucklers. The girl was very quick. Korathan supposed she had to be; her aunt was not a gentle or forgiving tutor.

"Keep your point up!" Phoria snapped, catching Elani's blade with her own and knocking it aside.

The girl recovered quickly and ducked under Phoria's guard, ending with the point of her sword under the queen's chin. They stayed like that for an instant, grey eyes locked with grey—so alike that to Korathan it was almost like seeing his sister at two different ages at once.

Phoria broke into a rare grin. "The advantage is yours, lady. Well done!"

Elani colored happily and lowered her blade.

Phoria turned to Korathan. "Did you see that? She could have cut my throat just then."

"Well done, Niece."

Elani bowed, graceful even in her leathers. "Thank you, Uncle."

"I've had the first message," Korathan told Phoria. "They are safely in Gedre."

Phoria tossed her practice sword to a page, exchanging it for a goblet of wine. "Good. Then the first toss is made."

"She will come."

"We will see."

"And will you be glad to see Aunt Klia, Elani?" Korathan asked, testing the waters.

"If it pleases the queen," she replied, her young face giving nothing away.

It chilled Korathan a little, to see how much Phoria's influence was already blossoming in such a young protégé.

Riagil í Molan and his wife, Yhali, met them at the gate of the clan house.

"Your arrival is unexpected but most welcome, Seregil of Rhíminee! And Alec, too," he exclaimed, clasping hands with them both when they'd dismounted.

Yhali offered a hand to each of them and led them inside. "Come in, and your escort, too. I've ordered a feast in your honor."

"You shouldn't go to such trouble for unannounced guests," Seregil replied, as etiquette required. Any guest—expected or otherwise: friend, enemy, or stranger—could expect such hospitality at any clan house in the land.

Traneus and his men were given rooms and the

use of the household bath chambers. Seregil and Alec, however, were given a bedchamber by the family's private bath.

"Your favor has improved here," Alec noted, sliding happily into the warm, scented water. After so many days in the same clothes, he was hardly even bothered by the presence of the bath attendants.

Seregil had no such modesty, ignoring them completely as he threw off his clothes and settled in the deep tub next to Alec's. "That means more than I can say, talí," he admitted with a deep sigh of satisfaction. "I guested here so often in the old days, with my uncle and kin, it was like a second home. I don't mind so much not having a name, so long as I have a welcome."

By the time they'd refreshed themselves, a meal had been laid out on the long tables under the trees in the central courtyard. The little fretted lamps nailed to the trunks were lit, too, just as Alec remembered.

Seregil was given a place of honor on Riagil's right. Alec sat at Yhali's left. Traneus, Alec noted with secret amusement, looked a bit put out with his place far down the table.

Yhali poured a cup of wine and passed it to Seregil for the guest's libation.

Seregil tipped a few drops onto the flagstones, then took a sip and passed the cup to his hosts. It was more than a ceremony; it was an unspoken pledge that neither party would harm the other while they shared the same roof.

"What brings you across the Osiat at such an unlucky time of year?" the khirnari asked as the spiced lamb and parsley bread were served.

"We're on the queen's business," Seregil replied. "Phoria has sent us to Bôkthersa to fetch Princess Klia home."

"Ah, she will be pleased!" Yhali exclaimed. "I think she's been homesick, though she's too proud to say so."

"And this is your escort?" Riagil raised an eyebrow at the small number of Skalans.

"I think we can ride from here to Bôkthersa without fear," Seregil assured him.

"Queen Phoria has sent new soldiers to attend her sister." Riagil paused, letting the observation hang on the air as he sipped his wine. "We thought that very odd."

"I'm not privy to the queen's thoughts," Seregil replied. "Captain Traneus, can you shed any light on the subject?"

The captain rose and bowed. "I fear not, my lords, though I'm sure her reasons were sound."

Riagil seemed satisfied and the conversation soon turned to talk of rains and trade, births and horses.

As soon as the meal was over, Traneus took his leave and went to see his men settled for the night. Seregil and Alec lingered a while under the flicking lanterns, enjoying the autumn night and the last of the year's night-blooming white flowers. A young woman fetched a harp, and Seregil obliged his hosts with some soft music, while Alec accepted a challenge to shoot against some of the young men who'd heard of his prowess with his Black Radly.

"It seems odd that the queen would not send you with a proper escort," Riagil observed.

Seregil smiled over his harp, still playing. "I know the way, and too many Skalans would only slow us down."

"I see. But you would perhaps not object if I sent a few riders with you, as well? As your host, I feel it is my duty. I've been meaning to buy more of your sis—" He paused and gave Seregil an apologetic look. "I mean to buy more of Bôkthersa's fine horses. I'll send my kinsman, Aryn í Arisei, and his servants to trade for me."

Seregil bowed his head respectfully. "We would be glad of their company."

They sat a while longer, then Yhali walked with them back to their room and bade them good night. She lingered a moment, clasping Seregil's hand. "Welcome back, Seregil í Korit. To me, you will always have a name."

Seregil swallowed around a sudden tightness in his throat. "Thank you, dear lady."

When she was gone, Alec took out Thero's yellow message stick and broke it in two, releasing the little burst of light. "I don't know what difference it really makes, but I feel a bit easier with that done, and with some Gedre riders on the road, too."

"So do I. I wasn't looking forward to being on a lonely stretch of road with Phoria's dog and his men." Then he grinned as he cast a meaningful look at the safely locked chamber door and the broad, clean bed. "Things are looking up, all around, wouldn't you say?"

CHAPTER 7

An Unexpected
Shooting Party

ALEC WOKE SMILING the next morning, bathed in early sunlight and trapped under Seregil's arm.

Seregil opened one eye. "Good morning."

"Good morning yourself. Move off. You're heavy."

Seregil rolled onto his back and yawned. "We stink. Bath."

Riagil found them there as they soaked, and introduced his young kinsman, Aryn. Alec covered himself as best he could with the sponge, blushing furiously. Both Gedre smiled and obligingly turned away a bit.

Seregil lounged at ease, uncaring as always, damn him.

"I mean to take the coastal route to Smuggler's Pass," Aryn told Seregil. "That's the fastest route to Bôkthersa, though we may encounter some early snow in the pass."

Seregil nodded. "Good. Give us time to dress and we'll meet you in the courtyard."

"Breakfast first," Riagil insisted. "Yhali won't forgive me if you don't have a proper send-off. My apologies, Alec í Amasa, for disturbing you."

Seregil held off until they were alone again, then threw a towel at Alec, laughing. "Tsk, such blushing! People will talk. Especially about that rather unfortunate mark I left there, under your left ear."

Scowling darkly, Alec climbed from the tub, found a small mirror among the bath supplies, and examined the purpling love bite. "I hate it when you do that!"

"I don't recall you—"

"Shut up!" Alec growled, fighting back a grin of his own as he wrapped himself in a towel.

"Well, at least we remembered to close the windows." Seregil stood up from the tub, water streaming down his lean belly and thighs and dripping from the beginning of fresh arousal between his legs. He gave it an amused look, then glanced up at Alec. "It's going to be a long ride to Bôkthersa."

Laughing, Alec threw the dripping bath sponge at his head.

Aryn í Arisei and a small escort of Gedre horse traders joined them for the morning meal, and their hosts sent them on with a string of provision horses, letters of passage, and a packet for Adzriel.

They set out north along the arid, rocky coastline, heading for what the Gedre and Bôkthersans called Smuggler's Pass. There were no farms here, just scattered fishing villages, and some goatherds. To the west, the jagged peaks of the Ashek range stretched into the distance like a great row of fangs for as far as the eye could see.

The Skalan soldiers were quiet at first, not knowing what to make of their unexpected companions, but the 'faie traders quickly won them over, practicing their Skalan on them, and acting as interpreters.

Traneus rode with Alec and the others at the front of the little column, and even he warmed up a bit, laughing at some long story Aryn was trying to tell him in broken Skalan.

Autumn had not yet taken hold along the coast. The trees still held their dusty leaves, and a few wildflowers still lingered on the wayside. Oxcarts laden with fruits, vegetables, cheeses, and cured meats rumbled past on their way to distant markets, interspersed with flocks of geese and sheep driven by children who smiled and waved to them.

"Smuggler's Pass, eh?" asked Alec as they rode along. "I seem to recall you saying something about you and your uncle using that route."

"On Traitor's Moon nights." Seregil smiled at the memory, and his hand strayed to the hilt of his sword. It had been a gift from that same uncle during their last visit, and the first Seregil had carried since Nysander's death.

"I remember you from those days," one of the older traders said, a man named Rien. "Your kinsman brought you out on the lantern boat to meet the Skalan traders." He grinned at Alec. "He spoke better Skalan than any of us, even back then. It's good to see you back here, Haba."

Seregil winced a little at the old nickname, which meant "little black squirrel."

Alec chuckled. "I thought only your sisters called you that."

"My friends, as well," Seregil admitted. "Don't *you* go getting any ideas, though."

"As you wish—Haba."

They spent the first night in a fishing village, sleeping four to a bed in the crowded inn, and headed off again before the sun rose. Yawning, Alec ate his cold breakfast in the saddle.

Aryn led them west today, following a winding road up into the foothills. By midafternoon they reached the tree line, following a river that flowed down from the pass. From here, it was five days' ride to Bôkthersa, in good weather.

The forest closed in around them, and the air grew noticeably cooler as the afternoon shadows slowly lengthened across the road. The riding was easy, the inn they were making for well within reach. The 'faie and Skalans talked and laughed, fast friends now.

"Your khirnari has lent us some fine horses, Aryn," Traneus remarked, admiring the sprightly bay he'd been given. "Do you think he'd sell her to me when we get back?"

"Perhaps. You won't find any better," the young 'faie replied proudly. "They're small, but they have spirit and—" He paused and consulted Seregil for the right word. *"Aluia?"*

"Endurance."

"Yes, much endurance. Why would one ride any other?"

"In Skala, only the rich can afford them," Alec explained, stroking the long silky white mane of his Silmai horse, admiring the way the mane and tail contrasted with her glossy black coat. Even here in Aurënen, they weren't common, bred by only one clan. "This one is just like the one Princess Klia was buying, the first time I met her." He noted the quick, sharp look Traneus shot him and feigned a mild look of surprise, thinking, *I'm not ashamed to say her name in front of you, you bastard!*

"I'm thinking of bringing a few horses back with me, too," said Seregil, perhaps sensing the sudden tension between the two.

"Do you keep a large stable in the city?" asked Traneus.

"No, a friend and I have a breeding herd at his estate."

"The war's driven the price up. A few years' worth of foaling will be worth—" Traneus broke off suddenly with a harsh gurgle, a black-fletched shaft protruding from his throat.

Shocked, it took Alec a few seconds to comprehend what had happened. Then the air was thick with the buzz and whine of flying arrows. Unshouldering his bow even as he kicked free of the stirrups, he slid off his horse, looking for cover as he nocked a shaft on the linen bowstring. This stretch of road was wide and lonely, and the thick trees that lined it were good cover for their unseen attackers. Arrows seemed to be coming from all directions.

"Get down, all of you!" Seregil shouted. He jumped to the ground and dragged Aryn from the saddle. All around them, riders cried out in pain or alarm.

Alec knelt at Seregil's side, using the enemy's arrow flights to target the unseen archers.

"Where are they?" gasped Aryn.

"Everywhere!" Alec sent another shaft into the moving shadows between two trees. More of their escort were falling. Alec's fine horse was bucking wildly, with an arrow in its glossy flank.

"But this is our *fai'thast*. Who would do this?" Aryn gasped.

"Doesn't matter now," Seregil told him, looking around sharply. "We've got to find cover."

But there was nowhere to go. The enemy had somehow managed to surround them. As Alec watched helplessly, the rest of their small escort was cut down, Aurënfaie and Skalan alike.

"This way, and keep your head down," Seregil hissed, grasping Alec and Aryn by the shoulders and propelling them toward the underbrush on their left.

They hadn't gotten ten feet when Aryn staggered, clawing at an arrow that had pierced his upper thigh.

Seregil dragged him to the ground and covered the Gedre with his own body. "Alec, check the wound. Did it cut the artery?"

"Yes." There was nothing they could do to save the man, and they both knew it. "We can't stay here!"

"What would you suggest?" Seregil snapped as an arrow sang over his head and another narrowly missed Alec's outstretched hand.

Then, unaccountably, the attack ceased as abruptly as it had begun.

Alec listened, but all he could hear were the cries of the wounded. Every member of their escort lay dead or dying. Aryn was dead. Seregil's friend Rien lay faceup with three shafts protruding from his chest.

"It's us they want," Alec whispered, standing slowly, an arrow nocked ready. "The only way they could have missed hitting us was if they meant to."

Seregil put his back to Alec's, braced for the next attack. "Who are you? What do you want?"

There was no answer. Sweat trickled down between Alec's shoulder blades as he waited for an arrow to find him.

"Show yourselves!" Seregil demanded, and was again answered with silence.

One of the Gedre riders pulled himself slowly to his feet, bleeding from a gut wound, and tried to reach them. An unseen archer put a shaft between his shoulders and he fell without a cry. Another man tried to drag himself to cover, only to be hit by two shafts that came from the opposite side of the road.

And still, not one shaft had hit either of them.

"They want us alive. If we can get into the woods, we might have a chance."

"Left or right?" Alec whispered.

Seregil looked around. The forest was thick here, and there was no telling what lay beyond the road.

He signed "left" and they broke into a run as they made for the trees.

They were within a few yards of cover when he heard a sharp clicking noise, like someone trying to strike a fire. Then the air in front of them thickened and turned black. Out of that blackness rushed two huge, hideously misshapen forms, each a misbegotten, misjointed parody of a man.

"*Dra'gorgos!*" Seregil cried, half in warning to Alec, half in shocked recognition. He'd run afoul of one before and hoped never to again.

He barely had time for the realization before the things were on them and the sun went out like a snuffed candle. Blind and disoriented, he seemed to feel a hundred hard, fetid hands clutching at him.

"Alec!" he yelled, striking out with his sword.

His blade hit something and exploded. There was no other word for it. For an instant he saw a flash like lightning. And perhaps it was, because the jolt of it sent a searing pain up his arm to the shoulder and slammed his teeth together so hard he bit the inside of his cheek.

"Alec!" Unseen arms were tightening around him like bands of iron, crushing the air from his lungs and reducing his voice to a hollow wheeze. "Alec, where are you?"

Lost in blackness and choking on the charnel stench, Seregil heard a distant scream.

Blind, chilled, and rapidly losing consciousness, Seregil tried to get to Korathan's wands inside his coat, hoping that breaking them all at once would alert the prince that something had gone terribly wrong. But the monster's grip was too tight. Desperate to leave some sign that would be recognized, he slipped Klia's ring from his finger and let it fall, and with it a prayer that it be found by a friend.

Alec had just had time to drop his bow and draw his sword before the blackness bore down on him.

"Seregil!" he yelled, caught in darkness and the grip of the black nightmare. A dra'gorgos—or at least that's what he thought he'd heard Seregil shout before the world went black. He tried to fight, but something hit his arm, numbing it except for a burning pain in his hand.

The hilt slipped from his fingers and his consciousness with it.

CHAPTER 8

No Stomach for Magic

SEREGIL WOKE IN darkness, chilled to the bone and caught in a wave of gut-wrenching nausea. His mouth was filled with the mingled bitterness of bile and iron; his teeth grated against a thin, flat metal plate that pressed on his tongue. He shuddered at the sensation and another wave of nausea threatened. The sour reek of vomit was strong, and a rushing, pounding sound filled his ears. Wherever he was, it was dark and moving. As his mind cleared, he recognized the sounds.

A ship. Bilairy's Sack, I'm in a ship's hold. How the—?

Moving his arms and legs carefully, he ascertained that although no bones seemed to be broken, he was shackled hand and foot. Gagging, he tried to sit up, but his head felt too heavy. He collapsed back on his side and felt rough planking against his bare skin. Metal dug into his temple, and the plate between his teeth shifted, cutting the side of his mouth. He was naked, too.

Just his luck.

They've got me in branks.

He rolled slowly onto his back, trying to ease the pressure of the iron cage around his head. Rough chain bit into the underside of his jaw, holding the wretched apparatus in place.

The last thing he recalled was the ambush in the forest. How in the name of the Four had he gotten on a ship? And in this condition, too?

What became of Phoria's message sticks? he wondered dully. *And what will she do when no word arrives?*

He was still too addled from the dra'gorgos attack to get further than that, but knew from experience that the illness was probably his usual reaction to magic. His first thought was that someone had sent him here by a translocation spell, but if so, the effects would be wearing off by now. Instead, he was still wretchedly sick, and it was making it hard to concentrate. And since he wasn't given to seasickness, something must be acting on him, probably some spell on the shackles. He never knew how a new magic would affect him, but more often than not it was unpleasant. This certainly fit the pattern.

He pulled weakly at the shackles and heard the dull drag of heavy chains against wood. There was a long bar between his hands, making it impossible to use them effectively, and another between his feet. He dragged his right hand awkwardly to his face and used his lips and cheek to examine the thick metal band around his wrist. It was a handspan wide, and he could feel neither lock nor seam. He twisted his wrists and the bands cut into his flesh; too tight to wiggle out of, even if he disjointed his thumbs. That was almost a relief; it had been a long time since he'd had to use such drastic measures and he was in enough pain as it was.

As his eyes slowly adjusted to the darkness, he found he could make out a thin sliver of light far overhead that was mostly likely a hatchway. Squinting, he made out the heavy staples his chains were secured to, and then, further away, the shapes of others bound as he was.

"Ah-ek!" It was impossible to speak properly around the branks. "Ar-ek? 'ere are you?"

Suddenly the darkness was filled with frantic voices, all of them as garbled as his own, and none of them Alec's.

Exhausted and sick, he lay still, trying to ignore the terrible discomfort, and the stink of his own vomit pooled near his head.

Over the rush of the waves against the hull, he could make out the thump of bare feet on the deck overhead, and voices. When he finally made out a few words, his heart sank even lower. They were speaking Zengati.

So, he was on a slave ship, and Alec wasn't with him.

Seregil clenched his teeth against the iron plate, using the shivery pain to fight down a burst of panic. He couldn't afford any distractions. He tried to tell himself that Alec could have escaped, but memories of the ambush in the forest won out.

Whoever his captors were, they had killed anyone they didn't mean to take.

And Alec wasn't here.

Panic won, and he thrashed in impotent rage, until he was bloody and too weak to move.

For the first time in a very long time, he was helpless.

CHAPTER 9

hobbled

ALEC WAS DEEP *under dark water, unable to breathe. He could see a light glimmering far overhead, and he tried desperately to swim up to it, but his body was heavy and his arms didn't work right. An undersea swell tugged at him and filled his ears with its soft roar. The more he struggled, the more he sank. Giving up, he used the last of the air in his bursting lungs to cry out for Seregil—*

The unpleasant scrape of metal against his teeth brought Alec out of one nightmare and into a new one. The sound of the sea was still in his ears, and the world was still moving, but daylight smarted his eyes. He was in a cramped, plank-walled room. A tiny window showed only a square of blue sky and a few white seagulls. Even without that, he could tell by the rolling motion of the room that he was aboard a ship under full sail.

How in the name of Bilairy had he gotten on a ship?

Badly disoriented, he looked down to find that his wrists were locked in wide metal bands, and a long bar was fastened between them to keep his hands apart. One end of a heavy chain was fastened to the middle of the spanner, and the other to a heavy metal staple in the wall. His fingers found metal straps between his eyes and around his head.

Someone had put him in branks, like the one Thero had worn when they were captives together on that Plenimaran ship. The same sort of wide, silvery bands of metal encased his wrists. Someone had mistaken him for a wizard and taken serious precautions.

Otherwise, he'd been made comfortable. He lay on a narrow bunk, warmly swathed in blankets. His clothing was gone, he noted uneasily, but otherwise, he seemed unharmed.

For now. Mardus and his necromancers had taken good care of Alec, too, as long it had suited them. How in hell had he come to be in the same damn situation twice?

He closed his eyes. He remembered the ambush, and something black and horrible rushing at him, surrounding him with numbing cold and a breathtaking stench. And Seregil yelling...

Panic rose again, stronger this time, as it sank in that he was alone.

He slid off the bunk and staggered unsteadily toward the window, but the chain wasn't long enough. He could get off the bed to stand, but no further. He climbed back onto the bunk and stood up on it to give him a different view out the window.

There wasn't much to see—just some taut ropes and a section of rail, and beyond that, open sea. He couldn't find the sun to judge the hour.

A chill, salt-laden draft caressed his skin, bringing gooseflesh out on his arms. He sat down and awkwardly dragged a blanket up over his knees with one hand.

The bunk was built into the wall—just bare boards under a thin mattress stuffed with wool. There was nothing loose lying about except two small wooden buckets on a shelf at the end of the bed. The empty one stank of piss, and was clearly meant for a chamber pot. The other held water. He leaned over and sniffed it suspiciously, but it seemed clean. Thirst overrode caution and he sucked up what he could, trying to wash the metallic taste from his mouth. Resuming his vigil, he tried to ignore the fear blossoming in his belly.

Where is Seregil? The thought throbbed in his mind like a heartbeat.

He could hear sailors talking somewhere nearby but couldn't make out their words over the sound of the wind and waves.

Finally, two men passed close by the window and Alec caught a glimpse of dark skin, long black curly beards, and a flash of distinctive striped clothing.

Zengati.

He slid down the wall and rested his useless hands on his knees, heart pounding as he realized how bad the situation really was.

He was still brooding on that when he heard the scrape of a bar being lifted outside his door.

Defenseless, he stayed where he was, his only protection the blanket pulled tightly around him.

The door opened just wide enough for a young boy to slip through, then shut behind him, and Alec heard the bar slam down again. His visitor, barefoot, and dressed in a long, belted shirt, was carrying a large wooden bowl. He eyed Alec for a moment, then quickly set the bowl down on the floor just within reach and scuttled back and banged on the door.

"Wait! Tell me where my friend is," Alec begged, or tried to. The words came out hopelessly mangled around the mouth plate.

The boy called out loudly in his own language to whoever was waiting outside. Alec didn't speak Zengati, but it was clear that he was scared of Alec, and none too pleased with his duty. As soon as the door opened, the boy dashed out.

Alec leaned over the edge of the bunk to inspect the bowl, which held some sort of bland, grey broth. He left it alone, drank more water, then settled cross-legged, back to the wall, watching the door and window. He pulled at the branks, but only managed to hurt his mouth. The wristbands were no better, smooth and seamless, sealed with magic.

Plenimaran magic, on a Zengati slaver's ship. He couldn't think of a worse combination.

Time crawled by and the light began to fade. Judging by the way the shadows moved across the floor, he guessed they were sailing north. North from Gedre lay Skala or Plenimar. Alec had no illusions about where they were headed.

Darkness fell and no one came, not even the

boy. Huddled in his blankets, Alec kept watch on the door, sick with worry for Seregil.

He must have dozed off, for he was completely unprepared when the door suddenly banged open and the cabin filled with people. Dark, bearded faces loomed over him and hard, hurtful hands held him down. Someone held a lantern aloft. Someone else grabbed the bar between his hands and wrenched it out sideways, so that his right hand was over the edge of the bed. An order was barked and some of the men fell back, giving place to a heavyset man wielding a small branding iron. Hands tightened on Alec's chest and legs and shoulders as the bastard grabbed Alec's wrist and pressed the iron to the inside of his forearm.

Alec screamed and swore and struggled as the smell of burnt flesh filled his nostrils, but to no avail. Flipping him over, they branded him on the back of the left calf, too.

It was over quickly, and they left him alone again, but that was little consolation. The pain of the burns was agony, and with his hands shackled like this, it was impossible to find a way to lie that didn't cause more pain.

He cringed as he heard the bar being lifted again. A tall, veiled figure slipped in carrying a basket and a small lantern. At first Alec thought it was a woman, but the legs and bare feet that showed below the short robe were a man's. His hair was hidden under something like a crude sen'gai, and a scrap of plain muslin hid his face below a pair of sad grey eyes.

Aurënfaie eyes, Alec thought, even before the

man unpinned the veil and let Alec see his face, and the thick iron collar around his neck.

He was 'faie, without any doubt, perhaps a bit younger than Seregil. He remained by the door as he held up his right arm, showing Alec the faded brand on his forearm. It was a symbol or letter of some sort, but nothing Alec could make sense of.

"Each slaver ship captain has his own mark," the stranger said in Aurënfaie, and the sound of that familiar language quieted Alec's fears a little.

"You're a 'lave?" Alec slurred around the branks.

The man gave him a dispirited shrug. "What else would a 'faie be, in such company? I've come to dress your burns. Will you let me?"

Alec nodded, trying unsuccessfully to cover himself.

The man set his basket down on the edge of the bed and pulled the blanket over Alec's lap and legs. "I know you're frightened, and in pain, but there's no need for fear. They like their 'faie slaves unblemished at the Riga markets, and that's where we're headed."

He took Alec's arm in gentle hands and applied a salve with a light, careful touch. Alec guessed he'd done this often. The salve smelled good, and soothed the burns considerably. Alec studied his helper closely as the man took strips of clean linen from the basket and bandaged Alec's arm. His tunic had short sleeves, and as he leaned over his task, Alec could see the telltale scars left by a lash peeking out across the back of one shoulder. "'ey 'ip you."

"I was stubborn, and proud," the 'faie replied

without looking up. "They beat that out of me, eventually. It doesn't have to be so difficult for you, little brother. In the end, you'll find it's best to submit."

" 'ubmit? 'oo what?"

"That all depends on who buys you. If you're lucky, being a half-blood, someone might only want you as a laborer, or an ornamental house slave. Turn on your side so I can dress your leg."

Alec rolled over to face the wall. "An' if I no' 'ucky?"

"Well, some would say your mixed blood has a pretty effect, and with that fair hair? You might end up in some rich merchant's bed."

" 'ever!"

"Or perhaps with a woman. The wealthier courtesans often keep boys as pets."

Alec shook his head furiously, heedless of the way the branks plate cut at the corner of his mouth, then let out a grunt of alarm as the man seized him by the shoulder and pulled him around to face him.

"I'm trying to do you a favor, little brother." Turning away, the slave grasped the hem of his robe and pulled the back up to his neck, showing Alec the netting of faded scars that ridged his skin from neck to knees. Then he turned and held up his penis in one hand, showing him the puckered scar where his balls should have been. "They're likely to take those anyway, unless they want to breed you. I'm lucky that master left as much as he did."

Yanking his tunic back down, he fixed Alec with a sorrowful look. "I was proud like you, little brother. But in the end I did all they wanted. You can spare yourself the suffering. Some masters can be quite kind if you're meek and tractable."

Alec squeezed his eyes shut and turned his face to the wall. Meek and tractable? He'd die first!

"Suit yourself, then."

"Wait!" Alec called after him. It was so hard to talk with this thing in his mouth! Choosing his words carefully, he asked, "'as there a 'an with 'e?"

"A man with you? A friend captured with you, you mean?"

Alec nodded. "Auren."

"I don't know. You're the only 'faie I've seen. Try to rest. It's two more days to Riga, and the sailors won't trouble you. The captain would have their skins for it."

He went out, taking the lantern and leaving Alec in the dark, and in despair. If Seregil was dead, then he had even less reason to be meek *or* tractable for anyone. He'd be more than happy to die.

CHAPTER 10

Rough Passage

SEREGIL WAS FAR too sick to gauge the passage of time, or to fight back when they came to brand him. He was barely conscious when dark figures held him down and burned his arm and leg, and only vaguely aware when someone came to tend the wounds. His physical misery was unrelenting.

Every so often the hatch overhead would open, and he roused a bit when they came down to sluice him off with icy seawater, washing away the vomit and shit. Then someone would hold his head up, using the branks for a handle, and force fresh water or broth between his teeth until he choked and swallowed. He usually just brought it up again, but somehow enough stayed in him to keep life in his wasting body. Sometimes in the night, they would come to stare at him, faces hidden behind the blinding glare of a lantern. Or maybe that was just a fever dream? He was too sick to tell the difference, or care.

The rough planking rubbed the skin from his body, and the branks were a continuous torment. His brands felt hot, and he knew they were infected. The only other constant during those miserable days was the hope that Alec was alive somewhere.

As he grew weaker, he slept more, but his dreams offered no escape. Long-dead enemies came to gloat over him. Delirious, Seregil woke once convinced that Mardus and his necromancer, Vargûl Ashnazai, were standing over him, laughing at his condition. In other dreams, he was at the Cockerel, with the headless corpses of Thryis and her family, or back at that sea temple again, looking down at Nysander's sorrowful, upturned face.

That was the only dream that made him weep, and for the first time in many years, he prayed in earnest.

Aura, Lightbearer, if Alec is alive, then help me. If not, then let me die.

He had little faith in answered prayers, but all the same, he lived, even as he sank ever deeper into darkness.

CHAPTER 11

Ho Good Place for a 'Faie

ALEC HOPED IN vain to see the veiled Aurënfaie again. He hadn't even asked his name. But no one except the boy came, bringing him food and water and taking away the slop pail. Alec tried to befriend him, but the boy kept his eyes averted and never lingered.

On the morning of the fourth day the breeze through the little window changed, carrying the scent of land. Standing up on the bed again, he caught a glimpse of white stone cliffs, bright in the distance. There was no sign of green—no forest or fields—and as he took more sightings through the day, his impression remained the same. Seregil had told him that Plenimar was barren in places, especially here in the south; that was why the Plenimarans tried so often to take the land of others. At least that was the Skalan view.

And they kept slaves. Alec looked down at the

scabbed brand on his arm, trying to imagine what lay ahead.

They made port late in the afternoon, and Alec began to feel sick. He told himself that it was just the rolling of the ship at anchor, but his heart knew better.

He'd eaten to keep his strength up. He'd watch for his chance and break for freedom at the first opportunity. He had no idea how he was going to get out of his shackles, but he could worry about that if he actually managed to get away.

That proved a vain hope. Three sturdy Zengati sailors came for him. They bound his legs together with rope and carried him out of the cabin on their shoulders like a rolled carpet.

The ship was a large one, long and lean, and there were dozens of sailors and armed men milling around. No one spared him a glance as he was carried past. Beyond the rail, he could see a waterfront teeming with people.

There was some sort of holdup at the head of the gangway, and he looked around wildly, realizing how futile his hope of escape had been.

At first glance, Riga was no different than any seaport city. The shadows were growing long, and there were lanterns lit along the streets. Tall warehouses lined the shore, and between them he got a glimpse of a large city that spread as far as he could see. Beyond that, in the distance, were white, rolling hills dotted with bits of dark green. It reminded him of Gedre.

On deck, a hatch had been thrown back and filthy, naked people were being led up. The smell was so bad that he retched around the mouth plate of the branks.

The miserable slaves were staggering in chains and, as Alec watched, two sailors came up carrying a limp body by the arms and legs. The man was filthier than all the others—emaciated and bloody, too—but Alec still recognized him.

"'eregil!" he shouted, thrashing in his captors' grip and cursing the branks that gagged him. "'eregil! 'eregil!"

He was terrified at first that Seregil was dead. The man was deathly pale under the filth, and his eyes were sunk deeply in dark, bruised-looking sockets. But as soon as the sailors stretched him on the deck, Alec saw him make a feeble effort to curl into a ball. The heavy metal bars fastened between his hands and feet were too much for him. As Alec watched, he went limp, only the whites of his eyes showing under half-open lids. Alec had never seen his talimenios so weak.

But he's alive and he's here!

Before he could tell anything more of Seregil's condition, Alec's handlers hoisted him higher and carried him down the gangway. Helpless he might be, but he was no longer without hope.

The last thing he saw before the deck rose out of view was the nameless Aurënfaie slave kneeling beside Seregil.

Help him, please! Alec silently begged, as he was carried ashore.

•   •   •

Alec?

Seregil was only dimly aware that the motion around him had changed. Then he was in sunlight, too painfully bright even through his eyelids. A fresh, cold wind cut through the stink he'd thought endless. Had he been asleep? Had he dreamed Alec's voice, calling to him?

It hurt too much to stay here, though, and he let himself sink back into the welcoming blackness.

Consciousness flirted with him, and he wasn't sure if he was awake or dreaming the sound of voices, coming to him faintly, as if from a great distance.

"I told you to hold him, not kill him!"

Seregil knew that voice from somewhere.

"We didn't know..."

He was too far gone to register what language was being spoken; he only knew that he understood it.

"Useless! He's dying!"

Who's dying? Not me, friend! Not until...

Alec's captors carried him down a long stone quay and into a market square. If he'd had any doubts about slavery here, they were put to rest now. There were iron cages full of naked men, women, and children, and beyond that, a raised platform where more people stood chained to posts in front of a crowd.

"Maker, save me," Alec whispered.

The sailors tightened their grip on him and

bore him down a paved street between the ware-houses.

The chill air was dry and full of dust. The street was crowded even at this hour and, for the first time in days, he was painfully aware of his naked-ness. Old women and young girls laughed and pointed, calling out in their own language. Alec's command of Plenimaran was far from perfect, but their jeering tone was enough. Still possessed of a deep-bred northern modesty despite all his time with Seregil, he burned with shame.

And he guessed there was worse to come. They were in sight of more auction blocks now, then among them. On one platform a fair-haired young woman was on display, with her hands tied behind her to keep her from covering any part of herself. Their eyes met in a moment of shared anguish. On the next block, two little boys stood weeping and clinging to each other as the auctioneer harangued the crowd. A blind fiddler stood on a street corner, playing a bright jig.

A sudden turn in the street spared Alec any more such sights, but it had been enough. Angry tears blurred his vision as he screamed and strug-gled, helpless to stop, as his captors hurried him into a long, low building.

It was like a barn inside, and lined with stall-like cages. They put him in one of these, laying him down carefully on a thick bed of straw and slam-ming the iron door shut behind them.

The place was brightly lit. Alec pushed himself up on his hands and looked around. The walls of his little cell were made of heavy boards, so he could only see out the front. Across the room, most of the cages held one or more captives.

Still hampered by the iron bar between his hands and the ropes cutting into his legs, he crawled to the back corner of his cage and covered himself in the straw as best he could. His heart was pounding, the sound of his own blood loud in his ears as he fought a renewed rush of panic. He had no tools, and there were people everywhere, talking or haggling loudly in languages he could not understand. He wished now he'd let Seregil teach him Plenimaran. After his last experience, he'd wanted nothing to do with this country, not even its language. Now he kicked himself for his stubbornness.

How long until someone dragged him back out to the blocks and put him on display? How would he know what was going on?

It was a busy place, this slave barn, not unlike a horse dealer's market. People of all sorts strolled up and down the line of cages, laughing and chatting together as they inspected the merchandise. Many stopped to look at Alec, but none came in after him. There were a number of Zengati about in their salt-stained boots and striped tunics. Most, however, had the look of nobles or merchants, and dressed more in the Skalan fashion. Alec studied them all carefully. Aside from Duke Mardus and his necromancer, the only Plenimarans he'd had any experience with were their marines, and they were a cruel, hard-bitten lot. By comparison, these people looked like any ordinary market crowd, except for the goods in which they were trading.

An elegantly dressed young woman paused to

stare at him, attended by several servants and friends. Her bodice was more modestly cut than that favored by Skalan women of fashion, but she had brilliant feathers and jewels in her upswept hair. Her face was covered in some sort of white powder and her lips were painted dark red. The unnatural cast of it, and the appraising look in her hard, dark eyes, made Alec nervous. She gestured at him, then moved on, casting back some remark that set her companions laughing and pointing.

Alec guessed she must be one of the courtesans the veiled man had mentioned. What little he'd ever heard about proper Plenimaran women was that they were kept at home and closely guarded.

I'll be damned if I end up the toy of some whore!

He tried to ignore the crowd after that, until a few ruffians crowded up to the bars and threw pebbles at him until he looked up. They were dressed like butchers, in leather aprons streaked with dried blood, and had curved knives and oddly made pincers dangling from their wide leather belts. One of them caught Alec staring and cupped his groin through his apron, making an unmistakable slicing motion with his other hand.

A distinguished-looking Plenimaran man spoke sharply to them and shooed them off. He was past his prime, but not old. He wore a black velvet surcoat with silver chains and wide cuffs of lace, a number of gold rings and a jeweled chain.

"Calm yourself, boy," he said to Alec in perfect Skalan. "If you are what I've been led to believe, then you are in no danger of the gelding knife."

The stranger was accompanied by a smaller

man in a deeply hooded cloak that obscured his face, and a small entourage of manservants, all of them dark-skinned, with close-cropped hair and beards. These looked more like the Plenimaran marines Alec had known, and he wedged himself more tightly into his back corner, even though he'd already guessed it wouldn't do any good.

There was no mistaking the look on the well-dressed man's face; he'd found something he'd been looking for, and Alec was it. He spoke softly to the hooded man, who in turn motioned forward someone who'd been concealed behind the others.

This one wore a veil over the lower part of his face, and Alec knew him at once for an Aurënfaie by his slighter build and light eyes. He wore a long, sleeveless tunic under his cloak and good leather shoes. A golden torque glimmered at his throat.

The hooded man and the man in the black coat spoke quietly with him in Plenimaran. The veiled man turned to look down at Alec, nodding agreement to something the men said.

"What're 'ou 'ooking at?" Alec spat bitterly in Aurënfaie, his words slurred around the branks.

The man in black said something to the 'faie, who then approached the bars and said in Aurënfaie, "My master bids you put your hand out through the bars. He won't hurt you."

Master? So this 'faie was a slave, too.

"Your masker can go fuck himsel'!" Despite the branks, he had made himself understood. Those eyes weren't smiling now.

"Softly, little brother. A bad temper won't do

you any good here. Come to the bars and put your hand through. You're in no danger."

"'o ta the 'rows, 'rai'or!"

"Please," the 'faie implored softly, stealing a look back at his waiting master. "Obey now, or they'll come in and force you. And that *will* hurt."

"He's quite right," the dark man told Alec, speaking Aurënfaie as fluently as he did Skalan. "And it will all end the same way, Alec of Ivywell. See? I know who you are. And I've been most eager to meet you. Now give me your left hand nicely, or those rough men in leather aprons will drag you out for me."

Defeated, Alec crawled awkwardly to the front of the cage and hesitantly extended his shackled hand out through the bars, half-expecting it to be cut off. The man grasped it and twisted the palm upwards, tracing the round, faded scar at its center with a thumbnail. Alec held still, watching as the man smiled to himself. It was almost as if he knew the history of that mark. Alec also noted that his fingers were stained with ink. Perhaps he was a wizard, after all or, worse yet, a necromancer.

"Just a little poke," the possible necromancer murmured, and before Alec could pull back he produced a thick needle from the folds of his robe and pricked the end of Alec's forefinger deeply.

Alec hissed at the pain and tried to pull back, but one of the servants reached in quickly and held him there while the master caught a large drop of Alec's blood on his fingertip. They released him then, and Alec quickly pulled back out of reach. The nobleman rubbed the blood between thumb and forefinger and a small tongue of muddy red flame licked up for an instant, then disappeared.

" 'ecroman'er!" Alec hissed, his worst fears realized.

The man wiped his soiled fingers with a spotless white handkerchief. "I'm nothing of the sort. And that's good news for you, I'm sure you'll agree."

The wizard, or whatever he was, turned to speak to the hooded man in his own tongue. Alec knew the Plenimaran word for blood—*ulimita*—and heard it spoken several times. The noble seemed very pleased about something, and so did the hooded man. Though Alec could still see nothing of his face, he heard him say something softly in Plenimaran. There was something familiar about that voice. Before Alec could tell for sure, though, the hooded man turned and strode away. Whoever it was, he had the gait of an old man.

The not-necromancer nodded to one of his companions and a weighty-looking purse changed hands with a slave dealer.

Turning back to Alec, he said, "My name is Charis Yhakobin. I own you now, Alec, and you will call me *Ilban*, which means master in my language. To address me in any other fashion is disrespectful, and will be punished."

"Kish my ash!" Alec snarled as a new wave of panic threatened.

"My tastes do not run in that direction, boy, and you will incur my great disfavor if you ever again suggest such a thing. You are a useful instrument to me. Nothing more. Nothing less."

At his order, one of the slave market men came

with a bunch of keys and opened the cage. Alec cowered back, but it did no good. His new owner gave orders to a pair of muscular servants. They entered the cage and cut the ropes around his legs, then roughly hauled him up by the arms.

"Come along, or my men will carry you out by force," Yhakobin advised.

Alec's legs burned as the blood returned to limbs too long bound. Even so, the urge to fight or run was strong. Alec hated feeling so helpless, but the memory of one of Seregil's early lessons came back, calming him a little.

Pick your fights carefully, talí.

So he feigned resignation, hanging his head as he shuffled out, but all the while surreptitiously glancing around for a way to run.

"I think we can dispense with this, as well." Yhakobin reached behind Alec's head and released the branks, then lifted the apparatus from his head. "The slavers can't tell the 'faie with power from those without. You're no wizard."

"Then what do you want with me?"

Without the slightest change of expression, Yhakobin struck him across the mouth so hard it snapped Alec's head sideways.

"Your first lesson, young Alec, is to address me with respect. Your second awaits outside. Cover him, Ahmol."

One of the older servants shook out a plain cloak and wrapped it around Alec, covering his bound hands.

Yhakobin turned to leave and the larger servants took Alec firmly by the shoulders and steered him to follow. Alec kept his head down, peering around from behind the cover of his dirty, unbound hair, looking for Seregil as they passed more of the cages, but there was no sign of him.

Night had fallen and the market crowd was even thicker. Even if he did manage to get loose, he was barefoot, weaponless, and practically naked. His fair skin and hair would be like a banner here, not to mention the fresh brands.

Everywhere he looked, Alec saw people in the same miserable situation, caged, chained, on display, or being dragged along behind Zengati traders or Plenimaran masters. Most of the slaves appeared to be from the Three Lands, but he saw a few 'faie among them, branked and bound, their eyes vague.

It was colder now, and the rounded street cobbles hurt his feet. Still unsteady, he tripped and would have fallen more than once if his guards hadn't held him so tightly. He stubbed his toes painfully and was limping by the time they dragged him to the edge of another large square.

"Here is a lesson every slave that comes through Riga is given." Yhakobin pointed to a line of half-naked wretches chained by the neck along a stone wall. Each one had a placard around his or her neck, and most had a bloody, bandaged stump where a hand or foot or arm had been.

"Slaves who run lose a foot." He nodded at a bone-pale boy with no feet at all. "That one has run twice, as you can see. He'll be hanged in a few days. Those who steal lose a finger or hand. I'm sure you can guess the rest."

He had his men lead Alec to a dispirited-looking woman chained near the end. She had all her limbs, but at Yhakobin's sharp order she opened her mouth wide, showing Alec the blackened wound where her tongue had been cut out.

"That is the penalty for speaking back to your master," Yhakobin warned. "I do hope you'll keep that in mind. I have no use for your tongue, and will happily have it out if it offends me again. Do you understand?"

Alec swallowed hard against the fresh bile rising in his throat, then said as humbly as he could manage, "Yes, Ilban, I understand."

Whatever role you play, play it to the hilt, Seregil's voice whispered in the back of his mind. Alec embraced all the fear and horror he'd been battling and let it show in his face.

"Very good." Yhakobin patted his shoulder. "Show me the proper respect, and you will find me a kind master."

They stopped next at what appeared to be a blacksmith's shop. It was warmer inside, at least. The smith greeted Alec's owner with a respectful bow, then motioned for Alec to kneel beside an anvil at the center of the shop. When he pretended not to understand, he was compelled to obey with a few rough shoves and a kick to the back of his knees.

Yhakobin took a thin, silvery-looking circlet from his robes and gave it to the smith. *A collar,* Alec realized, just as the golden torque the other slave wore must be a sign of his station.

The silver collar had a gap in it, with pierced flanges on both ends. The smith bent it out wide enough to place it around Alec's neck, then forced his head to the anvil. One of Yhakobin's men held Alec down while the smith fitted a copper rivet through the holes, set the tip of a blunt chisel against it, and struck it a single sharp blow with his hammer, so hard it jolted Alec's head against the iron.

"Sit up." Yhakobin slipped a finger under the collar and gave it a small tug. "Not too tight, is it? Have you nothing to say to me?"

"It's not too tight—Ilban," Alec managed, hating the cold weight of the metal against his skin just as much as the fetters on his wrists.

"The brands mark you as a slave, and every Plenimaran knows where to look. This collar marks you as my property, and it won't come off as easily as it went on. Keep that in mind as you dart those sharp eyes of yours around, looking for your chance to run."

Alec colored guiltily and Yhakobin laughed. "You do have spirit, don't you? Quite wasted on me, I'm afraid."

At his order the men marched Alec out to a waiting carriage. It was small, but well made, and decorated with inlay and polished woods. The glow of the brass lanterns set beside the driver's bench shone on the glossy flanks of a pair of Silmai blacks harnessed to it. This Yhakobin must be a lord of considerable wealth.

The liveried footman jumped down to open the door. Yhakobin climbed in and sat down on a seat covered in tufted red leather. Alec's guards shoved him inside and he was made to kneel at his new master's feet. The driver whipped up the horses and they set off through the darkness. Yhakobin took some papers from a pocket under the window and perused them, ignoring Alec as if he'd ceased to exist.

Alec seized the opportunity to study Yhakobin more closely. Like the carriage, the man's clothing and fine shoes spoke of wealth. Seregil had taught him to look beyond first impressions, however, and Yhakobin's hands told another story. In addition to the ink stains, the man had a scattering of small white scars on the backs of his hands—the sort of marks common among smiths and chandlers. *Or wizards,* he added silently. He tried to remember what the necromancer's hands had looked like, but his memories of them were vague now, overlaid by the torment he'd known in their grasp.

"Where are we going . . . Ilban?" he ventured at last.

Yhakobin didn't even look up. "Home. Be quiet now."

Alec gritted his teeth and pondered jumping from the moving vehicle while Yhakobin wasn't looking. But he was still manacled and at too much of a disadvantage. He wasn't going to risk losing a foot this early in the game. Instead, he contented himself with staring out the window. His low vantage point cut off most of the useful view; he caught only the impression of tall buildings and narrow streets, then an orderly line of trees, interspersed with lamp poles, which suggested a park. After that there was little to see except the rising moon.

The road grew bumpier and Alec was hard-pressed to keep his balance. One hard jolt threw him against Yhakobin's knees. The man righted him and ruffled his hair, as if Alec were a hound.

"What's this?" He pushed the hair back from Alec's left ear and examined the blue-stained dragon bite on the lobe.

"Is it some sort of clan mark?"

"It's nothing, Ilban," Alec lied. "Just decoration."

Yhakobin released his ear and went back to his reading.

Alec twisted his wrists in the manacles, pressing the spanner bar between his wrists. *I could strangle him and jump from the coach.*

And then what, aside from the broken bones and the lack of clothing? the Seregil in his mind asked wryly.

Before he could come up with a better plan, the carriage took a sharp turn, and then slowed. Alec glimpsed an arched stone gate, then heard the crunch of gravel under the coach wheels. A moment later they came to a stop and the door flew open. Men dragged him out by the spanner bar and hustled him quickly across a walled courtyard and through a low door. From there he was rushed down a narrow servants' stairway, to a long, dank, brick corridor. They took several turns as Alec looked around frantically, trying to make sense of where he was. The few doors they passed were closed. His guards halted in front of one that looked no different from any other and opened it to reveal a tiny, whitewashed room. One of them took the cloak, leaving him naked again.

Someone spoke curtly behind him; Yhakobin had followed them down here.

He took something from his pocket and palmed it before Alec could see what it was. But when he then touched each of the manacles, they cracked in half and fell to the floor, taking the wretched bar with them.

"Thank you, Ilban." Alec almost meant it this time.

Yhakobin frowned at the raw skin on Alec's wrists. "Those fools, risking infection for no reason."

At his order, the man called Ahmol produced a small pot of salve and rubbed it over the damaged skin.

Yhakobin seemed satisfied. "There, that should heal well. In you go, now."

They shoved Alec into the room and slammed the heavy door behind him. He heard a bar fall into place and shuddered. Shut in, and helpless again.

"Rest now," Yhakobin called in to him. "I'll have food brought down to you." There was a pause, then he added sternly, "It is customary for a slave to thank his master, Alec."

That was too much. "I'm no slave, and you'll *never* be my master!" Alec yelled, forgetting Seregil's lessons and the sight of the slave with her tongue cut out as he slammed both fists against the door.

It opened so fast he would have fallen into the corridor if one of the guards hadn't caught him and locked an arm around his throat. The collar bit into his neck as he was jerked off his feet and shoved face-first against a rough stone wall. Yhakobin was close behind him now, breath warm on Alec's cheek as he held up a short, thick riding crop.

"I will be lenient this time, since you are new and we are not in public." Stepping back, he struck Alec hard across the back. It hurt like hell, but didn't break the skin. Nine more blows followed, then Alec was grabbed by the hair and thrown back into the cell. He came down hard on the stone floor, banging his right elbow painfully and scraping the bandaged burn on his arm. The pain drove him back to his feet. He faced the doorway, braced to fight.

Yhakobin regarded him for a moment, then smiled. "Perhaps it's a good thing, this strong spirit of yours, though it will not make your life here an easy one."

"It's not my choice to be here, *Ilban*," Alec snarled, shaking with anger.

"No, but it is your fate." With that, the door closed and the bar fell again.

Alec listened as the footsteps faded away. The stripes on his back stung like fire, but the pain cleared his head. He was acting foolishly, fighting when there was no hope of winning, and antagonizing the man who held his life in his hands. Yhakobin could have just as easily had them tear out his tongue. For some reason he'd refrained, but it would be foolish to push the man.

The cell was cold and dark. A tiny barred window set high in the wall across from the door let in a little torchlight—just enough to make out that the walls were smoothly plastered and whitewashed, and the floor was paved with bricks set in mortar.

As his eyes adjusted to the dimness, he saw a pallet bed piled with folded quilts over in the far corner.

A long robe had been laid out for him, too. He pulled it on, surprised at how soft and clean it was. The wool gave off a faint scent of lavender and cedar, as if it had been stored in a proper clothes chest. The plain quilts smelled like fresh air and sunlight. The pallet, too, was a thick, well-aired feather tick.

It was a relief to be dressed again. He wrapped himself in one of the quilts and circled the room, looking for anything he could use to his advantage. The walls were solid and gave back the dull report of stonework under his knuckles. The door was hinged on the outside, and there was no lock to pick, even if he'd had something to work with. Stymied for the moment, he sat down on the pallet with his sore back against the cold wall, and pulled more quilts over himself.

"I'm alive," he whispered, shivering from the pain now and feeling a little sick. "*He's* alive, too, and we're both on dry land again. We *will* find each other."

All he had to do was bide his time and keep himself in one piece. Sooner or later, an opportunity would present itself.

CHAPTER 12

Bargains in Flesh

CHARIS YHAKOBIN WAS not a man who took any particular pleasure in disciplining his slaves. He usually left that to someone else, but this young Alec was quite a special case, and he'd already decided that no one else was going to lay a hand on him.

He climbed the stairs to the main level of the villa and crossed the central courtyard to find the Virésse khirnari waiting for him at a small wine table by the fountain pool. Ulan í Sathil was still wrapped in his cloak against the evening chill, with the hood thrown back. His white hair glimmered in the torchlight.

"You are satisfied with our bargain, Charis?" the khirnari asked in that cold, level voice of his.

"Most satisfied, though it's a pity the boy is a half-blood."

"But you can still make use of him?"

"Oh yes."

"And the other one?"

"You don't use his name, I notice. I haven't heard you speak of him directly once."

"He has no name. He is an outcast, and no concern of mine. I trust he will be dealt with appropriately?"

"I can assure you, he will never see Aurënen again, my friend."

"Yes, but will he suffer?"

"I have no doubt that he will, with his new master. And now, for my part." He took a leather folder of documents from inside his coat and laid it before Ulan. "Emancipation papers for forty-two Virésse and Golinil clan members. They will be on your ship by dawn."

Ulan paused, hand poised over the folder. "You promised me forty-four."

"Two have since died. Their remains have been prepared. You can still return them to their families. I do apologize, but it happened before I could purchase them."

"Ransom," Ulan corrected. "They are ransomed. We 'faie do not involve ourselves in the buying and selling of flesh."

"Of course. I misspoke. Those whom I ransomed, as my part of our bargain, then."

"Thank you. And as to the other part of our bargain?"

"As soon as a rhekaro is perfected—if indeed it is possible—and properly assessed, one will be sent to you."

Ulan raised an eyebrow at that. "If? This is the first time you've shown any doubt."

"I hadn't seen him, much less tested him when

we struck our bargain," Yhakobin reminded him. "I had only your word that he was of that bloodline at all. And the boy is half human, after all, and that's strong in him. I can only do so much." He paused and sipped his wine. "Tell me, Khirnari, are there truly none in Aurënen who know of this blood property? That seems so odd, given the length of 'faie memory."

"I knew nothing of it until you contacted me about all this. And if I knew nothing, then it is highly unlikely that anyone else does, with the possible exception of the rhui'auros at Sarikali."

"Ah, yes. Your mysterious, mystic priests. Are they the keepers of your people's secrets?"

The khirnari answered that with an enigmatic smile. "There are many stories about why Hâzadriël gathered her followers and fled north, though no one knows the truth, or so the rhui'auros would tell you. But some say that she was gifted with a vision by the *bash'wai* spirits who inhabit Sarikali."

"Mystics and ghosts! My, but you are a colorful people." Ulan's smile disappeared. He did not move, but the air around Yhakobin suddenly felt cold and dense. "I meant that as a compliment, of course."

"Of course." Ulan kept him pinned with his sharp-eyed gaze a moment longer, then looked down at his wine.

Yhakobin relaxed slightly as the atmosphere returned to normal. "So, I will endeavor to make the *rhekaro* with what I have to work with, and then we shall see."

"I should like to see your texts, which speak of this magic."

Yhakobin nearly refused; no alchemist shared his precious store of knowledge, and most certainly not with an outsider. And he did already have the young Hâzadriëlfaie in hand. All the same, Ulan í Sathil was too powerful a man to trifle with. "Very well. Please wait here while I retrieve it."

As he unlocked his workshop door, he glanced back suspiciously, but Ulan still sat at the wine table, gazing at the fountain or statuary now. After that little demonstration of displeasure, however, Yhakobin wondered if the man was somehow co-ercing him into revealing his precious texts. Safely inside, he went to one of the tables and placed a bit of sulfur in a crucible and poured a few drops of several tinctures over it, then drew the requisite symbols on the table. He lit the sulfur with a coal from the forge and watched the flame, which flared up yellow, then turned a deep green; Ulan was exercising no magic on him, or at least none he could identify.

Satisfied, he went to the small pavilion at the far end of the room and crawled inside to open the large casket hidden there. The lock opened at his touch, and he took out the lesser tome and carried it back to Ulan. He doubted the man, for all his apparent wisdom, knew how to read the Arcana.

"Here, Khirnari," he said, opening the book to a chapter marked with a black ribbon. Ulan took the tome and slowly followed the tiny characters with a finger, nodding slowly. "According to this, the longevity properties are not predictable."

"Most likely because of the differing distillation processes employed by the few alchemists who practiced this science. Each lineage has its own methodology, rather like the inherited magic of your people. And no one in those ancient times ever thought to use a half-blood, when the pure strains were so readily had."

"The history of your people's depredations on our shores is nothing to speak of lightly," Ulan said quietly, and the air grew a little heavy again.

"Of course not, Khirnari. I only meant to give you an explanation of why my endeavors in this matter may be unpredictable. But rest assured, the purification and decoction of blood strains is a great strength of mine. And at the risk of seeming arrogant, I daresay you will not find another alchemist who is more adept at the art than I."

"I do not doubt your expertise, Charis. If the process produces the elixir I hope for, then I will be pleased, of course. If it does something else, then you will of course share that knowledge."

"Of course. And regardless of the outcome, I will continue to keep our bargain. Any member of the Virésse clan I find in the markets or households of Plenimar will be purchased—ransomed, that is—and returned to you."

"And your traders will continue to have favored status in my ports, and in my fai'thast."

Ulan rose and bowed to him. "Good night, my friend, and good luck."

"Won't you stay the night with us, Khirnari? My wife has prepared a banquet in your honor."

The old Aurënfaie's hesitation would not have

been apparent to a man less astute than Charis Yhakobin. "I will be most honored to dine with you, but these old bones of mine will sleep better rocked by the tide in an Aurënfaie berth. One of the many prices of age, my friend. One becomes overly attached to the familiar in small things."

"And great ones, as well." It was no secret that the pact between Skala and the Gedre khirnari had hurt more than Virésse's trade and shipping interests. It had hurt their pride. What Seregil í Korit's role had been in that was unclear, but Yhakobin had been more than happy to benefit from the rift. If not for Ulan's animosity toward the young Bôkthersan, Yhakobin might never have gained the prize he now had safely locked away in his cellar.

He let his gaze wander to the dark, slender figure standing at a respectful distance in the shadows and gave a slight nod to show that all was well. Yhakobin was a wealthy man, and a powerful one, but merciful when it suited him. He could afford to be generous now, especially to one who had brought him his heart's greatest desire.

Ilban

FOR TWO DAYS Alec was left in peace, but he was clearly being punished; his gaolers brought him nothing but water. They didn't speak to him when they came with the pitcher, or to take away the pail, but no one abused him, either. He had no doubt, though, that he was being closely observed.

His belly ached and growled, but he'd known worse deprivations. By the second day he was a little light-headed, but the worst thing was the boredom. There was nothing to do but count the bricks in the floor and watch the patch of sunlight crawl across the wall. He'd tried to get up to the tiny window, but it was too high. Sitting in his nest of quilts, he spent hours listening intently, trying to imagine what lay beyond this room.

There were often footsteps in the corridor outside his door, and the muffled sounds of conversation. He couldn't understand the words, but it sounded like servants' talk. Occasionally he made out Yhakobin's voice—a calm, even murmur that was always answered with respect.

Birdsong came in through his window, and the ordinary sounds of a household—footsteps, the clank of a pail, the sound of wood being split, the crowing of a rooster at daybreak, the occasional snuffle of a dog near his window, women's voices, and the occasional laughter of children.

Just after dark the second day, his keepers came in carrying a lamp and a chair. Alec remained on his pallet as they set these things against the wall by the door, then stepped back to let in their master.

Yhakobin sat down and motioned to Ahmol, who carried in a wooden bowl and a small brown loaf. Alec's mouth watered painfully as the smell of warm oat porridge drifted across to him. Instead of bringing them to Alec, however, Ahmol stayed by the door and looked to his master.

"How does this night find you, Alec?" Yhakobin asked, crossing his legs and smoothing the fabric of his dark robe over his knee.

The smell of the food made his traitorous stomach growl. "Well enough, Ilban," he replied, respectfully dropping his gaze.

"Hungry?"

"Yes, Ilban." There was no use denying it. He could see the game that was being played, but standing on pride and getting any weaker wasn't going to get him anywhere.

"You're more reasonable tonight. I'm glad."

"Hunger is a good teacher, Ilban."

Yhakobin nodded to Ahmol. The servant set the

food down in front of Alec and went out, closing the door.

"Please, eat," Yhakobin said, as if Alec was a guest at his table. "I took my supper upstairs."

"Thank you, Ilban." Alec picked up the bowl and took a sip of the porridge. It was thin and milky, flavored with honey. He had to force himself to eat slowly so he wouldn't sick it back up. After a few sips he tore off a bit of the bread and used it as a sop. It was still warm from the oven.

He ate in silence, aware of the man's eyes on him, and the slight smile on his lips. Yhakobin had a sharp, intelligent face. The ink stains caught Alec's attention again; this man certainly had the look of someone more at ease with a pen than a sword.

He finished the porridge and set the bowl aside. "Your prison is better than some inns I've stayed at, Ilban."

"You are not in prison, Alec. This is where I put new slaves, especially excitable ones like yourself. A few days of peaceful rest to help you accept your new position."

"I'm glad you don't have your whip tonight, Ilban."

Yhakobin chuckled. "It's close by, I assure you. It's up to you whether I need it again. I am not the sort of master who delights in abusing his slaves for no reason."

Alec nodded and nibbled at another piece of bread.

"You may ask me questions."

Alec considered for a moment, then asked, "How do you know my name?"

"I've known about you for some time now. Plenimar has ears and eyes in Aurënen, as well as in Skala."

"Spies."

"Of course. And it was not difficult, with you and your companion making no secret of your mixed blood. Bragging about it, it seemed. Most unwise of you. Your people should have taught you better than that."

"My people?"

"The Hâzadriëlfaie."

Alec frowned and looked away. "They aren't my people. I never knew them."

"I see. Of course, you're not a pureblood. The color of your hair suggested it, and I've already verified the fact, back at the slave barns. That was a disappointment, but the strain is still very strong in you. So, you are the child of a runaway. Tell me, was it your mother, or your father?"

Alec kept silent, trying to comprehend what he was being told. *This is why they'd been captured? It's my fault we're here?*

"Well, it's of no consequence for now," Yhakobin said, still watching him closely.

"What do you want from me . . . Ilban?"

"All in good time, Alec. Tell me, do you know what an alchemist is?"

"An alchemist?" Alec searched his memory. He'd heard the term once or twice around the Orëska House, and always in disparaging tones. "I once heard someone call it kitchen magic."

Yhakobin smiled at that. "No, Alec, alchemy is one of the highest Arts, the marriage of magic and natural science. It's far more powerful in its way than all that hand waving your Orëska wizards do, and nothing at all like necromancy."

"But you used my blood for a spell, Ilban. I saw you."

"Blood can be a powerful element, Alec, no different than salt or sulfur or iron. The necromancers also make use of it, of course, but not at all in the manner of alchemists."

The food went heavy in Alec's belly. "You're going to kill me, and take my blood?"

"Kill you? What a shameful waste that would be! Whatever made you think of that?" He paused, then shook his head. "No, Alec, I would never kill you. I intend for you to live a long and comfortable life here with me. If you behave and do as I ask, that life can be very pleasant indeed."

Alec suddenly sensed an opportunity. Seregil had often praised his ability to look young and innocent. He played to that strength now as he widened his eyes and asked, "Then you really aren't going to kill me, Ilban? Or use me in your bed?"

"You have my word. Those are the furthest things from my mind. You know, not all Plenimarans are like those you've met on the battlefield. Our warriors are very fierce, but they are chosen for that, and trained to it. I've traveled a bit in your land and we ordinary folk are not so different from yours. You'll come to appreciate that in time. Get some rest, and after you've had another meal tomorrow, *if* you behave, I'll take you out of here and begin to familiarize you with your new home."

"What will my duties be?" he asked, then quickly added, "Ilban." This was getting very tiresome.

"You strike me as an intelligent young man. Perhaps you can assist me in my work."

"In alchemy?"

"Yes. I believe you'll be a very great help in time."

Alec picked up his bowl and knelt to place it at Yhakobin's feet. "Thank you for the food, Ilban, and your kind words. I'm less fearful now, for hearing them."

Yhakobin cupped Alec's chin and raised his face to look him in the eye. "That's very nicely said, Alec. Of course, I don't believe a word of it, and that's your second mistake." He hooked a finger in the smooth metal collar and gave it a playful tug. "You will not get far with this around your neck, my coy little nightrunner. Even if you slice the brands from your skin—and you wouldn't be the first to do so." Giving him a final firm pat on the cheek, Yhakobin rose and went out. The guards collected the chair and lantern and locked Alec in again.

He groped his way back to his pallet and lay down, heart thudding dully in his chest.

Nightrunner. Where in Bilairy's name was the man getting his information?

CHAPTER 14

The Power of Memory

HABA.

Still lost in darkness, Seregil dreamed of gentle hands easing his pain, soothing his skin.

Haba ...

Cool fingers traced the planes of his face. Warm lips covered his. In vain he fought to open his eyes. A dream ... only a dream.

He thought he was in his bed at Wheel Street. He turned his cheek to that touch ...

Alec. Talí ...

Fingers brushed his lips.

No, Haba.

No, of course not. Alec had never called him that ...

Darkness claimed him, pulling him deeper.

Haba!

"You're still abed?" Mydri called through the

tent flap. "Get up, Haba, you lazy thing. Father's waiting for you at the assembly."

Seregil curled deeper in his blankets, squeezing his eyes shut and trying to pretend he hadn't heard.

"Suit yourself, brat," his sister muttered, and strode off.

The air was already warm and filled with the drowsy buzz of cicadas. He could tell by the slant of tree shadows across the painted canvas that it was well past dawn. He threw back the blankets and sat up, knowing better than to keep his second sister waiting too long. Adzriel or Illina might shout for him, or come in and tickle him awake. Mydri was more likely to fetch him a nasty slap.

No breakfast again, he thought glumly, unless he could charm one of his aunts or cousins into giving him something behind his father's back. Or he could steal something from one of the other camps; that was a favorite game lately, among his friends.

He pulled on his long white tunic and tried to brush out the wrinkles. One more thing for Mydri to scold him for. He stuck his tongue out at the thought and laced on his sandals, then made a hasty job of combing his long brown hair with his fingers. He took more care with the dark green sen'gai. When it was wrapped and twisted into a proper shape around his head, he paused a moment, then let the long ends fall over his left shoulder.

He pressed his fingers to his lips, cheeks going warm with the memory of last night's stolen kiss in the shadow of the forest. *I have a lover.*

Grinning, he lifted the ends of the sen'gai and let them fall down his back. They weren't *really* lovers yet. And even if they were, Seregil certainly wouldn't give that fact away to his father by wearing his sen'gai tails over his shoulder like that.

Ducking out through the low doorway, he buckled on his knife belt, cinching it tight around his slender waist. *You've no more hips than a snake does* Auntie Alira was fond of pointing out.

She was the most likely prospect for breakfast. He was wondering if he had time to get to her tent before Mydri came looking for him again when Kheeta came barreling out from between the tents, the tails of his green sen'gai flying behind him.

"So there you are!" He came to a breathless halt and punched Seregil on the shoulder, then hooked an arm around his best friend's neck. "Your father's had us looking everywhere for you! He's already poured the morning blessing. He wasn't happy when you didn't show up."

Seregil shrugged as he wrapped an arm around his cousin's waist and set off for the council site. "He's always angry with me. At least now he has a good reason. I'll be your brother today. Will Mother feed me?"

"Not likely. And it's a good thing you're not my real brother. Father would take the switch to you!"

Seregil hugged Kheeta, glad of a moment's peace before having to face his father's unspoken disapproval. Again. As Korit í Meringil's only son, he was expected to make at least a token appearance at his father's side, though it was Adzriel, as the eldest, who served as her father's aide.

He sighed. "I wish we were really brothers."

People from outside their clan often mistook the two boys for twins. They were the same age, with the same lanky build—all arms and legs and restless energy—and with the same glints of copper in their dark hair. Kheeta and his family lived in the rambling clan house, too; he and Seregil had been cradle mates, and best friends since they could crawl to find each other.

Some of their other friends—clan mates and boys and girls they'd made friends with here at the summer assembly—joined them as they hurried to the open pavilion where the khirnari and elders were already gathered.

They sat on carpets and cushions spread on the grass, sipping tea as the endless arguments began for another day. Seregil wondered why so many of the other khirnari were against his father's plan, but beyond that, he didn't much care.

His father glanced up at him over the heads of the crowd, frowned, then ignored him.

"That's what I thought!" Seregil muttered under his breath, though he kept his expression respectful as he bowed, knowing others were watching.

Someone always seemed to be watching him, Korit í Meringil's useless youngest child. He did his best to ignore the sharp looks he was getting from some of the adults, resisting the urge to cross his eyes and stick out his tongue at them. Even Adzriel wouldn't let him get away with that.

He stood respectfully until his father waved a hand in curt, silent dismissal. As he turned to go, he caught someone else staring at him from across the pavilion, and his heart skipped a giddy beat.

Ilar was leaning on a tent pole, looking bored. The third son of one of the minor eastern clans, he had few real responsibilities. Even though he was older than Seregil and his friends—almost man grown, really—he still found plenty of time to slip away with them, fishing, swimming, and telling stories.

Seregil paused and gave him a hopeful look. Ilar smiled and shook his head, but his gaze never left Seregil. The boy could feel it like heat on his skin as he reluctantly turned away.

He forced himself to walk calmly from the pavilion, for the benefit of anyone staring at his back. The minute he was outside, however, he grabbed Kheeta and broke into a run, leading the others off for another delicious day of freedom. The broad river plain and surrounding forest were theirs to roam.

Really, it hadn't been a bad summer, overall.

Years away, leagues away, Seregil moaned softly in his sleep and faint spots of color rose in his pale cheeks. In the dream, Ilar came to find him, and he thrilled to the touch of those strong, gentle fingers against his cheek.

CHAPTER 15

Tricky Business

ALEC REMAINED CONFINED in the little cellar room for four more days. Ahmol brought him water for washing, took away the chamber pot, and tended the healing skin on Alec's wrists. Alec tried to speak with him, but either the man didn't understand or was under orders not to talk to him.

It might have seemed his new master had forgotten about him, if not for the fact that each morning Ahmol also brought him a new book to read, along with his food. They were written in Skalan, mostly collections of ancient ballads and courtly romances. The tomes were finely bound and well cared for. He tried to read them, hoping to pass the time more quickly, but his mind often wandered, worrying about Seregil, and the driving need to find some way to escape. So far nothing had presented itself. The grate over the tiny window was solidly mortared, and too small to get out of, anyway. Apart from trying to smother someone with the feather tick or strangle him with a quilt, there was nothing in the way of a weapon to be had, and Yhakobin was always well attended by burly servants. As the alchemist had pointed out, he wasn't the first slave to be held here. And, of course, Yhakobin knew what he was.

The food was ample now, but plain. Each morning he received a generous portion of the same thin, sweet oat porridge and some fresh bread. The midday meal and supper consisted of more bread, an apple or some grapes, boiled vegetables, and thick lentil porridge flavored with onions and bay. It was filling, but he soon longed for a bit of meat and cheese. But meal after meal, he wasn't given so much as a sausage.

All in all, it was a most baffling sort of captivity.

As he finished with breakfast on the fourth day, the men who'd dragged him here from the slave market appeared at the door. One of them held a sturdy chain and lock in his hands, the sort one tethered a dog with. Both had thick wooden truncheons hanging at their belts.

The one with the chain motioned for Alec to come to him.

Alec eyed the chain with distaste, but complied. At least he'd get out of this damned room. He stood still, hands at his sides, and let them lock the chain to his collar. The other man thrust a scrap of white cloth into his hands.

Alec unfolded it and saw that it was a sort of handkerchief, with white ribbons sewn to two corners. The guard glowered expectantly at him, then snatched it back and tied it over Alec's face as a veil, just like the one all the 'faie he'd seen so far had worn. The man adjusted it with a few rough tugs, so that it covered Alec's face completely below the eyes, then gave the chain a jerk and led him out.

Alec wondered if all slaves had to cover their faces like this, or just the 'faie.

He took careful stock of his surroundings as they passed along the brick corridors. It was quite a labyrinth. His guards led him in the opposite direction from the way he'd been brought in, and this time they passed open wine cellars and storerooms. After three turns, he was led up another narrow stair. At the top lay a proper passageway. There were rushes underfoot, and as they passed more open doorways Alec caught glimpses of fine rooms decorated with frescoes and mosaics of fish and wild animals.

They emerged at last into a large courtyard with a black-and-white mosaic floor. A long, rectangular pool lay at its center, with sparkling fountains down the center and statuary on both sides. The house had two stories, and formed a square around this courtyard. At the far end was a large archway, and what appeared to be gardens.

Rooms on the ground floor opened into the courtyard; on the upper, there was a pillared gallery, lined with doors and windows. Under different circumstances, he'd have found it a beautiful, peaceful place.

As they walked past the pool, he glanced through a very wide doorway and saw a large room furnished with a heavy dining table with gilded feet shaped like bulls' hooves. There was a large bowl of flowers on a stand beside it, and the walls were painted with scenes of groves and harvests. At the far end of the room, an enticing open archway overlooked a wooded hillside. In the far distance, he could see the dark curve of the sea against the horizon.

Even this tiny bit of new knowledge gave him hope. If he could get to the coast, he could steal a boat. His handler gave the chain a jerk as Alec paused, trying to gauge the distance and obstacles.

As they continued on toward the far archway he caught a glimpse into a room where a dark-haired noblewoman sat beside a fire with an embroidery hoop. He heard a child's voice and looked up to see two young, black-haired children on the gallery with a veiled woman. Her eyes were grey: another 'faie, perhaps, and certainly a slave. She looked away quickly, whispering to her charges.

As they neared the archway at the back of the courtyard, Alec caught the scent of meat cooking, so rich and strong that he paused again, savoring it. This time his handler cuffed him on the side of the head and nearly yanked him off his feet by the chain.

They passed under the arch and down a short flight of marble stairs into a smaller courtyard. This one was planted with trees and herbs, all ripe or gone brown with frost. On the far side stood a long stone cottage decorated in the same style as the villa. The courtyard wall to the left of it featured a large, elaborately carved fountain niche.

Lots of handholds there, thought Alec.

To his right he saw the entrance to yet another walled courtyard, where a large central fountain tinkled and splashed in a broad white basin.

His guards hurried him across to the cottage and knocked at the door. Ahmol let them in.

There were no windows; instead, skylights let in the morning sun, illuminating a large workshop that reminded Alec at once of Thero's rooms at the Orëska House. It even smelled just as bad as they sometimes did when the wizard made fire chips: a mix of hot copper, sulfur, and shit that made his eyes smart.

The center of the room was dominated by a cylindrical brick furnace, which the Orëska wizards called an athanor. It was about four feet tall, with small windows near the top, through which the flames showed like a pair of flickering yellow eyes. A big-bellied glass retort sealed with a clay plug sat atop it. Inside, something that looked like dull green mud bubbled and roiled.

At the left end of the room, furthest from the door, stood a miniature pavilion painted with rings of symbols he'd never seen before. The right-hand wall was dominated by a brick forge. An array of iron tongs and tools hung from hooks next to it, and baskets full of rough stones and thin rods of different metals were lined up underneath these. Small ingots of gold and silver lay in neat stacks on a shelf. Several small anvils took up a bench in the corner. A much larger one stood between the forge and the athanor.

The remaining walls were lined with book-cases, workbenches, tall cabinets, and polished chests with small, carefully labeled drawers. One table held a collection of glass vessels on iron stands. Some of these were very like ones he'd seen Nysander and Thero use. A large glass distillation vessel was currently bubbling on a tripod over a brazier, half-full of a thick blue liquid. A long snout arched from the top of the vessel, guiding drops of condensed steam into a white crucible.

The largest apparatus was comprised of a pear-shaped clay vessel sitting on a heavy wrought-iron tripod. A crazy array of thin, curly copper tubes stuck up from the lid like a madwoman's hair. Some kind of distillery, he supposed.

Overhead, hundreds of colorful cloth bags and strings of desiccated animals hung from the ceiling beams. There were frogs, rats, birds, lizards, squirrels, rabbits, and even a few fingerling dragons among the latter, he saw with a shudder of revulsion. Assorted skins and bones took up table space near an inner door, which, like the little tent, was covered with strange symbols.

Alec rubbed his smarting eyes. There were other, more familiar instruments scattered about: a set of brass sextants, a large brass astrolabe, chisels, saws.

One of his guards pulled him over to the large anvil and secured the end of his chain to a heavy ring on its base. Giving it a good shake to show Alec how strong the lock was, they left him there and went out, leaving the door to the garden slightly ajar.

When Alec was certain they were gone, he went

back to his appraisal of the room. Those metal rods could probably be used as weapons, and where there was an anvil, there must be hammers. If he could just smash off the lock before anyone came back—

The chain was about only an arm span long, though, and try as he might, there was nothing within reach. The anvil was far too heavy to drag. Still listening intently, he got down on his hands and knees, looking for something, anything that he could use on the lock.

The floor was made of wide, bare planks, and he ran his fingers along each crevice as far as he could reach, hoping to find a loose nail. He'd nearly given up hope when one fingertip snagged on something sharp. He picked frantically at it, peeling a fingernail back in the process, but at last pried out a thin metal needle file as long as his hand.

Thank the Lightbearer! He crouched by the lock at the anvil and inspected the keyhole. It was large enough. This could work!

He squeezed his eyes shut for a moment and took a deep breath to steady his nerves, then set to work. He examined the padlock closely, looking for any sign of wards or traps. Among those he'd been made to practice on, some had holes where spring-primed needles could jab out, coated with some nasty poison. He saw no signs of those, though, and set about probing delicately into the works with the sharp tip of the file.

The lock was large and heavy, but of a simple design—probably no more than three tumblers to shift. The file was a crude pick, but it was enough.

One after the other, the tumblers clicked back. Alec pulled the hasp loose and unhooked the end of the chain.

The sudden sound of clapping startled him so badly he dropped the lock and the file. Yhakobin stood in the open doorway, applauding him. Alec hadn't heard him approach. The alchemist was dressed in a long, embroidered robe today, and had the short horseman's crop tucked under one arm.

"An excellent demonstration of your talents, Alec," he said, stepping into the room, followed by the two guards.

Alec grasped the loose end of the chain in both hands and tried to swing it at the men as they came for him, but they caught him and threw him to the floor. One sat on his back. The other yanked his feet up in the air and held them together tightly.

"I guessed that you were clever, but never imagined you'd be this brash," Yhakobin told him. "Under different circumstances, I'd reward such a performance. But alas."

The guards held him tighter as Yhakobin brought the crop down hard across the soles of Alec's bare feet.

The pain was unbelievable—far worse than the whipping he'd had before. The first stroke stole the breath from his lungs, and by the third he was screaming. He couldn't keep count, but just when he thought he'd go mad from the pain it stopped.

The men yanked him up to his knees and held him by the hair and arms. The alchemist tossed the crop aside, then went to one of the tables and picked up a tiny glass flask with a funnel-shaped mouth. Using this, he carefully collected the tears from Alec's cheeks.

Alec gritted his teeth, hating himself for his weakness and for being such a fool as to tip his hand so easily. Seregil would never have made such a blunder. He held very still, keeping his eyes averted until Yhakobin finished.

"There, nothing wasted," the alchemist murmured, corking the bottle and setting it aside. "It gives me no pleasure to discipline you. I do it for your own good. If you actually had escaped and were caught by the slave takers, even I could not save you from the axe man's block. We have laws here, and they must be obeyed. I hope in time you will come to appreciate my leniency. Now, what have you to say to me, Alec?"

Alec drew in a hitching breath and bowed his head. "I'm sorry I tried to get away. Thank you, Ilban, for your . . . kindness."

"Hmm. Someday I will begin punishing you for lying, but for now, that will do."

The men dragged Alec back to the anvil and secured his chain with a new, larger lock. At Yhakobin's nod, one of them grasped Alec's left wrist and jerked his hand up. Yhakobin produced the bodkin from his sleeve and pricked Alec's finger again, as he had that day at the slave market. He performed the same procedure, collecting a droplet of blood and somehow igniting it. It licked up in a long tongue of dull red fire this time.

The alchemist murmured something in his own tongue, sounding pleased, then went to a table near the forge and came back with a small lead triangle inscribed with symbols of some sort, and fixed with a small bail, like a pendant.

"You will sit still while I do this." Yhakobin pointed meaningfully at the whip, which lay in easy reach, then bent and affixed the triangle to Alec's collar with some wire and a set of pliers.

When that was done, he took a tall, thin flask from a row on a nearby shelf, broke the wax seal, and poured out some liquid into a silver beaker.

"You will drink this. Every drop," he ordered, holding it out to Alec.

"What is it?" he demanded without thinking.

Yhakobin slapped him, hard.

Alec clamped his lips tight together and kept his eyes averted.

"Drink." The cup was thrust under his nose. The contents looked like plain water.

"Please, Ilban, what is it?" Alec braced for another blow.

"Don't turn up your nose at it, boy. That is Tincture of Lead, and noblemen have paid a great deal for smaller doses than this."

"Why? Ilban," he added hastily, still suspicious and not inclined to believe him. Who would pay to drink something as common as lead?

"It is the first step of your purification. It drives out foul humors. Drink, Alec, or I will whip you again."

The alchemist held the cup to his lips and the man holding Alec's head pulled it back by the hair, making it hard to keep his mouth shut. Yhakobin tipped some of the tincture between his parted lips and it seeped through his clenched teeth. It had a faintly metallic taste and was oily against his tongue. Alec gagged and tried to turn his head away.

Yhakobin gave another curt order. Alec was thrown down on his back, and a leather funnel was forced between his teeth to the back of his throat. The alchemist pinched Alec's nose shut with one hand and poured the rest of the draught into the funnel with the other. Alec had to swallow or choke.

"There now, was that really worth a second beating?" Yhakobin asked.

"No, please!" Alec gasped, but men held him down and the alchemist gave him five more lashes across the soles.

Alec managed to hold back his cries this time, but the pain was even worse as the crop fell on already swollen flesh. He was panting harshly through his teeth by the time they dragged him up to his knees.

"That is all for today. I will see you the day after tomorrow in the morning, Alec, and you will be given another draught. I suggest you remember the lessons of today."

His guards pulled him to his feet and Alec choked back a cry of pain. His feet were swollen from the beating and burned like fire. They laughed as they hoisted him by the arms and dragged him from the room.

By the time they reached the cellar stairway he was beginning to feel queasy, and by the time they reached his cell, his bowels were boiling and his throat was filled with bile. He barely made it to the slop bucket before erupting at both ends.

The bastard did poison me! he thought in despair as spasm after excruciating spasm ripped through him. *What a shameful way to die.*

He didn't die, but ended up sprawled shuddering on the floor, one cheek pressed to the cool bricks. Ahmol appeared soon after and quickly cleaned up the mess, carrying away the muck. Alec was too weak to resist or care when the man returned with a basin and cleaned him, then dragged him onto his pallet and threw the quilts over him.

"Ilban say, this good," Ahmol told him in halting Skalan.

"This is *not* good!" Alec groaned.

Alec lay there panting and cursing Yhakobin for a liar as the servant finished doing whatever he was doing across the room. Raising his hand to his collar, Alec gripped the strange amulet—for he guessed it was something of the sort—and tugged weakly at it. It was warm to the touch and bent easily between his fingers.

Ahmol was suddenly there and pulled Alec's hand away, shaking his head. For the first time, Alec saw the slave brand on the man's forearm. It seemed he'd been right about the veils. Only 'faie slaves wore them.

The other slave patted his shoulder and said something in his own language, probably urging him to sleep. Alec curled up on his side and realized he felt a little better. Perhaps he'd purged whatever poison the alchemist had fed him. The thought gave him some satisfaction as he drifted into an unhappy doze.

He slept deeply that night and dreamed that

Seregil was somewhere outside, calling for him. In the dream, the cell door opened at a touch and no guard stopped him as Alec stole cautiously out into the courtyard. The place was deserted, silent save for the sound of the fountains. He could still hear Seregil calling but couldn't tell where he was. His voice seemed to come from all sides at once.

He woke in a sweat. The cell was dark and silent. Throwing an arm across his face, he slept again, caught in the same frustrating dream.

kindness of kindred

ALEC WOKE FEELING exhausted and achy, with no appetite for his morning porridge, even though it smelled of honey and nutmeg today.

Must be my reward for surviving the night, he thought sourly, turning his back on it.

They left him alone that day, and he spent most of it sleeping. When nature forced him up to the slop bucket, he could barely walk, his feet were so swollen and sore. By evening he felt well enough to eat the bean soup and bread Ahmol brought him. He sat awake in the dark afterward, unable to sleep.

It was maddening, having nothing to do, and unable to see anything except a little patch of moonlit sky through the bars. He prayed in earnest, softly singing songs to Dalna, his cradle patron, and wondered if the Maker listened to him anymore, after so many years following Illior. All the same, it left him feeling a little better.

• • •

The guards came for him after breakfast the next morning. They thrust him into a clean wool robe and marched him upstairs on bruised feet to begin the whole nasty procedure again.

Just as before, he was chained to the anvil and left alone. The glass vessels were empty today, the braziers all cold, but a metallic smell hung over the room, underscored by other odors he did not recognize.

This time he knelt where they left him and didn't move until Yhakobin entered.

"Being a good fellow today, I see," the alchemist said, smiling that placid smile of his. "How are you feeling?"

"You—I was unwell, after that draught you gave me," Alec managed, then added a hasty "Ilban."

"That's good. Tincture of Lead does have a purgative effect. Your finger, please."

Knowing what would happen if he balked, he held out his hand. Yhakobin took the blood and this time it burned a much brighter red.

Alec blinked at the brief flash of color and resisted the urge to ask questions. The alchemist was clearly pleased.

Yhakobin removed the lead amulet and replaced it with another that looked like lead but was lighter against Alec's throat, with black symbols incised on it. The guards held Alec's head as Yhakobin poured something into the silver cup.

"This is Tincture of Tin," Yhakobin told him, holding the cup down where he could see into it.

"The effects are quite different. I do not think you will find them unpleasant. It is only a tonic, to purify the blood."

This tincture looked exactly like the last draught to Alec. Before he could stop himself, he jerked back, kicking Yhakobin by accident. The contents splattered across the front of the man's dark robe.

Yhakobin looked more resigned than angry as he nodded to the guards. This time they held Alec down over a bench and Yhakobin whipped the backs of his bare thighs. It was bad, but nothing like the beating of his feet. He didn't make a sound this time, and he didn't cry.

When it was over they held him down and jammed the hated funnel between his jaws. This new tincture burned as it went down and warmed his belly like Zengati brandy. The feeling persisted as he was dragged back to his cell, but this time the only effect it had on him was a heavy lethargy. He couldn't keep his eyes open. Giving up, he collapsed on his bed and wrapped a hand around the new amulet. As he slipped into a daze, it occurred to him that this one was once again probably of the same metal as the tincture. It made no sense to him, this use of metals, but clearly there was some magic to it.

He slept deeply all day and into the night, rousing only when a servant brought him water and a bland vegetable broth to drink. Though still groggy, he roused enough to realize that it was a different person than the usual guards or Ahmol leaning over him.

"Hello, little brother. Are you awake?"

This man was Aurënfaie, with a long braid of dark hair. Alec lurched up and reached for him, thinking it was Seregil, come to free him at last, but as his eyes adjusted to the light of the small lantern the stranger had brought, he saw that this man was older, and that his eyes were hazel-colored, like Nyal's, rather than Seregil's clear grey. Could this be the slave who'd been with Yhakobin at the market? He hadn't been able to tell the color of that man's eyes.

"No veil," Alec mumbled, blinking, as he tried to wake up.

The slave held up a square of lace-trimmed linen and winked at him. "Promise not to tell? I thought you could do with the sight of a friendly face."

Alec managed a wan smile as he caught sight of the collar the man wore. It was thin and polished, very much like his own, but was made of gold, or gilded. "Thank you. You're the one I saw at the market, aren't you?"

"Yes," he whispered, holding a cup of water to Alec's lips and helping him drink. "Ilban thought the presence of another 'faie might reassure you. My name is Khenir."

He wore a slave's long, sleeveless robe, but his was made of fine dark wool, with bands of white embroidering at the neck. Glancing down, Alec saw that he wore wide golden bracelets, too. The slave brand on his forearm was old and faded, like Ahmol's.

Khenir pressed a cool hand to Alec's brow. "How are you feeling?"

"So tired," Alec mumbled, still thick-tongued from the draught but determined to stay awake and talk to this man. "What clan are you?"

Khenir shook his head sadly. "If you knew how long it has been since anyone asked me that! I was from Tarial clan, a minor family in the south, near Datsia. And you?"

Alec sat up and rubbed at his face to clear his head. "No clan. I'm ya'shel, from—" He paused, catching himself. He wanted to trust this man, but he couldn't let himself forget that he was just a slave, owned by the same man, and possibly loyal to him. Alec had made enough stupid blunders already. "From Skala."

Khenir pointed at Alec's left earlobe. "You didn't get that dragon bite in Skala."

"I've been to Aurënen," Alec admitted. "But my father was Tír."

"Ah. Drink some more. You need it," Khenir urged, placing the cup of broth in his hands. "I've never known Ilban to purchase a half-breed before. He's usually so particular."

"Why's that?" Alec asked, between sips of broth. His belly growled, hungry for more substantial fare.

"The high-ranking men of Plenimar prefer pure blood in their slaves, just as they do with their horses and hunting dogs," Khenir whispered, more resigned than bitter. "The ya'shel usually go to merchants' households, or the brothels, or get sold off to the countryside as farm labor. You're very lucky."

That was a matter of opinion. "Are there others in the house? I saw a veiled woman."

"A few. That's Rhania, the children's nurse." He took the empty cup from Alec and gave him one filled with water. "You're to drink this, and this." He held up a wooden pitcher. "Ilban means you no harm, but his purifications can be a bit hard on the body."

"Is that really all this is?" Alec fingered the amulet at his throat. Khenir's collar was un-adorned.

"Don't worry. Ilban would never harm you."

"Oh, really? Have a look at my feet."

"That was just a beating. We've all had those. But Ilban is very kind, as masters go. Now let me tend your brands."

Alec held out his arm and Khenir untied the bandage. The burn was healing clean, and quickly. There was hardly any redness around the scab. "I'm starving. Doesn't Yhakobin ever give his slaves meat?"

Khenir gave him a warning look. "Even be-tween the two of us, you must refer to Ilban by his title. What if someone were to overhear? As for meat?" Khenir shook his head. "You're a slave, Alec, so you'd have to please Ilban a great deal to get any of that. I can't think the last time I tasted any. They think it keeps us docile."

Alec didn't feel docile yet, just resentful and hungry.

Khenir dabbed an aromatic salve on the burn.

"They have many ways of taming us, little brother. They've made an art of it. I hear it's worst for those with manifested powers."

"I'm safe, then. That slop pail has more magic to it than I do. I suppose I should be glad. A slave on the ship showed me the scars where he'd been whipped. And gelded. At least they didn't do that to me."

Khenir carefully worked the bandage away from Alec's leg. This one had seeped and the wrappings had stuck to the scab. "Not yet," he murmured.

"What do you mean, 'not yet'? He told me he wouldn't!"

Khenir shrugged. "Perhaps Ilban means to breed you, then, or sell you when he's through with you. Intact young slaves often fetch a better price."

Alec pondered that uneasily. "He said it's my blood he wants."

"Well, Ilban is an alchemist, after all. It must be something to do with that."

He leaned forward to work at the soiled leg bandage and his tunic pulled back from one shoulder, revealing the faded white stripes of lash marks, just like the ones Alec had seen on the 'faie aboard the slaver ship.

"Did he do that to you?" asked Alec.

"Oh, no! Ilban is not my first master."

"You fought back, too, didn't you?"

"For all the good it did."

"And did they—?" Still rocked by what Khenir had implied, he glanced down at the other man's lap before he could help himself.

Khenir looked up sharply. "You *never* ask a slave that! Do you understand? Never!"

"I'm sorry. I spoke without thinking."

Khenir sighed and went back to work. "You're new to all this. Sometimes I forget what that's like. I've been here a very long time, you see."

"I'm sorry," Alec said again, feeling miserable. Khenir's reaction was answer enough.

"Drink your water."

Neither spoke as Khenir finished with the bandaging and gathered up the soiled linen strips and empty cups.

"I didn't mean to offend you," Alec ventured, as Khenir stood and fastened the lace-trimmed veil across his face. "Do you have to go?"

The man leaned down and stroked his hair. Without thinking, Alec closed his eyes and leaned into the touch; it felt like years since anyone had touched him with anything like kindness.

Khenir smiled sadly and trailed his fingers down Alec's cheek. "I'll be back as soon as it's allowed, I promise. Just do as you're told. It will be better for you if you do, and perhaps Ilban will give you more freedom in the house."

He went out and took the candle with him. Alec groped in the dark for the pitcher. The tincture had left him thirsty.

More freedom, eh? Alec pulled the quilts up to his chin. A little moonlight found its way through the grate, and he could see the white puff of his breath on the air.

He knew he shouldn't get his hopes up too much, but Khenir had unwittingly given him a great deal of useful information. There were at least two others like him here, and if he could lull "Ilban" into giving him the run of the house, as Khenir and the nurse evidently had, then sooner or later he could find a way to escape. Given the very real possibility of having his balls cut off, sooner would be better. So, he reasoned, he'd play the good slave and take the tinctures, and use every opportunity he had to learn the layout of the house. But he'd have to be very careful. Yhakobin had made it clear that he knew too much of Alec's past to be fooled easily.

Burrowing down into the deeper warmth of the quilts, he kissed his palm and pressed it to his heart. *Keep well, talí, and don't think I've forgotten you. I'll get out of here and I'll find you, no matter what it takes.*

As he drifted off to sleep, hoping for dreams of Seregil, it occurred to him to wonder what had happened to the other slaves Khenir had alluded to, the ones their master preferred.

kind Words. Bad News

"HABA?"

Cool fingers and Adzriel's scent brought Seregil close to the surface of waking again. He dreamed of her face, sometimes smiling and kind as she almost always had been, during the years she'd raised him. But in other dreams he was a child again, standing before the judges at Sarikali with blood on his tunic, and she was weeping.

And always that pet name—Haba, "little black squirrel"—whispered close to his ear. Adzriel had called him that first, and then only the ones who loved him—his friends, Kheeta, his sisters . . .

Another, too.

Haba, come back to us.

Haba, wake up.

Wake . . .

"Are you awake at last? Open your eyes and show me." A woman's voice, speaking in Aurënfaie.

Seregil let out a soft groan as someone lightly slapped his cheek. "Mydri, don't. Sick."

"Wake up, now. You must drink something."

Consciousness returned slowly. At first he was aware only of a tremendous heaviness, then that scent, and of how hard it was to open his eyes. Something cool and moist passed across his eyelids, then his brow and cheeks. Someone was washing his face.

"Adzriel?" It came out a faint, cracked whisper. His mouth was so dry, and his tongue felt thick. "Where—?"

He didn't recall reaching Bôkthersa. Something had happened . . .

"Open your eyes, young son."

Young son? It was said in the formal style, rather than familial. His gummy lids parted at last and he found himself in a curtained bed in a dimly lit room. A candle burned somewhere beyond the bed curtains and someone sat beside the bed, a dark shape, with no visible face. A scrap of memory stirred—a dark, faceless shape lurching at him, a horrid, rotting stench . . .

A dra'gorgos!

But there was nothing but the scent of wax here, and the faintest whiff of Adzriel's perfume still lingering in the air. Too weak to reach out or even turn his head, he blinked up at the woman, needing to hear a friendly voice.

"Ah, that's better." A woman, certainly, but not any of his sisters.

"Where—?" he asked, his voice a raw whisper.

"Hush, now, and stay still. You've been terribly

ill." As she leaned forward and brought a horn spoon to his lips, his saw that she was very old. A long white braid hung over one shoulder, and what he could see of her face above an embroidered veil was lined with age.

Cool sweet water trickled over his parched tongue and he swallowed eagerly, though it hurt like fire. He opened his mouth for more.

The faded blue eyes above the veil crinkled at the corners, revealing her hidden smile. "There now, a little more. Slowly though. We didn't think you'd live, young son."

"Who didn't?" he rasped between sips.

She just shook her head a bit as she gave him more water.

"My sister," he tried again, thinking she might be a bit deaf. "I thought—"

"Adzriel, is it? You called on her more than once. That's your sister?"

"Is she here?" He hadn't dreamed her scent. He could still smell it.

"No, and be thankful for that," she replied, shaking her head.

"What? Please, tell me where I am," Seregil begged.

"In the house of our master, of course." Age-knotted fingers stole to a silvery circlet at her withered throat. Then Seregil noticed the faded round brand on her forearm.

"You're a slave?"

"Of course. As are you." She reached out and tapped something around his neck.

"What is that?" he demanded, though he already had a pretty good idea.

"Your collar, young son. You're a slave now, no different than the rest of us. Seeing the size of that dragon mark on your hand, I'm surprised you ended up here. Maybe the luck of it ran out, eh?" She rose slowly and stepped away from the bed. "Rest now. I'll bring you something to eat in a little while."

"No, wait. Please!" He heard the soft sound of a door closing.

Frustrated and confused, he stared helplessly up at the dark canopy over the bed. He had to gather his wits, and soon!

But it was so hard. He felt sluggish, drugged. The struggle to think made him short of breath, as if he were climbing a mountain rather than lying flat on his back.

He'd been deathly ill, she'd said, and he certainly felt like it. His body hurt all over, and there were spots of a stronger, throbbing pain on the underside of his right forearm, and on the back of his left calf where it rested against the sheets.

Sheets? His wandering mind veered of its own volition. He flexed the fingers of one hand and felt smooth linen and the give of a soft mattress. What slave was given this sort of bed? Had the veiled woman been lying? Had he misunderstood?

But no, he remembered that much from the ship—rough, grasping hands, then pain and the smell of his own flesh being seared, cutting through the fog of illness.

"Fucking hell! Fucking, rotting balls of hell!" he whispered helplessly.

He was tucked in tightly under heavy quilts. It took all the strength he could muster to slowly work his right arm free. There, black against the pale underside of his forearm, was a small, scabbed brand in the shape of the letter S. He reached up and touched the metal collar around his neck. It was about a finger's width in thickness, the metal rounded and very smooth.

"Aura Illustri!" He let his arm fall and closed his eyes, fighting down a rush of nausea as more fragmented memories seeped back.

The ambush. The smell. The shock of seeing the hideous black dra'gorgos bearing down on him. How could such an abomination appear on Aurënfaie soil? It could only mean that one of their attackers had been a necromancer; no one else could summon the unclean things.

And screaming. He was certain he remembered someone screaming.

"Alec!" Real panic set in then, and he managed to raise his head enough to see that there was no one else in the bed, and no sight of anyone else in what he could see of the room.

He'd called out for his sister, but not his talimenios? Panting, sick, and overwhelmed with guilt, he fell back against the pillow as tears welled in the corners of his eyes.

Screaming. Who had been screaming? Was it Alec? Was he dead, like all the others?

No! he told himself fiercely. *No, I'd know. I'd remember that!*

Yet try as he might, he couldn't be certain, any more than he could summon the memory of what had followed.

The slaver's mark was all he had to go on, and that was the worst possible news, for there were only two places he could be right now: in Plenimar, or in Zengat.

And yet for slavers to venture so far inland on Aurënen soil was unheard of in that part of the country. And what would they be doing with a necromancer?

He tried again to move, but the last of his strength had deserted him. As consciousness fled, however, a sudden realization followed him down into the darkness.

"Betrayed!" he mumbled to the empty room. "Phoria, I'll see you dead!"

Caged Doubts

FOR THE FIRST few days, Seregil didn't have the strength to get away even if they'd left the door open for him. Instead, he had to settle for alternating between fretting over what could have become of Alec and making what observations he could make from his bed.

From what little he could recall from the ship, his captors had probably placed some sort of magical ward on him, and apparently he'd had his usual reaction to it. His skin was still sallow and he'd lost a considerable amount of weight. His belly was sunken and his ribs were more prominent than usual. The magic had eaten into his muscles, too, and his arms looked thin. In addition to the brands, he had sores and scabs over a good part of his body. The old woman had been right in thinking he'd nearly died.

He had no way of knowing what the collar around his neck looked like, or was made of, but it was very hard metal. At least it wasn't magicked. He wouldn't be feeling as well as he was if it had been.

Despite his dire situation, he was glad to be clean and comfortable. Even his hair and nails had been neatly trimmed. He knew better than to mistake this for kindness on the part of whoever had bought him, but that didn't mean he couldn't enjoy it for now. It was certainly better than the condition he'd been in, and it gave him a chance to start recovering his strength.

Judging by the slant of light through the window, and the slice of blue sky he could see, he guessed that his room was on an upper floor. It was a surprisingly fine chamber for a slave. Though sparsely furnished with a bed and a heavy armchair by the hearth, the walls were paneled with polished wood; here and there the patina showed lighter in places where some hanging or furniture had been removed. The stout door was locked from the outside and no one came in except for the old woman. He caught a glimpse of an armed man at the door whenever she entered.

He slept a great deal and thrashed through nightmares of the ambush—dreams in which Alec lay dead on the ground with the others. He woke trembling and sweating, sick with not knowing whether it was a memory or a phantasm created by his fears.

Interspersed with these dark dreams were others, more snippets and flashes of his own past—of Adzriel and events from his childhood, before he'd been banished. Some were clear, others jumbled and confused, with only the impression of gentle hands touching him. At times they were innocent and he thought it must be his sister, but at others those hands roamed over his body, stirring his flesh and making him ache for more. No matter how he tried, he could not see who his dream lover was. He woke from these feeling sick in a different way, and strangely guilty.

The old woman came to him several times each day, bringing him food and helping him bathe. He was kept to milk and bread, and thin broths, but the servings were generous and he ate everything offered, in order to gain his strength back. But it was a frustrating battle and his body was slow to mend.

His nurse was a hard one to draw out. She was kind to him in her way while he was weak, but grew more shy and nervous as he regained his strength. He kept at her not only because she was his only link outside this room but because it distracted him from his fears.

With some charm and persistence, he learned that her name was Zoriel and that she'd been a possession of "the master's" family for generations, since she was a young girl. She couldn't even remember the name of her clan. Looking into those faded blue eyes, he saw no spirit there, only long-ingrained resignation and lingering traces of fear. She spoke of the "master" with reverence but refused to tell Seregil anything of him, not even his name.

"I daren't," she said, nervously fingering the worn metal band at her throat.

Seregil didn't press her but instead tried to get a sense of the household and whether there were any other 'faie there.

"A few," she told him, eyes going vague. "But I'm not to talk to you about that, either. Please, don't ask any more, young son. It's not for me to say."

"Please, just one more question," Seregil said, taking her hands. Her fingers were bent and chapped by years of hard work. "Is there a young man with long blond hair here? He'd have arrived the same time I did, most likely as a slave. Please, old mother, he's dear to me, and I don't even know if he's alive."

"I've seen no one like that." She pulled free and began gathering up the day's soiled linens and empty dishes. "You're the only new slave I know of, and you're my only concern. I don't know what the master will say when I tell him of all your questions! It's not proper for a slave to act so, and the sooner you know that, the better!"

"I'm a slow learner," he muttered, feeling tired and sulky.

She shook her head sadly. "Then you'll find yourself at the wrong end of the whip soon enough."

"Didn't you ever try to get away?"

This was met with a look of blank incomprehension. "Get away? Where would I go?"

Seregil positioned himself for a good look out the door as she went out. Yes, the door was most certainly under guard, but only by one man. A few more days, he promised himself, and he would be strong enough to fight his way out.

But after three days, he was only just strong enough to leave his bed for a little while and limp slowly about the room. When Zoriel brought him a soft woolen robe to wear, he noticed that she seemed distracted.

"Is something wrong, old mother?"

"Getting above himself, the scoundrel," she muttered, then began fussing over him as she helped him over to the chair by the window.

"Who is?"

"That's no concern of yours," she snapped, tucking a blanket over him.

Seregil spent the morning there, glad to have something to look at besides these four walls.

As he'd guessed, he was on an upper floor. There were iron bars over the casement on the inside, set in new mortar. The window was thickly leaded and glazed. Peering out through the rippled panes, he could see part of a small garden courtyard with a fountain in the middle and a pillared colonnade. A nobleman with dark hair walked there for a while, and later, a pair of small children appeared with a dark-haired woman with a veil over the lower part of her face. Another slave, no doubt.

"You don't want to tire yourself out, your first day up," Zoriel scolded when she returned with his midday meal. "Back to bed with you now!"

Seregil wasn't about to argue. He'd used up

what strength he possessed just sitting up. His legs were dangerously wobbly as he crossed the short distance to the bed. He played up the weakness for her benefit, and even went so far as to beg her to feed him his soup. She clucked her tongue at him, but his request must have pleased her, for her old eyes were kind as she spooned it into him. She was less fearful when he seemed weak, he guessed.

Seeking to capitalize on her good mood, he finished off the soup and bread, then asked, "You've never told me the master's name. Why is that?"

He caught a flash of the distaste he'd noted that morning as she sniffed and replied, "I haven't been told to tell you." She dabbed a bit of broth from his cheek with a napkin.

"Well, I wish I knew whom to thank." He sighed happily, folding his arms behind his head. "I knew worse accommodations when I was free. Does the master treat all his slaves like this?"

"No," she told him curtly, and that curtain of fear came down between them again.

Trying a different tack, he gave her a sad look. "I'm not asking you to disobey any orders, but it eats at me day and night, wondering what my fate's to be." He dropped his gaze and let his voice falter a little as he plucked at the metal collar. "I'm scared, old mother, if truth be told. And all this, it just makes me more fearful. Why would he be treating me so well, unless he meant me for—" He managed a convincing grimace. "For his bed. Is he like that?"

"Him?" She scowled and shook her head. "That

wouldn't be for me to say, even if I knew. Here, finish your own bread and leave the tray on the floor. I've tasks waiting." She went to the door, but paused before knocking for the guard. "Savor your leisure while you can, young son. You'll soon learn that, in our way of life."

Seregil mulled over her words as he finished the last of the bread. At best, this nameless master of hers must be strict in his ways; at the worst? That remained to be seen.

He tried to rest, but his thoughts turned to Alec and set his heart pounding uncomfortably in his chest. He got out of bed again and made his way slowly back to the window. Sweating and winded, he collapsed into the chair and rested his arms on the sill.

It appeared to be a formal courtyard. There were no stables or workshops, just neatly planted beds laid out between paths made of something very white—stones or shells, probably—around the fountain. He couldn't see a gate from this angle, but guessed that if he did somehow manage to get out through the window and down to the ground without breaking his legs, he'd still have to make his way through the house or go up a wall and over the roof. He wasn't capable of either just yet.

Of course, that all turned on how he was going to get out. The window was not an option—the bars were solidly set and too closely spaced even for someone as slim as he to wiggle through. The window casement was nailed shut, and the glass was so thick he couldn't even hear the splashing of the fountain.

He felt stronger the next day, and as soon as Zoriel left him alone after breakfast, he made a slow circuit of the room, looking for anything he'd missed so far. He didn't much care if anyone knew. Deep down, some rebellious part of his nature hoped word would get back to "Master."

It took a discouragingly long time to finish looking under the bed and between the floorboards for something he could use as a tool or a weapon, but he forced himself to finish. There had to be something, anything that would be of use!

But he found nothing. "As if he's going to leave a knife under the bed for me, or a hank of rope," he muttered, slumped in an exhausted heap by the door. All he had to work with was a wooden pitcher, which might do in a pinch, once he was strong enough to swing it. Zoriel didn't even leave the chamber pot in the room. He had to ask for that— a humiliating necessity—and she took it away when he was done.

He fingered the collar again. It was getting to be a habit. He'd found where it was riveted shut, but the seam was tight, with no play in it at all. No surprise, there.

The bed was too sturdy to pull apart. The mattress was a heavy one, stuffed with straw and feathers. He dragged himself into bed and rammed an ineffectual fist into the single pillow he was allowed. That wouldn't make much of a weapon, either, unless he wanted his keepers to laugh themselves to death.

You've got me well and truly penned, whoever you are! he thought, twisting a corner of the pillow between nervous fingers. He didn't know much about how the Plenimarans treated their slaves, but he was convinced that this situation was unusual. If not for the brands on his skin, he'd have guessed he'd been taken instead for a ransom.

Not that there's anyone left in Rhíminee who'd pay to have me back.

Defeated for now, he closed his eyes and tried instead to summon some new memory of the capture or the sea passage, hoping for some sign that he'd seen Alec alive after the dra'gorgos attack.

And still, nothing more came to him. *He's not dead! I'd know if he was dead. I'd feel it!* The thought consumed him. The talimenios bond ran deep between them, a joining of souls; *I'd know if that was broken!*

He clung to that, but the cold black fear crept back anyway. Curled up under the warm bedclothes, clean and safe for now, guilt overwhelmed him. Everyone in that ambush had been targeted for death—everyone but him. *Oh talí! If you were killed, because of me...*

"Damnation!" He hurled the pillow at the door in impotent rage, then lurched out of bed and threw the pitcher after it. It bounced ineffectually off the door, spraying water everywhere, and landed back at his feet, mocking him. He kicked it across the room, hardly noticing the flash of pain as he cut one bare toe on the handle, and staggered across the room to pound on the door.

"Show yourself!" he yelled. "Tell me why I'm here, you coward! Let me out of here, you pus-dripping horse prick!"

His only answer was the thump of a fist from outside and the muffled sound of someone laughing at him.

"Bastard!" Seregil slid down the wall with his head in his hands and choked back a sob. "Dirty bastards!"

Alec is not dead!

He could be.

No, he's not; he's not!

I might never know . . .

Weak, scared, and frustrated beyond all telling, he pressed both hands over his mouth and cried.

An Unexpected Reward

ALEC'S INTERACTION WITH Yhakobin followed an unchanging pattern. Every other day he was taken out to the workshop and his amulet was changed to one corresponding to the tincture given. Every moment he was out of his cell he watched for an opportunity to get away, but so far it had been impossible. He was kept under close watch every moment he was out of his cell. If this continued, he'd be forced to make a break for it from one of the courtyards and hope for luck.

The one between the main house and the alchemist's workroom appeared to be the best bet, and he'd memorized every tree, rough bit of stone, and vine. The wall fountain was very promising, as was the thick climbing rose that grew up the side of the workshop. It would tear the skin from his hands and feet for sure, but that would be a small price to pay.

The alchemist had seemed very pleased when,

the day after he'd spoken with Khenir, Alec began accepting the silver cup without a fight. The tin amulet was exchanged for one of iron, then one of copper.

Yhakobin hadn't bothered with the blood flame spell for several days, and today was no exception. As soon as Alec downed the tincture, the alchemist motioned to the guards and went to the forge.

"Ilban? May I ask a question?" Alec asked quickly as the men closed in on him.

Surprised, Yhakobin turned back to him. "What is it?"

"That slave called Khenir says this is a purification. Please, Ilban, what is it you are purifying out of me?"

"He told you that, did he? Well, no matter." Yhakobin chuckled as he turned and tossed the used amulet into the forge. "It's nothing you'll miss, I assure you. Here, I have a new book for you, a reward for your good behavior."

Alec accepted the volume with a humble nod, and his guards led him away.

And so the days went: one to himself, and the next back to the workshop. The copper amulet was changed for one of something Yhakobin called sophic mercury, and he was made to drink Tincture of Quicksilver. This one tasted especially foul, and cramped his belly a little, but even so, he found he was feeling remarkably well in spite of his situation and the wretchedly bland food. His mind was wonderfully clear, and he felt stronger, even with the lack of meat.

He'd hoped to see Khenir again, but that day

passed as usual, with no sign of him. With nothing else to do, he perused the new book. This one was a history of the coming of the first Hierophant. Plenimar had been his seat of power, according to this writer, and Skala had broken away, waging war unjustly to gain control of all the Three Lands, and the sacred isle of Kouros.

Alec read half of it out of sheer boredom, and then paced his cell restlessly, listening to the mundane noises from outside and wishing desperately he was out there. He'd happily work in the kitchen or split firewood, just for something to do!

The following day was just like the last. He was too restless to read, and instead spent the afternoon pacing and performing some strengthening exercises Seregil had taught him during the long winter months they'd spent in the cabin. He'd need to be fit when it came time to run. Without knowing it, the alchemist was preparing him well for that, he thought with a smile. How pleasant it would be to thank him at the point of a knife.

As he dropped into a crouch, preparing to practice his leaps, the slant of light across the bottom of the door caught his eye. There was something scratched into the wood, visible only from this angle. At first glance it looked like lines of random marks, but on closer inspection, he saw that it was writing and most of it in Aurënfaie. He had to lie on his belly to read it, with his body at a slant so as not to block the light.

The lettering was crude, almost unreadable, and Alec wondered whether the author had lain here, at the end of his strength, and what he had used to write with. He traced the line of scratches with a finger to find the beginning and read: "Malis, son of Koris." Just below it, he found another name that made his heart skip a beat: it read simply "Khenir, without hope." And at the corner of the panel, another: "Ulia, daughter of Ponia, my curse be on . . ."

This one was unfinished. *Were you interrupted,* he wondered, *or did you just give up?*

He searched the bottom of the door and found over a dozen more such inscriptions, some with names, others anonymous expressions of fear, grief, and despair. Several of the curses mentioned Yhakobin by name. In other places, there were tiny crescent moons, Aura's symbol, incised with a fingernail.

Here are the others, those who came before me, but where are they now? Why are Khenir and the children's nurse the only ones left?

He found a clear spot and used his thumbnail to inscribe a crescent moon, and his own name: Alec, son of Amasa. He sat back, sucking his sore thumb. It had been an impulse, to add his name, but he suddenly wished he hadn't. Those listed there, save Khenir, had all disappeared, their fates unknown. Was this his fate, as well?

His dreams were wild that night—all battles and killing and running through dark forests. He even dreamed of escaping and finding Seregil. In the dream, he stole through the house in the dark, checking door after door and finding them locked, until at last one upstairs opened and there was Seregil, waiting for him with open arms and that beloved crooked grin. Alec ran to him, but woke before they could touch. The dream had been so vivid that he lay awake for a long time, heart pounding, sunk in renewed despair. If he disappeared here, like those others, Seregil would never know what happened to him. He'd be nothing more than a name on the door, lost in the shadows of this wretched little room.

There was a brief delay at Yhakobin's door the following morning. When the guards finally led him inside, he saw that the alchemist was not alone. A very tall bearded man dressed in a red surcoat stood by the little painted tent at the far end of the room. His eyes were black and hard, and he fixed Alec with a sharp look as he took his usual place near the anvil. The stranger spoke with Yhakobin for a moment, looking at Alec all the while. When they were finished, Yhakobin turned to Alec and smiled.

"You are looking very well! Let me have my drop first." Yhakobin was in unusually high spirits today and Alec wondered if it had anything to do with the mysterious visitor.

Alec held out his finger, uncomfortably aware of the stranger's intense gaze.

Yhakobin pricked it and repeated the blood spell. This time the flame burned a vivid blue and lasted for some moments. He spoke to the visitor again, obviously pleased.

Apparently satisfied, the other man bowed and took his leave.

"Excellent! Better even than I'd dared hope," said Yhakobin.

Alec wasn't sure if he was referring to the color of the blood flame or his visitor's reaction to it. "If I may, Ilban, who was that man?"

"That, my young friend, was Duke Theris Urghan, cousin to and legate of his Majesty, the Overlord. He was here inquiring after my progress with you. And I must say, I was able to give him a very good report." He took Alec's chin between his fingers and inspected his face closely, turning it this way and that. "Oh yes, much better than expected. And I daresay you're feeling quite well, too."

The alchemist's elation made Alec nervous. What was it Yhakobin was seeing that pleased him so much? Alec thought of those who'd left their names on the door. Had they seen this same gleam in the man's eyes?

"My, you are serious today." Yhakobin took a polished metal mirror from one of the tables and held it up in front of him. "See what I've done for you, boy, and show a bit of gratitude."

Alec took one look and let out a choked gasp, shocked at the stranger he saw in the reflection. Far from growing pale from lack of meat, his coloring had heightened. His eyes looked bluer, and his hair, though lank from lack of washing, seemed to shine a brighter gold.

But that wasn't the only change. He looked more 'faie somehow, as if the very planes of his face had been altered.

"I don't understand!" he gasped, touching his cheek with superstitious awe. "What have you done to me, Ilban?"

Yhakobin held out the daily draught to him, but Alec balled his fists on his knees and shook his head. "Why do I look different?"

"Not so different, and nothing that will do you the least bit of harm, as I promised. I am a man of my word, Alec. Behave now, and drink this without a fuss. It's far too valuable to spill."

"No!"

He knew it was futile, but he fought anyway as the guards held him down and pinched his nose shut. Yhakobin thrust the leather funnel down his throat and poured the contents of the cup in. They held him until he gagged down every drop, then dragged him up to his knees at Yhakobin's feet.

The alchemist shook his head as he fastened a silver amulet to Alec's collar. "I should thrash you, but I'm too pleased with your progress."

"What did you do?" Alec demanded again, gagging at the sweet taste that filled his throat.

"All I've done, Alec, is refine your Aurënfaie blood, cleansing it as best I can of the taint of your human parent. I can't remove it completely, and the effects last only as long as the tinctures do their work, but at this moment you are more 'faie than you have ever been in your life."

Alec pressed his clenched fists against his knees, fighting the urge to fly at the man. Tainted? His father—his human father—was the only family he'd ever known! He could have cried at the thought of losing what little connection he had left to him, but he wouldn't give these bastards that satisfaction again. Instead, he closed his eyes and bowed his head. *Play the role, Alec. Play it to the hilt.*

"Forgive me, Ilban. It was the shock. I—I wasn't prepared."

To his surprise, Yhakobin went to the forge and lifted out a kettle that had been warming on a hook by the fire. He poured two steaming cups and handed one to Alec, motioning him to a low stool.

Yhakobin sat down in a large chair next to him and took a sip from his cup. Alec sniffed his. It smelled like a very good, strong tea, nothing more.

"You've had your draught for the day," the alchemist assured him. "This is tea from southern Aurënen, the best in the world. See, I'm drinking it, too."

Alec took a cautious taste, and then another. By the Four, he'd missed the taste of good tea almost as much as meat. This was delicious; the warmth of it spread through him, and with it thoughts of home.

"Thank you, Ilban," he said, and for the first time he actually meant it. "But I'm surprised. You drink Aurënfaie tea?"

Yhakobin smiled at that. "Surely you aware that many of the clans trade with us, and have for centuries. Virésse, for instance. Ulan í Sathil and I are on very good terms."

Alec froze, cup halfway to his lips. He and Seregil had had dealings with the leader of the Virésse clan during Klia's negotiations in Aurënen.

Ulan was a smooth, ruthless man, and one not likely to forgive them for their role in breaking up the Virésse monopoly on Aurënen's trade with the Three Lands.

Could it have been him who betrayed us? What was a year's time for an Aurënfaie to wait, who counted time in decades? Perhaps all Ulan had to do was bide his time until they came back to Aurënen. And there'd been no secrecy about their mission.

"Is there something wrong with your tea?" asked Yhakobin.

Alec shook his head and took another sip of the fragrant tea, letting it wash away the lingering aftertaste of the tincture.

"The world is a large place, Alec, and I think you have seen only a little bit of it in your young life. You've been taught things about my country that are not true."

I knew you kept slaves, Alec thought, but wisely held his tongue.

"And you know nothing of alchemy, do you? Would you like to know more?"

"Yes, Ilban," Alec replied eagerly, though not for the reason Yhakobin probably thought.

Yhakobin filled both their cups again. "Alchemy is the art of manipulating the consciousness that exists in all matter. With skill and knowledge, an alchemist can effect great transformations."

"Turning lead into gold?" Alec asked, skeptical.

"That is certainly one of the better-known applications, the epitome of the lowly puffer's art, but one of very minor importance to any serious alchemist.

No, we seek a deeper spiritual transformation, to heal the inner disharmonies of individuals, and of the world."

He pointed to an elaborate tower of glass vessels, now brewing on the athanor. They were the round-bellied type, with down-curving, snout-shaped outlets, each shedding drops of something into a small, three-legged cauldron covered in raised symbols.

"The distillation vessel is one of the more common implements. One of our great arts is that of refining and transformation. It was an alchemist who discovered the smelting of iron from base ore a great many years before our ancestors came to this part of the world. Others perfected the elegant balance of alloys to create hard steel, bronze, and other high metals. And we discovered the combinations of metal, symbols, and auspicious hours that give power to objects, such as that amulet you're wearing.

"But most importantly, we learned to extract powerful medicines from metals, minerals, common animal matter, and herbs. These tinctures I've given you are of that nature. They cleave to and bind impure energies in your blood, so that they can be removed by the natural functions of the body." He smiled. "In that way. I have been your physician. Or, if you prefer, your body has been like one of my distillation vessels. By combining the right elements under the proper conditions, I have transformed you into what you saw in the mirror."

"But why go to the trouble when you could

have just bought yourself a pure 'faie?" Alec asked, intrigued in spite of himself.

"Because never before have I found one of your exquisite lineage. You are unique."

Alec kept his attention on his tea. While many people in Aurënen had made a fuss over his Hâzadriëlfaie blood, he'd been more of a curiosity than a wonder. No one had thought him particularly special. Khenir's talk of breeding and gelding came back to him, making his skin prickle uncomfortably.

"May I ask, Ilban, why that's so important? I'd been given to believe that the Hâzadriëlfaie were only a minor clan."

"They are not a clan at all, but a group of individuals united by a unique accident of nature. I assure you, Alec, you are a very special young man. With your help, I will perhaps be able to make a very powerful medicine, indeed. One that may well cure all the ills of the body. Is that not a worthy goal?"

"And you need Hâzadriëlfaie blood for that?"

"Only that will do. And according to the texts, an even purer elixir can be distilled to prolong the human span of life to that of a 'faie. A very long time ago, longer even than 'faie memory, an alchemist from my land discovered the secret method of distilling it. The Hâzadriëlfaie selfishly wanted no part of the work, though. That's why they took themselves away as they did, and the few Aurënfaie who knew the truth are long dead, and the memory is lost there. But here in Plenimar the secret teachings have been passed down in certain lines. I am the scion of one of those lineages."

"What would happen if a 'faie used the elixir that makes their life longer?"

"A very interesting question. Now, I must get back to work. And despite your earlier unruliness, I believe you deserve a reward today. Would you like to walk in my meditation garden with Khenir?"

Alec bowed deeply to hide his sudden rush of excitement, both at seeing the closest thing he had to a friend here and at the opportunity for a better look at that garden. "Thank you, Ilban. I would like that very much."

"Good. It must give you some comfort, having another 'faie to converse with."

"It does, Ilban." And it did.

When the guards came for him as usual, Khenir was with them. He wore a cloak over his house robe, and held up another for Alec, and a pair of thick, felted wool slippers.

Alec started to thank him, but Khenir caught his eye and made a quick, nervous nod in Yhakobin's direction. Alec turned and made a small bow. "Thank you again for your kindness, Ilban."

"And the veil, Khenir," Yhakobin reminded him.

Khenir handed Alec a veil similar to the one he was wearing and helped him tie it on. The guards let them out, but gave Khenir charge of the chain attached to Alec's collar.

"I'm sorry. Ilban's orders," Khenir whispered with an apologetic smile.

"It's all right. I understand," Alec whispered back, too eager to get into the garden to care about it.

One of the guards growled at Khenir as they left the workshop and he immediately bowed and said something servile. It hurt Alec to see it; the Aurënfaie were a proud and dignified people. He thought again of the lash marks he'd seen on Khenir's shoulders, and on the back of the slave on the ship. It made him ashamed again of how easily he'd acquiesced so far, even if he did have good reason.

The guards escorted them through the small side gate to their left and into the fountain court. A covered portico encircled it on three sides. The inner walls were painted a brilliant blue and bright, fanciful scenes of sea life showed through the white pillars. Neatly laid out paths of crushed shell led through tidy herb beds and leafless bushes to a large round fountain at the center of the garden. A slender pillar of white stone supported four stylized fish, whose spouting mouths filled the basin below.

Alec took all this in at a glance, then turned to more important elements. This courtyard occupied the angle between the main house and the workshop gardens, and was solidly enclosed on those sides. Over the east and south walls, however, he saw treetops and sky. There were two more guards, as well, stationed at the far end of the garden. The two who'd escorted them here remained on guard by the gate, leaving Alec and Khenir at least the semblance of privacy for a little while.

Khenir kept a grip on Alec's lead but linked his other arm companionably through Alec's as he led him around the portico to admire the frescoes. The simple friendliness of the gesture brought a lump to Alec's throat.

"What did those guards say to you before?" Alec whispered.

"They don't like us speaking our own language, which they can't understand. We're well contained here, though, so they're less concerned. They've agreed to let us walk about while they and the others keep watch."

It was such a relief to be out in the fresh air that for a little while Alec let himself forget about tinctures and masters and guards and simply lost himself in the pleasure of being outside. It was a fine day; the cold, sweet breeze carried the smell of pine and the sea. Gulls circled high overhead, shining white against the deep blue of the sky.

"Are we close to the coast?" he asked.

"About five miles," Khenir replied. His hand tightened on Alec's arm as he whispered, "I know what you're thinking, and you must put such thoughts from your mind. Ilban's men are trained slave trackers."

"You've never tried?"

Khenir glanced nervously back in the guards' direction. "I did—once, before I came here. I was fortunate that the master who held me then didn't want me maimed. But he punished me so badly he might as well have. It's a different world here, Alec. You must accept that."

"So I should just give up?" Alec hissed bitterly.

"Yes. With that face and that hair, you wouldn't get a mile before you were caught."

Alec knew a thing or two about not being seen, but held his tongue.

They left the portico and walked along the shell paths. Khenir took off his veil and turned his face up to the pale sun. Alec did the same, savoring the feel of the breeze against his bare skin. He didn't think he'd ever get used to wearing the hated scrap of fabric. He'd worn masks nightrunning, but this was a badge of shame.

"Why do they only make 'faie slaves wear these?"

"As a reminder of our bondage," Khenir replied. "But they also protect us, shielding us from the eyes of other masters."

"What do you mean?"

"If a noble of higher standing came here and decided he wanted you, Lord Yhakobin would have no choice but to sell you to him, or even give you away if his guest was of a very high rank. It's not uncommon for such things to happen, especially with comely slaves like you."

"Bilairy's Balls!" Alec pulled away and stared at him in disbelief. "We really are just chattel, aren't we? Like a hound or a horse."

"True, but it's not always a bad thing."

"How can you say that?"

Khenir hushed him, shooting another nervous look in the guards' direction. "Please behave. I don't want to be sent in so soon."

"What do you mean, it's not a bad thing to be owned?" Alec whispered angrily.

Khenir was quiet for a moment as they continued on. He looked so sad that Alec slipped his arm through the other man's again, covering the hand that held the chain with his own. Khenir gave him a grateful look that melted Alec's heart.

"You don't have to talk about it, if you don't want to," Alec told him.

"Actually, it's a better memory for me than most. I've had a number of masters, most of them far more . . . demanding. The last was the cruelest of all, the one I ran away from, and he nearly killed me. Master Yhakobin saw me during a visit to the man's country estate. He was so . . ."

Khenir paused, blinking back tears. "He saw the wretched condition I was in and took pity on me. He took me away with him the next day. I am so grateful for that! He saved my life with his elixirs, and ever since he's been the kindest master I've had."

"How many have you had?"

"Too many," Khenir replied, and Alec thought again of the terrible scars he had seen on his shoulders.

"Well, he must think very highly of you, to trust you with me like this." It struck him then that if he made a break for the wall now and did manage to escape, it was probably Khenir who would pay the price. *So I'll just have to take him with me when I go.*

"Your collar is a lot fancier than mine, too," he went on. "I took it for jewelry the first time I saw you."

Khenir touched it self-consciously, as if he'd forgotten about it until Alec mentioned it. "I've earned his favor."

"Do masters ever let a slave go?"

To his surprise, Khenir nodded. "Sometimes, if the slave has done some extraordinary service. Or sometimes, a favored slave is bequeathed his freedom when the master dies. Usually, though, we're passed along to the heirs with the rest of the household goods, or sold off to buy new, younger ones. It's a frightening time, when a master dies. You don't know where you'll end up."

Once again Alec sensed there was a great deal going unsaid and too many painful memories. He tightened his arm through Khenir's and said, "There was a nobleman with Master Yhakobin today."

"The Overlord's legate. I served him breakfast this morning. A very powerful man, that one. Ilban was quite nervous about his visit, and what news he'll take back to Benshâl. I hope you behaved yourself?"

"I must have. Ilban gave me tea and talked about alchemy."

"See? It's just as I said. Behave yourself and he'll treat you well."

"Do you know a lot about alchemy?"

Khenir smiled and shook his head. "I just do what he asks of me, grinding elements and cleaning the glassware."

"He doesn't have much good to say about Orëska magic, but I don't see much difference."

"Well, it's all the same to us, isn't it?" Khenir drew him over to the fountain. "Come see the fish."

"Fish?"

As they approached the broad basin a pair of

white doves that had been drinking there took wing. Coming closer, Alec saw that there were water lilies growing there, and clumps of small, striped rushes in sunken clay pots. Large, sleek fish were swimming among the submerged stems. They were shaped like trout, but their markings were like nothing he'd seen before. Their bodies were white as fresh snow, with spots of brilliant orange and velvety black.

Khenir took a crust of stale bread from his pocket and showed Alec how to make them swim up for crumbs. The largest would take the bread from their fingers.

Alec grinned as a very large one with an orange face sucked greedily at his finger. "I wonder how they taste?" His mouth watered at the thought of a few of those plump swimmers spitted on a green stick over a bed of good hot coals.

Khenir chuckled. "Don't let Ilban hear you say that. These are imported from some land beyond the Gathwayd. Any one of them would bring a better price than either of us."

"Master Yhakobin must be a very rich man."

"And a very powerful one, as well. He's among the chief alchemists in Plenimar. The Overlord himself consults with him often, about his son."

"What's wrong with him?"

"The boy is very young and frail, and suffers from fits no physician or priest has been able to cure. Master Yhakobin's tinctures are all that keep him alive, or so I'm told. A courier comes once a week for new ones, sometimes more often if the child is doing very poorly. And the legate, too, as you saw today."

So that's why my blood was so important! If Yhakobin could cure the Overlord's son, then he'd probably be the most favored man in Plenimar. "Why isn't Ilban at court in Benshâl?"

"I suppose it's a mark of how important he is that the Overlord lets him potter about down here in the country. They are on very good terms. His Majesty visits occasionally."

"You've seen the Overlord?"

"Yes. A powerful and ambitious man."

Alec tucked that information away. "You're sure alchemy isn't necromancy, using blood and all that?"

"Oh yes! The master despises necromancers even more than he detests wizards." Khenir looked around, making sure the guards were still by the gate at the far end of the garden. "He also worries about the hold they have on the Overlord. They don't practice openly in most parts of the country, but he keeps some of the most powerful at court, and Ilban thinks he relies on them far too much. It's rumored that he uses them against his own people, just as his father before him. Despite what you Skalans think, the Plenimaran people have no love for necromancy. It's a blight on the land, and there are those who say that the young heir's illness is a punishment from the Immortals."

Alec considered this as he watched the fish nudging about among the plants, looking for more crumbs. His only experience of Plenimarans before now had been at the hands of their soldiers and necromancers, but if the people were not all like that—if they hated their ruler and his filthy minions—then maybe he could find help of some sort when he escaped.

"He said that I'm important in some way, because of who my mother's people are."

"Oh? What clan are you?"

"Hâzadriëlfaie."

Khenir looked at him in surprise. "Those who went north? I've never heard of them mixing with any outsiders. Some even say they all died years ago."

"I never knew my mother's people, and I don't know how she met my father. He never told me anything except that she was dead. But later I found out that, after I was born, he took me away before her people could kill me, as they do all ya'shel. They murdered her, though, before my father could save her."

"That's very sad. I'm sorry."

"Well, it's not like I remember her. I didn't know anything about her until—" He hesitated, but damn it, he was sick of being so guarded with the only person here who'd shown him any kindness. "Ireya. Her name was Ireya ä Shaar. An oracle showed her to me. That's all I know, really." *Except that she died to save my father's life. And mine.*

"Then you don't even know where her people are?"

"Not exactly. The Hâzadriëlfaie kill outsiders on sight, so no one goes near their lands. Those who try don't come back."

"That must be difficult, not knowing the 'faie part of your family, when you resemble them so much."

Alec shrugged. "It doesn't matter much to me. Like I said, I never knew about them."

That was a lie, of course. Ever since he'd been given that vision of his mother, he'd dreamed often of her face and the anguished look in her eyes as she'd placed her infant son in his father's arms. He'd thought a lot about certain passes in the Ironheart foothills, too—places his father had steered clear of. Everyone around Kerry knew the legends about the 'faie who lived somewhere beyond Ravensfell Pass, though most thought they were just a legend. But all the old stories told around tavern fires spoke of a dark and dangerous folk who killed unwary hunters who strayed too close to their borders.

"Do you know what Yhakobin wants with me?" he asked, tossing another crumb to the fish.

"As I said, Alec, I only do what I'm told. He does not confide in me." Khenir stood with his face to the sun again, eyes closed and smiling now, as if he'd found refuge in better thoughts.

Seeing him like that, Alec suddenly found himself thinking, *By the Four, but he's handsome!*

The traitorous thought surprised and shamed him. Where the hell had that come from?

Fortunately, Khenir took no notice.

Alec fixed his attention on the fish again, guilty and heartsick as he recalled the silly fight he and Seregil had gotten into when Seregil suggested he find a willing girl to have children for him. And here he was now, looking at another man.

Forgive me, talí!

After nearly two weeks of rest and decent food, Seregil told himself he felt a little stronger today, but after a few circuits around the room he knew otherwise. Frustrated, he acquiesced glumly when Zoriel moved the chair to the window for him and left him there with his bowl of morning gruel and a blanket over his knees, like an old man. Whatever magic the slavers had used on him, it had taken a more lasting toll on him than anything he'd ever experienced, except perhaps for the amulet he and Alec had inadvertently stolen from that Plenimaran duke soon after they met. He still had the scar on his chest from that mishap.

He gazed down into the garden, docketing again all the possible routes of escape—a tall tree, some stonework that offered good handholds, a climbing rose. From what little he could see over the wall, this was a country house, which presented other problems. A city was an easy place in which to lose oneself; open fields, probably bare this time of year, were the worst possible option.

No use worrying about that before I'm strong enough to do something about it. Feeling more useless than ever, he rested his chin in one hand and watched the sparkle of the fountain. There were some large fish in the basin that he hadn't noticed before. That was a sure sign of wealth, though he'd already guessed as much.

Doves were drinking and bathing there, too, but scattered as several people walked into view in the covered portico. He expected the children and their nurse, but it was two taller, veiled figures. They passed from view, then reappeared on one of the paths leading to the fountain.

"Alec!" The breath locked in Seregil's chest as he lurched unsteadily to his feet, clutching at the bars for support. There was no question; even with the veil and shapeless robe, his lover's build and gait, and that braid hanging down the back of his cloak were unmistakable.

He's alive! He's alive and he's here, in this house!

"Alec!" he shouted.

When Alec gave no sign of hearing, Seregil reached through the bars, pounding at the thick window. It would not give, and even that sound did not seem to reach the men in the garden. That didn't stop him from shouting himself hoarse. Caught between relief and frustration, he sagged against the bars, tears rolling unnoticed down his cheeks as he drank in the sight of his talí alive and apparently well.

He's alive! Thank the Light, Alec is alive! The words throbbed in his head in time to his frantic heartbeat. *I didn't get him killed!*

He'd paid scant attention to the other man, but he scrutinized him now and saw that he had Alec on a chain like a dog, fastened to some sort of collar around his neck. He silently vowed to cut off the hand of the man who'd put it there.

Though Seregil couldn't make out their faces, it appeared that they were on friendly terms. That gave Seregil hope. If there was one thing Alec excelled at, it was charming people and disguising his own motives.

The other man wore a golden collar around his neck, just visible under the edge of the veil. He also had the dark hair and build of a 'faie. *Well done, talí. Perhaps you've found us an ally!*

Alec and his companion walked together, arm in arm, while Seregil watched like a drowning man sighting land across the waves.

As they reached the fountain, both of them pulled down their veils. For a moment Seregil only had eyes for Alec; he looked well—better than well, actually. Even through the wavy glass, Alec had never looked more beautiful. It made his heart ache to be this close and yet so hopelessly apart. Just then, however, Alec's companion looked up in Seregil's direction and smiled.

Seregil's elation curdled in his throat. He knew this face, this man. He'd haunted Seregil's memories all the days of his exile, and his dreams, too, since he'd been here.

Ilar í Sontir. First lover. First betrayer. The man who'd engineered Seregil's downfall all those years ago.

He slammed his fist against the window again. "You whoreson bastard!"

In the garden below, Ilar took Alec's arm as if they were the best of friends. Seregil shuddered, feeling like he was caught in a horrible dream when he saw the way Alec smiled at him.

Seregil clutched the bars that kept him from kicking out the window and leaping down to kill

Ilar for putting hands on Alec. *Just one more reason to kill you, Ilar!*

Ilar looked up again, almost as if he'd heard Seregil's thoughts.

You meant for me to see, didn't you, you bastard? You had Zoriel put me here, to be certain I'd be watching.

What followed took on the feel of a staged performance, which it probably was. Ilar touched Alec often, and they stood close together, talking like friends as they threw bread to the fish. Alec actually reached out and took Ilar's arm. Seregil stood there, fingers going numb around the bars, hating Ilar with a passion so strong it made black spots swim in front of his eyes.

He stayed there until Alec and Ilar passed from view again, then sank down in the chair and put his head between his knees, feeling sick.

When the nausea had abated he fell back in the chair, staring out the window at the grey-backed gulls circling above the house. His heart beat so hard it ached.

How can this possibly be?

Where has Ilar been all these years, and what is he doing here?

Think, damn it! I can't even stay on my feet. What am I going to do?

When his head stopped spinning, he slowly pushed the chair into the corner of the room furthest from the door and huddled there, sweaty and winded, clutching the empty water pitcher in both hands. He felt absolutely ridiculous, but right now he didn't have much in the way of options.

Zoriel came at the customary time with his midday meal and found him there. "What's this?"

"I saw your 'master,' down there in the garden," he growled. "Turns out he's an old friend of mine."

Zoriel set the tray across his knees. "You're talking nonsense. Eat your food."

"Tell him I'd very much like to renew our acquaintance, won't you?" Seregil called after her as she went out. "Tell him it's been far too long!"

"Fool!" she threw back as the guard slammed the door.

Seregil smiled crookedly as he ate the bean soup, brown bread, and honeyed milk she'd brought. His circumstances hadn't changed, but knowing where Alec was, even if it was with Ilar, was the first firm ground he'd had under his feet in weeks.

It had been over half a century since Seregil had met Ilar that summer at the clan gathering by the river.

My last summer there, he thought bitterly. *Is that why I dreamed of it again, after all this time? Did I know he was so close?*

Thanks to Ilar, he'd killed that Hamani clansman. And, in doing so, betrayed his own father, his clan, and destroyed the fragile negotiations before they could come to fruition.

Ilar was several decades older than the green boy Seregil had been then. He'd been so handsome, so charming, always with time for his young companion. He'd made Seregil feel like he was someone special instead of his father's great disappointment.

Seregil rested his head in his hands with a soft groan. Ilar hadn't had much trouble seducing him, and in more ways than one. He secured Seregil's needy heart first, with caresses, kind words, and false praise, playing the smitten swain when all the time he'd been sounding out the khirnari's son, finding the best way to ruin him—and through Seregil, his father's negotiations with the Zengat. Too late, Seregil had realized that this had been his "lover's" real goal, all along.

Even after all these years, the memories were stained deep with shame. Adzriel had tried to warn him against the older man, and in time even Kheeta had grown concerned about Ilar's hold over Seregil.

But Seregil hadn't listened to any of them, and in the end he'd been cheaply bought. Ilar had made a game of giving him little challenges: steal a bit of food from this camp, go to the heart of another and bring back proof he'd come and gone unseen, and the like. Puffed up with his successes and the older man's approval, he'd willingly gone to the tent of the Haman khirnari, looking for a document that would supposedly aid his father in his negotiations. Little did he guess that as soon as he was safely off on that errand, Ilar had convinced one of the Haman khirnari's kinsman to go there as well, on some pretext.

It had been dark, and the man had surprised Seregil. They both drew weapons, but Seregil was quicker with his knife, striking out of fear and panic before he could weigh the consequences. Seregil hadn't meant to kill him. The act had sickened him to the heart and he'd made no effort to get away.

Ilar and those who'd been his fellow conspirators were long gone by the time Seregil appeared in the council tent, shattered and in tears, with the first blood he'd ever shed still warm on his hands and white tunic.

Ilar was never seen in Aurënen again...

Seregil didn't realize he'd been poisoned until the half-empty soup bowl slipped from his hand and clattered to the floor in front of him.

"No!" he whispered, as the room began to spin. Why would Ilar kill him now, after going to all this trouble?

But he didn't die, or even lose consciousness. His body simply went to sleep, leaving his mind awake and frantic.

Time passed and he sat frozen, slumped in his chair, mind racing. At last he heard the grate of a key in the door. He wasn't at all surprised when Ilar stepped in and closed the door behind him. The veil was gone.

"Ilar í Sontir," Seregil rasped, forcing the words out.

"Haba. I do hope you enjoyed your meal." And he gave Seregil that warm, false smile he remembered so well as he crossed the room and bent over Seregil. He slipped a finger under Seregil's collar and gave it a little tug. "This suits you. And I'm known as Khenir now, but you can use my old name if you wish. It doesn't mean anything here."

He picked Seregil up in his arms as if he weighed nothing and laid him on the bed. He placed the pillow behind Seregil's head, pulled his robe down over his knees, and smoothed a stray lock of hair away from his face, mocking him with seeming tenderness, all the while with that unsettling look in his eyes. When he had Seregil arranged to his liking, he pulled the chair over and sat down beside him.

"I trust you're comfortable, Haba? Do say so if you're not." Cruel glee began to show through the solicitous mask.

"What . . . Poison . . ."

"No, just one of my master's tinctures. It's not the first time you've had it, you know. Been sleeping well since you came here? Have your dreams been especially vivid?" He held up a silver perfume flask and pulled out the stopper, waving it under Seregil's nose. The scent of wandril flowers. Adzriel's scent.

"Bas—"

"What's that? Do speak up." Ilar set the flask aside, then leaned close and stroked Seregil's hair and cheek. Then he leaned closer still and kissed him, thrusting his tongue deep into his mouth.

Seregil tried to bite him and Ilar pulled back, wiping his lips. "You used to like it when I did that." This time he stroked his fingers down Seregil's bare arm and across his chest, sending an involuntary shiver through him. Ilar paused as his fingers found the scar in the middle of Seregil's chest.

"What's this? Ah, but you can't answer." He traced the outline of the round mark, then examined the dragon bite on Seregil's hand. "That's a most impressive mark. Who knows all the things you've done, to get so many interesting scars since we last met." Ilar stroked his cheek again. "I've been so very patient, all these years. I waited a very long time to see you again, my little Haba. Oh, I've enjoyed our evenings together lately, but it's so much nicer with you awake."

Seregil thought of those dreams he'd had, of an unseen lover touching him, coaxing his aching response. He'd have gagged if he'd been capable.

I'd know if he raped me. I'd know. Oh, Illior!

"You looked younger in your sleep, more like the boy I loved."

Seregil managed a low growl of disgust.

Ilar's hazel eyes went distant for a moment. "I did, I think. I was certainly very fond of you by the end. It was so hard to see it through, the commission given me by the khirnari of Virésse."

He laughed as Seregil's eyes narrowed. "You didn't think he'd stand by and allow your father to succeed, did you? But then, you were only a child, and not thinking of such things." He stroked Seregil's hair again. "But you're a man now, aren't you, and all grown up? Still, those pretty eyes of yours are the same, though I don't believe I ever saw that kind of anger in them back then." Without warning he slapped Seregil hard across the face. "What have *you* to be angry about? How does that compare with what happened to me? They let you live. They set you free!"

A cold chill rippled unpleasantly over Seregil's skin. "You—knew?" he managed, his voice a ghostly rasp.

"Do you think I haven't made it my business to know where you were, and how you were prospering? Poor little exile, weren't you? Queen's Kin!

Lord Seregil, with your fine house and fine friends. And your *freedom*!" He struck Seregil again, and the coppery taste of blood welled along the edge of his tongue.

"You—your—own—fault."

"My fault?" Ilar gave him an incredulous look. "You weren't supposed to *murder* anyone! You were only supposed to be caught and made an embarrassment before your father. To upset his plans. That's what I was paid to do. But you, you little monster, you killed a man! And I was the one who paid the price. That was your choice, but I've borne the curse of it."

Seregil rolled his eyes, chancing another slap. He didn't believe him, and he didn't care. "Alec?"

"Ah yes. Alec. Word came from Aurënen that you'd returned, and that you had an Hâzadriëlfaie with you." The hand that had slapped him traveled down Seregil's belly and under the covers to caress his limp cock through his robe.

"So?" Seregil was for once glad of the drug, for the way it dulled him to the movements of that hand.

Ilar's smile returned, thin and nasty, as he sat back and crossed his arms. "You really don't know, do you? Or any of the khirnari of the Iia'sidra. No one remembers why Hâzadriël gathered her followers and disappeared, all those generations ago. But there are those here in Plenimar who do."

Seregil waited, intrigued in spite of his distrust. To his dismay, Ilar only chuckled and stood up.

"Sleep well, Haba. Perhaps I'll visit you again tonight."

"No! Alec..." Seregil croaked, as his body lay there like so much carrion.

"He's no longer your concern, is he? Oh, but just so you know?" Ilar pushed back his right sleeve and showed Seregil the underside of his forearm. The slave brand was smooth and faded, white against the pale skin. "This will be burnt over soon, marking me as a freedman. Your lover is the price of that freedom. And can you guess what *my* price was, for finding him for them?"

He paused, leaving Seregil to wonder who "them" might be.

"My price, little Haba, was you."

CHAPTER 20

The Price of Loneliness

ALEC WAS ALWAYS left to himself the day after a visit to Yhakobin, so he was as much surprised as pleased when Khenir appeared at his door that afternoon.

"Would you like to take another walk?" he asked, grinning.

Alec was so glad to get outside again that he hardly minded when one of the waiting guards fastened the chain to his collar.

Once again, four guards were there to watch them. Making a break for it in daylight probably wasn't going to be an option, Alec decided. That was not a cheering thought, but he couldn't help enjoying being out of that cell again. It was a bit warmer today and he relished the warmth of the sun on his face as they strolled around the garden, enjoying the splash of the fountain and the cries of the gulls overhead.

After a while Khenir took Alec's hand in his as

if it was the most natural thing in the world. Alec blushed guiltily as the warmth of the other man's palm against his own sent a rather pleasurable tingle up his arm.

What's wrong with me? Am I really that lonely?

He tried to pull free without insulting the man, but Khenir gave him such a sad look and said, "Humor me, won't you, little brother? It's so lonely here."

Alec was too kind to refuse him that, and Khenir gave him a grateful look.

They walked on like that for a while, then the other man sighed. "Your frown tells me there's someone you're faithful to, yes? Is she very pretty?"

Alec gave a noncommittal shrug.

"No?" Khenir smiled knowingly. "Or maybe not a 'she'?"

"I'd rather not talk about that."

Khenir seemed to shrink in on himself as he turned away. "Keep your secrets, then," he said softly. "What am I in your eyes, after all, but filth and spoiled goods?"

"No, that's not it at all!" Alec laid a hand on the older man's shoulder. "I appreciate your friendship, Khenir, more than you know!" He paused, wanting to undo the hurt but knowing better than to give away that kind of information, even to a fellow slave.

Khenir still refused to face him. "No, I shouldn't have presumed. It's just—well, as I said, I've been lonely here . . . Please, say we're friends?"

He turned around and held out his hand. There were tears on his cheeks. Alec took his hand again.

"Of course we are. It's just . . ." What could he possibly say? "It's just that my heart is broken, losing him, and I can't think of anyone else. Not yet."

Khenir touched Alec's cheek. "I . . . That is . . ." He glanced back at the guards. They seemed to be engrossed in their own conversation. He leaned closer, lowering his voice. "I'm not asking for your heart, Alec. But if we could just find a little comfort together . . ."

And Khenir kissed him.

Alec tried to pull away but Khenir got an arm around his waist and gripped the back of Alec's head, whimpering a little as he prolonged the kiss.

Alec twisted out of his grip and shoved him away. "Stop it!"

Khenir stumbled back against the edge of the basin and sank down on it, covering his face with his hand.

Alec wiped his mouth with the back of his hand. "Damn it, Khenir!"

The man was weeping in earnest now, shoulders shaking under his cloak. The guards were on their way over to them, but Khenir quickly said something that sent them back to their post by the gate. Looking up at Alec, he drew a shaky breath. "Forgive me. You see what I'm reduced to, shaming myself and my clan in front of you? What must you think?"

Alec kept his distance as much as the chain allowed, but his outrage slowly gave way to pity. He could only imagine what it must be like, lost in an enemy land for so long, stripped of every shred of dignity. "It's all right. I understand," he said at last, then regretted his choice of words when he saw renewed hope flicker in Khenir's reddened eyes.

"Then perhaps—?"

"I'm sorry. No." Then, to show there were no hard feelings, he took Khenir by the hand and pulled him up. "Let's walk some more before they make us go in."

Khenir tried to pull his hand away, and Alec knew he should probably let him, but he wanted to make it clear that he held no grudge. And even now, he had to admit that the simple clasping of hands was a comfort to him, too.

It's just because he's the only one here who's been kind to me, he thought, but he still felt torn.

Khenir was very quiet for a while as he collected himself, then slowly he told Alec a little about his lost home. His eyes misted again as he haltingly named friends, family, and a lover long missed. In return, Alec found himself telling him of his father and the free life they'd lived in the northlands. That seemed like a safe topic since it had nothing to do with Seregil or their profession.

"How did you come to Skala?" asked Khenir, calmer now.

"I went to Rhíminee after my father died, looking for work." That was close enough to the truth.

The weight of the chain pulled his thin metal collar uncomfortably against the side of his neck, and he reached absently to shift it. His fingers strayed to the amulet and he traced the marking on it. "Did you ever have to wear these things?"

"No. It must be part of the special purification."

"Because of my impure blood."

"Most likely."

"Do you see the change in me?"

"Of course, but I didn't know if he'd shown you." Khenir gave him a shy, sidelong look. "You're very handsome. You were before, but now you look more like a full-blooded 'faie than a . . . Oh, no. I don't mean anything by it! I'm not . . ."

"It's all right." Alec gave his hand a reassuring squeeze and chuckled. "I've been called a lot worse."

Khenir fell in step beside him again, but the silence that followed felt rather strained. "I saw your name," Alec told him.

"You did? Where?"

"On the door," Alec whispered.

Khenir looked honestly perplexed. "What door?"

"In my cell." Perhaps it had been another man of that name. Whatever the case, Khenir seemed to have no idea what he was talking about.

But after a moment Khenir nodded sadly. "Oh yes, down at the bottom. I'd forgotten. That was a dark time."

"I'm sorry. I didn't think—"

Khenir patted his hand. "You apologize far too often, and for things that are not any fault of yours. It's enough for me that I have someone I can talk to. You see, I was half-dead when Ilban brought me here, and I wasn't kept down there very long. As soon as I could speak again, I pledged my life to him. I've kept that promise."

Alec couldn't really fault Khenir for that; he had been pretty damn grateful, himself, the night a stranger who'd turned out to be Seregil had gotten him out of that north country dungeon the night before Alec was to be sold to Plenimaran slavers. It was ironic, really. Everything that he'd done and become since then had landed him here anyway, with a collar around his neck.

"There were more names. What happened to all those people?"

Khenir shrugged. "Who knows? It's a very old house and they could have belonged to Ilban's family."

Just then they were interrupted by shrill, child-ish laughter. A small boy dashed into the garden, clutching a toy horse to his chest and looking back over his shoulder with a challenging grin. Somewhere behind him, another child wailed an-grily. Alec didn't need to understand the language to guess that the boy was teasing his sister.

A woman called out sharply, and the child stuck out his tongue. He turned and made for the foun-tain, but halted as he caught sight of Alec and Khenir in the shadow of the portico. The child's mischievous expression changed to open disdain. He snapped something at them, and Khenir hastily bowed and put on his veil.

"Cover your face!" he whispered to Alec.

Alec pulled his up, but not quickly enough to suit the little tyrant. The child stamped his foot and shouted at them.

Khenir replied with a deeper bow, but that only made the boy angrier. He snatched up a stone from beside the pathway and cocked his arm back, ready to throw. Khenir just stood there, hands at his side.

Alec stepped between them, glaring at the child to make him stop.

The boy's eyes widened and the hand holding the stone lowered a bit. But there was no mistaking the malice in his eyes.

"*Buko!*" he cried angrily, and it sounded like either a threat or an insult.

The veiled nursemaid appeared before things could get any worse and hurried to catch the boy. Forgetting about Alec and Khenir, he dropped the stone and darted out of reach, laughing again as he disappeared the way he'd come.

Rhania paused a moment, looking at them, and Alec saw the unmistakable tracery of Khatme clan tattoos on her face above the veil. More surprising still was the naked animosity in her dark eyes as she looked past him to Khenir.

He spoke sharply to her and she flinched as if he'd struck her, then hurried away, hissing something back at him under her breath.

"What was that about?" asked Alec, wishing he'd had a chance to speak with her.

"She hates me," Khenir explained. "I took her place in the master's esteem, and now she's just the nursemaid."

"She's a Khatme."

"Yes, and no one holds a grudge more deeply. You'd do well to watch out for her. She's a spiteful, ill-tempered one, that woman."

"What did the boy say, before she came out?"

"Oh, he was just playing the little master, upbraiding us for having our faces bare. The whole household spoils young Master Osri, and his father worst of all. I hope I didn't get you in trouble, letting you go without your veil again. If Ilban says anything, just put the blame on me. It was my fault anyway, and he's less likely to punish you that way. Now come, let's walk a little more before they make you go back."

That evening Alec stared down at his supper tray in surprise, thinking, *Yhakobin must be really pleased with me!* First the unexpected walk in the garden with Khenir, and now this; in addition to the usual bread, soup, and apple, there was a thick wedge of white cheese.

His mouth watered painfully as he sniffed it, but he resisted the urge to wolf it down. Instead, he ate the bread and soup first, then savored the cheese a nibble at a time, between bites of the apple. If the alchemist had visited him then, he might have thanked him outright, not for his kindness, but for food that would give him that much more strength when he finally escaped.

That thought carried a twinge of guilt. Once again, he might have been able to pull free from Khenir and make for the walls before the guards could catch up with him. And of course, there was that business with the kiss.

With Khenir or without him, I've got to get out of

here, and soon! He kissed his palm and pressed it to his heart. *Soon, talí. I swear I'll find a way . . .*

He woke at Micum Cavish's house to the familiar smell of sweat and woodsmoke, and the wail of the high wind off the mountains. It moaned through the tall pines outside and drove rain against the shuttered windows and down the chimney. Droplets glittered a moment in the smoky red light, then died, hissing on the smoldering embers.

For the first time, he and Seregil had shared this guest room at Watermead as lovers rather than friends. Already drained by the emotion of Seregil's near escape, and hampered by his own inept and embarrassed awkwardness, Alec had thought to wait a little longer, but Seregil had conquered his fears with kisses and caresses, and treated him tenderly, showing Alec the first ways of pleasure rather than taking his own.

Now, snug and happily dazed under a pile of furs and blankets, with Seregil curled warm against his back, Alec lay there lost in awe of the experience. What was it the Oracle at Rhíminee had told Seregil, soon after they first met? "Father, brother, friend, and lover."

Seregil had truly been all four to him now.

Lover. Talimenios. He couldn't even think the words yet without blushing hotly, but there was no shame, and no regret. Just wonder.

And he couldn't get back to sleep. When he finally pushed up on one elbow to see if daylight was showing through the shutters yet, Seregil made a sleepy sound of protest at the sudden draft sucked under the covers by Alec's movement and snuggled closer, tightening his arm around Alec's waist . . .

Only now they weren't at Watermead at all, but in the winter-locked cabin in the mountains. That wasn't rain hissing on the embers and filtering down through the loose shingles but sparkling white snow. And Alec hadn't been a blushing innocent for a very long time.

"Go back to sleep. It's early, *talí*," Alec whispered. He lay down and pulled the blankets up over both of them, trying to remember what they'd put by for breakfast.

The hunting had been poor for days. A half-frozen venison haunch and a brace of stiff grouse hung from the rafters overhead, the last of their meat. The little root cellar under the floor was empty, too. It had snowed hard for the past week, stopping at last the night before, and they were out of bread, cheese, and sausage. Both of them had more bones showing than they had in the fall.

"We're going to have to make it into town today somehow," Alec muttered, not relishing the idea of such a long trek on snowshoes over the unpacked expanse of powder, or the same trek back with the weight of supplies on their backs.

"Mmmmm. Later," Seregil mumbled sleepily, running a hand down Alec's chest, then lower.

Suddenly the food situation didn't seem so pressing. With a happy sigh, Alec turned over to face him and return the caresses of his lover, his friend.

This lonely cabin was their haven, their refuge against memory and sadness. Seregil had vowed never to set foot in Rhíminee again, and at moments like *these, Alec didn't regret it. Seregil hadn't dreamed of Nysander for nearly a week. In fact, he'd slept well for days, and was content and even more passionate than usual.*

So it was now as they made love, and soon the heat of their bodies warmed the room more than the meager fire. Before they were done they'd kicked the blankets back, sweating in the red glow.

When it was over Alec fell back against the musty pillows, spent and happy. He reached for Seregil, but he wasn't there.

He wasn't there . . .

The cabin, the bed, the sound of the wind and the smell of the damp embers—it all faded away, melting like the snow had melted soon after that long-ago morning.

Instead, he was shivering in a dimly lit room, caught in the grip of Yhakobin's guards as Ahmol carefully cleaned the cooling white spendings from Alec's belly with a wooden scraper into a metal bowl.

Oh hell. The cheese. When will I stop being a fool?

Alec instinctively tried to jerk free and cover himself, but the men held him fast until Ahmol was finished.

"Why?" Alec snarled, still struggling. "Why are you doing this?"

Ahmol gave him a disgusted look. "Ilban say. Need your *bura*."

Bura?

Ahmol moved hastily back as Alec began to retch. Nothing came up, but the others released him, letting him curl into a miserable ball. As he did so, he suddenly noticed that the door of his cell stood open.

He uncoiled and shot up from the pallet, shoving his startled gaolers aside as he broke for freedom.

In retrospect, it wasn't a particularly well thought out escape. He didn't quite make it to the door before one of them caught his braid and yanked him backward off his feet.

I've really got to cut that off, he thought as he fell awkwardly, scraping a hip and the heel of one hand painfully on the bricks.

A guard pinned him to the floor with a boot on his chest while the others went out.

"Ilban not be so good, you run," Ahmol warned over his shoulder.

"Ilban *not* good anyway!" he spat back, but held his hands out at his sides to show the guard that he was done fighting. It was pointless now.

The guard took his foot away, collected the lantern by the door, and went out, securing the door firmly behind him.

Alec scrambled to his feet, shuddering with indignity and the cold. He found his discarded robe and pulled it on, ignoring the lingering stickiness on his belly. There was a strange bitterness at the back of his tongue that wasn't bile.

He gave me something to make that kind of dream! How else would he have known when to send his men?

Back on his pallet with the quilts pulled up to his chin, Alec swallowed hard to keep from being sick again. *Ilban* would probably want to save some of that, too, the pervert!

Another shudder ran up Alec's back as he thought of the way Yhakobin had collected his tears in a little bottle.

Nothing wasted.

He couldn't even enjoy the memory of the dream, knowing those bastards had been watching. That thought was too much for him. Throwing back the quilts, he barely made it to the bucket in time.

Alec sat awake the rest of the night, waiting for the nauseous effects of the drug to wear off. The night passed slowly, and he watched the tiny window brighten from black to blue to pink, then to yellow as the sun came over the courtyard wall outside. It was easier to think now that he could see, easier to marshal his careening thoughts away from the shame of the night. One thing he was quite certain of: Yhakobin was mad. It was disconcerting to think that about someone who seemed so rational, but what other explanation could there be for a man who kept the tears and blood and spendings of another?

Ahmol brought his breakfast at the usual time the following morning, and Alec left it untouched. When the guards came to collect him, he did his best to ignore their knowing smirks.

"I trust you slept well?" Yhakobin said, pouring Alec a cup of tea.

Alec gave him a sullen shrug, waiting until Yhakobin poured himself a cup and had taken several sips before he dared taste his own. It was the same good, strong Aurënen brew as before; it cut the bad taste in his mouth and soothed his aching stomach.

"You're angry with me, I think."

Aware of the whip lying ready on a nearby table, Alec kept his gaze on his tea. "No, Ilban."

"Indeed. But perhaps a little shocked, yes? I don't blame you, but it was the only way. It's not as if you'd have given up such vital fluids willingly. Really, now, it did you no harm, except perhaps to your pride. You shouldn't even have awakened."

Alec's fingers tightened around the cup. "Why do such a thing, Ilban?"

"Each of the body's vital essences contain valuable elements, no different than metals and minerals, and each has its use."

Alec's eyes widened. "You mean, you make something from . . . from that?"

Yhakobin smiled. "Oh yes, something very precious. I'm almost ready to begin. But not quite yet." He rose and took a flask down from the tincture shelf. "We come to the final draught, at last. Come here. We must change the amulet."

Alec shuddered at the touch of the man's cold fingers as Yhakobin removed the silver amulet. He tossed it into the forge, as always, then held up a heavy lozenge of gold for Alec to see. It had more symbols on it than the others.

"You are most favored, Alec. I told you that rich men would pay dearly for the Tincture of Lead; they would give more than money for this Tincture of Gold, the highest of the natural elements." He fixed the pendant in place and patted Alec's cheek.

It was only with an effort that Alec kept himself from knocking that hand away.

Yhakobin saw and cast a meaningful glance in the direction of the whip. "This is a very special day for you. Don't spoil the moment with one of your pointless tantrums."

Alec hastily dropped his gaze again, tensing. Something was going to happen now. He needed his wits about him to take advantage of any opening.

He swallowed the tincture without a fight. It tasted like pure spring water, and had no immediate effect.

"What are you going to use me for, Ilban?" he asked, weary, scared, and pleading. It was only halfway an act.

Yhakobin just patted his shoulder. "You will see soon enough. And don't worry. It's not your life I need. Sleep well, with my promise that no more indignities will be visited upon you."

Alec held his tongue. Yhakobin's promises didn't count for much.

CHAPTER 21

Distractions

THERO PUSHED THE ornate scroll aside and rubbed his eyes. It had been a parting gift from Seregil's sister Adzriel. It was an exciting project, to be sure, but he'd just realized that he'd already translated the same passage at least three times and he still didn't know what it said.

The afternoon had slipped by and the workroom was in shadow except for the light of the lamp at his elbow. Thero absently snapped his fingers, lighting others around the room. Leaning back in his chair, he stretched his stiff neck until he was staring up through the leaded glass dome above the workroom, where the last orange and gold of the sunset still lingered.

There were magical emblems worked into the patterns of the glass up there. Ever since he came to this tower as a boy, he'd tried to discover exactly how many there were. After all these years, he still came up with a different count each time, depending on which way the sunlight or moonlight struck the tower. Nysander had never solved the puzzle, either—though he was of the opinion that his old master, Arkoniel, had intentionally magicked the glazing to confound and amuse his successors. He'd created the mural in the sitting room, too.

For the past several days Thero hadn't been able to concentrate on anything as well as he'd have liked. It was Seregil's fault, of course. The fool had probably forgotten to break the second message stick. He and Alec were no doubt soaking in some luxurious Bôkthersan bathhouse right now, or hunting with Klia in the fragrant pine forests.

"You're allowing yourself to fall back into bad habits," he muttered aloud, but in his mind he heard Nysander's gentle chastisements. He'd wasted years being jealous of Seregil—of his freedom and irreverence and the deep bond he shared with the old wizard. Alec's arrival had softened the rivalry a little, and Nysander's death had ended it, but old habits were hard to break.

The truth was he *was* jealous of both of them right now, being in Bôkthersa with Klia.

Thero and the princess had become good friends in their shared exile, and what Alec had begun for him, Klia and the Bôkthersan people had completed. Thero had found a way out of his emotional exile— given up being a "cold fish," as Seregil loved to put it—and learned to find pleasure in simple daily interactions with ordinary people. Especially with Klia, though she was far from ordinary.

He sighed, thinking of her: her good nature; the intelligence that shone in those eyes; the way her hair swung in a heavy braid against her back at sword practice with Beka or while riding.

He sighed again, then caught himself at it. He had no illusions about his standing with her, of course. She'd never consider him more than a friend and ally. *What would an eagle want with a crow like me?*

But he was also a man who'd discovered he had a heart, and wished he hadn't. It sometimes distracted him from more important considerations, like why Phoria had suddenly recalled her sister's loyal bodyguard. For over a year Urghazi Turma had languished in Aurënen, apparently forgotten. Then, out of the blue, came a new guard, all strangers, and orders to stand down and sail home. Beka Cavish and her riders had threatened mutiny, and had been roundly chastised by Klia for it. Every last one of them had wept openly as they rode away, men and women alike.

As Thero and Klia had grown closer, she'd finally admitted that she believed her days might be numbered. Queen Phoria had never been close to her youngest half sister, and Klia's great popularity—both with the army and with the people—could be construed as a threat. But Thero knew Klia would never betray the throne. She was too honorable for that. Unfortunately, she was also too honorable to disappear when she had the chance. She would obey her sister's summons and accept the consequences, whatever they turned out to be.

The day they'd parted, Klia had set his heart reeling when she'd kissed him on the cheek and whispered, "Good-bye, my good friend. If we don't meet again, know what you have meant to me."

He'd ridden away that day with tears burning his eyes and his heart scorched with a love that could not be.

Giving up on the scroll, Thero climbed the stairs to the gallery and gazed out across the city—past the dark bulk of the Palace and over the harbor to the expanse of dark blue sea.

Dark blue, like her eyes in the shadow of the forest . . .

There were ships on the horizon, their sails black against the setting sun, and he wished very badly that he was aboard one of them, sailing south.

"Fool!" he muttered, and headed for the gardens to clear his head.

He'd actually begun to make some headway with his translation that night and found the beginning of a very interesting transformative evocation, when Wethis hurried in without knocking.

"Prince Korathan is downstairs, asking for you, my lord."

"And you left him standing there?" Thero snapped. By ancient protocol, only the queen herself could enter the House without the invitation of one of the wizards, but this was ridiculous. "Bring him up at once! I'll be in the sitting room."

The young servant bowed and dashed out. Thero hurried downstairs to make ready for his royal visitor.

He summoned a jar of wine from its resting place in the snows of Mount Itheira, and set out the crystal goblets Nysander kept for special guests. By the time Wethis ushered Korathan in, his stomach was in an uneasy knot. What except bad news would bring the prince here at this hour?

To his relief, Korathan did not appear to be particularly distraught as he entered. He'd put aside his court robes and chain of office for practice leathers, and his fair, grey-streaked hair was pulled back into a long tail.

"Have you heard anything?" Korathan asked before he'd even taken his seat.

"I'd have sent word, Highness," Thero assured him. "And so I take it that you've not, either?"

Korathan accepted a cup of wine. "How long does it take to ride from Gedre to Bôkthersa?"

"Less than a week, without delays, but this time of year they might have been caught in bad weather in one of the passes."

"I see. Then you're not concerned?"

Thero traced the edge of his cup with one finger. "Not yet. Are you?"

"Phoria is growing impatient."

"And she expects Klia to defy her? All the princess talked of, through all those long months of exile, was returning to fight for Skala."

"I know, and I believe you. I believe in *her*. But the longer this war goes on, the more restless Phoria becomes. She's going to formally adopt Elani at the Sakor Festival."

"Then her succession is secured and she has nothing to fear."

Korathan nodded, looking suddenly weary. "Let's hope it sets the queen's mind at rest."

"I'll feel easier when those fools send the signal. If they've forgotten, I'll turn them both into rats when they get back."

Korathan chuckled. "You don't really believe they would."

"No, of course not. But it's better than the alternative."

Alchemy

IN SPITE OF Yhakobin's assurances the night before, Alec sensed trouble when Ahmol failed to arrive with his breakfast. Since he hadn't done anything worth punishment, something was afoot.

That assumption took on more weight when the guards showed up and marched him through the house to the workshop.

Suspicious as he was, Alec was not prepared for the sight that greeted him there.

Yhakobin was standing by the slate-topped table, wearing a leather butcher's apron over his robes and holding a short, blood-smeared knife in one bloody hand. The normally cluttered table had been cleared and what looked like a sheep's stomach lay there in a puddle of bright fresh blood.

I'm next on that table. Maker save me!

Suddenly Alec wasn't in the sunny workroom; he was miles and years away on that Plenimaran ship, watching Vargûl Ashnazai hack open the chest of one of his sacrificial victims. Alec had struggled then and he struggled now, locking his knees and desperately trying to wrench free of the hard, strong hands that held him.

But as always, it was useless. They pulled him into the room and kicked the door shut.

"Such a fuss!" Yhakobin exclaimed. "Take him through."

"No!" Alec fought even harder as they lifted him and carried him toward the door at the back of the shop, the one he'd never seen open.

He lashed out with elbows and feet, and finally managed to catch the man on his left in the face with his arm. The man grunted and loosened his grip just enough for Alec to jerk free, then twist his other arm loose. He broke for the garden, but they caught him and threw him to the floor.

One of them got an arm around his throat and held him still while Ahmol jammed the hated leather funnel between his teeth. Oddly enough, Yhakobin didn't seem angry at all as he bent down to pour something into the funnel.

"Drink, Alec. This won't hurt you. It will make it easier."

Alec choked and sputtered, but most of the liquid went down his throat, spreading numbness as it went. The world went dim, then black. His last thought was of Seregil. *I'm sorry, talí. I really have failed you this time.*

Consciousness returned very slowly. Alec was cold, and he was lying facedown on something very uncomfortable.

I'm not dead yet, anyway. That's something.

He was hanging facedown in some sort of flat metal cage suspended six or seven feet above a dirt floor. His hands and feet were shackled to the frame, his body supported by crossbars. More metal pressed across his back and thighs. It was like being caught between two barred doors. Judging by the way the metal dug into his flesh, he was naked again.

He could turn his head a little and, looking around, saw he was in a cellar. The room was large enough that the single torch burning by the narrow stone stairway did not light all the way to the far wall. A musty, damp smell hung in the air, with a sour tang to it, like a root cellar full of spoiled fruit. Right below him a hole had been dug, large enough to bury a good-sized dog. A mound of displaced earth lay to one side, and a spade.

Alchemy was starting to look a great deal like necromancy again.

Yhakobin came down the stairs, still in his apron. Ahmol followed, carrying a large basin.

"What are you going to do to me?" Alec demanded, straining against the shackles.

"It is time for you to serve your purpose," the alchemist replied. He was carrying a small mallet rather than the knife. "I've told you many times how special you are. This is the final test."

Yhakobin took a drop of blood from Alec's bound right hand and did the fire spell. This time it burned longer, in a bright fan of every color that shifted and shimmered like the nacre on the inside of a seashell.

"That is the proof. You have been purified properly, and the Hâzadriëlfaie blood is ready."

"For what?" Alec gasped, struggling harder against the restraints.

Yhakobin reached under his apron and took out what appeared to be tap and stopcock, like a tavern keeper would knock through a barrel bung to serve his beer. But this one was far too small for that, just a few inches long, and made of gold.

"You've seen my refining vessels," the alchemist went on. "But they are not always made of glass or clay. Your strong young body is the final alembic for this process. In you, I have carried out the seven steps."

Ahmol knelt and tipped the contents of the basin into the hole. It was the stomach Alec had seen earlier. Both gut holes were tightly tied up with black cord, and it was covered in black symbols, like the ones he'd seen on the amulets. There was something inside that made it bulge.

"You must have thought me very odd, for gathering your various essences; now you see the purpose. In this bag, together with various mundane elements, are your tears, your hair, your blood, and the spendings of your loins, mixed with sulfur, salt, and quicksilver, the water of life."

"Kitchen magic," Alec snarled, covering his rising fear with bravado. "It sounds like a foul pudding you've put together."

Yhakobin smiled as he stooped under the edge of the cage with the golden tap and the mallet.

Alec could only hang there and scream as the alchemist drove the sharp end of the tap into his chest.

CHAPTER 23

Treachery

IT WAS TOO soon to look for his kinsmen's return. Riagil í Molan had no reason for concern until a trader of the Akhendi clan named Orin í Nyus brought him a handful of bloodstained Gedre sen'gai, an earring that belonged to Aryn with a wizened bit of flesh still clinging to the silver hook, and a Skalan gorget.

He rode out at the head of a search party that same day, with the Akhendi as their guide. The trader led them a day and a half up the coast, to a little ravine in a wooded pass. He'd seen the crows circling over it, he explained, and followed them to the pile of stripped bodies piled by a stream at the bottom.

Aryn was there, with the rest of the escort. Of Seregil and his talímenios, however, there was no sign.

"Could they have done this, Khirnari?" his

cousin Nurien asked, with one hand over his nose to block out the stench.

The old man bent to examine the bodies more closely. In addition to sword wounds, he found the stumps of broken-off arrows in most of them. He pondered this for a moment. Then, asking his kinsman's forgiveness, he cut one of the broken shafts from Aryn's body. The barbed, intricately incised steel head was unmistakable. "This is the Zengati work."

Nurien shook his head. "Slavers, this far inland, and this far east?"

"It's less than a day's ride to the sea from here," Orin í Nyus pointed out. "They could have put in at any of a dozen smuggler's coves."

Riagil nodded and turned to wash his hands in the stream, already composing a letter to Queen Phoria.

∝ Change of Scenery

"I MUST SAY, I liked my previous accommodations much better," Seregil croaked, licking blood from a split lip. Ilar had finally made the mistake of thinking him tamed, not realizing how much of Seregil's strength had returned. He'd visited him that afternoon without having his pet prisoner drugged first.

Seregil had looked up out of habit as soon as the door opened, expecting Zoriel. But it was Ilar instead. Seregil was on his feet with his hands around the bastard's neck before either of them guessed he was going to attack. In the blink of an eye, he had Ilar on the floor under him, digging his thumbs into the man's windpipe under that golden collar and watching his eyes bulge.

Looking back on it now, Seregil had to admit that it hadn't been the wisest course of action. If it had just been the two of them, his rage might have carried the day. But naturally, the coward had guards just outside the door, and they'd made short work of Seregil, hard as he'd fought. To his credit, it had taken three strong men to pry him off Ilar. The last of his strength was gone by then, leaving him with no choice but to curl up like a pill bug as they beat and kicked him unconscious. He did, however, have the satisfaction of seeing Ilar hanging back, clutching his throat and looking suitably shaken. Seregil would have much preferred him on the floor dead, but beggars couldn't be choosers.

It had been early afternoon then. When he'd come to in this cold little cell, the light through the single tiny window was colored with the slanting glow of sunset.

They'd left him his slave's robe, at least, but the brick floor under him was damp and cold and his collar was digging into the side of his neck. His abused body felt like it was stuffed with broken glass as he rolled slowly onto his back and tried to take stock of his new surroundings before he lost the light.

It was a task made more difficult by the fact that there appeared to be two of everything: two windows, somewhat overlapped; two doors, both sadly lacking an inner handle or lock hole; two smelly slop buckets against one wall; and, against the other wall, a weirdly elongated sleeping pallet.

When he tried to sit up, his head threatened to explode, so he quickly gave that up. Instead, he forced himself back over onto his belly and crawled to the pallet, which drifted frustratingly in and out of focus and insisted on bobbing like a boat on the tide.

He made it at last and dragged himself onto it.

There were a few faded quilts and a dented pillow. As tempting as it was to just collapse on top of them, the room was already too cold for that. Whimpering a little, he used up the last of his strength to crawl under the covers, face crushed into the pillow.

Suddenly he was surrounded by the scent of Alec, stale, but unmistakable. Alec had slept in this bed, this cell!

"So this is where you've been, talí," he whispered, sniffing the quilts and finding traces of his lover's scent there, too—musk and sweat and unwashed hair. He let out a hoarse noise caught between a laugh and a sob and pressed his bruised face to the pillow again. "But where are you now?"

The double vision warned of a bad head wound. He dragged himself up with his back to the wall and pulled the quilts up to his chin, trying very hard to quell the nausea burning in his throat. He pressed his cheek to the cold wall, hoping it would help. He found if he sat very, very still, he didn't feel quite so much like dying.

Stop whining and think!

But thinking turned to Alec, and those thoughts soon turned to worry. Where in Bilairy's name was he?

He'd been struck on the head before, with similar effects, and Micum had gone to great lengths to keep him from sleeping, claiming it was dangerous. Seregil had no one but himself to rely on this time and it was difficult. His body kept trying to betray him. Time and again he caught himself nodding off, and paid for it with pain and nausea when his head snapped up. Would dawn never come?

It was still dark when a faint scratching at the door awoke him from another light doze. He'd been dreaming that he was in bed with Alec back at the Stag and Otter; in his confusion he tried to get up and go to the door, thinking it must be the damned cat wanting to be let in.

Moving, however, proved a worse idea than ever. His bruised muscles had stiffened while he slept; even this slightest movement was too painful, and his head felt like an inflated bladder on a stick. He gave up. "What do you want?"

The scratching became a soft tapping, brief and faint.

"Who is it?" he demanded more loudly, wondering if he was in fact addressing a rat.

"You are Seregil, of Bôkthersa clan?" a woman whispered in Aurënfaie. "Come to the door."

He tried again, but the prospect of dragging himself across the floor was too much right now. He was still seeing double and felt dizzy just raising his head. "I can't. Who are you?"

"Zoriel sent me. She fears for you."

"Tell her I'm fine." He waited, but there was no response. "Please, where is the young man who was here before me?"

Again silence. He waited, but his mysterious visitor was gone. Why hadn't he asked about Alec first? In the back of his mind lurked the very real possibility that Alec was gone from the house—sold off, or dead—

Focus, damn it! You've gotten out of worse scrapes than this.

Then again, he didn't really know what sort of scrape he'd landed in just yet. Alec had been kept here, and the few times that Seregil had seen him in the garden, he'd looked well enough.

He stared up into the darkness, assessing the strange, brief conversation. He was surprised that the old woman cared enough to ask after him. And it seemed she'd had to convince a third party to do it for her, and apparently at some risk. His visitor had spoken Aurënfaie, meaning either she was a slave or that someone intended for him to believe she was.

Dawn found him still awake. Using the wall to brace against, he managed to get on his feet and limp around the confines of the little room, trying to work some of the pain from his body. His vision was better now, at least.

A thorough search left him depressed and disappointed. Whoever had built this cell had known what he was doing. There wasn't a damn thing he could make use of, unless he could take down the guards with the pail. Which wasn't completely out of the question.

Time passed and no breakfast appeared. Forcing himself up again, he searched again, looking closely at every inch of the place. While examining the door, he came across the scratched names. Khenir's was there, and Alec's, too. Seregil traced the awkwardly incised lettering with the tip of his finger, then added his own beside it, in case they changed places again. "I'll find you, talí. Hold on."

He was given no food or water that day. No one came near him at all. That night he moved the pallet across to the door, hoping his unseen visitor would come again, but the night passed in silence.

The following morning a sullen man brought him a pitcher of water and a stale crust of bread, but no water for washing. Seregil ate sparingly and was glad when they had no ill effect.

He wasn't so lucky that evening. The morning meal had been too small, and by suppertime he couldn't resist the temptation of warm bread and cheese. Nor was he surprised when the numbness of the drug stole over him again. He almost welcomed it, assuming that it meant Ilar would soon arrive to taunt him. Perhaps he could get him to let slip where Alec was. If nothing else, it was good not to be in quite so much pain for a while.

He'd guessed right. Ilar approached him more carefully this time. It amused Seregil, but he was too far gone to laugh. Lying there, helpless and numb under the quilts, he noted with satisfaction the bruises showing on Ilar's throat above the neck of his robe. He could make out the marks of his own fingers on the pale flesh behind the golden collar.

Just give me another chance to finish that job.

Ilar squatted down by the pallet and gripped him by the hair, giving his head a painful shake. "I suppose you're very proud of yourself." His normally deep voice was thin and raspy. "Still the same little monster I remember. I should have known. Fortunately for me, that garshil of yours is more tractable."

"Alec. S'name's Alec." Seregil mumbled, anger cutting though his daze. People had called Alec that in Aurënen, too: mongrel. It was the worst of insults, and he wasn't surprised to hear it on Ilar's lips. "Where—?"

Ilar gave him a sour smirk, then stood and waved to his escort. The men pulled the blankets from the pallet, fastened a heavy chain to his collar, and dragged Seregil unresisting from the room.

Walking was out of the question. He could barely hold his head up. His bare feet scraped over cold brick as they passed along an ill-lit corridor outside. At the end of it they carried him up a narrow stair, and through a very fine courtyard paved with a black-and-white mosaic. As they passed a long, rectangular fountain, he caught sight of a veiled woman with two small children, watching him from the far side.

She was 'faie and Khatme, too. There was no mistaking the clan markings on her face above the veil. How had the slavers gotten hold of one of that clan? Perhaps she'd been a traveler, or a merchant.

She pulled the children close as they passed, but Seregil didn't miss the slight nod she gave him. Perhaps this was his night visitor?

He tried to flex his limp arms and legs as they dragged him down a broad stair into a different court, but his body was dead weight in their hands.

They stopped at the door of an outbuilding and Ilar grabbed him by the hair again. "I'm going to do you a great favor. In fact, I'm probably granting your most heartfelt wish. I do hope you'll show me some gratitude afterward."

Seregil's heart beat faster as they took him through a large, sunny workshop. The large athanor dominating the center of the room and various alembics steaming away on a table suggested alchemy. He didn't have time to form much of an impression otherwise; his handlers wrestled him roughly through another door on the far side of the room and down a staircase. It stopped at a landing where there was another door, then continued down into a cellar below.

It stank of damp earth and blood here, and something else he couldn't identify. It was sweet, but with an underlying stench of decay, like moldy apples.

The men lowered him to his knees, but kept a grip on his arms, holding him upright. His head lolled limply, but his eyes quickly adjusted to the dim light cast by a single lamp, and he saw that part of the dirt floor had been disturbed. There was loosely mounded soil there and, as he watched, a drop of something dark and glistening fell on it. As the droplet sank in, something underneath the soil moved.

"Ah, I see you've brought your friend to visit," a deep, cultured voice remarked from somewhere across the room. The words were Aurënfaie, but the accent was Plenimaran.

"Yes, Ilban. Thank you for allowing it," Ilar replied.

Ilban. That was the Plenimaran word for master.

Seregil turned his head slightly, wanting to see what sort of man owned Ilar. He managed a glimpse of a tall, robed figure on the far side of the disturbed earth—the alchemist, perhaps—and another, taller man in black.

The loose earth heaved again, and Seregil was suddenly afraid of what might be about to emerge.

"Why . . . ?" he managed to croak.

"I was hoping you would ask," Ilar rasped. "Let him see."

His keepers released him and Seregil slumped forward in an ungainly heap. The cloying stench of the damp earth against his face was overwhelming. He gagged, then let out a startled grunt as they turned him over onto his back. He found himself staring up at some sort of grillwork suspended from the beamed ceiling. No, he realized as his eyes adjusted to the light; a cage.

Ilar lifted a torch close to it and Seregil let out a low whine.

Alec hung there, splayed facedown and naked. His eyes were closed and his face was slack and deathly pale. He was thin, too. Seregil could count his ribs through the bars.

Oh Illior, he's dead! Seregil thought in despair, but then saw that this was not so. Corpses didn't bleed.

There, in the center of Alec's chest, was a tiny metal tap, just large enough to funnel a slow, steady fall of blood, drop by slow, small drop. Every time a drop landed on the mound of earth, whatever horror lay beneath moved in response, as if it shared a pulse with Alec.

"Killing...him!" Seregil whispered between suddenly chattering teeth.

"I promise you, I am not," the robed man assured him. "If my labors here prove fruitful, I will be keeping your friend alive for a very long time. He will be my precious and most prized alembic, brewing wonders for me. At the moment, I'm keeping him comfortable and asleep."

As if he'd heard, Alec suddenly stirred in his bonds. His hands clenched and his eyes moved behind closed lids, making his lashes quiver.

"Alec!" Seregil croaked.

Alec's eyes remained closed, but his cracked lips moved. No sound issued, but Seregil was sure they formed the word "talí."

Ilar leaned over him, gloating. "And it's all thanks to you, Haba. If not for you, I'd never have known this boy existed. I wanted you to see what's become of him and show you that you are helpless to stop it."

Seregil glared up at him. "Kill...you!"

"This one has spirit, too," the alchemist observed in Plenimaran. Seregil kept very still, not letting on that he understood. "I wonder if he'd be any use to me? Which clan is he again?"

"A Bôkthersan, Master."

Seregil gritted his teeth, imagining himself hanging in a cage like Alec's.

"But I don't know if he's strong enough, Master," Ilar murmured. Seregil couldn't see his face but caught a distinct hint of hesitation.

"Nonsense. A little bloodletting won't hurt him. And do I need to remind you that until I see fit to free you, both you and he are mine to do with as I choose?"

"No, Ilban!" Ilar replied, obsequious again. "Kheron, take him up at once!"

"Wait." The man in black, who'd remained silent until now, looked more closely at Seregil. Nudging him with the toe of his boot, he asked, "This is the one who killed Duke Mardus?"

"So I'm told."

"He should be executed, though I suppose he did us all a favor in the end. Ambitious fools like Mardus always end up as liabilities. He did have his uses, though."

"I assure you, Your Grace, the fate of this 'faie will not be an easy one."

"See that it isn't."

"Take him up!" the master ordered, and one of the guards hoisted Seregil in his arms and carried him upstairs to the workshop. Seregil cast a last desperate look back at Alec, cursing his own help-lessness.

Once upstairs, he was placed facedown on a slate-topped table, with his left arm over the side. The guards held him, and the alchemist nicked a vein in Seregil's wrist and held his hand over a bowl, collecting his blood. While this was going on, he and Ilar talked casually over Seregil, as if he weren't there, still speaking Plenimaran.

"He stinks, Khenir." Apparently Ilar's master didn't know his real name. "I thought you'd been taking better care of him."

"It's part of his punishment, Master, for attacking me."

"Ah, I see. Well, I suppose it's more humane than the prescribed flogging."

"I hate to mark him, Master."

"He is a particularly fine-looking specimen, even for a 'faie. You could set yourself up quite nicely, contracting him to the breeders."

"Perhaps when I'm done with him, Master."

The master bent to look at the back of Seregil's hand. "Hm. Another simple tattoo. The boy has one as well. What do you know of these?"

To Seregil's surprise, Ilar replied, "Nothing, Ilban. My clan didn't use such marks. How fares the rhekaro?"

You lying bastard! Seregil nearly laughed. As usual, Ilar was playing his own game, even against the master he professed to worship. And he'd changed the subject nicely, too. *He'd probably have made a good nightrunner.*

"As you saw, it quickens nicely," the master replied, none the wiser. "I expect it will be complete by tomorrow. The moon phases have been more of a factor than the treatises led me to believe. Or perhaps it's the boy's mixed blood. Whatever the case, I'm glad, for he isn't as strong as I'd hoped. He's not stirred in over a day."

Seregil closed his eyes, feeling more desperate than ever. They were killing Alec, and for what? He'd never heard the word "rhekaro" and had no idea what it meant, except that it was probably whatever unclean thing was moving about under the dirt, fed with his talimenios's blood. Given the presence of the nobleman here, this wasn't just some minor experiment and yet the bastard spoke as calmly of it as Nysander might of some interesting spell he was working on.

"Do you know yet if the rhekaro will yield what you hope, Master?"

The alchemist chuckled at that. "Are you really in such a hurry to leave me?" When Ilar said nothing the man patted his shoulder. "Don't worry. Something has quickened, and I will keep my word. If all goes as we hope, I will emancipate you."

Ilar stroked Seregil's hair. "And this one will truly be mine, Master?"

"Yes, though why you should want such a wild and dangerous creature as that is beyond me, especially one that has betrayed you in the past."

"I look forward to breaking him, Master."

Seregil bit the inside of his lip. *Oh, I will kill you slowly!*

"Hmm. You know, Khenir, some wild things are meant to be tamed, rather than broken."

The alchemist wrapped a bandage around Seregil's wrist, then sniffed the blood in the bowl and dipped his finger in it. He rubbed it between his thumb and forefinger, like he was testing silk, then the smear burst into a bright blue flame. "Yes, that's good strong western blood in those veins. A Bôkthersan, you say? They make very strong dra'gorgos, I hear. I know of several necromancers who'd pay well for a flask of this. You might make a bit of a profit on him that way, until he's manageable. I will give you letters of introduction."

"Of course. You are the kindest of masters, and the greatest of alchemists."

So I was right! thought Seregil. That explained the tidy workshop. He'd always understood them to be benign, like wizards, but what he'd seen in that cellar spoke of darker workings. He hoped Ilar and his master would speak more of Alec and whatever this rhekaros thing was, but it seemed they were done with him for now. The alchemist looked down at him for a moment with something like pity in his dark eyes. Seregil marked him for death, too.

"In the meantime, I think I will try a few experiments of my own with this." He set the bowl aside and covered it with a white cloth.

"Of course, Master. He is yours, to do with as you please."

For now, thought Seregil, sensing something other than abject respect in Ilar's voice again. Perhaps the deal between them wasn't such a sure thing, after all.

"If I may, Master, might I have some more of the rosefish elixir? It's a very great help in handling him."

The alchemist took a small flask from a shelf and handed it to Ilar. "Mind you don't use too much on him. Only in small doses is it safe. I do hope you will remember what you have learned here in my house. In the end it is only kindness that wins them over—though a firm hand is necessary, as well."

Ilar bowed deeply. "In you, I have had the best of teachers, Master."

"Perhaps. But remember, too, that some can never be broken, and sadly, they must be put down to preserve the public safety. The penalties for harboring a dangerous slave are severe, and more so for freed-men."

"I will be careful, Master. Thank you for your concern. Martis, Kheron, bring him back to his chamber. I will be there in a moment."

Seregil's keepers had names, now, though he had no idea who was who.

The elixir was wearing off. He had strength enough now to twist in their grip, looking for Ilar, who was following close behind. "What is he doing to Alec?" Seregil wanted to ask what a rhekaro was, but that would tip his hand.

"A great work. He is creating something beauti-ful and useful from that half-breed of yours. You should be proud."

"Liar!"

Ilar smiled. "Not this time, dear Haba."

They carried Seregil back to his cell under the house and deposited him on the pile of quilts.

Ilar had them unhook the chain from Seregil's collar, then hold his head steady as Ilar forced a few drops of the elixir between Seregil's clenched teeth. "Come now, it will be so much easier for you, this way."

"It" was probably going to involve the horse-man's crop Ilar was holding under one arm, Seregil decided with a certain weary resignation.

The numbness spread through him, different than what he'd felt earlier. He couldn't move, but unfortunately, he could still feel perfectly well as Ilar drew his head into his lap and stroked the hair back from Seregil's eyes. "I must admit, I had be-gun to have thoughts of taming you nicely, as my master suggested. When you were asleep all those days, I was taken in by that face of yours, just as before. But you've shown your true colors again, haven't you? I should thank you for bringing me back to my senses."

" 'r welcome," Seregil whispered, trying to summon a decent sneer. His lips wouldn't cooperate.

Ilar laughed. "Do you know what I dreamed of, through all these years of shame? I hoped that one day you would suffer as I have suffered, and, my dear Haba, that day has come." He smiled and stroked Seregil's cheek again. "You're lucky I don't want to mark that fine skin of yours any more than it already has been."

Seregil could not fight back when the men turned him over, and his screams were weak and hoarse as Ilar beat the soles of his feet with the crop. It went on for some time, until the pain cut through the effect of the drug and he finally managed to struggle a little, trying to escape the torture.

Ilar relented and tossed the crop to one of his men. "That's enough to start. Know, my dear Seregil, that I've endured far worse. And so shall you, before I'm done."

Seregil was feeling remarkably clearheaded now, and full of the strange elation that comes when pain ceases. "You want fear from me, or sympathy?" he slurred thickly. "Go fuck a dog."

Ilar kicked him onto his back and rested a slipper-clad foot heavily on Seregil's chest, making it hard to breathe. "Fucking is something else they took from me, Haba, long before I came to this house. Will your friend still want you when you've been gelded, I wonder? What will you have to offer him then?"

With that he swept out of the cell, leaving Seregil to curl up in a ball in the darkness, hands clenched protectively between his thighs.

Gelded? Panic cut through the pain and lingering effects of the drugging, and an hysterical little laugh escaped his lips. *Poor bastard. No wonder you're so bitter.* Slavery was bad enough, and the abuse, but to have your manhood taken, too? *And now he's planning the same for me.* He knew it was no idle threat.

He was cold, and still too numb to get himself under the covers. His feet burned and felt like they might be bleeding. With a little flailing and grabbing, he managed to pull a corner of the quilt over his chest and looked for comfort in Alec's fading scent on the fabric. *What would you do, talí, if they did do that to me?* The thought was sickening, but even so, he knew in his heart that Alec would never turn his back on him, any more than he would if Alec had suffered the same plight. Not that it made the thought of having his own favorite parts cut off any less horrifying.

But even that fear paled in comparison to the sight of Alec hanging in that cellar. Regardless of the alchemist's reassurances, it looked like they were slowly bleeding him to death.

Sleep wouldn't come, and so he had no defense from his own wandering thoughts.

If it weren't for you, Haba, I'd never have known he existed.

Remorse overwhelmed him again, closing a fist

around his heart. It was true. He'd put Alec on the road to that cage the night he'd found him in that northern dungeon. Seregil had always claimed not to believe in fate, but now he wasn't so certain. And if that had been fate, then what of the rest of his life?

Ilar said I wasn't meant to kill that Hamani. And if I hadn't? He lay there a long time, cold and sad and aching, pondering the question in a way he hadn't before. The Haman had drawn steel first. If he'd only shouted, or grabbed for him, would the boy Seregil had been then still have drawn a weapon? Ilar called him a monster, blaming Seregil for all that had happened to him since, whatever that had been.

Just like I do him.

He quickly quashed that thought. They were nothing alike!

It's not my fault! If he hadn't seduced me in the first place—

Then what? he wondered for the first time. Would he ever have known Nysander, or Micum? Or Alec? He thought of all that had befallen his friends, for having known him. The chains of fate, or plain ill luck, hung heavy on him.

They'd all have been better off without me. The thought slipped insidiously across his mind before he could crush it.

"Stop your damn whining!" he muttered angrily. There was only one thing he could afford to dwell on right now, and that was how to get out of this cell and get Alec away from that madman.

And kill Ilar, he amended with a dark, crooked grin. *I'll show him what a monster really is!*

CHAPTER 25

Rhekaro

"ALEC? ALEC, OPEN your eyes."

Khenir?

Awareness returned slowly. Gradually, and in no particular order, Alec realized that he was no longer hanging facedown, that the center of his chest hurt like a bitch, that he was warm, and that he was very hungry and thirsty.

The sour, earthy smell was still all around him, but so was the unexpected aroma of cooked meat. He forced his eyes open and found that he was wrapped in warm blankets and propped in a corner of the cellar. Khenir knelt beside him, holding a mug to Alec's lips.

Alec drank, and nearly wept with relief as the rich salty taste of mutton broth flooded his mouth. He gulped frantically, dribbling down his chin, until Khenir pulled the cup away.

"Slowly now. There's no need to make a mess."

"More!" Alec rasped, and was amazed at the effort it took to speak.

Khenir let him drink again, and the warmth spread through Alec's belly and limbs. He slipped a hand under the blanket to where his chest hurt and found a small scab there, between two of his ribs, right next to his breastbone.

Memory flooded back—Yhakobin approaching with the golden tap and the hammer. Alec clenched a hand in the blankets, shuddering, but grateful to be lying here now, even in this cellar. Anything was better than hanging in that cage.

"How long?"

"Four days," Khenir replied. "Ilban is very pleased with you."

"Indeed I am," Yhakobin said, coming down the stairs with a larger lamp. Duke Theris was with him. Ahmol and one of Alec's warders followed, carrying small spades.

As they approached, the light spread, and Alec saw that where Yhakobin had buried the foul bag, the earth was now mounded and moving.

"What is *that*?" he whispered.

"Let's see, shall we?" Yhakobin replied.

The two servants removed the top layer of soil, then stepped back. The alchemist knelt by the heaving pile and gently began brushing the loose soil aside to reveal the strange, elastic mass beneath. The duke looked on from a slight distance, covering his nose in distaste.

The sheep's stomach was swollen, and darkly mottled with decay. Ahmol assisted his master and as they uncovered more of it, Alec could see strange protrusions under the flesh—odd, moving lumps and bumps.

Yhakobin gripped the covering and tore it open, releasing a horrid stench. Alec gagged, and Khenir and the duke buried their noses in their sleeves, eyes watering.

A small, grime-smeared hand thrust up through the opening and clutched at Yhakobin's wrist. It was perfectly formed, even to the fingernails, but glowed an unnatural fish-belly white under a glistening layer of filth.

Yhakobin said something softly in his own language, and reached deeper into the foul sack to lift out . . . A child.

"Maker's mercy!" Alec made a warding sign under the blanket.

It was curled tightly in upon itself. He could see nothing from his place in the corner but the curve of a thin back, and a sodden mass of white hair.

Yhakobin cradled it in the crook of one arm and turned to show the duke its face. It was almost like a real child, but softer, as if it wasn't fully formed yet. The cat-slanted eyes were tightly closed, and both arms were wrapped across its chest. The alchemist slipped a finger into its mouth and scooped out some sort of clear slime, then turned it this way and that, frowning a bit.

"What's wrong, Ilban?" Khenir asked.

"The oldest treatises described wings, but this has none. Oh well, it's alive, and appears suitable otherwise. Now you must play your part again, Alec. Bring him closer."

Alec shrank back in his corner, too weak to fight. Khenir got an arm around his shoulders and whispered close to his ear, "Do as Ilban says, please!"

"N—no!" Alec gasped. "Don't! Why are you helping him?"

"Because he is our master," Khenir replied, dragging him the rest of the way across the packed earth floor.

"Don't be afraid, Alec," Yhakobin said, drawing out the hated bodkin. "I only need a drop." He gave Ahmol an order. The slave grabbed Alec's clenched left hand, pried the forefinger loose, and then held it steady. Yhakobin stabbed the tip and pulled the bleeding finger down toward the white creature's mouth.

Alec struggled harder, but it was no use. Those colorless lips closed around his finger and sucked, like an infant at the breast. It had felt just like this when Luthas had sucked on his finger for a pacifier.

The thing's eyes opened wide, and Alec was stunned to see that they were the same dark blue as his own but empty as a doll's. "What is it?" he gasped.

"A rhekaro, Alec. A being created through alchemy."

The rhekaro thing released Alec's finger and he wrenched his hand away in disgust, clutching it to his chest. The rhekaro slowly uncurled and wobbled to its feet.

It was no larger than a five-year-old child, perfectly formed in every way, except for the white skin and matted mass of white hair, and the lack of genitals between its thighs. Once on its feet, it just stood there beside its creator, without the slightest hint of animation in its expression.

"Why would you create such a thing?" Alec asked, aghast. There was something horribly familiar about that blank mask of a face.

"That is not your concern. You can take him to the bedchamber now, Khenir. See that he's properly bathed and fed. I won't be needing either of you tonight."

Khenir got Alec on his feet and tried to help him limp away toward the stairs. After a few steps, however, Alec's legs gave out under him. One of the guards carried him up the stairs.

Alec suffered the indignity, staring back over his shoulder at the strange white thing that had been fashioned from his own essences.

You shall father a child of no woman . . .

"No," Alec whispered brokenly. *O please, Illior, Dalna, don't let this be the meaning!* He knew why that thing's face had looked familiar. The same visage had looked up at him from the washbasin when he was small. The thing looked like him!

They reached a landing and stopped at a door there. More stairs led up to an open door. Through it he could see the dried carcasses and bags hanging from the workshop ceiling.

Khenir took out a key and opened the door. Beyond lay a room very much like the one Alec had been kept in all these weeks, one that must be directly under some part of the workshop upstairs.

This cell had a proper bed against the far wall and a small bathing tub full of steaming water.

Khenir had the guard carry Alec straight to the tub and lower him into it. "You don't smell very good, my friend." He handed Alec a rough cloth. "Wash yourself. I'll go fetch your supper."

He and the guard went out and Alec heard the key grate in the lock.

The tub wasn't large enough to stretch out in. Huddled there with his knees under his chin, he dipped the washcloth and scrubbed weakly at his face and chest, then squeezed it over his greasy, tangled hair, longing for a sliver of soap. A little lantern on a hook by the door cast a warm glow over the room. Alec was glad of that; he couldn't have stood being locked away in the dark.

It was no use. He didn't have the strength to do any more. Leaning back against the side of the tub, he tucked his chin to get a look at the wound on his chest.

It was tiny, and seemed to be healing well. The skin around it wasn't even bruised. He wondered if the golden tap had gone all the way to his heart, and if Yhakobin's strange purifications had aided the healing.

He turned and scrutinized the door. This one had a keyhole! Alec's lips stretched in a thin, slightly crooked grin as he looked around again at the host of new possibilities the sparse little room offered to a trained eye.

His gaolers were getting careless.

Khenir returned with a tray, towels, and a large book under one arm. He set them on the bed and locked the door from the inside, then knelt by the tub.

"Is that more meat?" Alec asked hopefully.

"Yes. Do you need some help?" Khenir asked, noting the abandoned washcloth.

Alec colored and glanced away. "Yes. What did he do to me? I can hardly move!"

"He bled you. We gave you what nourishment we could but he kept you asleep, to make it easier on you."

Alec grimaced. "How thoughtful. So, do you know what that creature is, or what it's for? I thought he said he was going to make some kind of medicine, not a monster!"

"I'm a slave, just like you. Ilban does not confide in me." He scrubbed gently at Alec's back. "But he did agree to let me care for you here."

"You asked him?"

"Yes. And look!" Khenir rose and went to the tray, lifting a bowl for Alec to see. "Boiled chicken and turnips! And he's sent you a new book to pass the time."

"He must be very pleased with me." Alec's mouth was already watering again, in spite of the broth still warming his belly.

Khenir finished with Alec's bath and helped him into a clean robe. When Alec was settled in bed with his back to the headboard, Khenir lifted the tray onto his lap.

Alec let out a small moan. Besides the chicken dish, there was warm bread, a wedge of blue-mottled cheese, and a mug of cider, too. But he didn't dare eat any of it. "What if it's drugged again?"

"I'm sure it's not," Khenir assured him. "I watched the cook myself as he prepared it. As Ilban said, he doesn't need you at the moment."

"But when he does?" Alec cocked an eyebrow at the other man. "Will you tell me when the drugs go in again?"

"I swear to you, I didn't know!"

Alec shrugged, then grabbed up the horn spoon and dug in. Food had never tasted so good.

As he mopped the last precious drops of gravy from the bowl with the bread, he said without looking up, "You have the key to this room."

"Yes."

Alec let the pause that followed ripen.

Khenir's eyes filled with fear. "By the Light, Alec, don't ask that of me!"

"But I *can* get away, if I get the chance. I could help you, too."

Just then they heard the sound of footsteps crossing the workshop overhead, then the low murmur of a deep voice.

"Keep your voice down! He'll hear you," Khenir whispered, trembling now. "I've survived this long with both my feet, Alec. I mean to keep them. There are slave takers out there, just waiting for fools like you. Not to mention the common, everyday folk who'd grab you in a heartbeat, for the bounty. I told you before; you won't get half a mile with that face of yours, and that yellow hair. And even if you did, all you'd have to do is open your mouth and they'd know what you are. No, don't think of it. You're too weak to get out of bed, much less out of the house."

"So you've just given up?" Alec hissed back. "I can't! There's someone..." He caught himself and held his tongue. "You have the key in your pocket, right? I can make it look like I attacked you, overpowered you."

"You don't know what you're asking," Khenir replied miserably, unable to meet his eye. "I'm sorry. So sorry. Go to sleep." He hurried from the room, locking the door securely behind him.

"At least you left me the lamp," Alec muttered. With light, he could make a thorough search, take the bed apart if he had to, to find something to work the lock. He tried to get up, but a wave of dizziness overtook him, and he fell back against the pillow. Yhakobin's foul blood magic had left him too weak to move.

His eye fell on the tray Khenir had left behind. The horn spoon still lay in the empty soup bowl! He grabbed it and tested its strength between his hands. It was thick and sturdy.

Had it been an oversight, or was this Khenir's way of helping him? It didn't really matter to him. Alec found a loose seam in the side of the mattress and slipped the spoon inside. *A little sleep and I'll be fine*, he thought, eyelids already slipping down.

He slept deeply and dreamed that the door swung open and Seregil was outside, grinning that crooked grin of his and gesturing for Alec to hurry. He started awake, expecting the door to be open, and felt crushed when it wasn't. He had no idea what hour it was, but the tray was gone. His throat and mouth burned with thirst, and he was glad to find a fresh pitcher of water beside the bed. He took small sips until his belly was steady enough, then drank half of what was left in long, thirsty gulps.

Feeling a bit better, he climbed stiffly out of bed and began a search, looking for anything that might help him get out of this wretched room. The bed was solidly pegged and the bed ropes were too thick to get free without a knife. He gave the frame a frustrated yank, then stopped, heart missing a beat.

The spoon. Did I dream that, too? He hurriedly felt along the side of the mattress, looking for the loose seam, and found it. With a shaky sigh of relief, he felt the spoon's hard outline through the coarse ticking.

"Thank the Light!" he whispered, leaving it there for now.

Other than that, he had a covered toilet bucket and the water pitcher.

Further searching only left him frustrated. He used the bucket, and then settled on the bed with the spoon, trying to break it lengthways into usable splinters.

He was still at it when the sound of a key in the lock startled him badly. He hadn't heard anyone coming. He managed to stuff it back into the mattress and pull a quilt down over the rent just as the door opened. He threw himself back against the pillow and tried hard to look as if he'd just woken up.

Khenir came in, carrying a covered tray. "Ah, you're awake at last."

"It's morning?" Alec asked.

"You missed morning by a long shot and the sun's down again. You slept the day away, my friend. I tried to wake you earlier, but you were too deeply asleep. I have supper for you, if you're ready."

Alec's belly let out a very loud grumble as he caught the scent. A thick slice of brown bread was covered in melted cheese, sharp and tangy. And there were two apples, and a mug of tea slaked with cream.

He fell on the food like a starving dog again, too hungry to be embarrassed. Khenir sat on the end of the bed and smiled, watching him. "I can bring you more. Ilban said you're to have all you want. But you must drink all the water in the pitcher first, then more. You gave him quite a lot of your blood."

"Gave? What will he do with me, now that he's got his—what is it called?"

"A rhekaro. And I'm sure I don't know. But he's been locked in his shop with it since the unearthing and hasn't eaten or slept. Whatever it is, he seems enchanted by it, even if it doesn't have wings."

"Wings? Oh yes, he said that, didn't he?" Alec rubbed at his eyes. "It all seems like something I dreamed."

"It's real, Alec. Here, give me the tray and I'll fetch you some more food."

"No, I'm full for now." Alec lay back and threw an arm over his eyes. He wondered if he should thank Khenir for leaving the spoon. But what if it had only been an oversight? He wasn't sure he wanted to know. "If he's got what he wanted from me, do you think he'll sell me to someone else?" The thought had haunted him since he'd woken up.

"Oh, I don't think so. You're far too rare. That's good, though, really. You're lucky your first master is a kind one. Be satisfied with that."

Never, thought Alec, but he didn't feel like arguing with Khenir right now.

They talked a little, then Khenir wished him good night, giving him a quick kiss on the brow. Before Alec could react, he was out the door.

Shaking his head, Alec levered himself out of bed again. He was still unsteady, but too rested to sleep anymore. After a few turns around the room, he settled down to read the book while the lantern burned, and shut his eyes when it finally failed.

He did sleep then, and dreamed of Seregil again, coming to save him.

"You always find me," he said, throwing himself into his lover's arms.

"Not always, talí. And when I don't, you take care of yourself," Seregil whispered in his ear.

Suddenly a scream ripped the air around them. Seregil was gone, and in his place stood Alec's father, maimed and bloody as he'd been the day Asengai's torturer finished him off.

"Father!" Alec cried out, fifteen again.

Another cry woke him and brought him bolt upright in the bed. It was coming from the workshop overhead. Terrified and disoriented, Alec shuddered uncontrollably as the cry came again, a high-pitched, ragged screech, like the sound of a wounded rabbit. But it was no coney Yhakobin was tormenting up there; it was the pale creature.

He lay back against the pillow, heart hammering under his aching wound. *It's not a person. It's a monster. An abomination. It doesn't matter.*

As the cries grew louder and more frantic, he pressed the pillow over his ears and curled into a ball, trying to stop the rising rush of horror and pity the sounds wrung from his heart.

Unnatural the thing might be, but hearing anything suffer like that was unbearable! And what monster made sounds like that?

The cries subsided gradually to childish sobbing, overlaid by Yhakobin's low, dispassionate voice.

Is it over? Please Dalna, let it be over!

Another scream dragged Alec from the bed. He stumbled to the door and beat on it with his fists. "Stop hurting it, you bastard! Leave it alone."

Mercifully, the cries did stop. Alec slid slowly down the locked door and came to rest with his head on his knees, unable to stop shaking. He sat there on the cold stone floor, feeling more miserable and impotent than ever.

Since I listened to my father dying ...

"No," he whispered miserably. "It's not human. It's not even real—"

But the whisper of the oracle stole into his mind again. *A child of no woman ...*

He pressed his fists to his temples, shaking his head. "No! No, no, no!"

All went silent upstairs, but he stayed where he

was, straining his ears for any sound. Presently he heard footsteps approaching and a key thrust into the lock. He crawled away as the door swung open. It was Ahmol.

"Ilban say come."

Alec went cold all over, but he was too weak to fight as the man lifted him effortlessly and climbed the stairs to the workroom.

The pale creature lay on the slate table, its slight body bound down with wide leather straps. The alchemist was washing his hands in a basin at the end of the table, still clad in his leather apron. The duke was there, too, looking rather ill. Two warders stood guard at the door.

"Ah, Alec. I need you. I've had some unexpected complications with this one."

Alec approached slowly, apprehension growing with every step. He'd reached the edge of the table before he could make himself look down at the creature. When he did, all his worst fears were realized.

At some point, Yhakobin had washed the filth from it. Its pale skin was a dull, dust grey. The matted white hair had been cleaned and raggedly shorn. What was left wasn't white, after all, but the palest silver, like moonlight on sea mist.

But Alec only noticed those details in passing, focusing instead on the atrocities that had been practiced on that little body. Where the left eye had been there was only a slanted, empty socket, weeping yellow fluid. Three fingers were gone from the left hand, and strips of skin had been flayed from its arms, legs, and chest. There was no blood, just torn white flesh, like that of a fish, and a little white fluid. Alec's stomach turned over as he noted the neat row of covered jars arrayed on a small table beside the alchemist.

"Why are you doing this?" he whispered, unable to look away from the ravaged little body. And it was gazing back at him with its single remaining eye. Alec thought he saw a sort of hopeless beseeching there, though otherwise the rest of the face was a masklike as before. But that eye! It was so much like that of a real child's that it broke his heart.

"How can you do this?" Alec demanded, glaring up at Yhakobin now. "Why did you make it, just to kill it?"

Yhakobin shook his head as he wiped his hands on a cloth. "I must admit, I did not expect it to have a voice. The writings indicated quite the opposite. I can only assume that your purification was not as successful as I'd thought."

"This—" Alec swallowed hard. "This is *my* fault? I'm not the one cutting it to pieces!"

"The rhekaro is not a pet, or a plaything, Alec," Yhakobin remonstrated gently, as if speaking to a stupid child. "They are created to be used."

"You cut off its fingers. And its eye!"

"And I may accomplish great healings with them, and strong spells. Or I might have, if it was better made. I won't know until I test them. But for now, I must ask you to give it another few drops of your blood."

Alec stepped back, but Ahmol was there, keeping him in place and reaching for his wrist.

"You're so concerned with its pain. Are you saying that you begrudge it a healing? I must know if that much is true. Give me your hand."

"A healing?" Alec clung to the only thing he'd understood so far and let Yhakobin prick his finger. As before, the alchemist guided the hand to the rhekaro's lips, and this time Alec did not resist as they closed around his fingertip.

It suckled harder this time, and Alec felt a strange twinge run up his arm. He'd have pulled away instinctively, but for the change that happened almost instantaneously.

The raw wounds on its limbs closed as he watched, leaving only the thinnest of scars. Where the three fingers had been severed, tiny white buds were already taking form, growing back like a lizard's severed tail.

The grey skin took on its former pale glow and, strangest of all, the fine hair also seemed to be growing; within a few minutes, it lay like a silvery white cloud around the thing's head.

The duke, whom Alec had quite forgotten about, suddenly appeared at his elbow, saying something to Yhakobin in hushed, awed tones.

"It is not human, for all that it may appear so," Yhakobin warned, studying Alec's face carefully. "It would be a great mistake for you to think otherwise."

"It screamed when you hurt it."

"Metals ring under the smith's hammer. It's nothing more than that." He pulled Alec's hand away.

Two blue eyes fluttered open as the rhekaro

tried to follow the finger with questing lips. The hair was down to its shoulders now. Alec couldn't resist testing the feel of it between his fingers. It was silky soft, like Gherin's.

"If you're done with it, it can stay with me," he offered, remembering this time to add, "Ilban."

The alchemist raised an eyebrow at him, then chuckled softly. "Good night, Alec." He gave an order to his men and they escorted Alec back to his new cell. The smell of the cellar wafted up from below, damp earth, old blood, and the sweet stink of the "birth." It was almost a relief when they slammed the door and shut out the stench of it.

Alec curled up on the bed and stared at his pricked fingertip. His blood had helped create that thing, and now it healed it. How was that possible?

Not just his blood, but *Hâzadriëlfaie* blood. That must be why they'd left Aurënen and disappeared into the north, all those centuries ago. They must have known what could be done with their blood, and they fled, far out of reach of Zengat and Plenimar. But what was the rhekaro used for, that the Hazâd would go to such lengths to keep such things from being made? And was it really going to be used to make medicine for the Overlord's child? And how? Would they cook it or boil it or drain its blood?

Oh Illior, why didn't you warn me? What's the use of an oracle, if not to keep something like this from happening?

There'd been no warning, though. He'd gone over the rhui'auros's words endlessly, trying to glean their meaning, but he couldn't see any way they'd hinted at such a horror.

Pondering this, he dozed off again, only to be roused by more sounds of pain from the workshop.

He pulled the pillow around his ears, trying to shut out the pitiful cries. When that proved impossible, he frantically pulled the horn spoon from its hiding place and staggered over to the door to inspect the lock.

Seregil had taught him many things over the years, and among the first of those lessons had been lock-craft. With his tool roll in hand, he could open just about anything, but Seregil had also taught him to make do with what he had, and for just such situations as this.

The lock hole was small. He put his eye to it first, but the light was wrong to make out the workings, and he couldn't get even the tip of his little finger inside to feel around. He went back to the bed and turned the horn spoon over in his hands, noting how the grain ran lengthwise down the handle. If he could snap it just so, it might yield the beginnings of a usable pick.

Upstairs the cries started again, weaker this time.

Don't listen. I can't do anything, not unless I can make this work. Just use what I have.

Sweat rolled down his face and back as he tried to break it between his fingers, but the horn was too strong. After several false starts, he found that he could jam the edge of it between the bed frame and the wall, like a vise, and use the lip of the pitcher to bend it.

The cries continued intermittently, making his heart race. As he worked, he couldn't help wondering what he'd do if he did manage to get the door open. In his current state, weakened and unarmed, he'd be no match for Yhakobin's guards, or the man himself, probably. But then, head-on fights weren't the nightrunner way; Seregil had done his best to instill that in Alec, who'd had more of a tendency for honest fights.

The cries grew weaker as he finally snapped off the bowl and broke the handle into two long spines.

He held them up, inspecting the taper and thickness. *Still too big.*

He didn't dare try breaking them again, so he settled on the floor by the bed and burnished the rough edges against the stone flags. His hands began to shake and sweat stung his eyes. To distract himself, he concentrated on recalling Seregil's various lessons on the subject. A bit of doggerel came to him and ran round and round inside his head.

A crafty nightrunner died of late,
And found himself at Bilairy's Gate.
He stood outside and refused to knock
Because he meant to pick the lock.

The silly little verse took him back to their old rooms at the Cockerel, sitting knee to knee with Seregil as he took some lock to pieces and explained how it worked. They'd spent countless hours at it. Some had one pin, others had as many as five. Others had wards or poison needles to stick the unwary thief, but they all could be tickled open if you had the skill.

After a considerable amount of rubbing and burnishing, he had a crude tool. Going to the door, he inserted it into the lock and gingerly felt around.

This lock, a simple two-pinner, was hardly a challenge, even with his makeshift tools. The horn pieces made little noise as he carefully probed the works. With a little careful twiddling, he threw the tumblers and heard each satisfying click as they fell.

All had gone silent upstairs.

That doesn't mean Yhakobin is gone, he reminded himself as he eased the door open and peered around it. The low murmur of voices came from upstairs—Yhakobin's and someone else's. Alec crept halfway up the stairs to hear better. They were speaking Plenimaran, so he had no idea what they were saying, but he recognized the other voice. It was Khenir. He was surprised at the tone: it sounded as if the two men were arguing about something. Khenir was using the humble "Ilban," but his tone grew less and less respectful as the debate went on. Alec caught his own name several times. Was Khenir arguing on his behalf?

The risk wasn't worth the toss, eavesdropping on a conversation he couldn't understand. What mattered was that when the right moment came, he was ready and had a way out!

He crept back to his room, locked the door, and hid the picks inside the mattress again with the rest of the spoon bits. As he lay back on the bed with his head on his arms, trying to calm his racing pulse, he wondered again about the rhekaro. He hadn't heard it making any noise. Perhaps Yhakobin would leave it alone now, having gotten whatever it was he was after from it.

Ahmol shook him awake sometime later, and the guards hustled him upstairs, where Yhakobin was waiting. Morning light streamed in through the skylights, and he could hear a mockingbird trilling somewhere nearby and the laughter of the children at play.

The slate table was bare, and scrubbed clean.

"Where is it, Ilban?" he asked without thinking.

The alchemist nodded toward a small tub by the door. It was covered with a cloth, and a single hank of silvery white hair hung out from beneath its edge.

"Oh, Illior. You killed it," Alec gasped. One of his handlers cuffed the back of his head for such insolence, but Alec hardly felt it. He felt numb, gaze still locked on that pitiful lock of hair, remembering the pleading look he'd seen in its eyes when he'd healed it.

"It was never alive to begin with," Yhakobin told him impatiently. "It was ill made, besides. Quite useless. We shall have to try again. Give me your hand."

Alec tucked both under his armpits. "Why? So you can torture another one?"

Yhakobin struck him across the face, sending him sprawling. The guards were on him at once, but the alchemist reached for his bodkin rather than the whip.

"I don't have time for this. I've redone my calculations, and if this proves suitable..." He jammed the bodkin into Alec's sore finger and performed the flame spell. It burned pale lavender. "Ah, good. I haven't lost too much ground, after all." He paused, and Alec realized he was staring at the dragon bite on his ear.

"I know what that is now, Alec. Khenir confessed it to me. It's such a small thing, and yet...? Well, no matter. We are where we are." He went to the tincture shelf. "I believe we can start with silver, this time."

"No!" Alec tried in vain to wrench free of the guards, but they knew his tricks now, and had little trouble holding him down on his back and pinching his nose shut as Yhakobin leaned over him with the funnel.

CHAPTER 26

Pride

SEREGIL HAD NO way of knowing how long Ilar had kept him drugged, but when he finally did wake up in that cold little cell, he was desperately hungry and thirsty. His ribs were sticking out again. The pallet under him was wet and reeked of urine.

Mine, no doubt, he thought wearily.

A wooden pitcher stood beside the bed. He rolled over and sniffed at it. Water. Not caring if it were drugged or not, he took several gulps. It was stale but cool, and it soothed his dry throat.

His next priority was to get away from the dirty bed. He rolled off and sorted out a few of the quilts that hadn't been soiled, then used the corner of one dipped in water to clean himself. His skin was sore where he'd lain in his own filth.

Wrapping himself in the musty quilts, he propped himself up in the corner and stared at the door. The spot of barred light on the wall told him it was late afternoon.

Alec could be dead by now.

Seregil hugged the quilts tighter around him, pondering that reality. Whatever this rhekaro thing was, Alec's blood was clearly an important ingredient.

It was no secret that the necromancers of Plenimar favored 'faie blood for use in their foul magics, a fact from which the slavers made a great profit. Hadn't the alchemist said that Bôkthersan blood was used for making a dra'gorgos? He wondered whose life had been given for the one that had attacked them in Aurënen.

But the alchemist also claimed to have no intention of killing Alec. *My precious alembic, brewing wonders for me.*

Seregil shuddered. *Not while I have breath in my body!*

Gathering his strength, he used the wall to push himself upright and then leaned on it as he walked around the room to test his strength. He was light-headed and unsteady.

I couldn't fight my way out of a rotten gourd!

He'd waited before, in the upstairs room, getting his strength back, and all the while Alec had been at the mercy of the alchemist and Ilar. Now, when he knew Alec was so close by, Seregil was right back where he'd started—limp and useless, trapped in a cell with no means of escape. He wondered if Ilar meant to starve him to death this time, but doubted it. That would end the fun too soon, and it had sounded like he meant to savor Seregil's destruction.

I've been in worse spots, he told himself again, but was hard-pressed to think of many. At least he wasn't bleeding and had no broken bones so far.

That was to the good—though from what Ilar had said, he wondered how long that would last. The future looked rather bleak at the moment.

He found himself missing Zoriel. She'd taken good care of him and cared enough to send that Khatme nurse to check on him.

He tugged absently at a strand of dirty hair. To get out of this wretched prison, he was going to have to use his wits. Fighting Ilar was hopeless. The bastard would enjoy it. No, it was time for a new strategy, and fast.

"Rhania, come pay me another visit, won't you, my dear?" he whispered into the gathering gloom. It wouldn't be the first time he'd found a servant just as useful as any lock pick.

But it was not Rhania who came to him after dark, but Ilar, and he had an escort this time. Seregil didn't stir from his corner. He'd had a long time to consider his options.

One of the men placed a stool and a lantern by the door. The other held a tray and Seregil's mouth watered at the aroma of some soup made with onions and spices.

Ilar sat down and regarded Seregil with obvious delight. "Awake, I see. I hope fasting has improved your temper?"

"I suppose it has," Seregil replied, purposely sounding fainter than he felt. "Please, what's happening to Alec?"

"I believe Ilban Yhakobin is preparing him to make another rhekaro."

"Another?" Seregil closed his eyes, fending off a wave of very real panic.

"Yes. The first one was not suitable," Ilar told him, relishing his discomfort.

"I want to help him," said Seregil. "Is there anything I can do that will sway you?"

"My goodness, this is a sea change," Ilar sneered. "And why should I bargain with you?"

"No bargains," Seregil replied. "I'll do anything you want, take any torture you like, if you can keep that man from killing him."

"You must think me quite a fool, Haba. I assure you, I'm not. I know the minute I turn my back on you, you'll try to strangle me again, or run away. Probably both."

"You think I'd leave Alec to die in this place?"

Ilar pondered that a moment. "Perhaps not, but I do find it hard to believe this sudden change of heart toward me."

"You have my word, Ilar—*Ilban*. By the love I once had for you, and the love I bear for Alec now."

"Words are worthless between us, Haba."

Seregil gathered his will, swallowed his pride and crawled to Ilar on hands and knees, letting the quilts fall away.

"What's this?"

Seregil crouched before him, kissed one slippered foot and then rested his forehead lightly on it. "My life for his, Ilban. Please, I beg you, my life for his."

Ilar grabbed the back of Seregil's head, fingers twisting painfully into his hair. "Be careful, Haba. I will not be lenient with you again when you betray me."

"My life for his," Seregil whispered.

"He is not mine to save, you know."

"But your master listens to you. As long as Alec survives, I will serve you."

"You will serve me anyway, one way or another."

"I will serve without resistance."

"A very interesting proposition, Haba, and one I will consider." He released Seregil and shoved him away, then stood abruptly. "Get away from me. You stink."

Seregil crawled backward, to all appearances a craven, broken man.

Ilar stood a moment longer, and Seregil could feel the man's gaze traveling over him, suspicious, but intrigued. "Well, we shall see."

Turning to the men, he spoke in their language. "Clean him up, and the room. If anything untoward happens, I'll have your guts on a trencher."

The men watched sullenly until Ilar was out of sight, then one growled to his partner, "That arrogant little dog's prick! Who does he think he is, ordering us around? By Sakor, I'd like to put him in his place once and for all."

"So you keep saying," the other one sighed, pushing past him to roll up the soiled bedding. "Count Yhakobin would have you flogged and sold if you so much as laid a finger on his precious pet 'faie, and you know it. And the lickspittle will be free soon, too, and of better standing than either you or me. So just hold your temper and wait. He'll be gone soon enough."

He leaned over Seregil and wrinkled his nose in disgust. "This one doesn't seem too high and mighty, does he?"

The other chuckled as he came over and yanked Seregil's head up by the hair.

Seregil was getting tired of this sort of treatment, but remained limp and passive.

"Not bad, for a 'faie. Look at those eyes!"

"And that mouth," the other rumbled, scratching suggestively at his crotch. "What do you think? Would he squeal to Khenir?"

Seregil carefully kept himself in check, not betraying that he understood every word. When one of them began to unlace his breeches, however, the meaning required no words. Neither did Seregil's answer. He bared his teeth and snapped them together a couple of times, glaring a challenge.

The other man laughed. "Give it up. He's not worth the beating, and I do believe he means it. Get that old bitch down here to clean him. She's been all in a lather over him since they put him down here."

They got their petty revenge, taking the bedding and leaving him naked and shivering on the cold floor. He chafed his arms and legs as he waited. He'd have to be careful with them. As much as they might hate Ilar, they clearly enjoyed tormenting Seregil more.

They returned in short order with Zoriel and several servants. Seregil was glad to see they were carrying a small tub and buckets of water, as well as fresh bedding.

The water was icy, but any bath was welcome and he endured it happily as Zoriel scolded him.

"I had you well again, and look at you now, young son! You're nothing but bones and bruises."

"My master isn't as kind as yours," Seregil

replied with a wry grin, wincing as she scrubbed his back with a rough cloth.

"You tried to throttle him, I heard." Leaning close, she whispered, "Some of us had a good laugh over that, and not just the slaves." She dumped a can of cold water over his head and started on his hair with the soap, saying loudly, "Don't you know who Khenir is? He's the master's favorite, and soon to be a freedman. You'll belong to him, so you'd best learn some manners."

Seregil sniffed and said nothing. He glanced at the guards to make sure they weren't paying attention, then murmured, "Did you send the Khatme woman to me?"

"I did. I heard at first that you'd been killed, but she said she saw you being dragged down here. She has the run of the house, more than I do."

"She's your friend?"

"I suppose you could say that. It takes a Khatme a while to warm up, as they say. Cold as their mountain fai'thast, most of them, and crafty. But she soon learned she's no better than the rest of us, when *he* came."

"Khenir, you mean?"

"Who else? He's a sly dog, that one. Smooth as silk with Ilban, and never a word to the rest of us that doesn't suit his ends."

"He was always like that."

She paused in her washing and whispered, "He said he knew you in the past, but I didn't believe him at first. So he's dragged you into slavery with him, has he?"

"To get himself out. It's not me your Ilban wanted, but my friend. Have you seen him?"

"The yellow-haired boy? Only a glimpse now and then when they'd take him through the house to the workshop, but not since they started keeping him there."

"And you've heard nothing more of him since?"

She hesitated, then shook her head and helped him from the tub and into a large towel. He locked eyes with her. "You *have* heard something. Please, tell me!"

"Well, a few nights ago the most pitiful sounds came from the master's shop."

Seregil gripped her wrist as she tried to dry his hair. "What kind of sounds?"

"Cries," she whispered. "Like someone was being murdered. It could have been an animal, but it sounded like..." She pursed her lips and blinked. "It sounded like a child! But no slave that young's been brought in, or any animal of late. Not that I know of, and I don't miss much that happens in the house. Rhania hadn't heard of any, either."

Seregil sank slowly to the floor and pulled the towel around him. "A few nights? When I was brought back here?"

"Yes."

"Bilairy's Balls. Is that why he laughed at me?"

"What's that?"

"Nothing. Thank you, old mother. I'm grateful for all your care."

She shook her head, then bent and kissed him on the top of the head as if he were a child. "No one's called me that but you, young one. Come and sit up so I can comb out that mess of hair of yours."

Seregil allowed himself to relax as she worked

through the tangles and helped him into a clean woolen robe. As she tucked him into bed, he even caught himself wondering fleetingly how he could take her with him when he got out. That was ridiculous, of course, but he did feel a bit guilty at the thought of deserting her.

Alec wouldn't leave her.

Zoriel retrieved the tray that had been brought earlier and set it across his legs. It was nothing more than the same old lentil soup, bread, and a sliver of hard cheese, but he was so famished it looked like a feast to him. He ate the meal one item at a time, expecting to end up drugged sooner or later. By the time he finished, though, he was still awake and clearheaded.

Zoriel carried the tray out, and the servants cleared away the bath things and took the lantern with them.

Seregil listened to the bar fall into place, then turned on his side. The new pallet and blankets were warmer than the last, but smelled only of fresh air and herbs, with no trace of Alec. They'd left him his pillow, and he pressed his face into it, seeking the lingering traces of Alec's scent.

The cries Zoriel had reported had sounded like a child or an animal, she'd said. He clutched the pillow closer and prayed it had been the latter.

The following day he was moved back to his upstairs room, with the view of the garden. No one came to beat or drug him, but he knew better than to get his hopes up yet.

At Ilar's command, Seregil sat by the window

that afternoon and saw him walking in the garden with Alec, arm in arm as before. Ilar was holding the chain attached to a collar around Alec's neck, as usual, but Alec seemed completely at ease with him. Every smile Alec gave the bastard was a knife in Seregil's heart, but at least it was proof that he was still alive and well.

And he looked very well, indeed. It was difficult to tell at this distance, and it was probably only the longing of his own heart, but Alec seemed to have a certain glow about him. Seregil had always found him handsome, but he looked even more so now— a far cry from the filthy wreck Alec had been in that cage only a few days earlier. Now and then, though, Seregil saw his hand steal to his chest, where the tap had been, and the smile disappeared.

As he watched, overcome with yearning, Ilar suddenly turned to the window and waved up at him, instructing Alec to do the same.

Seregil caught his breath and waved back. Alec waved again, then turned away, unconcerned.

Seregil's heart broke a little at that, and at the way Alec suffered it when Ilar slipped an arm about his shoulders and led him to the fish basin. He sank back in his chair, for the first time wondering if Ilar was seducing Alec, as he had Seregil so long ago. He pushed the unworthy thought away as soon as it arose, but he couldn't shake off a sense of foreboding.

It hurt his pride to call it jealousy, so he didn't.

"Who is that?" asked Alec, waving up at the indistinct figure behind the thickly glazed window.

"I think it must be Rhania," Khenir replied. "That is her room."

"Oh." Alec waved again and thought he saw her wave back. Khenir took his arm and they resumed their walk. "You know," said Alec, keeping his voice low. "I can hear what goes on in the workshop from my room."

"I don't doubt it. It's right over your head." Khenir patted his arm. "It must have been very hard for you, hearing the rhekaro cry out."

"It was horrible!" He walked on a little further, gathering his courage, and wondering how much he could really say to this man, friend or not. "I wish there was some way to get free, before he can make another. Wouldn't you . . ."

Khenir clasped Alec's forearm, and ran his thumb over the shiny pink skin of the brand. "This is all you are now, or ever will be, Alec. Accept that, and save your worry for yourself. That's what the rest of us do."

"You wouldn't even try to get away?"

"I told you before, Ilban is a good master. He takes good care of all of us, as long as we know our place." He looked down ruefully at his own brand. "It's not like I have anywhere else to go."

"Not even back to your clan?"

Ilar went very quiet, then said very softly, "I'd die first."

CHAPTER 27

The Pale Child

ALEC BIDED HIS time over the next few days, looking for a chance to get free. But Yhakobin was in the workroom constantly, and others with him. Alec could hear the sound of them moving about every hour of the day and night. The alchemist even brought his tinctures to him down here. When Alec was alone again he stuck his finger down his throat and vomited them up again, but it didn't do any good. Every time Yhakobin did the flame spell, the color had changed.

There were no more walks, either, and no more invitations to tea. He was left on his own, anxious and frustrated. When they finally dragged him back into the cellar, he fought harder than ever but of course, it was no use.

Thankfully, Yhakobin drugged him again, and when he woke a few days later, weak and sore and sick, Khenir was there to comfort him.

He held a cup against Alec's lips. Alec tasted water, took it, and drank in slow, careful sips, not wanting to lose a precious drop.

As he watched, Ahmol helped Yhakobin dig up the new rhekaro and place it on a cloth. It stayed curled up, helpless as a newborn babe. The hair and skin looked white through the filth, just like the last one, but this one was a little bigger. And just like the last one, it had no wings. Alec was almost sorry; he'd wondered if they were like a bird's, with feathers, or just skin, like those of a bat or the tiny dragons he'd seen in Aurënen.

Yhakobin gave a terse order and Ahmol brought him the silver tincture cup. The alchemist gently pried one of the rhekaro's hands from its chest and pricked one small fingertip. Something oozed out, but it didn't look like blood. Instead, it was almost clear, like water or new sap. Alec thought of the wounds on the previous rhekaro. For all that they looked nearly human, they had no more blood than an oak tree.

Yhakobin caught the drop in the cup and peered in. Whatever he saw pleased him, judging by the smile that broke across his face. Khenir said something hushed and excited. The alchemist clapped him on the shoulder, then wrapped the rhekaro in the cloth and carried it over to Alec, still huddled in his corner.

"You know what is required," Yhakobin said quietly, unable to take his eyes from his new creature.

Alec held out his hand—the left this time, since the fingers of his right hand were all sore and scabbed—and let the alchemist prick him and place the bleeding finger to the rhekaro's lips.

Like a questing infant, it made a few false tries, then found the finger and sucked hard.

Alec nearly pulled away from that hunger. It felt like the thing was sucking the life from his body. His arm went numb to the shoulder.

"Steady," Yhakobin warned, clamping a hand on Alec's elbow to keep him in place. "This one is stronger than the last—a good sign."

The rhekaro took one last pull, then opened its eyes and looked up at Alec. This one's eyes were not dark blue, but a silvery grey, hardly darker than the whites around them. Like the last one, though, it wore his own younger face, but with a stronger 'faie cast to it. Alec touched its moist, cool cheek and thought again of salamanders. It gazed up at him placidly.

Yhakobin chuckled. "Even you are moved by it, aren't you?"

"Please, Ilban, don't hurt this one."

"You really are far too sentimental. I've told you before, it's not a person. And you have nothing to fear, for now. It has passed the first test."

Alec looked over at Ahmol, who still held the cup. Something dark was floating in it, but the slave turned and carried it upstairs before Alec could tell what it was.

The rhekaro's cool eyes were still fixed on Alec, and he looked in vain for some sign of intelligence there. All the same, he couldn't bear the thought of that little body being ravaged and tormented.

A child of no woman.

His child. Looking into this rhekaro's face, remembering the screams of the other as it had been torn to pieces, his chest ached with sorrow and guilt. He thought of his picks, still safely hidden in his mattress.

It was time.

Khenir helped him down to his room, where supper had been laid out. The tub had been made ready for him, too. After hanging in that cage, Alec was almost glad to come back here to such simple comforts.

Neither spoke as the slave gently cleaned and dressed him. Alec was too tense to enjoy it, straining to listen for any sound of pain from above. But none came.

"Something different happened this time?" he asked, sinking gratefully into bed and starting on the cold meat and cheese laid out for him.

"I do hope so, for your sake. Perhaps he'll leave you alone if it is what he wants it to be."

"Maybe." Alec took another bite of the meat. "What was in the cup?"

The other man didn't answer, just smoothed the blanket over Alec's legs.

"You saw. Tell me!"

"The color of the water changed. I don't know what it means," Khenir replied, not looking at him.

And Alec knew that Khenir had just lied to him. The realization weighed like a stone in his belly.

The door was closed; the guards were outside. "What's to stop him from making more if they're so important to him? How many times do you think I can go into that cage and come out alive at the end of it?"

"Don't talk like that, please!" Khenir begged. "If he has what he wants, then I'll beg him to make you a house slave, like me. It's not so bad, really."

Alec caught his wrist and pulled him closer. "I am no one's slave! Have you been here so long you've forgotten what it is to be free?"

"Perhaps I have. But what can we do? Accept your lot and make the best of it, like the rest of us."

Alec wanted to tell him about the horn picks hidden in his mattress. He wanted to ask for his help, and somehow find Seregil and offer Khenir his freedom in return, too, but the lie earlier made him hold his tongue and Alec said nothing as Khenir kissed his brow and took his leave.

Just for now, he told himself, unwilling to give up yet on the only ally he had. *When the time comes, if I can help him, I will.*

He reached into the hole, needing to touch the picks, his keys to freedom.

They were gone.

And his meal tonight had come with no implements.

Stunned, he kneaded the mattress over, then turned up the edge to peer inside.

Every piece of horn was gone, the picks and all the broken bits.

Alec felt cold and sick all over. Anyone might have been in here—the guards, Ahmol, Yhakobin himself. But he knew for a fact that Khenir *had* been.

What was the old saying? *Smiles conceal knives, talí.*

He curled up in a tight, miserable ball under the covers, wondering what the punishment would be this time.

For the first time since his capture, he felt like a slave.

The following morning he was summoned to the workshop before breakfast. He expected to find the alchemist ready with the whip, but instead there was a tray of warm apple pastries and another pot of the excellent Aurënen tea. Alec eyed both distrustfully, wondering what new drug they concealed.

Yhakobin laughed. "Come now, don't look like that! This is a day of celebration, and these excellent pastries are your reward."

"For what?" Alec asked, still wary. Was it possible the man didn't know about the picks, or was he just playing with him?

Yhakobin took one and bit into it. "See? They're very good."

Alec sat down slowly on the stool and picked one up, but couldn't make himself take a bite.

Yhakobin sighed, then cut his own in half and gave the bitten part to Alec. It oozed juice and spices. He could smell the butter in the crust. Seeing that Yhakobin ate his own portion without hesitation, Alec took a small bite from one corner. It was the best thing he'd tasted in weeks, and it showed no signs of killing the alchemist.

"I don't know what's wrong with you today," Yhakobin said, cutting another pastry in half and letting Alec choose which part he wanted.

As Alec wolfed down his second piece, the alchemist rose and went to the strange little painted tent at the far end of the room. He pulled open the front of it, and inside Alec saw an iron cage. The rhekaro was huddled inside, skinny arms wrapped around its thin, sexless body.

Its hair was paler silver than the last one's, and had already grown down to its waist. When it looked up and saw Alec, it let out a weird, high-pitched whimper.

"It's hungry, too. You must come and feed it."

Alec froze, and the pastry went dry in his mouth.

Yhakobin raised an eyebrow at him. "That's the second time you've shown me disrespect today, Alec."

Alec swallowed the mouthful he'd been chewing. "Forgive me, Ilban. I'm just—I don't know what to make of any of this."

"That's better. It subsists upon your blood. That alone sustains it." He pulled out his bodkin. "Come here, Alec. It's only a few drops. Surely you don't wish the poor thing to suffer?"

The words struck home. Resigned, he rose and let Yhakobin prick him, then squatted down and held his hand in through the bars, wondering what to expect.

The rhekaro sniffed sharply, then sprang forward on its knees and clutched Alec's hand, sucking greedily at his finger. It was startling in its ferocity, and the strength in those pale little hands. He could feel the sharp edges of new teeth breaking through its pale gums. Shock quickly gave way to fascination. Though nearly as big as Illia, and better formed than its predecessor, it seemed more like an infant in its actions.

"Does it speak, Ilban?"

"Speak? Of course not! Why would it speak?"

Rebuffed, Alec kept his questions to himself and concentrated on the rhekaro. Its hand was cold against Alec's, but he could feel muscle and bone in all the proper places. Apart from the lack of genitals or a navel, and its distinctive complexion, it seemed human enough. It looked up at him just then, and he could have sworn it smiled. The colorless lips, still sucking, flexed a little and its weird silvery eyes crinkled slightly at the corners. Only then did Alec realize that he had been smiling at it.

He was relieved to see that this one appeared to be unharmed so far, except for some reddened spots on its fingertips.

"You use its blood, too, Ilban?"

"What runs in the veins of this rhekaro is your blood, but in a more highly purified form."

Hâzadriëlfaie blood, Alec thought.

"This creature's body is at once the vessel and the athanor which refines it," Yhakobin went on.

"What do you want it for, Ilban?" he asked before he could stop himself.

But the man's patience was at an end. "That's enough, Alec. It does not concern you."

Alec went back to his cell in a daze, the taste of the pastries still filling his mouth. The rhekaro, whatever it was, needed him to live, which ensured a very narrow scope for Alec's life if he didn't find some way to get out.

And if I do escape, it will starve and die. It surprised him, how much the thought of that bothered him.

And then there was the matter of the missing picks. Was it possible that it hadn't been Khenir who'd taken them? And if not, then who had them, and why?

CHAPTER 28

Seregil Follows his Own Advice

ILAR SEEMED PREPARED to take Seregil at his word regarding his pledge. The beatings ceased, and for several days Seregil was left to himself, except for Zoriel's brief visits to see to his care. He had a few books now, and sat by the window much of each day, reading and watching for any sign of Alec. But the garden remained empty, save for when the household children came to feed the fish.

Just when he thought he'd go mad, Ilar came one evening to visit him. He was dressed in a finer robe than usual and carried a jar of wine and one cup.

"So, are you ready to make good on your pledge, Haba?" he asked, taking the chair by the window. "We will try this for a little while: I will visit you as if you are my concubine and let you serve me wine."

"As you wish, Ilban," Seregil said, sinking to his knees by the bed, trying very hard to sound submis-

sive. Concubine, indeed! Bold talk for a man with
no tack between his legs.

The door remained ajar, and there were several
guards posted in easy earshot, lest Seregil get any
more untoward ideas. If he'd been on his own, nothing could have stopped him from breaking for it right
then and there. But there was Alec to think of, and so
he used every last shred of self-control he possessed
to gracefully pour and pass the cup, when every instinct screamed for Ilar's blood. But he played his
role, and played it well.

Ilar drank, then reached to stroke Seregil's
cheek as he knelt by his feet. "Hmm, this does have
its charms. Very well, then. Let's see how long you
can be a good boy."

Seregil forced a smile. "More wine, Ilban?"

Thankfully Ilar asked no more of him than that,
and after a few nights Seregil's subterfuge began to
bear fruit. Ilar did not trust him, and probably
never would, but Seregil could be very charming
when he chose, especially with one so easily flattered. Little by little, Ilar began to lower his guard.
He spoke more freely, revealed a bit more about
Alec and what was being done to him. Evidently a
second rhekaro had been made, but Ilar seemed
strangely troubled about something.

And still the door stayed open and the guards
visible, and Seregil played the chastened slave
and humbly performed the tasks required, all
the while watching and listening, and biding his
time.

One evening a week or so after their truce, Ilar came in hobbling a little and lowered himself into the chair with care.

"Are you hurt, Master?" Seregil asked, trying not to sound too pleased.

Ilar scowled and shook his head. "It's nothing."

"You're in pain. What happened?"

Ilar gingerly raised the hem of his robe to show Seregil a dozen or so angry red welts across the backs of his calves.

Seregil stifled a grin; they were clearly the marks of a whip. Putting on a mask of concern, he touched a finger to one of the wounds, making Ilar hiss in pain and jerk away. "Did Master Yhakobin do this to you?"

"It's your whore's fault!" he snarled, shoving Seregil away. "His blood is so tainted by Tirfaie filth that the rhekaro is not right. The first was useless, and the second is an enigma."

"Maybe your master is not doing it right?" Seregil asked without thinking.

Ilar cuffed him on the ear. "You forget yourself, Haba. I'm already in a foul mood. See this?" He held out the arm with the slave mark. "That should be branded over by now. I should have earned my freedman's mark the day that boy was delivered. It's not my fault he's a half-breed! Ilban knew it when he made me his promise. But still I wait and bear the brunt of his frustration. How many of the wretched things does he get to make before he holds up his end of the bargain, eh?"

Seregil bowed his head. "Forgive me, Master Ilar. I'm sorry to add to your cares." He nodded at the stripes. "That must have hurt a lot."

"Oh don't pretend to care! Just make yourself useful. Here." He took a small pot of salve and some linen wrappings from his pocket and tossed them to Seregil.

So Seregil tended the wounds. The alchemist had probably wounded Ilar's pride more than his body, he thought, disgusted at such a fuss over so small a matter. The skin was hardly broken. Ilar had hurt him far worse and not given it a second thought. Lips pressed tightly together to hold back any snide observations, he dabbed the salve carefully over each welt as if they were war wounds, then set about wrapping the linen.

"You have a deft touch, Haba," Ilar murmured, watching him with rapt attention. "But I suppose you must have needed it in your former line of work?" For once he wasn't sneering. He sounded tired and discouraged.

"I did. But I wonder how you know about all that, Master?" Seregil replied softly, still concentrating on his bandaging. This was new ground.

"You know of a necromancer named Vargûl Ashnazai?"

The name was like a hot poker pressed to Seregil's heart, linked as it was to memories of blood-streaked walls and severed heads chattering on his mantelpiece, and a hank of Alec's hair knotted around a dagger, left for him to find. "He was a very memorable man," he managed at last.

Ilar chuckled at that. "His uncle, Duke Tronin

Ashnazai, is a good friend of my master. It was from him that I heard of your adventures against Duke Mardus and his cabal. Duke Tronin had the story from a nobleman who was with Mardus's entourage. Seems he'd witnessed you killing Mardus, and that Orëska wizard—what was his name, Haba? Ander? Nander, or something like it?"

"Yes," Seregil whispered. "Something like that."

"It was most perplexing news, too, as I'd understood that the man was your patron in Rhíminee. Tell me, Haba, do you kill all your friends in the end?"

Seregil sat back and kept his clenched hands pressed to his thighs, biting the inside of his cheek as he forced himself not to lash out. "No, not all of them. And I didn't kill that necromancer, though I'd have been happy to do the deed. Alec had that honor."

"Ah. Well perhaps we'd better keep that between us, eh? Oh, and this as well." He reached into a pocket and took out several long black slivers of what appeared to be broken horn. "Your protégé is a very clever boy in some ways, even if he is quite gullible. I left a spoon within reach and he did exactly as I'd expected, making a lock-picking tool. Earlier he even picked a padlock with a file. You must have been a very good teacher. Not that you'll need such skills here. But you are neat-handed—a fact I mean to make use of." He reached into another pocket and passed Seregil a clay oil vial, then propped one foot in Seregil's lap.

Swallowing another morsel of his pride, Seregil obediently warmed some of the rose-scented oil be-

tween his palms and began to massage the offered
foot. It was something else he was good at, and
though Ilar never took his eyes off Seregil, he relaxed noticeably.

"I think I like this tame new Haba, even if I
don't trust him one little bit."

"Thank you, Master. The feeling is mutual."

Ilar slapped him hard on the cheek so fast
Seregil didn't have time to brace himself. He went
sprawling and the flask of oil spilled over his lap
and the rug.

"You are my property now, Seregil, and you'd
do well to remember that. I can do whatever I like
with you, even torture and kill you, and no one
would lift a hand to protect you. You are of no more
worth than a candle or a glove—something to be
used and discarded at my whim. What do you think
I should do with you?"

Seregil pushed himself up, righted the flask before it could empty, and lifted Ilar's foot back into
his lap. "I wouldn't be much use to you dead," he
observed, working his thumbs up the arched instep
in a way that made Ilar gasp.

"Don't be too sure of that, Haba."

They were quiet for a while. Seregil kept his
eyes on his work, trying not to choke on the heady
aroma of the oil. "What will you do with your freedom when you get it, Master?" he asked, when he
sensed from the occasional low moan that Ilar's
mood had improved sufficiently. "Where will you
go?"

"Go?" Ilar was resting his head on one hand now,
eyes hooded with unabashed pleasure as the massage

continued, but the question drew his brows together. "Alec asked me the same thing, you know. So common with new slaves who haven't come to terms with their situation."

"What did you tell him?"

"Where would you have me go? Home to Aurënen? Like this, with the brands of shame on my skin forever? Have you ever seen a freedman in Aurënen?"

"Not that I know of," Seregil admitted, slowly working the stiffness from Ilar's toes. "But maybe they avoid the baths."

Ilar snorted softly. "Even without these marks, I doubt I'd be very welcome. I'm certain you told them of my role in your downfall?"

"I didn't have to. You ran away—Master. That spoke for itself."

"It was that or the fate of the two bowls, wasn't it? Tell me, how did you escape execution?"

"*Teth'sag* was declared against me, but the rhui'auros spoke for me and they exiled me instead. It might have been the same for you. You weren't the one who committed the murder."

"No, but your father and sister had their eye on me all summer and would have accused me as your seducer."

Seregil forced himself to stay gentle as he worked his fingers over the delicate sinews and bones of Ilar's ankle. "You did seduce me—Master," he murmured.

"Perhaps, at first," Ilar replied, suddenly wistful. "But I told you before, I began to love you, too."

Seregil paused and took a deep breath, but he

couldn't hold back any longer. "So much that you sent me to that tent that night, knowing what had to happen?" he asked, fighting to keep his voice low. "Even if I hadn't killed that man, I'd have been ruined anyway. That was what the Virésse were paying you for, right?" He broke off and rubbed oil carefully over Ilar's long toes again, as if that could smooth his outburst.

"I never meant for you to kill anyone," Ilar murmured, resting his head against the back of the chair, more relaxed than Seregil had ever seen him. "I thought you'd get a beating, nothing more."

Seregil found that hard to believe. It had been an unforgivable breach of hospitality and one that reflected on his entire clan.

"I would have taken you with me, if I could have," Ilar added quietly. "We would have been happy together. If not for Ulan í Sathil, I'd have been your talimenios."

Seregil could tell that whatever the truth had been at the time, the man believed his own story now, and thought he meant what he'd just said. But then, they'd both had four decades to dwell on the events of that summer. Did either of them remember anything more than they really wanted to?

Ilar sighed. "You don't believe me, do you, Haba?"

"What does it matter, Master?" Seregil replied, fighting down the sudden rush of doubt.

Ilar leaned down suddenly, caught him by the collar, and pulled him into a hard kiss. The oil flask fell again, and the scent of roses engulfed them. Seregil made no effort to resist or participate, and he was gratified to see the hint of disappointment in the other man's eyes as he pulled back. He stayed very still as Ilar cupped his face in both hands and looked into his eyes. After a moment he laughed softly and released Seregil. "Even after all these years, and all that's befallen me, I'm still tempted. You should be flattered."

"I suppose I am, Master." Seregil forced the lie out, shaping it with a grudging sincerity. Let Ilar think he'd been moved by something other than disgust.

Perhaps the act rang true. Ilar grabbed him by the arms and pulled Seregil into his lap as if he were still the green young boy he'd been that long-ago summer. Seregil kept himself pliant and unresisting as Ilar ran greedy hands over his face, shoulders, and chest, then pulled him close to breathe in the scent of his hair.

And for one brief, traitorous moment, Seregil's body remembered that touch.

Suddenly Ilar pushed Seregil from his lap. He landed on his ass and the bastard gave him a push with one oiled foot, sending Seregil onto his back.

"Feh! It's like handling a corpse. Do you think you'll win me over like that?" Ilar barked an order and one of the men outside came in and handed him the whip.

Seregil cowered on the rug, one hand on the wet patch of carpet where the oil had spilled, as Ilar rained blows down on his bowed back and shoulders. "Forgive me, Master! I didn't dare presume. Do you want—?" *Forgive me, Alec.* "Do you want me tonight?"

With a bitter laugh, Ilar threw the whip down and pulled up the hem of his robe, letting Seregil see the ruin there. "What use would I have for you, like this?"

Seregil couldn't suppress a shudder of sympathy; everything had been taken from Ilar. He had nothing left between his legs but scars.

"Oh, Master!" Still not ready to give up the game, he carefully placed a hand on the man's thigh, just below the hip. "You wouldn't be my first eunuch."

Ilar stepped back and dropped his robe, but for just an instant Seregil caught the fleeting glimpse of a naked emotion in those hazel eyes: want.

"Really?" Ilar sneered. "What an interesting life you've led, being free all these years. Would you play the clever whore for me, too, for the sake of that half-breed of yours? Or are you planning to insinuate yourself into my bed so you can strangle me there?"

Seregil sat back on his heels and met his tormentor eye to eye, unflinching. "I gave you my word, Master Ilar: My life for his. I won't harm you as long as he remains alive."

And once again, he saw that hesitation, that hint of vulnerability. And once again, it passed.

Ilar shook his head and put his clothing back in order. "No? Well, perhaps I will consider your very generous offer, but not tonight."

He picked up the whip and went to the door. "Oh, and to answer your earlier question, Master Yhakobin is generously setting me up in a house of my own, once he's achieved success. Freedmen with a patron like mine live very, very well here. You'll be my very first slave, an ornament for my household. So enjoy your glimpses of your talimenios while you can."

Seregil remained on his knees for some time, surrounded by the overpowering smell of roses. Time was growing short. He silently thanked the Four that Ilar had revealed as much as he had. It stuck in his throat, to play the broken, docile slave, but tonight's work made it all worthwhile.

Now, to learn how long he had.

The scent of the oil clung to Seregil's hands even after he'd scrubbed them in the basin. It pervaded his dreams as he lay in the dark, chasing sleep.

Wild white roses were blooming along the river by his father's encampment that summer. Ilar had plucked one for him the first time they'd kissed. He carefully broke off the thorns and tucked it behind Seregil's ear.

"You're lovely."

"I'm not. You just want to kiss me again."

"You are, and I do."

And he had.

Seregil handed him a rose, but instead it was a dagger and he plunged it into Ilar's beautiful throat, as unerringly as he had with the Haman he'd killed . . .

Now it was the young Haman lying at his feet. Moonlight turned the blood black on the dead man's skin and clothing, and his hair was like a halo of snow. And Ilar was there in the shadows, sobbing, with blood

*running down his thighs... No, it was Alec. They'd
gelded Alec! And something pale and frightening was
struggling beneath the bushes, rustling in the dead
leaves...*

Seregil sat up in the darkness and put a hand to
his cheek. He was crying. But for whom?

The sound of the rustling leaves came again,
startling him badly, until he realized it was someone scratching at his door.

He went to the door and pressed an ear to it,
whispering, "Who is it?" He had an idea, but was
careful not to betray any potential ally if it was Ilar
out there, playing with him out of spite.

"It's Rhania." She spoke so softly he could
hardly hear her.

"What do you want?"

"Are you a 'runner in the night,' as they say?"

"Did you wake me just to ask me that?"

"Does a runner in the night know how to run
away from this house?"

Seregil waited, saying nothing.

"Can you get out of here?" she whispered ur-
gently.

"As you can see, I can't even get out of this
room."

"But if you could?"

"Perhaps. But they cut off the feet of those who
run away. Zoriel told me so."

"Only those who are caught."

"You want me to help you escape?"

"Shhhh!" A pause, then, "Yes! Until now I have
had no hope, but I heard Khenir speak of you to

some of the others, bragging how he had brought low so clever a man as you."

"Did he, now?"

"Yes. You hate Khenir, do you not? Perhaps even as much as I?"

"Oh, I think I have more practice at it than even you, my lady. Do you know how soon he is leaving this house?"

"I don't know. A few weeks, perhaps? A house is being made ready for him."

"Have you seen a blond half 'faie here? In the workshop, perhaps?"

"Yes, he's there. He's closely watched." She paused, then whispered more softly still, "Someone is coming! Think on what I have said."

Seregil didn't hear so much as a whisper of a footstep, but when he heard several pairs of heavy feet pass by a moment later without incident, he knew she was gone.

He went back to bed with his heart racing. It was too soon to get his hopes up, but this was the start he'd hoped for. He whispered a blessing aloud across his left palm, "*Marös Aura Elustri chyptir!* Hang on, talí. I'll be with you soon!"

CHAPTER 29

Cross Purposes

KORATHAN APPEARED AT Thero's door without warning one morning as the wizard was sitting down to breakfast. He rose, intending to invite him to share his humble meal, but the look on the prince's face killed the pleasantries, unspoken.

"You've had news."

"Of the worst sort. The khirnari of Gedre has sent word. It appears that our friends and their escort were ambushed less than two days out of Gedre. The escort was killed. Seregil and Alec are missing."

"When did he learn this?"

"Only recently. The bodies had been hidden, and no one in Bôkthersa knew to look for them until some trader stumbled across them. Zengati arrows were found with the bodies."

"I see. What does the queen say?"

"She is upset, of course, and means to send a second delegation."

"That's it? What about Seregil and Alec?"

"My guess is that they were taken by slavers. I was hoping that you could be of assistance and look with that wizard eye spell of yours."

Thero had to take a quick breath to calm himself; why was it that everyone thought wizards could just snap their fingers and do anything that was needed in a heartbeat?

"With all due respect, your Highness, they could be halfway to Khouimir by now. Or in any of the hundreds of Zengati slave markets between there and the border." He sat down, overwhelmed by the enormity of the task. "Or in Plenimar, for that matter. I have no firsthand knowledge of either place, aside from a bit of the western coast of Plenimar."

But his mind was already racing. "But if it is Plenimar, then they'd most likely be taken to Benshâl or Riga first, from what I've heard. But again, there's no way to know which direction they were taken, or to what land. Such a search would take a hundred wizards months, if not years, to accomplish. I'm sorry, Highness, but it's virtually impossible that way, like looking for a couple of lentils in a crib of corn."

"What would you suggest, then?"

"If it were anyone else we were looking for, I'd say to send Seregil and Alec," Thero replied grimly. "Or Micum Cavish."

"We still have him. I suggest you send for him at once."

Thero sent off a message sphere to Watermead, and had word back in an instant that Micum was on his way.

Breakfast forgotten, he locked his tower door and went into the casting room. He chalked the proper circle, then knelt in the center and paused, considering his next move. He suspected that Phoria would consider what he was about to do disobedience at the very least, but that was why the windowless casting room was protected from prying eyes of all sorts by more than walls and locks.

A message spell was too limited, and a translocation to Bôkthersa, while certainly possible, was far too risky for now, and would involve Magyana, the only wizard left proficient at the powerful spell. Instead, he had dusted off one of the oldest tomes in Nysander's library and found a spell created by his master's master, Arkoniel. It was a precursor to the translocation magic, based on something so unlike traditional Orëska magic that Thero had always suspected it was from some other source. Nysander had hinted as much the one time he'd shown Thero how it worked.

He'd called it a "window spell," and that was the simplest way of imagining it. Cast correctly, it opened a portal through distance, allowing a wizard to look through to where another person was, no matter how far, and speak with him. Useful as that might be, Nysander had disliked it, and cautioned Thero against using it because it was crude, and dangerous both to the caster and the one who was sought through it. To illustrate this point, he'd opened a window to a distant valley and swung a dead rat by the tail through the opening. Only the severed end of the tail had swung back.

Klia would be alone in her room, probably still asleep, at this hour. Thero knew her rooms at Bôkthersa as well as he knew his own here, and carefully focused on a spot far enough from the bed that she would not inadvertently reach out and be injured.

Following Master Arkoniel's carefully written directions, Thero spoke the words and cupped his hands together, then folded them open like a pair of shutters. The space between, about the size of a small hand mirror, shimmered for an instant, then filled with shadow and color. It had worked. He was looking into Klia's room.

Just enough light came through a parting of the long curtains to illuminate a fall of shining chestnut hair, and one bare shoulder above the coverlet.

"Klia," he called softly, not wanting to alert the bodyguard outside her door. There was no telling who was there anymore, or where their loyalties lay.

She stirred, but only to pull the covers up under her chin. She was a deep sleeper, when not in the field. The hand that remained resting near her ear was the maimed one. The first and middle fingers were gone, but what remained was strong and graceful, and beautiful to Thero, who knew what she'd endured. She'd allowed him to kiss that scarred flesh once and his lips still tingled at the memory.

He caught himself woolgathering and tried again. "Your Highness, wake up!"

She sighed deeply, then pushed back the covers

and sat up, rubbing her eyes. Her hair was a dark, tousled mess, and her nightgown hung askew off one shoulder. He caught himself with a guilty start as he leaned dangerously close to the aperture.

"What? Who is it?" she asked sharply, reaching under her pillow for the dagger he knew she kept there.

"Over here," he called, and widened the opening so that she could see him better.

"Thero?" She slid out of bed and threw on a shawl. "What in the world is this?"

"Stay back, please!" he warned, then gave her a brief explanation of the spell.

"I see." She kept her distance, frowning. "Well, my friend, I've missed you badly, but what brings you into my bedchamber at this hour and by such a strange method?"

"Seregil and Alec. Have you had any word from them recently?"

She was awake now. Mention of Seregil always got her attention, he thought with a stab of envy. "No, nothing. What's going on?"

"Phoria sent them to fetch you. I know they landed at Gedre over a month ago, but nothing's been heard of them since." He hesitated, hating to be the bearer of bad tidings just yet. "They were carrying letters from the queen. She's recalled you to Skala."

"Really?" Klia sounded less than convinced. "And why didn't she let me return with my own bodyguard?"

"I don't know. Perhaps it's a test. She still doubts your loyalty and your response to the summons is to be the touchstone. I suppose she didn't want Urghazi Turma there defending you if you—" He broke off, not wanting to insult her.

"But I never got any message!"

"No. It appears they were ambushed before they could reach you. I hoped they might have escaped and continued on, but they should have reached you by now."

Even in the muted light of the bedchamber, he could see the anger flashing in Klia's blue eyes. "Do you think my sister may have had something to do with their disappearance?"

"No!" he said hastily, for the benefit of any spying listeners. "Of course not. In fact, there is evidence that they were taken by Zengati slavers. The odd thing is, the rest of the Aurënfaie escort and the Skalans were killed and left, Captain Traneus among them."

Klia pushed her hair back over one shoulder and gave him a wry look. "Can't say that I'll shed any tears for that man. What does Korathan say to all this?"

"He's tasked me with the search."

"Good. I'll set out for Rhíminee as soon as I can."

Thero hoped his disappointment wasn't too clear on his face. "I will contact you again as soon as I've figured out what to do."

An awkward moment passed as she waited for him to disappear and he couldn't help hesitating just a moment longer. "Stay well, Highness." With that, he broke the spell and passed a hand across his forehead. He was sweating, and not because of the magic.

Thero's page, Wethis, met Prince Korathan as he was leaving his chambers to join his sister for breakfast.

"Your Highness, Lord Vicegerent," the young man said, bowing politely and holding out a folded parchment sealed with Thero's mark. "Lord Thero sends a message."

Korathan dismissed the page and read the letter as he continued on down the long corridor between his rooms and his sister's. Phoria had finished with her breakfast and gone out to the gardens outside her salon. He found her there, walking slowly along the eastern path, admiring the last of the autumn flowers. She was dressed for court; her hair was twisted into looping braids behind her head, and her blue velvet gown and cape were stiff with gold embroidery.

She waved him over and linked arms with him. "Walk with me, Kor."

He covered her hand with his own and fell into step beside her. "I've had word from Thero."

"What did your wizard have to say? Can he help?"

"Yes, but not in the way I'd hoped. He feels it would be best if he went to Aurënen to view the site of the massacre. He means to take Sir Micum Cavish of Watermead with him."

"Another Watcher, I believe?" She plucked a

yellow aster and twirled it absently between her fingers.

"Perhaps, but he's a fine tracker, and he knows Seregil's ways. If they managed to leave any kind of sign, Micum is the one to find it. Let Thero and Cavish attend to this for you."

"Very well," she replied, frowning.

Korathan was used to these sudden changes and took no offense. "They are the best suited to the task."

"I trust your judgment, Brother. And if Klia sails into Rhíminee Harbor at the head of an Aurënfaie fleet?"

"If she did, Phoria, it would be to support you."

"So you say." Her frown deepened as she crushed the blossom. "You always take her side."

He gave her arm a reassuring squeeze. "Only when you are unfairly suspicious of her."

"She was always Mother's favorite."

"And yet you are the queen. She was the youngest, that's all. Mother always cared for you."

Phoria tossed the ruined flower away. "Be that as it may, my patience is nearing its end. And, Kor?"

"Yes?"

Her hard gaze softened to concern. "You won't let your heart blind you, will you?"

"About Klia?"

"No . . . *him*."

"That was a long time ago, Phoria. You know where my loyalty lies. And my heart."

She kissed his cheek. "My good brother. You know you're the only one I can trust completely."

Korathan gave her an awkward, one-armed hug. "Always, dear sister. Always."

Taking his leave, he called for his horse and rode to the Orëska House. He'd been here so often lately that no one stood on ceremony anymore. One of the house stewards escorted him directly upstairs.

The sunny workroom was deserted. The steward pulled out a chair for him, then went to a side door and knocked softly.

Thero emerged, dressed in a stained robe and apron. He was flushed, and there was ash dusting his hair and shoulders and chalk dust on his knees.

"I've interrupted you."

"Not at all, Highness." Thero rubbed at a small burn on his cheek but only managed to smear more soot there. "I attempted a few other searching spells, but they were no help."

"Phoria is getting impatient but has agreed to let you and Micum go south."

"Ah." Thero walked over to the table and poured them each a cup of tea. Handing Korathan his, he sat down beside him. "Then perhaps you will not be angry with me for the steps I've taken. I've exhausted all methods. I've cast dozens of wizards' eyes. I can find no sign of them between Bôkthersa and Gedre, but I may have missed them. It's a very large area. But I can tell you now with certainty that Klia has had no word from them, either."

"You've spoken with her?"

"Well, yes, actually." Thero looked a bit embarrassed at the admission, then explained the spell he'd employed. "I apprised her of the situation. She assured me that she remains completely loyal to the queen and plans to return at once. I wanted to speak with you before I passed the information on to her Majesty."

"Bilairy's Balls, man, if you could do that, why did Phoria have to go to all the trouble of sending Seregil?"

"You'd have to ask her that. I did offer, the day I came back."

"I see." Korathan pinched the bridge of his nose, feeling the start of a headache behind his eyes. "Tell me what Klia said and I'll couch it properly for Phoria's ears. In the meantime, I want you to go there at once. You can do it quickly, can't you, with one of those sort of traveling spells?"

"A translocation? I've never managed it, but Magyana can cast them. I'll speak with her, and we'll go as soon as Micum arrives. But you do understand that even if we learn what direction they were taken, it's no guarantee that we can track them?"

"Do what you can and report to me directly."

Thero smiled and bowed. "Of course, Highness. But you're not suggesting I reinstitute the Watchers against the queen's express order?"

"Certainly not. But as Vicegerent, I'm entitled—no, obligated—to protect the Throne in any manner I can, and I'd not be the first to have spies of my own. Anything you might need, I will provide."

"Thank you, Highness." He paused a moment, then added, "I don't believe Seregil would do anything to provoke trouble between Phoria and Klia, regardless of his feelings toward either one. It had to be an ambush."

"I believe that, too, Thero, but this business of them being the only ones not killed worries me. If it really was slavers, why not take them all? Are you prepared to deal with them if they actually have deserted?"

"I'm sure that won't be necessary," Thero assured him, keeping to himself that his solution would be to tell them to keep on running. "Trust in them as you would me, Korathan. They would not betray your trust of their own volition. Something's gone very wrong. If they're anywhere to be found, Micum and I will find them."

The prince clasped hands with him. "Go, then, with my blessing and the queen's."

Watcher Business

MICUM WAVED OFF the Orëska doorkeeper who mistook him for a stranger. It had been a while, he supposed.

He took the stairs slowly, hampered by his bad leg and stick. As soon as he reached Thero's landing, however, he straightened and concentrated on striding normally. The thick scar on the back of his thigh always stiffened during a long ride, but once he got moving he could get around well enough, so long as he didn't have to sprint.

Thero answered his knock, already dressed for travel. The young wizard's time in Aurënen had changed him, and for the better. The sallow complexion and thin-lipped, brittle demeanor were gone; Thero was sun-browned and looked fitter than he had in Nysander's time. Seregil had always maintained that Thero needed to spend more time outside the Orëska House, and it appeared he'd been right.

"Magyana's on her way," Thero told him, hustling him to the workroom, where a small pack and several bags sat ready on a bench. "Have you eaten? I'm sure the khirnari will feed us when we arrive. He's expecting us soon and I—"

Micum laughed. "It's all right, Thero. I'm ready when you are, and just as anxious to be off."

Thero paused and gave him an apologetic smile. "Sorry. I haven't been able to think about anything but leaving. Thank you for getting here so quickly."

"Well, you did interrupt a good breakfast yesterday with that message light of yours," Micum reminded him.

Thero looked blank for a moment. "Oh! I disturbed your lady."

"In more ways than one."

"She's not happy to see you back to Watcher business, is she?"

"No." And if it had been for anyone but Alec and Seregil, she would have thrown more things at him than she had, and sharper ones, too. Being the cause of her tears, and Illia's, had hurt far worse, though.

Magyana came in without knocking. "Here I am. Shall we begin?"

"Are you certain you can send two of us at once?" asked Micum. Magyana had aged terribly since her old friend's death. She looked frail as a dry twig today.

Magyana chuckled. "It has been a while since I've done it, but I'm sure I haven't forgotten how. Go on, hang on to your baggage there and be ready to step lively. I can only hold the portal open a few moments."

Thero shouldered his pack and made to slip a

hand under Micum's arm. The older man raised a bushy red eyebrow at him with an unmistakable frown and Thero hastily stepped back.

"I'm not a complete cripple either, you know," Micum grumbled, tucking his walking stick under one arm. "I'm fairly certain I can walk a few feet without falling on my ass."

"Sorry." Thero was smirking, the bastard!

"If you're quite done?" Magyana interjected.

Micum nodded. "We are, Mistress. Whenever you're ready."

Magyana pressed her fingertips together in front of her face and began the muttered incantation. A spark of darkness coalesced in the cage of her fingers, and she spread her hands, stretching the darkness into a shining, spinning mirror of blackness large enough for the two men to step through.

Micum caught himself holding his breath, as if he were about to jump into deep water. He'd only done this a few times and didn't care much for the feeling. Steeling himself, he grabbed Thero by the elbow and together they stepped into the spinning darkness and disappeared.

Magyana let the portal collapse, then dusted her hands and sniffed loudly. "'Are you certain you can send two of us at once?' What cheek!"

Magyana knew Gedre well, and her aim was true. Micum and Thero stumbled out in the middle of the sunlit courtyard at Riagil í Molan's clan house.

The whitewashed buildings were long and low, with round white domes here and there and brilliant flowering vines still in bloom.

A loud whistle came from somewhere overhead and Micum looked up to find a young girl about Illia's age sitting in the branches of the huge tree that dominated the courtyard. She was dressed in a long tunic and trousers, and her bare feet were dirty. At her signal a number of people emerged from the house, led by a distinguished old man with a pretty young woman on his arm.

They came to Thero and kissed him on both cheeks. "Welcome back, Thero í Procepios. And welcome to you, Micum of Cavish. You are the friend of Gedre's friends and welcome in our house."

"Khirnari, and lady, I am honored to be here, even under such sad circumstances. I grieve for those whom you have lost."

Lady Yhali bowed to him. "And we grieve for the fate of Seregil and young Alec. I know they are close to your heart. Come. Refresh yourself and eat at our table."

Micum glanced up at the sun, gauging how much daylight was left.

"You're anxious to be off," Riagil noted with an understanding smile. "The place of the ambush is a day and a half's ride from here. I'll send for your escort at once, if you would prefer."

"If you would not think us rude, Khirnari?" Thero replied.

"Of course not," Yhali said, patting his arm. "Come and have some tea while your escort assembles."

They sat at one of the tables under the tree and servants brought them cold tea flavored with crushed mint and borage leaves, and plates of soft little cakes filled with nuts and honey.

"I've called for forty riders to go with you, and all of them skilled at arms," Riagil said as he rejoined them. "I only wish I'd had such foresight with the others. It is a heavy shame to bear, for guests to come to such a pass."

"How could you have foreseen a slaver raid, this far east?" Thero replied kindly. "Seregil and Alec will hold no grudge against your house, rest assured."

"I understand a few things were recovered from the site of the attack?" Micum asked.

Riagil motioned to a man standing nearby, who went to fetch a large wooden tray. On it were half a dozen Zengati arrow points, a broken silver neck chain, several scarves bearing Zengati clan designs, and a bone button.

"That's all?" Thero asked, disappointed.

"There were more arrows, but they were all the same."

"And the bodies?"

"Buried, of course. They'd already begun to bloat when we found them."

"Of course," Micum murmured, examining each item closely. Seregil was the best of them at reading a corpse. Thank the Flame his or Alec's hadn't been among the dead.

Distracted by such thoughts, he very nearly missed a detail. He picked up the button again and looked more closely at it. "This isn't Zengati work.

See how it's drilled with four holes rather than two, and the way the edges are rubbed smooth? It's from Plenimar, or Skala."

"Any Zengati could have eastern clothing, either from trade or slave taking," Thero pointed out.

"Perhaps, but it's too soon to rule out anyone yet," Micum replied. "If the Zengat could make such a raid, anyone could have been with them."

Yhali gave him a perplexed look. "Why would a Skalan mean them any harm?"

Micum exchanged a quick glance with Thero. It wouldn't be politic to admit that the person they most suspected was the Skalan queen.

CHAPTER 31

A Change in the Wind

SOMETHING WAS WRONG.

Yhakobin was as polite as always when Alec came upstairs each day, as long as Alec was docile and cooperative, but there was a tension in the air that hadn't been there before. He had no doubt it had something to do with the new rhekaro and the cries that still occasionally came down from the workshop.

Yet unpleasant as the circumstances now were, Alec was glad to get upstairs for any time at all, if only to break up the boredom of the day. It was good to see if the sun was shining or the rain was falling, good to smell the wintry breeze through an open window and hear the sounds of Yhakobin's children playing outside in the gardens.

Over a week had passed since the making of the new rhekaro. Each day Alec was brought up to feed it, and each day he was sent back to his little cell immediately afterward, with nothing but new books to amuse himself. Yhakobin had little time for him anymore, which in itself seemed a blessing. The smaller furnaces around the room were cold now. Only the athanor was stoked and it burned continuously, heating some greenish-brown mess in the large retort atop it.

While the rhekaro fed each day, Alec looked it over carefully, hoping the alchemist would not notice. At first there were only the bodkin pricks on its pale fingertips, but as the days went by, bandages slowly appeared on both its arms and legs. The memory of the bucket by the door, with that bit of hair hanging out, made his heart race and his guts roil.

Whatever this creature was, Alec could not deny the fact that he was connected to it by blood. Even if it was a monster, no creature deserved to be cut up alive, as the first one had been.

Or deserved to be kept naked in an iron cage, either. It reminded him too much of that nightmarish journey his first time in Plenimar, creaking along in that filthy bear cage.

There was no waste bucket in there, or any water. Did it need such things, he wondered? With its strange eyes and skin, and stranger blood, it simply wasn't a real child. *Except for the way it looks at me.* Those silvery eyes locked on his face each day as it sucked hard at his fingertip, and he was almost certain now that he saw some sign of intelligence there. And though it was hard to tell with it huddled over all the time, he thought it looked larger than it had at first, too. Could it be growing, on nothing more than a few drops of blood a day? Its hair was certainly longer. The long, silvery tresses pooled about it like a shimmering cloak.

It's not a child! he reminded himself time and again, but each day he wondered more and more what it really was.

Alec hadn't seen Khenir in all that time, but one afternoon as he sat reading on his bed, the door opened and there he was. Alec regarded him with a new coldness, convinced that he'd taken the horn picks. But his heart ached a little, too, torn between conviction and regret.

Khenir noticed the change in his demeanor at once, of course. With a sigh, he sat down on the bed beside him. "You're angry with me?"

"I think you know why."

Khenir nodded slowly. "That day I saw that the spoon was missing and realized my mistake in leaving it behind. If Ilban had found out?" He shuddered. "You put us both at a terrible risk with such a foolish act. If you got away because of my carelessness, it would have been my life in payment."

"I was planning to take you with me," Alec told him.

Khenir stared at him in disbelief. "You'd really do that?"

"Of course!"

"That was very good of you. I never guessed— But you don't think those splinters could really have worked in the lock, do you?"

Alec kept to himself the fact that they'd worked perfectly well. "Why are you here?"

"I've been worried about you! I was afraid Ilban was taking his anger out on you, as he has on me more frequently." He lifted the hem of his robe and showed Alec a few red stripes across the backs of his calves.

"What's he so upset about? He's got his white creature and I'm keeping it fed for him. And those cries?" Alec hugged himself, feeling miserable and helpless. "By the Light, does he make them just to torture them? What is it he wants?"

Khenir sighed. "He's pursuing a great secret, Alec. The rhekaro made from Hâzadriëlfaie blood are said to yield the necessary elements for a perfect elixir."

"To do what? Heal the Overlord's child?"

"Yes. That's what he told me, at least."

Alec narrowed his eyes at the older man. "You think there's something else it does?"

"I have no idea, but I do know that he's made many healing elixirs over the years without going to such lengths."

"Say all you want about 'alchemy'; it all looks like necromancy to me, and it causes suffering."

"But for a higher purpose."

Alec shook his head and looked away.

Khenir squeezed his shoulder and gave him a little shake. "I'm sorry about taking your things, but it was to protect you as much as myself. I keep telling you, you haven't been a slave long enough to understand the danger."

"And how would I, shut up in a cell for weeks on end?"

"I know it's difficult for you. If only Ilban's

experiments work, things will surely change. In the meantime, I'll ask if you can go out in the garden with me again."

Alec had expected to work harder than this to get another chance at the garden. "Thank you. I'd like that."

"Then you forgive me?"

Alec forced a grudging smile. "Forget about it. It doesn't matter anyway. I guess I'll have to settle for another walk on my chain, eh?"

CHAPTER 32

On the hunt

MICUM AND THERO found horses saddled for them at the head of the escort waiting by the courtyard gate. There was a stone mounting block near the gateway, and Micum swallowed his pride and used it. Once he was on horseback, he was any man's equal.

The khirnari was the next to use the block, climbing stiffly into the saddle of a fine chestnut mare. "I will be your guide."

Thero bowed in the saddle and Micum did the same, glad of more time to get to know the man. Seregil had always spoken fondly of him.

They rode along a coastal road until dusk, and guested at a lonely farmstead. The farmer and his family were clearly honored to have their khirnari under their roof and made their Skalan guests welcome with every comfort they had.

The following morning they turned up into the wooded hills, following a well-traveled road. Micum kept one eye on the trees, but the khirnari assured him that bandits were rare in these parts. Micum nodded, but kept watch anyway; this was perfect country for an ambush. Wasn't that why they were here?

They reached the ravine that afternoon and Riagil led them down to the spot where the bodies had been found. Thero seated himself on a rock by the stream and closed his eyes, intent on seeking any lingering energies that might be here. Micum left him to it and walked slowly up and down the bank of the stream. The soft ground was still marked by footprints, but not from a battle. It looked more like the bodies had simply been dumped here after they were killed.

"Why would they have turned aside?" wondered Thero. "That water doesn't look good to drink, except perhaps for the horses."

"Why indeed?" Micum dismounted stiffly and walked slowly up and down the side of the ravine. It had been weeks since the attack—weeks of rain and wind, but he could still tell that the attack hadn't happened here. There was no sign of a fight.

Leaving his horse with one of the 'faie, he grabbed his stick and worked his way slowly back up to the road, following the faded signs that were left. The Gedre had mucked up much of it when they came for their dead, but he could still make out some drag marks, and the deep impressions left by men carrying a burden.

The trees were thick on either side of the road and would have provided ample cover for archers.

Given the number of arrows found in the bodies, that must have been the main type of attack. Beginning with the ravine side of the road, he limped slowly into the forest, gaze and stick sweeping the ground. Fortunately, there wasn't much undergrowth, and he soon found numerous groups of small depressions, where the archers had stuck handfuls of arrows into the ground, in easy reach as they shot. The tree cover had protected footprints better in here, and he guessed there had been at least thirty ambushers.

Going to the far side of the road, he found similar signs and a rusted knife of Skalan make, which he pocketed.

Chin on chest, he walked the roadside for nearly an hour, searching for old signs along the verge while the others milled about, trying to stay out of his way. He found nothing more on the far side of the road, so he crossed over and tried again on the ravine side.

He had better luck here. The grass was longer between the road and the trees and looked to have been trampled some time ago. He used the tip of his stick to brush it this way and that, looking for tracks. Instead, the tip struck something that gave back the clink of metal. Feeling around, his hand caught on something sharp enough to cut his fingertip. He drew back, then let out a low whistle of satisfaction. It was the hilt of a sword, and one he recognized by the curled, fern-head ends of the quillons. It was Alec's, or what was left of it; the blade had been shattered. The remains of it, no more than a few inches long, were razor-sharp and darkened to an unusual blue.

A few moments more searching uncovered the hilt of Seregil's sword in the same condition. It was Aurënfaie work, made by Seregil's uncle to replace the one he'd destroyed killing Nysander. Not only was the blade of this one shattered and dark, like Alec's, but the smooth round lozenge of Sarikali stone that had formed the pommel was gone, leaving nothing but the empty bezel.

He crouched for a long time, holding the hilts in his hands; this was where his friends had made their stand.

"Show me something, boys," he murmured, smoothing his mustache thoughtfully. Neither would have gone without a fight; the swords were proof of that. And Seregil at least would have tried to leave him some sign. He always had.

Micum gave the hilts to Thero and continued his search. A few feet from where Seregil's hilt had fallen, the point of Micum's stick struck something small and metallic. He went down on both knees and parted the grass. There, half-buried in a small ants' nest, glinted the ring Klia had given Seregil. He picked it up and polished the red stone on his sleeve, cleaning the dirt from the princess's portrait. *Oh my friend. If you let this fall, it must have been very bad indeed.*

A few yards away, he found a few of the message sticks under a clump of wilted clover. Rain had washed away most of the paint. He wondered if the magic had washed away, too, and why neither of his friends had managed to break any of them.

Whatever happened here that day, it happened fast, or they'd have gotten away.

By the time Micum was done, he'd found an untarnished Plenimaran silver coin mashed into the ground inside a footprint from a Skalan boot, very likely Seregil's from the size. There was also a stained ivory toothpick, and a human front tooth that had been broken off rather than pulled. He carried these to where the others were waiting and lined them all up on the ground beside the hilts.

Riagil looked rather chagrined as he examined the collection. "My men searched this area for two days."

"Micum has sharper eyes than most and more experience with ambushes of this sort, Khirnari." Thero knelt and passed his hands over the items slowly. "The tooth belongs to a Plenimaran soldier named Notis. He was here for the attack. A Silmai trader dropped the toothpick sometime more recently. He was on his way to Gedre. It has nothing to do with the attack."

As his left hand drifted over the sword hilts, however, Thero shivered and picked up Seregil's. Pressing it between his palms, he closed his eyes, lips moving soundlessly in some spell, as Micum and the others looked on. "Someone set a dra'gorgos on them."

The khirnari's eyes widened. "On Aurënfaie soil? The audacity!"

"And where there's a dra'gorgos, then there's a necromancer, too," said Micum.

Thero repeated the procedure with Alec's hilt, with the same result.

"Are they dead?" asked Riagil.

"I don't see that. But what this proves is that there were Plenimarans with the Zengat."

Micum frowned. "Then I'd say that they were taken east, rather than west. Can you use these to find them?"

"Perhaps. . . ." Thero examined Seregil's hilt again. "If there was a bit of blood, even a drop, I might . . ." He set Seregil's hilt aside and picked up Alec's. After a pained moment, he looked up. "There's a tiny bit of Alec's blood here."

"You use blood magic?" Riagil asked, surprised.

"It's not necromancy, but something my master's master learned from the hill folk."

"The Retha'noi, you mean?"

"Yes, Khirnari. I believe they are closely related to the Dravnians in your own mountains. Such spells are in my lineage of magic now, though this one is not very powerful. The only thing I use it for is findings."

Thero scratched the bit of dried blood from the hilt and pinched it between his thumb and forefinger. With head bowed, he whispered the blood calling to blood spell, then waited silently for the images to appear.

But nothing came to him except a distant blur of light, dancing just out of reach. *Alec! Alec, come to me.*

But nothing else did, except that strange blur, and it told him only that Alec was probably alive.

He broke off in frustration and opened his eyes to find everyone watching him. "I think he's alive, but I can't place him, or even see him. Something's shielding him, but it's like nothing I've ever encountered."

"But he *is* alive?" said Micum.

"I'm quite sure of it."

"Well, what can you make of this, then?" Micum took the hilt from him and pressed the tooth into Thero's hand. "You can bet this bastard bled. If we can find him, maybe he can tell us where they were taken. Where is he?"

Chagrined at not having thought of it himself, Thero smiled up at Riagil. "I told you he's a clever man."

He clasped the tooth between his palms and whispered the spell again. This time the images came at once, fast and clear. The man who'd lost the tooth was alive and laughing with some others. By their speech, dark complexions, and beards, he knew them for Plenimarans. Some noble's own men-at-arms, by the look of them, or brigands. With Plenimarans, it was often difficult to tell the difference.

"They're calling him by name . . . yes, it's Notis." Thero strained to see more of the man's surroundings. The spell was a hard one, and made his head pound as he pushed himself to his limit. Sweat was beaded on his brow and upper lip by the time he opened his eyes. "Virésse! By the Light, the man is in Virésse, in some sort of barracks or on a ship. I can't tell which, but he's most certainly there. I recognize the harbor."

"What's a Plenimaran slaver doing there, of all places?" wondered Micum.

"He may not be a slaver by trade," Riagil told him. "Not even Ulan í Sathil would stoop so low as to trade in bodies. But this Notis may be in service to one who does, and that man may be a trader in other commodities."

"The point is, he's in Aurënen!" Thero exclaimed. "We have to find him and make him tell us what happened. That's the only link we have to where they might have been taken."

"Khirnari, can any of your people do that traveling spell that brought us here?" asked Micum.

"No. That, like the blood spell, is no part of Aurënfaie magic. But if we ride hard, we can be back in Gedre soon enough, and there I can put you on my fastest ship. Whatever you need, you have only to ask."

Thero stood and bowed to him. "We accept your kind offer, Khirnari, with our deepest thanks. It's still a great wide world to search in, but this gives me hope."

"Thank the Four," Micum murmured, leaning heavily on his stick. "If they are alive, then I won't stop until I find them and bring them home!"

Child of No Woman

THE FOLLOWING DAY, Alec and Khenir were allowed in the garden again, veiled and under guard, as usual. Apart from the ever-present escort, this was the best place for a potential escape, and close to the cell he was in now. He was glad that they hadn't thought to put him back in the first cell under the main house, at least not yet. All he had to do was get the cell and workshop doors open some night when the workshop was empty, slip out here, and over the wall. Of course, he'd have to find a way to carry the rhekaro when he went . . .

That last thought brought him to a sudden halt by the fountain. He kept his gaze on the fish swimming lazily after Khenir's crumbs, but his mind was racing. There was no telling what the alchemist would do to the pale little creature, now that it, too, was proving unsuitable to his needs.

Hell, with me gone and no one else's blood good

enough to feed it, it will die anyway. I can't just leave it—can I?

His heart already had the answer. It was a child, born of no woman.

His child.

So that's settled. Maybe that will finally make Seregil shut up about me finding a girl, too.

Khenir looked up and chuckled. "It's good to see you smile."

"I like the fish. Can I have some of that bread to give them?"

Khenir passed him the crust he'd brought and they sat together on the rim of the fountain, watching as the fish thrust their blunt heads and gaping, whiskered mouths up out of the water to beg like puppies.

Khenir still had charge of his chain, but Alec had room enough to move away a little, and as he bent to look more closely at a yellow snail crawling along the bottom of the pool, he caught sight of something lying in the shadow under the wide basin.

It was a child's bronze hairpin.

Without any change of expression, he knelt and rested one arm on the edge of the basin, trailing his fingers in the water for the fish to nibble at, while letting the other fall. It only took an instant to palm the pin.

He had no sleeve or belt to hide it in, so he pinched it in the folds of one curled palm and prayed to Illior he didn't have cause to use his left hand until his got back to his room.

Khenir rested a hand casually on Alec's shoulder. "I'm glad you like the fish so much. You look like a child, kneeling there."

Alec grinned up at him. "They're very pretty. The whole garden is. It's good to get out of that room. And . . ." He glanced away shyly. "And to see you, too. There's no one else I can talk to here. I've really come to understand what you said about being lonely. It's awful, isn't it?"

"It is." Khenir's hand moved from Alec's shoulder to his hair, and he combed his fingers through the loose strands around Alec's face. The tips of his finger were cool and soft as they brushed his cheek, and Alec was once again torn between sympathy and distrust. He turned his face away from that touch.

"Still pining for that lost love of yours?" Khenir asked sadly.

"Yes. But it's good to have you here."

Khenir leaned closer and whispered, "Would you really take me with you, if you got out?"

"Yes, I would."

"And do you think you could really get away? How would you do that?"

Alec looked back at the fish. Did he trust Khenir or not? His head told him one thing, but gut instinct made him hold back. It was a bad feeling, especially if he was wrong and Khenir really was his friend.

Caution won out, all the same. He shrugged. "I don't know. Get on a ship headed west, I suppose."

Khenir laughed outright at that. "That's your whole plan, is it? Find a ship? Hmm, I think maybe I'll take my chances and stay here, then. You'll be chained in the market without a foot before the next full moon."

Alec shrugged. "You're probably right."

He kept the pin hidden in his palm until he was

alone in his cell again. He waited until the lock ground into place, then sat down and examined his find.

It was a child's hair stick, just less than three inches long, with a carved ivory finial. *Illior must have heard me, after all,* he thought, for the pin was made of bronze, rather than soft gold or silver. However, his horn splinters had been longer.

He knew that Khenir's evaluation of his so-called plan was apt. Even if he did get out of this room, and the villa, he wouldn't get very far without some way to disguise himself, and the rhekaro, too. He glanced up at the ceiling, wondered if there was any sort of dye in the workshop.

And, of course, he'd have to find Seregil, too.

He had little appetite that night but ate his turnip stew and bread anyway to avoid any undue attention. Ahmol took the tray away when he was done and Alec lay down to wait.

Without a window, it was impossible to gauge the passage of time. Instead, he fixed his gaze on the candle flame in the niche by the door and began counting softly to himself to mark the passing seconds. He recalled Seregil once telling him how long it took a candle to burn an inch but couldn't remember what the actual time had been. It was boring work, and he lost count several times, dozing off, but when the candle finally burned almost to the socket, he judged that it must be late.

He went to the door and put his ear against the wood. All was silent beyond. Encouraged, he inserted the pin into the lock and gently caressed the tumblers, seeing what he could reach. The first pin gave easily, but the second was a hairbreadth out of reach.

"Bilairy's Balls!" He sat back on his heels and turned the hairpin over between his fingers. It was metal, so there was the chance that he could pound it out a little to make it longer, but with what? He carried it over to the corner with the slop pail. The pail was carved in one piece from a length of log and quite thick at the bottom.

It had also been used several times today.

Alec kicked it over to make it look like an accident, but was careful to send the contents away from the bed. Stale urine spread across the floor and soaked into the mortar. Satisfied, Alec carried the bucket away from the mess and sat down to work on the pin.

He soon discovered that wood was no fit tool for shaping cold bronze. At first all he managed to do was dent the bottom of the pail and leave traces of metal on the floor. Just as he was about to give up, however, he accidentally struck the ivory bead on the end of the pin and shattered it, revealing a precious length of knurled metal that had been hidden before. He picked up every broken fragment and hid them in the mattress, then went back to the door.

The extra little bit of length was enough. The lock gave and he inched the door open on darkness. There was no sign of light from the cellar below, or from the workshop. He crept up the stairs and put his ear to the door. More silence there.

He took a deep breath, then tested the latch. It lifted with a faint snick of metal and he opened the door a tiny crack. The workroom was in darkness except for the red glow from the athanor's furnace.

A fire needed tending. He pushed the door open a little further and looked around for the alchemist and his servant. But the room appeared deserted.

Or so he thought until something moved just outside the dim glow of the furnace.

It was the rhekaro. It was clad in a short slave's tunic that left its limbs bare. Alec saw more bandages than had been there this morning. As he watched, it squatted by the athanor, stared a moment at the fire within through one of the ports, then took a handful of woodchips from a basket and fed them one by one into the chamber.

It's not a mindless thing, thought Alec, pleased but wary. If it served the alchemist, it might just be loyal. Well, there was only one way to find out.

He stepped slowly into the room, watching the rhekaro for a reaction.

It paid him no attention until he came up behind it and touched its shoulder.

It turned and looked up at him, then its lips made a little sucking motion.

"Are you hungry?" Alec whispered.

The creature made no reply but fixed its gaze on Alec's hand.

"All right, then." He went to one of the tables and found a bodkin lying next to a bowl of flowers. He stabbed his finger and offered it. The rhekaro took it eagerly and sucked, looking him in the eye as it always did.

"Do you know me?" he asked softly. "Can you speak?"

As always, there was no answer. Perhaps it lacked the ability to speak or understand, thought Alec. And despite the number of wounds it clearly had, he hadn't heard much screaming, either.

The rhekaro made no move to resist when Alec untied one of the bandages around its left arm to inspect the damage. He expected to find skin sliced away, but instead he found a painted symbol similar to those he'd seen on the amulets Yhakobin had made him wear.

Other bandages revealed similar marks. Some looked inflamed, but there was no serious wound. So the alchemist was taking better care of this one, at least. The little thing was clean and its long hair shone in the firelight.

"What are you for?" Alec murmured, retying the bandages.

As soon as he was finished, the rhekaro squatted down to feed the fire again, seeming to forget all about him.

Alec left it to its task and began searching the shop for anything that might help them escape. There was nothing like a weapon, except for the bodkin, and that wouldn't be much good against a sword. What knives Yhakobin used were stored away out of sight. Once again, he cursed his lack of Plenimaran. The drawers of the alchemist's cabinets and cupboards were all carefully labeled in clear but incomprehensible script.

"Damn! I can't even find the tea, much less a knife," he muttered aloud.

The rhekaro straightened again and went to the tallest of the cabinets, the one with scores of small drawers. Without any hesitation at all it pulled one out and reached in, then came to Alec and held out a pottery jar with a leather top. Surprised, Alec opened the lid and sniffed at the contents.

It was tea.

Meanwhile, the rhekaro went to one of the tables and grasped the handle of a drawer there. When it would not open, it just stood there, apparently baffled.

"Is that where the knives are?" Alec asked, not expecting an answer.

The rhekaro touched the handle again, then let its hand fall to its side.

Alec made short work of the simple lock and opened it. Inside was a neatly arranged array of knives that would have made a butcher happy.

He clapped the rhekaro on the shoulder. "Thank you. Now, you don't know if he has any dyes, do you?"

The rhekaro went to another large cupboard and opened it, showing Alec a pile of leather pouches, many of them stained from the contents inside.

"Brown dye?" Alec tried.

The rhekaro selected a pouch and carried it to him.

"Do you know how to mix it?"

Stymied again, the rhekaro just stood there.

"That's all right. You're a good helper." It was impossible not to speak to it as if it was an actual child. "Keys?"

Again there was no response.

"Food? Bread?"

Nothing.

"Flower?"

Despite the fact that the flower bowl was only a few feet away, the rhekaro paid it no mind.

"Let's see. What would be useful? Rope?"

It went to a closet and returned with several hanks of rope, some of it stained and stiff with what appeared to be blood.

"Seregil?" Alec tried. As expected, that got him another blank look. It seemed that the rhekaro's education was very limited. "Well, let's try this. Alec?"

The rhekaro immediately came to him, took his hand, and sucked on his finger.

Alec chuckled and pulled his hand free. "At least you didn't come at me when I said 'food.'" He took those cool little hands in his and pressed them to his chest. "Alec. My name is Alec. Alec is me. Do you understand? Name?"

The rhekaro gazed up at him and he could have sworn he caught a fleeting look of confusion. Perhaps, having no name of its own, such distinctions meant nothing to it. "Alec" was probably the same to it as "chair" or "rope" or "tea": just another useful item to be found in the workshop.

There was no question that it was focused on him now, though. As he stole to the outer door to listen, it followed right behind on bare silent feet.

There were guards somewhere outside. He could hear them talking. No use going out the front door, then.

It would have been helpful if the place had a window into the smaller garden, but no such luck. The skylights were no more help, either; there were bars across them now. When had that happened?

Perhaps it was a night barrier, set in place when the alchemist finished for the day? The rhekaro followed him like a lost pup as Alec hastily searched further, looking for any other way out.

In the process he found a cupboard containing a few of Yhakobin's stained work robes. They were a bit large, but had sleeves and were not slave garb. There was a pair of worn shoes, too.

He paused, keeping one ear attuned to the door, and took stock. So far he had access to clothing, knives, tea, a dye he didn't know how to use, and a lock pick that worked.

And no idea where Seregil was.

He paused by the athanor, watching the contents boil sluggishly. It still looked like mud to him.

"What is he up to, I wonder?" he murmured.

Cold fingers closed around Alec's wrist. Surprised, he looked down to find the rhekaro staring up at the retort as well, and it had a hand pressed to its chest, just as he had when he'd tried to make it understand his name.

"What? You have a name?"

As expected, there was no answer except that it lowered its hand.

"You want a name?"

That little hand went back to its chest, over its heart—assuming it had one.

"Can you tell me what you mean, or is that just something you saw me do?" he wondered. "But I should call you something, I guess. I've never named anyone before, except a horse." He studied the little creature for a moment, then said, "How about Sebrahn?" It was the Aurënfaie word for moonlight. He touched the rhekaro on the chest. "Sebrahn. That's you. What do you think?"

The rhekaro looked at him a moment, then slowly pointed at the retort and then at itself, and held up a finger, showing him the white line of a scar.

Alec held its hand a little closer to the waning glow of the fire. A scar? And it had healed without the help of his blood, too. He looked at the roiling mass, then back at the creature. "He put something of you in there, didn't he? He made you from me, and now he's trying to make something from you."

Sebrahn went to the knife drawer, selected a small, sharp blade, and brought it to Alec, then held out its hand.

Alec put it back and closed the drawer. "No. I won't do that to you."

Just then he heard a louder voice outside: Yhakobin, speaking with the sentries.

Alec looked frantically at all the open cupboards and drawers. He'd let himself get distracted by the rhekaro, forgetting that the alchemist worked all hours!

Cursing silently, he flew around the room, trying to put everything back to rights. It was only when he stumbled over Sebrahn that he realized that the rhekaro was still following him. The voices were getting closer now. Ahmol was with his master.

Alec took the rhekaro by its thin shoulders and whispered, "Tend the fire!" then bolted for the stairs. A final glance found the creature squatting by the athanor again with its basket of chips, but it was looking at him.

Alec just managed to get the stairway door

pulled shut when he heard the workroom door
open. It hadn't been locked!

Damning himself for all kinds of fool, he crept
back to his room and locked himself in with shaking
hands. It took several tries, and he had just gotten the
pick hidden in the mattress when he heard steps on
the stairs outside his room. He braced for the worst,
but they continued on downstairs to the cellar.

Alec quickly moved the pick, since Khenir already knew that hiding place. Reaching under the
bed, he wedged the brass pin between the mattress
and the bed ropes. That done, he sagged back across
the bed, limp with relief, until he heard the rhekaro's
first thin squeal of pain from the cellar. It took every
ounce of will he had not to pick the lock again and
dash down to stop whatever was going on. Instead,
he pounded on the door, yelling, "Leave him alone.
Stop hurting him, damn you!"

It did no good, of course. The cries continued
for a little while, then stopped just as abruptly. He
kicked the door in frustration. "You heartless bastard! He's just a child. How can you do that?"

He jumped back quickly as a key rattled in the
lock. The door swung open and there was the alchemist, whip in hand and furious. Ahmol stood just
behind with Sebrahn's limp little body in his arms.

"You killed him!" Alec snarled.

Yhakobin strode in and grabbed Alec by the
hair, dragging him back to the doorway.

"Him, you say? Look at its hand," he ordered,
giving Alec's head a hard shake, and then shoving
him to his knees for a closer look.

The rhekaro's left arm hung limply down, and

Alec saw that its entire hand had been cut off this time. Something was dripping from the terrible wound, but it wasn't blood. As with the last one, it was thicker, and almost clear.

"You are a fool, Alec, if you think this *thing* is in any way human," the alchemist said sternly. "And you are a greater fool to insult me. I've no patience with you—or it—tonight."

He barked out an order and two strapping men appeared and held Alec while Yhakobin drove the bodkin into Alec's finger and yanked his hand to the rhekaro's slack lips. After a moment the lips closed around it and it sucked weakly, but its eyelids didn't even flutter.

Yhakobin shoved Alec's face closer to the severed wrist and he saw five little nubs protruding from the stump, the same sort as he'd seen when Yhakobin had cut the fingers off the first rhekaro he'd made. It was the beginning of a new hand.

If it was healing, then perhaps it wasn't dead, after all.

His relief was short-lived. Yhakobin handed his whip to one of the men. "Good night, Alec. Pleasant dreams."

The beating that followed involved not just the whip, but fists and boots as well. By the time it was over Alec was spitting blood and both eyes were swollen shut. They left him on the floor. The last thing he heard was the door locking after them.

As consciousness spun away, he comforted himself with the knowledge that his new pick was still hidden. Freedom was his when he chose to grasp it. Next time he wouldn't hesitate.

The Watchers Go forth

THE WEATHER TURNED rotten before Micum and Thero could set sail from Gedre. Lashing rain and high seas held their vessel in port for three days, then the wind was against them, forcing the captain to tack endlessly to make any progress at all. The Osiat was deeper than the Inner Sea, and the storms fiercer, especially heading north toward the Strait. But the ship was a sturdy, sleek little caravel, lateen-rigged and well ballasted, under the command of a Gedre named Solies.

It took nearly a week to reach Virésse. Thero used the tooth to keep track of their quarry; so far Notis was still in the harbor town. The Gedre khirnari had given them letters of introduction, but Micum seemed increasingly uneasy as they neared the port.

"Would it be fair to say that Seregil and Ulan í Sathil aren't exactly on cordial terms?" he mused as they sat in the galley, trying to keep their salt meat and turab from sliding off the table as the ship pitched and rolled.

"I've been thinking the same," Thero admitted. "And if Seregil were here, I think he'd be reminding us that he's never one to go in the front door when he has a chance to do otherwise."

Micum grinned. "Are you turning nightrunner on me, too?"

"I wouldn't go that far, but there's much to be said for caution."

"Can you magic us somehow, so we don't stick out in the crowd?"

"I could, but remember where we are going. My magic is more likely to call attention to us than it is to shield us. I think an attempt at stealth might be the better plan."

"Well then, I guess we'd better ask Captain Solies if he knows of any back doors."

As it happened, the captain did, and put in that evening at a secluded inlet a few miles west of Virésse harbor. Sailors swam their horses ashore for them, and Captain Solies went with Micum and Thero as they were rowed ashore, looking less than pleased with the plan.

"Keep those letters with you in case you're challenged," he warned. "I'll be left explaining our anchorage here if anyone comes asking."

"We'll be back in a few days," Thero promised. "And I'll do my best to send you word if it all goes wrong."

• • •

They spent the night under tall pines, wrapped in their blankets against the damp chill.

"I had my first taste of this with Alec, when the Plenimarans took us," Thero admitted, huddled near the little fire Micum had coaxed to life. "I must admit, I miss my tower rooms at times like this. Nysander and Magyana were better at this sort of thing."

"You've hardened up nicely, though." Micum lifted the little kettle of tea off the coals and poured Thero a cup, then took out his pipe for a smoke. Settling with his back to a tree trunk, he took a few puffs. "It's been a while for me, too. Feels damn good to be sleeping rough again."

The following morning found the forest thick with fog. Thero would have been hopelessly lost, but Micum, who seemed to have an infallible sense of direction, soon found a narrow cart track leading in the right direction.

Micum kept up the horses at good pace through the morning as the mist burned off under the rising sun. By the time they dismounted by a roadside spring to eat, Thero noticed that his limp was more pronounced.

"I think I can help you with that," Thero offered. "Nysander taught me a bit of healing, and I learned more from Mydri in Bôkthersa."

Micum sighed. "I can't say no to that, I suppose. What should I do?"

"Just sit on that rock there. I'll have to put my hands on you."

"Go on, then." Micum sat down and stuck out his bad leg.

Thero knelt beside him and carefully pressed a hand to the front and back of Micum's thigh. He'd never laid hands on a man before, and felt a little awkward, but Micum just watched with interest and showed no sign of discomfort.

Thero hadn't seen Micum's wound since it had healed, but he could easily trace the long, uneven ridges of scar tissue through the thin leather of Micum's breeches. They ran from behind his knee to just below his buttock. Closing his eyes, Thero whispered the healing charm Magyana had taught him to take away pain. The tense muscles under his hands relaxed a bit and he heard Micum's grateful sigh.

"That's a bit better."

"Wait a little." This time, Thero summoned the deeper healing Seregil's sister had taught him—one he'd used often to help Klia through the long, painful days of healing, when her remaining fingers threatened to curl permanently into withered claws. As the spell took hold, he could feel the rush of blood through muscle and the tension of tendon along bone. He imagined warm sunlight and sent the heat of it deep into the flesh.

"By the Light!" Micum murmured.

Thero held on until he felt the thick, hardened skin loosen under his fingers, then sat back and opened his eyes. "I can do more later. Do you think you can ride some more?"

Micum stood and tried the leg. "Hell, I think I can run! Now, is our friend Notis still there?"

Thero took the tooth from a pouch at his belt and pressed it between his palms. "Yes, and he's ashore, too. I think I can find him now that we're closer."

They reached the outskirts of Virésse that afternoon. The sprawling white city embraced a deep, broad port, and was protected at its back by mountains. Pausing on a hill overlooking the harbor, Micum sat on a stone fai'thast marker and counted well over a hundred ships of all sizes moored there, and not a few of them carrying the striped sails of Plenimar.

"It's no secret that the eastern clans trade with them," Thero observed. "Still, it's a bit daunting, seeing so many of them here."

"I see a good many Skalan vessels there, too. We should be able to pass unnoticed if we don't call attention to ourselves."

Thero took out the tooth again and cast the seeking spell and a wizard's eye at the same time. The result was a quick, dizzying mental flight to a tavern inn at the waterfront. The signboard in front bore no words, but showed a dragon wrestling with a sea serpent.

"That shouldn't be too hard to spot," said Micum, rubbing absently at his game leg. "Let's hope their food and ale are good. How's your Plenimaran, by the way?"

"I can make myself understood, though I'm sure to be known for a Skalan as soon as I open my mouth."

Micum nodded. "I've still got my northland accent. Better let me do most of the talking until we get our man cornered. It'll draw less attention."

CHAPTER 35

The Good Slave

ILAR'S VISITS WERE becoming more frequent, and more varied. There were still whippings now and then—sometimes when Seregil let his careful mask slip, sometimes at Ilar's own strange whim—but only at Ilar's own hands now, and those Seregil could easily bear.

Ilar came earlier in the day and stayed longer, too. Seregil played his role with increasing ease. As long as he kept Alec in his heart, he could feign obedience to Ilar with ease, pour wine for him without spitting in it when Ilar wasn't looking, and even manage to converse with the man, listening again and again to Ilar's version of the days they'd spent together. He learned of the man's family and, when Ilar had had more wine than usual, his regrets at the shame he'd brought on his kin and clan. Seregil even shared a little of his own past, when pressed, and took a certain degree of dark pleasure in recounting his exploits in Skala, for the pain and envy it kindled in Ilar's eyes.

As the days passed and they grew more accustomed to each other's company, Seregil sensed that, despite Ilar's cool façade, he was increasingly troubled. Seregil guessed it had something to do with the fact that there had been no more mention of Ilar's freedom. Intrigued, he bided his time and chose his moment carefully.

One evening, when Ilar seemed especially tense, Seregil poured the wine and brought it to him. Standing respectfully beside his chair, he reached out, and then pulled his hand back as if reconsidering the action.

"What is it?" Ilar demanded irritably.

"You seem out of sorts, Master." Ilar relished hearing that word from his lips, and Seregil used it as often as possible, playing the obedient slave.

"And what if I am?"

Seregil slipped his hand under Ilar's long hair to stroke the nape of his neck. "Yes, you're very tense. If I may, Master?"

Ilar glanced up warily. "Stay where I can see you."

Ilar was no fool, and still had a healthy distrust of Seregil, but it had also become obvious that he was starved for touch in this house. If approached carefully, Ilar was particularly susceptible to the slightest show of kindness. So Seregil chanced it now, kneading the back of Ilar's smooth neck with expert fingers.

The man was slow to relax. He sat stiffly, still drinking, one eye on Seregil.

"It would be easier if I stood behind the chair, Master," Seregil suggested, sliding his fingers down the neck of Ilar's robe to massage between his shoulder blades.

"Easier to what? Throttle me? I prefer you where you are."

"Then how about this?" Seregil boldly straddled Ilar's legs, settling on his knees to bring both hands into play. It brought their faces close together and Seregil kept his eyes lowered for a time, then looked up through his lashes. Even a eunuch could be seduced if you knew what he liked; Ilar liked to be touched.

"What is it you want?" Ilar muttered.

"To take that frown from my master's face."

"'Coy' doesn't suit you, Haba," Ilar sneered, but Seregil could already feel the tension easing from the muscles under his fingers.

"What *do* I want, then?" Seregil worked his fingers up and down the back of Ilar's neck. "My freedom, certainly. And Alec, of course."

Ilar chuckled at his honesty. "What else?"

"Something's wrong, isn't it? Master Yhakobin hasn't released you as he promised."

"He will."

"When?"

Ilar locked eyes with him. "What's that to you?"

"I am yours, Master. My fate lies with yours, hand in glove. I can't help being curious."

"Well, if you must know, your half-breed may not be bleeding the right sort of blood."

Seregil kept up his gentle work as he took this in. He couldn't ask about the rhekaro without tipping his hand. Fortunately, Ilar was in a talkative mood.

"Mmmmm, yes, Haba. Right there." He sighed

as Seregil began kneading the stiff muscles at the base of his skull. "Since you are so agreeable today, I'll answer your question. The master seeks to make a particular kind of creature, one that has great power. It can only be made with the blood of an Hâzadriëlfaie."

A monster made from 'faie blood, just like the dra'gorgos! "That's why he wanted Alec?"

"Yes. As soon as word came from Aurënen that one had appeared, Master Yhakobin was determined to be the one to capture him."

"Who sent word?"

"Spies, I suppose. It doesn't matter."

It does to me, Seregil thought darkly. Assuming that Ilar was telling the truth, this seemed to point to someone other than Phoria. Seregil was a little disappointed.

"Fortunately, I was able to assist him, since I knew that the young man's talimenios was you. So when word arrived that you were both returning to Aurënen—Well, you know the rest."

"Were you there?" Seregil kept his voice calm and his fingers working.

"Of course not! But I knew your name and face, and that was enough for the slavers. You certainly made no secret of your movements."

"Why didn't they come after us in Skala?"

"They don't raid that far north, do they?"

"I suppose not."

"And Rhíminee is not such an easy place for spies, since Mardus's failed attack on the city."

"I'm glad to hear it. So, Alec is well, Master?"

"You've seen him."

"And he doesn't suspect you being anything other than a fellow slave?"

"Apparently not."

Seregil very much hoped Ilar was wrong about that.

"Oh, by the way. It seems your blood is as useless as his. Master Yhakobin attempted to use that which he took from you that day. It doesn't transmute properly at all."

"Do give him my regrets, won't you?" Seregil said without thinking.

Strong hands clamped over his wrists, pinning them together in front of his face. "Are you missing the whip, Haba?"

"No, Master! Please, forgive me."

"Then watch that tongue of yours, or I'll cut it out. Now prove to me that you are sorry."

Seregil leaned in to kiss him, only to be shoved off Ilar's lap. With an inward sigh, he prostrated himself and kissed the toe of his slipper. Ilar pulled his foot away and used it to shove his face into the carpet. "Don't forget your place, Haba. And don't forget your bargain."

"I won't, Master." The thick pile of the carpet got into his mouth and he coughed.

Ilar gave him a last light kick in the head and swept out, slamming the door after him.

"Ingrate," Seregil muttered, wiping his mouth. In spite of the indignity, it had been a good evening's work. It didn't sound like Ilar would be leaving the house anytime soon.

CHAPTER 36

Nightrunning

RHANIA CAME TO Seregil's door again that night.

"Have you thought more about what we spoke of?" he asked, cheek pressed to the door.

"Yes. Do you really think it possible?"

"Get me out of this room and I'll prove it to you."

"And you would take me with you?"

"Yes."

"You give your word?"

"By the honor of Bôkthersa, I swear it. But we'll need a few things. Weapons, clothing, food. Can you put your hands on those?"

"Yes!"

"Don't do it all at once. Someone might notice. Just a bit at a time, and hide them somewhere you can get to quickly at night."

"I understand."

"Now, how are you going to get me out of this room?"

There was a long silence. "Let me think on that. I will find a way."

Once again, he heard no sound of her leaving. That might be a good sign. She was brave and quiet, and must have a steady nerve to come to him like this. He might actually be able to keep his promise to her.

Rhania stole to his door almost every night, whispering to him about what supplies she'd been able to cache, and telling him of any glimpse she'd had of Alec. It seemed he was still being kept in the outbuilding and was sometimes allowed to walk in the garden with Ilar. As far as she could tell, they'd become friends.

That news was like a knife in Seregil's gut.

Ilar visited Seregil every day, and his visits grew longer. It was clear he delighted in having Seregil under his sway and making him do all sorts of menial tasks.

Seregil played the perfect body servant, letting Ilar believe that he was becoming resigned to his fate. Day by day Ilar grew a little more at ease with him, a bit more open.

Today, after some subtle prompting while massaging Ilar's feet, Seregil had gotten him to talk about some of his former masters and what he'd suffered at their hands. As Seregil listened, he found himself caught between pity and disgust. His expression must have betrayed him, though; Ilar had suddenly kicked him away and stormed out without a word.

Seregil sat up and staunched his bloody nose with the bottom of his robe. For once, he didn't hold it against Ilar, when his own collection of wounds had been gotten as a free man, doing his chosen work. Not that it made him hate Ilar any less, of course.

That would be weakness.

Lying in bed that night, though, he spent a long time trying to chase away the images Ilar had summoned in his mind. But they followed him into his dreams, and he was glad to be woken sometime later by the familiar sound of soft, persistent scratching on his door.

He walked over and pressed his ear to the wood. "Yes?" He was always careful not to use her name, or sound as if he were expecting anyone, in case it did turn out to be someone less friendly.

Tonight his answer was the sound of a key in the lock. A cloaked figure slipped inside, armed with a large carving knife. Seregil jumped back quickly, braced for an attack. Rhania pushed back her hood and removed her veil.

She wasn't young but was quite beautiful under the tracery of Khatme clan markings. Seregil read them quickly: she was a person of middle standing, without magic. There were large holes in her ears where the clan jewelry had been stripped from her. One earlobe had been torn and healed badly.

"Here, take these!" She reached under her cloak and handed him a wadded tunic. Inside he found a belt, some ragged trousers, his worn old poniard, and Alec's boot dagger with the black-and-silver handle.

"Where did you get these?"

"Ilban Yhakobin had them displayed in the library downstairs, as trophies. The slavers include belongings in the price of the sale."

"That's all there was? No swords, or a bow?"

"There was nothing else."

"Damn." Seregil's uncle had made his sword for him. Alec's—together with the Black Radly bow—had been gifts from Seregil. "I wasn't expecting you to act so soon. Has something happened?"

"The master visited my bed tonight." Rhania raised her chin proudly, daring him to judge her as she held up a large key. "I took it while he slept and came here at once. We must leave before he knows it's missing. He's sure to know I took it."

"Bravely done."

"Come on, then. Kill Khenir with your knife and flee with me!"

But Seregil wasn't ready to let go of all caution just yet; somehow, it felt too easy. "It's a good tale, my lady, and believe me, nothing would please me more. But why should I trust you any more than I do him? How do I know it's not Khenir putting you up to all this, just to get me in trouble?" That would probably suit Ilar very well, watching him lose a foot on the block.

She fell to her knees and clasped her hands. "I give you my pledge: 'Though you thrust your dagger at my eyes, I will not flinch!'"

"Are you sure?" asked Seregil, grasping the tip of the knife she was still holding and moving it away from his crotch. The oath was more than mere poetry among the 'faie. He drew the poniard and leveled it at her face. Even when he made a quick feint at her left eye, she remained absolutely steady, her gaze locked with his.

"Please. Don't doubt me now," she whispered.

He pulled her to her feet. "Will you show me to where my friend is being held?"

"Yes, but it's dangerous."

He grinned as he changed his slave robe for the clothing she'd brought him. "At this point, what isn't? I'm not going without him."

"I know. But we must go quickly!" She pulled back her cloak to show him a satchel she had over one shoulder. "See? I have food, water, a flint, and the rest you asked for."

She took him by the hand and led him down a narrow stair and through several turns of a narrow passageway. He smelled dust and mice—a back passage, one that let servants move through the house without offending the eyes of the master and his household.

They came out in a shadowy room full of bulky furnishings. At the far end a set of double doors stood open. Seregil stole up to the edge of the doorway. It was a crisp, overcast night, with no moonlight to betray them. Intentionally or not, the Khatme had chosen her moment well.

Peering cautiously outside, he froze as he made out a line of figures outside. As his eyes adjusted to the light, however, he realized that they were only statues, lined up along the sides of a long fountain pool.

I've been here! He recognized the black-and-white mosaic paving. It was all he did remember, having been drugged to the gills the only other time he'd been here.

Overhead, there was a second-floor gallery, with doorways and lots of darkened windows.

"There, the watchman," Rhania whispered, pointing out a dark figure slumped on a stool near an archway to their left. An overturned cup lay at his feet.

"Drunk?" asked Seregil.

"Dead, I hope. He helped himself to me once too often, so I gifted him with a bit of one of the master's special elixirs in his wine tonight."

"You were planning this long before I ever showed up."

"Yes. Aura sent you, and I am ready."

"Take what the Lightbearer sends and be thankful, eh?" Seregil shook his head, wondering how a woman like her had ended up a slave in the first place.

Rhania pointed to an arched gateway at the far end of the courtyard. "Through there. Your friend is in Ilban's workshop."

"Good. Stay close to me."

Keeping to the shadows under the gallery, he started for the gate.

Suddenly someone on the gallery overhead shouted, "There they are."

Rhania cowered back against the wall as the sound of running feet came from all directions. "That's Ilban!"

"There!" a woman screamed, and Seregil prayed it wasn't Zoriel.

"No!" Rhania gasped, looking around wildly. "No, I can't . . . I won't!"

Before Seregil could stop her, she clasped the carving knife in both hands and drove it deep into her breast. She fell without a cry.

"Shit, shit, *shit*!" Seregil bolted across the court-yard, dodged between two startled guards coming the other way, and dashed into the garden beyond. The workshop Rhania told him about was right there in front of him, but it might as well have been on the moon for all the good it did him right now.

A pursuer caught him by the shoulder. Seregil paused just long enough to plunge his poniard through that man's throat and into the chest of the one who'd come with him, then ran across to a large, ornate fountain on what appeared to be an outer wall. Using the carvings for purchase, he scrambled up. At the top, somehow still clutching the bloody poniard, he looked over and saw a shad-owed fold of ground below. Ditch or gorge, it was impossible to tell.

He kept low and ran along the top of the wall, trying to find a better place, but the declivity fol-lowed this side of the house.

If he did jump and didn't break his neck, he still might not be able to get back inside easily for Alec. And just where exactly was he going to go if he did run—branded, dressed in stolen, ill-fitting clothes, with blood on his hands, and no knowledge of the countryside?

He followed the top of the wall past the workshop and around the smaller garden with the covered walkway and the fish pool. He caught sight of movement below just in time to flatten himself into the angle between the wall and the tiled walkway roof.

"What are you doing in here?" a man demanded.

"The master said to search everywhere," another replied.

"Don't be a fool. You can see where he went over the wall. There are bloody handprints all over the fountain. Get the dogs and search the gully first. He's likely lying there with a broken leg, the damn fool."

"That'll be the least of his worries once the master has him again."

The voices faded away. Thunder rolled in the distance, and a few drops of cold rain pattered down, spattering on the tiles and soaking through the back of Seregil's thin tunic. A moment later the skies opened and rain came down in sheets.

Seregil mouthed a silent prayer of thanks. The rain would cover the fact that there were no tracks beyond the wall. He cautiously raised his head and looked around. Directly across from where he lay was the wing of the house where he'd been held in the upstairs room. Several small wooden grilles were visible just below the eaves, and most likely let into an attic. In his experience, attics of large houses could be very useful places.

He carefully crawled along the walkway roof, but the rain was so heavy now that he could barely see the fountain and guessed he was equally hidden.

It was hard work, clambering over the uneven tiles, and his palms and knees were sore by the time he finally reached the first wooden grille. It was old and a little rotten. Using the dagger, he easily pried it from its frame and wriggled in.

It was dusty and cold inside, and pitch-black at first. He crouched where he'd landed, letting his eyes adjust. A flash of lightning gave him a glimpse of jumbled trunks and broken bits of furniture. Seregil resisted the urge to explore just yet and leave telltale wet footprints in the dust.

His caution was well warranted. Servants soon appeared with lanterns and proceeded to search every corner of the rambling space. Seregil was kept busy skulking from one shadowy hiding spot to another. He eventually managed to get behind them in an already searched area and hunkered down under a large pile of moth-eaten bedclothes, clutching the bloody poniard.

It wasn't the best hiding spot: the musty comforters were alive with beetles and mice, and he nearly ruptured his eardrums stifling several violent sneezes.

The lights finally disappeared and the attic went silent again. He stayed where he was, breathing though his mouth, for some time, but no one came back to catch him out. The storm still raged outside, with thunder treading on the lightning's heels.

With any luck, Yhakobin would give up the search for tonight, and find the trail cold tomorrow.

Safe for the moment, Seregil arranged himself more comfortably in his dusty, itchy hiding place to rest while he could.

"Take care, talí," he murmured softly. "I'm coming for you soon."

Closing In

THE MILKY LIGHT of early dawn was slanting
through the broken slats when Seregil cautiously
emerged from his hiding place. He braced for some
lurking guard to jump him, as they had last night,
but it seemed he was alone with the mice for
now. He brushed himself off, slapped a spider off
his neck, and looked around. His pursuers had
done him a favor. There were fresh footprints all
over the dusty floor. No one was likely to notice a
few more.

The attic ran all around the top of the house,
mirroring its shape, and he soon found a small window overlooking the alchemist's shop and garden.
There was no sign of anyone there at the moment.
He hoped that they hadn't moved Alec back into
the cellar. If he went back the way he'd come, he
should be able to climb down onto the roof of the
covered walkway around the garden and from there
break into the shop.

"You did me a good turn, Rhania, giving me these knives back," he whispered, clasping the poniard's stained grip. "May your soul continue on in peace."

Having satisfied himself to his position and plan for the night, he turned his attention to the contents of the attic and soon found enough old clothing to outfit a regiment, some cracked leather boots that fit, and, most useful of all, an old wicker basket containing a lady's sewing kit. There were a few ivory needles, some rusty shears that, with the application of a little spit, could still cut, and even some serviceable thread.

He chose the two best-looking coats and breeches and tried them on. They were all too large, so he sat down under one of the grates to alter them.

The morning passed quickly, and he was glad to be busy; it took his mind off his empty belly and parched mouth. He held one of the ivory needles in the corner of his mouth and sucked on that while he worked, trying to get a little spit flowing.

By early afternoon the rain had stopped and he'd altered two coats and bundled them into a pair of moth-eaten cloaks. Bored now, he went back to searching, and soon found a place over the main part of the house where he could hear voices. Stretching out on his belly, he pressed an ear to the floor. It sounded like servants' chatter, and from what he could make out, the household was still in an uproar. Grinning, he softly moved on, looking for anything else that could be useful.

The alchemist had no weapons or coin lying

about up here, but Seregil did find something nearly as valuable in a locked casket. With the help of the shears he pried the hasp up and spilled out a small pile of jewelry. Most of it was small items of worked silver, set with inferior stones—a child's collection, perhaps, but there were a few gold lockets and a set of ivory and gold combs set with a nice bit of blue chalcedony.

Valuable, and portable. My favorite combination. He added them to his stock of useful items.

Further on, he ran across a box of rusty tools, and among them was a lathing hatchet with a cracked haft. It had a flared blade on one side and a hammerhead on the other.

"You'll do quite nicely in a pinch," he murmured happily, testing its weight. It could cave a man's skull with either side. He also found a worn whetstone, and carried both back to the window and set about sharpening the hatchet blade. He didn't have much spit left by now, but it was enough to grind an edge of sorts. He was looking around for something to bind up the haft when the sound of a commotion burst out in the direction of the workshop. Someone was crying out, and one side of his mouth curved up in a lopsided grin, for he was quite certain he recognized that voice.

Alec awoke to the sound of shouting upstairs in the shop. He went to the door and pressed his ear to it. It did little good; what he could make out was in Plenimaran. But there was no doubt that Master Yhakobin was furious with someone. A moment later he heard the sound of a blow and a cry, then a babble of craven apology.

That was Khenir's voice.

The tirade ended with the sound of someone being dragged down past his door to the cellar, and the slam of the heavy door there and the tramp of ascending boots.

Things went quiet for a long time after that, but he was sure he could hear the sound of ragged weeping now and again, floating up from below. Time dragged on. His belly told him it was long past time for breakfast, but still no one came. What could Khenir, the master's favorite, have done to warrant this sort of treatment?

At last Ahmol appeared with some soup and bread.

"What's going on?" Alec asked, not really expecting to be understood.

"Slave run," the man replied sullenly.

"Khenir tried to escape?"

But Ahmol shook his head. " 'Faie slave."

"Rhania?"

Ahmol snorted at that, then sneered with evident enthusiasm, "*Khenir* slave."

Alec wondered if he'd understood the man's broken answers correctly. Hadn't he just said it wasn't Khenir who'd escaped? And if this escaped 'faie wasn't Khenir or Rhania . . . "Is the slave who ran a man?"

Ahmol gave him a grudging nod and went out. Hadn't Khenir told him that there were no other 'faie slaves in the house?

He sat staring at the door, heart beating loud in

his ears. There was no reason to think it *was* Seregil, but he couldn't quash the sudden rush of hope that it might be. Perhaps the alchemist had purchased both of them that night. Maybe Seregil had even been in the same slave barn, and Alec hadn't seen him. *To have been that close!*

And if it *was* Seregil, and if he *had* gotten out, then he was out there somewhere, looking for a way to get Alec out, too.

But only if he knows I'm here.

He decided not to think about that right now. No matter what, it was time to get out. He reached under the bed and felt for his pick. It was still there.

Alec paced and fretted, wishing he had a window to tell the time by. He slept and woke and paced some more, empty belly reminding him that no one had appeared with a meal for too long. He was still at it when the door swung open and two of Yhakobin's warders stormed in and dragged him upstairs to the workshop garden. It was late afternoon, or at least he thought so. Black clouds hid the sun, heavy with the promise of rain.

A dozen or more household servants were there, along with a great number of armed men. Alec recognized several as those who had dragged him back and forth from his cellar prison. They all stood around a stout post that had been set into the ground. Beside it, on a litter, lay the nursemaid, Rhania. A cloth had been bound across her eyes and another under her jaw; she was dead. Flies buzzed around the blood staining the front of her rain-soaked gown.

If it was Seregil who'd escaped, why would he kill another 'faie?

Yhakobin stood by the post, holding his crop in one hand. Alec began to tremble, wondering what in Bilairy's name he'd done to deserve this?

But it soon became apparent that this wasn't about him. More men emerged from the workshop, dragging Khenir between them. The fine golden collar was gone, replaced by one of cruder iron. Alec was shocked at his appearance. The normally reserved man was screaming and struggling, hair wild about his face as if he'd been tearing at it. And he was naked.

Worse, the scars of Khenir's gelding and terrible whippings were revealed for all to see.

Alec watched, grief-stricken, as the struggling man was dragged to the post and chained by his collar to it.

"Ilban?" Alec gasped faintly.

"Watch well, Alec." Yhakobin flexed the crop between his hands. "This wretch Khenir, whom I loved and trusted above all others, has brought shame on my house, and death. He begged a slave of me and promised to tame him, then allowed him to escape and kill poor Rhania." He looked down at the dead woman and shook his head. "Such a waste!"

Khenir had a slave? One who needed taming? Is that what Ahmol had been trying to say? But how could a slave own another slave?

Yhakobin brought the crop down on the cowering

man's bare shoulders and back. "You are cast out of my household!"

The alchemist continued to vent his rage on the huddled, screaming man. Watching helplessly, Alec forgot all his suspicions and questions for the moment; Khenir had befriended him, comforted him. And Alec couldn't save him.

Yhakobin whipped Khenir until he was out of breath, then threw the crop aside. "I should have you skinned alive for this, but in light of your past good services, I am sparing your life. You'll be flogged, and tomorrow you'll be taken to the markets and sold, with your sins known."

"Please, Ilban, no! Kill me if you will, merciful Ilban, but not the markets, I beg you!" Khenir wailed.

When Yhakobin turned his face away, Khenir grew more frantic. "The door was locked! I know it was locked! It had to be locked. The key. I have it. Please, Ilban, let me show you!"

"Silence! He was your responsibility and you failed. You know the laws, Khenir. Your shame falls on me."

Men tied Khenir's hands and hung him from a large peg set high on the post. Another unlimbered a short, thick drayman's whip and took his place.

"Thirty lashes," Yhakobin ordered. "Don't cripple him. I want him fit for the block."

Alec closed his eyes, but there was no escaping the screams that followed.

Seregil lay with his face pressed to the wooden screen, and was surprised at how little pleasure he took in the sight of Ilar being brought low. How many times had Ilar endured the whip, he wondered, thinking of all the scars on the man's body. And who knew what sort of person would buy such damaged goods?

He was so beautiful once...

No! This is my doing, my revenge. I should be glad! But his heart wasn't in it.

When the whipping was over, and Ilar had subsided to ragged moans, someone came forward and threw handfuls of something onto his back. Judging by the renewed screams, Seregil guessed it was salt. Alec was still being held at the front of the crowd, and even in this light, Seregil could see his lover's anguish.

The master gave another order and Ilar was cut down, still chained by his collar to the post. They left him there, broken and alone.

Something tickled Seregil's cheek and he brushed at it, expecting to feel another spider, but it wasn't.

He wiped his face angrily. *Why should I waste any tears on that bastard?*

But he couldn't seem to look away from the broken wreck of his enemy, or block out the pathetic sobbing.

CHAPTER 38

Lovers and Lying Bastards

ALEC SAT ON his bed, watching the candle burn down, glad to be shut down here, away from masters and whips and the sight of Khenir hanging on that post. He couldn't get the man's cries out of his head, or the sight of his scars. But mixed with that was the memory of that day in the garden, and Khenir's faltering attempts to woo him. Or seduce him. Had Seregil been in one of those upper rooms? Was he the shadowy figure at the window Alec sometimes caught sight of?

Oh, talí, what did you think?

Khenir lied to me.

"Alec, I was half-dead when Ilban brought me to this house . . . I pledged my life to him. I've kept that pledge . . ." He'd been telling Alec the truth then.

And he'd admitted to taking the first pick Alec had made.

But he didn't tell Yhakobin about that. It could

*have been me on that post, and Khenir certainly
would have been rewarded if he'd told.*

He didn't know what to believe at this point,
only what he wanted to be true.

He rested his face in his hands, trying to calm
his racing thoughts and pounding heart.

Breathe, Alec. Just focus on your breath, Seregil
whispered to him from long ago.

In.

Out.

Slow.

Deep.

He continued like that for a long time, until
grief, doubt, confusion—all of it—receded, leaving
in their place that same calm silence he felt right
before he released his bowstring and let an arrow
fly.

He reached under the bed, reassuring himself
again that the bronze pin was still there, and settled
back to watch the candle's progress.

By midnight, the house below had fallen silent.
Seregil felt around in the dark, making sure he had
everything he needed. The clothes he'd altered fit
well enough and despite the musty odor that clung
to them, he felt more himself than he had in weeks,
free at last of his slave's garb. He had a suit of
clothes ready for Alec, too, rolled tightly around a
pair of boots he hoped would fit.

The poniard, dagger, and lathing hatchet were
tucked securely into the belt Rhania had given him.
The bits of jewelry, his boots, and Alec's clothing

were tied in the cloak and slung over one shoulder, and with them the severed braid of his long hair. He regretted having to cut it, but that, as much as his face, would have been a flag to any slave takers. What remained hung in ragged hanks around his face. Between that, his patched-up, faded, ill-fitting clothing, and a day's worth of dust on his face and hands, he cut a rather fine figure as a beggar. He tied a stained kerchief around his neck and went to the window to see if the coast was still clear.

He'd seen two sentries so far, and they came and went. No doubt the alchemist had the rest still scouring the countryside for him.

The night was overcast but the clouds were broken and fast-moving, letting enough starlight through to make out Ilar, still huddled beside the post. If there were guards posted to watch him, Seregil couldn't see them from this angle.

Slow and careful, now. He climbed out onto the walkway roof and set the grille back in place. His bare feet made barely a whisper as he retraced his steps around the small courtyard to the edge of the workshop garden.

From here he could see the pair of sentries at the arched entrance leading back to the house. Leaving his bundle on the roof, he crept along the wall to a dark corner furthest from Ilar and the guards, dropped silently into an herb bed, and drew Alec's dagger and his poniard. He had one chance at this, and he meant to make it count.

The two men were standing together just inside the entrance to the garden. One was smoking a pipe and the sweet smell of the tobacco permeated the night air. Keeping close to the wall, Seregil silently closed in on them, glad their attention was focused on conversation rather than paying attention to their work. As he got closer, he saw with a certain degree of satisfaction that these were the men who'd beaten him so badly.

Perhaps Yhakobin had his best men out on the hunt. These two went down without a sound. He cut one throat, then the other before either of them realized what danger they were in, then stabbed each one through the heart. The death rattles were hardly over before he'd stripped them both of their sword belts and buckled one on. When he was done he arranged the bodies slumped against the wall, as if they'd fallen asleep on duty. With a last glance into the central courtyard of the house, he retrieved his bundle from the roof and ghosted across to the workshop door.

"Seregil..." Ilar rose unsteadily to his knees and held out both hands to him, whispering, "Seregil, please... help me."

Seregil walked back to him, sword in hand. "Help *you?*" he whispered in disbelief.

"Kill me, then! I can't face the markets again." He broke off with a strangled little sob. "Please, Haba, take your revenge, I beg you!"

Why am I hesitating? Seregil wondered. *Isn't this what I've dreamed of, all these years?*

But this wasn't how he'd imagined it, with his prey already bound and humbled by another's hand. *Just be done with it. It's a kindness if nothing else...*

As he raised the blade, a hand closed over his wrist.

Badly startled, Seregil whirled around, ready to strike.

But it was Alec. The younger man was dressed in an ill-fitting robe and armed with a kitchen knife. Seregil slapped the blade aside and grabbed him in a desperate kiss, knowing they could both be dead before the night was out. Alec's fingers dug into his back as the younger man clung to him.

It took an act of will to pull away, but Alec's lips tasted of metal and Seregil quickly checked him for blood. "Are you hurt? How did you get out?"

Alec took what looked like a hairpin out of his mouth. "I used this. I heard a 'faie had escaped and hoped it was you," he whispered back. "Why were you going to kill Khenir?"

This was no time for proper introductions. "He asked me to. You heard what Yhakobin said."

"I know. That's why we've got to take him with us."

"I can help you," Ilar quavered. "I know a way out of this house. Under the workshop."

"And you never used it?" Seregil muttered, skeptical.

"I didn't dare. Not alone. I—I took care of Alec. I protected him!"

"He did," said Alec. "I can't just leave him."

"He's in no condition..." Seregil began, then gave up. It would be quicker and safer to get them all inside, then see if Ilar was lying.

That was what Seregil told himself, anyway.

Alec kissed him again and thrust the makeshift

pick into his hand. "Meet you in there. I have to get something." He disappeared into the workshop as silently as he'd come.

Seregil rounded on Ilar again. "And I'm supposed to trust you? So you can get back into your Ilban's good favor by betraying us?"

"He can't go back on his word. It's the law," Ilar whispered, clutching Seregil's knees. "And the men who will buy me . . . Oh Aura! If you won't take me, then kill me!"

This was the moment. He could kill Ilar or leave him to his fate in the markets.

Only he couldn't do it.

"Shut up and hold still!" The lock was simple and the hasp gave quickly.

"Thank you, Haba!" Ilar gasped as the chain fell away.

Seregil yanked him to his feet by his collar. "Call me that again and *nothing* will save you," he hissed, their faces almost touching. Satisfied with the fear in Ilar's eyes, he pulled him by the collar into the workshop.

Inside, the large athanor was burning and threw just enough light for him to see that Alec wasn't alone, either. He held a young child by the hand—a thin, pale little thing, in a ragged, oversized robe and head scarf.

"Bilairy's Balls, Alec! Are you going to take the whole damn household?"

"Trust me. I'll explain later."

That makes two of us, talí.

Seregil gave Alec the pick, his dagger, and the other sword, then unrolled his bundle and handed him the clothing he'd prepared for him in the attic. Alec pulled his robe off, and Seregil satisfied himself that, apart from some bruises, he wasn't injured. Between the two of them, Alec appeared to have been handled more gently, except for those times in the cellar. He pulled on the new clothing quickly, slipped his dagger into the top of one stolen boot, and looped his sword belt over his shoulder.

While Alec changed, Seregil started to help Ilar roughly into Alec's discarded robe, but stopped at the sound of the man's strangled whimper. The stripes on his back weren't deep, but they were bloody, and still crusted with salt. Every movement must be agony.

A water bucket stood by the athanor and Seregil used it to rinse away what he could from the wounds. Ilar trembled but stayed silent.

Seregil pulled the loose robe over the man's head, keeping the fabric from pulling at the wounds as best he could, and handed him the worn pair of shoes Alec had discarded. "Now, where's this escape route?"

Ilar went to one of the smaller anvils near the forge. "Here. Underneath."

Seregil grabbed it by the horn and heel, and strained to lift it. It tilted slightly, and a crack of darkness appeared under the section of floor it was bolted to. Alec joined him, pushing from the other side and together they tilted the trapdoor back until the edge of the anvil was resting on the floor. The underside was sheathed crossways with wooden planks, with a large iron ring in the middle. A small, timber-braced shaft led straight down into darkness. A wooden ladder was bolted to one side.

"I overheard Ilban telling the children about it," Ilar explained. "It goes down to a tunnel leading away from the house, in case of invaders."

Seregil turned to look for something useful to take, but Alec held up a bundle of his own. "We're ready."

Alec had also fashioned a cloth sling like the ones northland farmwomen used to carry their small children on their backs as they worked the fields. He hoisted the child into it and showed Seregil how it left both his hands free. The boy clutched the back of his coat, skinny bare legs dangling against Alec's hips.

Seregil sighed. Sling or no sling, sooner or later the little one would be a hindrance. But at least he was quiet; he hadn't made a sound.

Seregil pushed Ilar toward the trapdoor. "You first."

The man gave him a shaky nod, then grasped the top of the ladder and slowly began the climb down, pain clear in every move. Little spots of fresh blood had already soaked through the back of his robe.

Alec went next, moving as if the child weighed nothing at all. The child didn't so much as whimper as Alec started down.

When the others were out of sight, Seregil slung his own sword belt over his shoulder, tucked the neck of his bundle through his belt, and set his feet on the ladder. It took both hands and all his weight to pull the heavy door down, and then he narrowly missed being brained as it fell heavily back into place. He ended up hanging by one hand from the iron ring in total darkness. He found the ladder with his foot and quickly made his way down by feel.

The shaft was very deep. He had splinters in both hands by the time he saw a faint light below.

Ilar stood at the bottom with the others, holding up a candle. The space here was not much bigger than the shaft itself, but just behind him was a sturdy-looking oak door.

"It's locked," Alec told him, yanking at the iron handle above a keyhole.

"Give me your pick."

"I tried it. It won't budge."

Seregil held out his hand and Alec shrugged and gave him the metal pin.

Kneeling, Seregil probed the wards inside. "Tricky."

"You cut your hair," Alec noted, running his fingers through the uneven fringe at the nape of Seregil's neck.

Seregil's skin tingled at the touch but he kept his mind on the business at hand. "Assuming I get this open, where does it lead?"

"I don't know," Ilar replied.

"Bastard!" Seregil growled, still grinding away. "Why am I even listening to you?"

"Because I'm the only bastard you have?" Ilar replied with just a hint of his old smugness.

Seregil's fingers clenched on the pick. "Hold the light over this way."

"Well, it must lead away from the house," Ilar

offered weakly as Seregil went back to work on the lock. "Alec, I think you should leave that behind. Master Yhakobin will stop at nothing to get it back."

"Shut up!"

Seregil looked sharply over his shoulder. "Stop at nothing to get *what* back?"

Just then the muffled sounds of footsteps and shouting echoed down the shaft from the workshop. Seregil gave the lock a last careful tweak and the door swung inward on what looked like the promised passageway.

Seregil stood back and made Ilar a mocking bow. "After you."

Alec gave them both a confused look as he followed with his candle.

When the others were safely through Seregil fastened the door again and turned to follow Alec. As he did, the light fell across the child's upper face, and his slanted, silver eyes.

Seregil caught Alec by the elbow. "This is what Yhakobin wants, isn't it? What the hell is it?"

"A rhekaro," Alec answered quietly, pulling his arm free.

The pick slipped from Seregil's fingers. "This is what I saw in that cellar, under the dirt?"

"No, that was the first one Ilban made," Ilar replied.

"You were there?" asked Alec, turning to face Seregil full on.

"Yes." *Because Ilar wanted me to see you like that, damn it!* "Why are you dragging it along?"

"Yhakobin tortured the first one he made to

death," Alec told him, clutching the straps of the sling. "If I leave him, he'll die!"

"Let it."

The shouting above was getting louder.

"He comes, or I stay," Alec said flatly. "I'll explain later. We need to go!"

Seregil snatched up the fallen pick. "Come on then, before someone figures out which way we went."

Alec slipped past him to follow Ilar. "Thank you, talí."

Don't thank me yet, Seregil thought darkly, sword in one hand, the poniard in the other.

The passageway was shored with timber and brick-paved. Nothing moved around them but their shadows, and there was no sound but the whisper of shoe leather against the bricks and Ilar's labored breathing.

Seregil had ample time to study the rhekaro as they went, or at least the back of it. Its thin legs looked bone white in the candle's wavering glow. A lock of hair had escaped from the scarf; it hung below the thing's waist and shimmered like silver.

What in Bilairy's name are you? he wondered, thinking of the writhing pile of dirt, stained with Alec's blood. No good could come of that! Why was Alec so adamant on having it?

Because it looks like a child, of course. And Alec had seen one tortured to death. No wonder he'd refused to abandon this one. *Trust me,* he'd said. And Alec had never given him reason not to. Ilar was a different matter, and Seregil kept a close eye on him.

The way ran more or less level for some time, and then began to slant up sharply. Seregil guessed they'd gone nearly a mile by the time the passage ended at a door similar to the one they'd left behind. The lock was the same and Seregil soon tickled it open.

"Put out your light."

When it was dark, he softly opened the door a crack and peered through. It was just as dark beyond, but a slight breeze carried the smell of horses.

A shaft like the one in the workshop led up to a trap door. Seregil pushed it up just enough to see. It was heavy, and the smell was much stronger now.

They were in a large stable. A flyspecked lantern on a nail illuminated the glossy haunches of several horses in stalls. Shit apples and straw covered the floor and the trapdoor. Bits of muck fell down the shaft, eliciting mutters of protest from below.

He lifted the trapdoor up a little further, braced for an outcry, but heard nothing but the night sounds of the horses.

"Stay down," he whispered to the others, then pushed the trap all the way back and climbed up.

The stable spoke of money and title, and the horses were good ones. Treading softly, he discovered a young ostler asleep with a jug in a stall near the door. Seregil could smell the wine on him from two yards off.

He crept back to the shaft and motioned the

others up. Ilar came first, then Alec, straining a little now under the slight weight of the rhekaro.

Seregil pointed to the drunken ostler, and then motioned for them to follow him out. He kept a close eye on the drunkard, poniard at the ready, but the man never stirred.

Outside they found a well-kept farmyard and corral, and a slope-roofed little cottage with darkened windows. A larger house stood on a nearby rise—a hunting lodge, perhaps, and also dark. This Yhakobin fellow was well prepared for a hasty departure should he ever need to make one.

Wary of watchdogs, Seregil led the way across a small onion patch and an herb garden, and into the shadow of a small orchard just beyond. A few apples still hung from the branches. They paused here and picked a few, letting the juice soothe their dry throats.

Ilar plucked nervously at his slave collar as he ate, as if the weight of it pressed on him more now that they were fugitives. Alec unwrapped the rhekaro from its sling and set it on its feet. It hunkered down beside him, completely still.

Seregil wanted more than anything to grab Alec, check him for damage, and never let go. After all the weeks of uncertainty and abuse, he ached to hold him and be held. If Ilar and the rhekaro hadn't been there, he probably would have, and damn the danger.

It hurt a little that Alec seemed more engrossed in caring for the unnatural creature. Seregil watched jealously as he bit off a small piece of apple and offered it to the rhekaro. The creature just stared at it, as if it had never seen food before.

As Seregil watched, Alec took out his knife and nicked the end of his own finger, then held it out. The creature grasped it eagerly and sucked it like a teat.

Seregil grimaced. "It eats blood?"

"His name is Sebrahn."

"Oh lovely. You've named it."

"That's right. And it's my blood he eats. Just mine. That's why I couldn't leave him. He'd starve. It's all right, though. He never needs very much. See? He's done."

The rhekaro sat back and licked a last dark smear from its colorless lips. Its tongue looked grey in this light.

"Bilairy's Balls." Seregil leaned over and pulled off the rhekaro's head scarf. Silvery white hair tumbled down its back, so long it brushed the ground behind it. "More hair to cut."

"I'm not sure it will do any good."

"Oh?"

"Things—grow back."

The child-like thing was watching Seregil now, its eyes white and blank as a corpse's in the starlight. Seregil's every instinct warned him to get Alec as far away from it as possible.

"Why didn't you kill the ostler so we could steal the horses?" Ilar whispered, eyeing them both as if they'd gone mad.

"If I wanted to leave no doubt of where we'd been, that's exactly what I'd do," Seregil snapped, taking it out on him. "Next you'll be leading us back to the seaport to find a ship. And eat that apple core or bury it. They'll have trackers on us soon enough."

"Where are we going, then?"

"Let me worry about that."

"You still don't trust me? I helped you!"

Seregil bit back an angry retort. If it had been just the two of them, he could have just stuck a knife in the man and been done with him. Ilar had served his purpose, after all. He was nothing but useless baggage now. Still, hiding the body would be a bother, not to mention the time it would take to calm Alec down.

"We've got to get as far as we can tonight and find a good place to lie up. And get these off." He tugged irritably at the iron collar around his neck. "Is there any magic in them?"

"Not that I know of," Ilar replied. "But you won't find a smith who'll do the job."

"I'm pretty handy with a chisel. We just need to find the tools. And what about these?" He pulled his sleeve back, uncovering the brand. "I suppose we could cut them off. Or burn them over."

"That's the first thing a slave taker looks for. When a slave is freed, that mark is branded over with another, larger one, to prove he's free."

"What sort of mark?" asked Alec.

"The crest of his master."

Seregil ran a hand back through his ragged hair. "No easy solution there, then, unless we can find one to steal. Stay here, both of you."

Leaving Alec to keep Ilar under control, Seregil

made his way back the way they'd come. After some searching, he found the tools he needed in a lean-to next to the cottage. If there were dogs here, they certainly weren't worth much as guards.

He returned to find the rhekaro curled up beside Alec with its head in his lap. It wasn't sleeping, though. Its eyes followed Seregil as he approached, shining like a cat's.

"These will have to do," he said, holding up the small mallet and a cold chisel. He waved the mallet at Ilar. "You first." If he was going to make any serious mistakes, it wasn't going to be on Alec's neck.

Seregil found a suitably large rock and had Ilar lay his head on it, bracing the loose part of the collar against the crude anvil.

"Hold still," he warned as he set the chisel point against the riveted seam in the metal.

The hammerblows were dangerously loud, but he struck well and severed the joint in three tries without doing any significant harm to Ilar. It took him and Alec together to wrench it open enough for Ilar to slip out of it. There was a ring of pale, shiny flesh around his neck where the golden collar had rubbed for so long, and a wider band of reddened skin from the new one.

Seregil had a fleeting urge to smooth his fingers over it.

Ilar raised a hand to his throat. "It feels so strange, not having it there. Thank you."

"It had to be done," Seregil replied gruffly. "You next, Alec."

When that was done, he handed Alec the tools

and held his breath as Alec struck off the hated metal band. When it was off he rubbed gratefully at his own neck. "That's better!"

Ilar was still doing the same, but now he looked more frightened than grateful.

"What's the matter? Do you miss it already?"

Ilar was trembling. "If we're caught without these . . ."

"If we're caught, that will be the least of our worries."

He left Alec to bury the broken collars and took the tools back where he'd found them, not wanting to leave the slightest clue behind. As he made his way back to the orchard, he found himself picturing Ilar's grateful smile again.

What is wrong with me?

They set off again, striking east, away from Riga.

"What are you doing?" Ilar demanded, balking almost immediately. "Mycena is north, and the coast that way! You're just leading us deeper into Plenimar."

"Then stay here," Seregil muttered. "Of course, I'd have to kill you."

As he'd expected, Ilar fell into step behind them, walking in sullen silence.

Alec caught Seregil's eye and made the hand sign for "Aurënen." Seregil nodded. If they could make it to the Strait and steal a boat, they could cross to Virésse, or better yet, coast along to Gedre, where they were assured of a warmer welcome.

He shot the rhekaro a dark look. *And what will they make of you?*

• • •

Alec, the better guide outside of a city, took the lead. The clouds were clearing and he kept the stars of the Great Hunter over his left shoulder to keep them going east. He wasn't troubled by Sebrahn's slight weight, or the odd coolness his little body gave off instead of heat. It was the simmering tension brewing between all of them that worried him.

The night air was cold enough that they could see their breath in front of them. It was poor country for shelter or hiding. Trees were sparse, and the few villages they passed were mean little places.

Seregil was grim, and Khenir wisely kept his mouth shut, though he was obviously in pain. Alec could feel the tension crackling between the two of them. And no wonder, if he'd understood Ahmol and Yhakobin correctly. He tried to keep his mind on the way in front of them, but his heart was in turmoil. This wasn't how he'd envisioned his reunion with his talimenios; Seregil was distant and clearly upset by Sebrahn's presence, as well as his obvious loathing of Khenir.

Alec felt betrayed. Hadn't there been signs enough that Khenir had lied to him? But deep down inside, he was also sorry to have his worst suspicions about the man realized.

When Khenir began to lag behind, however, it was Seregil who fell back and took his arm to support him.

"Are you going to kill me now?" Alec heard Khenir whisper.

"Shut up and keep walking," Seregil growled back.

They'd gone another mile or so when he heard the sound of moving water. Veering to the right, he soon found a small spring. Alec put Sebrahn down to the ground and stretched, easing his stiff shoulders. Ilar collapsed where he was, shaking with exhaustion.

The spring water was sweet and cold. Each drank his fill, then sat a while to rest. Seregil settled beside Alec and hugged him close, obviously not caring what the others might think. Alec hugged him back. Khenir watched them with an almost hungry expression.

Alec glared back at him. "All that time, you knew, and you lied to me."

"I—I didn't dare tell you," Khenir stammered. "Not while we were still in that house. Once Ilban had freed me, I would have explained."

"I'm sure you would have, and enjoyed it, too," Seregil said, in that dangerously calm tone that always boded ill for someone. "There's a lot you didn't tell him, isn't there? Alec, I'd like to introduce you to an old friend of mine. This is Ilar í Sontir."

For a long moment Alec felt numb. Then the pieces began to fall into place. "Then...why is he still alive?"

Seregil sighed. "When I figure that out, I'll let you know."

Alec barely heard him. He jumped to his feet, sword drawn, and advanced on the cowering slave. "Ilar? *Ilar?* You bastard! The spoon, and those walks . . . You played with me and lied to me, and all the time . . ."

Seregil caught him before he lunged at Ilar, locking his arms around Alec's chest as he fought to get loose. "Listen to me! Right now we need to find somewhere to hide before the sun comes up." Seregil held him fast and brought his lips close to Alec's ear. "Trust me, too, talí."

Alec lowered his sword, but any compassion he'd felt for his false protector was gone. Ilar was now his betrayer, too.

Seregil took Alec by the arm and drew him away from the others.

"Let it go, talí," Seregil whispered. "Ilar's a silky customer, and always was. Whatever happened between you—"

"You think something happened?" Alec sputtered, stung by the notion.

"I saw you two down in the garden, by the fish pool," Seregil told him, sounding pained to have to speak of it.

Alec took his hand. "He tried to seduce me. Even though I trusted him then, I wouldn't betray you. I wasn't even tempted."

Seregil raked his fingers back through his shorn hair, the way he did when he was particularly uncomfortable or exasperated. "It's all right. But I remember what he was like—what he's still like."

"And yet you didn't kill him?"

"You stopped me, remember?"

Alec clenched his fists in frustration. "And now we have to anyway, or keep dragging him along so he doesn't betray us."

Even in this light he could make out Seregil's strained little half smile. "I've never been much for killing in cold blood, and neither are you. I suppose we're stuck with him, at least until we're far enough away from Yhakobin that it doesn't matter."

"I still don't understand. You always said you'd kill him on sight!"

Seregil shook his head. "I've seen his scars, talí, and what's been done to him all these years. He's not the man I remember. He's—broken."

"You *pity* him?"

"You're no more surprised than I am. But what could I do to him that his life here hasn't done already?"

Alec paused, trying to take that in. "Were you with him, all the time we were apart?"

"No, not for the first part. There was an old woman who looked after me while I was sick."

"I saw you, on the ship. At first I thought you were dead."

"I damn near did die from the magic they put on me. I don't know how long I slept, or what he did to me while I did, but when I woke up it was just the old woman for a long time. Ilar showed up later, after he made sure I saw you two together in the garden."

"That bastard!" he hissed. "How was he with you?"

"He had me at his mercy, and he enjoyed it."

Alec thought he caught just the slightest hint of uncertainty in his lover's voice. "Did he force you—"

"You saw what they did to him. But if that had

been what it took to get to you, I would have, without a second thought." Seregil pulled him close again. "Would you have hated me for that?"

Alec looked deep into his own heart. "No," he murmured, and felt Seregil's sigh of relief.

"Besides, I attacked him the first chance I got," Seregil added, clearly pleased at that. "After that, he knew I'd kill him the minute he let his guard down. Whatever else Ilar is, he's no fool. Come on, now. We've got to find someplace to lie up before the sun rises."

"How far to the Strait?"

"I'm not sure, but if we turn south tomorrow, we're bound to strike it."

"And then?"

Seregil gave him a crooked grin. "We take what the Lightbearer sends. Hopefully in the form of a nice swift little boat, eh? Luck in the shadows, Alec. It hasn't failed us yet."

"And in the Light," Alec murmured, hoping the Immortal in question was listening.

As they moved on, Seregil half expected Alec to drop the rhekaro and attack Ilar again.

Instead, when Ilar fell behind, Alec resumed their earlier conversation. "So, who do you think betrayed us to Yhakobin in the first place? The queen, or Ulan í Sathil?"

"I don't know. Maybe both. But having had a good long time to ponder the matter, I'd say that if the queen was looking for an excuse to cast doubt on her sister's loyalty, our disappearance with the only missive might be a good starting point."

"What about Prince Korathan? Would he do something like that to you?"

Seregil frowned. "I wouldn't have said so, but who knows? If things are really that bad, there isn't much point in going back to Skala."

"Do you think Micum knows we're in trouble yet? Thero must have figured out there was something wrong when the messages didn't come."

"We don't know that they didn't get them, Alec. Whoever caught us might have figured the sticks out and used them. There's no way of telling. It's just us, talí. We're on our own."

Alec shrugged. "Well, we're free, and we're together. That's a start."

Seregil's grin was all the answer he needed.

CHAPTER 39

Thero Turns Nightrunner

LED BY THERO'S sightings, he and Micum entered Virésse as travelers and lost themselves in the crowds of one of the seedier dock wards. They soon located the tavern with the dragon and serpent sign—a low, dirty place frequented by Skalan and Plenimaran sailors, Zengati traders, and other rough sorts. There were no 'faie there, apart from the proprietor—a one-eyed Golinil clansman named Wharit. He was as dirty and disreputable as his clientele, distinguished only by his lack of facial hair and his filthy brown-and-white sen'gai. The barmaids and potboys were all foreigners, as were the whores plying their trade there.

Micum stopped just inside the door and wrinkled his nose at the stink of smoke and unwashed bodies, then said softly, "This isn't quite how I pictured Aurënen."

"Virésse port is a meeting place for all sorts."

Micum adjusted his sword belt for the benefit

of anyone taking his measure. "That's all right, then. I know how to act here."

They sat down at a small table and Micum called for a pitcher of turab from a passing barmaid, holding up a silver half-sester piece and giving her a rakish smile. The woman's smile was bright and false as brass, but she brought them their beer and settled on Micum's knee.

"You got the sound of a Skalan, my dear," she purred, eyeing the silver piece. She had a Riga accent and dark, sharp eyes.

Micum tucked the coin between her ample breasts and squeezed her thigh, while Thero looked on with poorly concealed surprise. "I'm a long way from home, my girl, and always glad to see a pretty face. Even if she is too young for me."

The woman, who was most assuredly not too young for anyone, wiggled suggestively and stroked his stubbled cheek. "You're a charmer. Will you want a room for sleeping, you and your friend?" She gave Thero a sloe-eyed look that made the younger man blush.

"Indeed we will," said Micum. "But not until we've had some hot food and a decent wash." He produced another coin and held it up. "Can you help us with that?"

"We have good food, and a tub in the yard out back." She eyed the coin meaningfully. "For men I like, I can get you hot, fresh water."

Micum laughed and gave her another squeeze and the coin. "Ah, you're honeycomb, girl, sweet as can be. What's your name, my dove?"

"Rose to you, handsome."

"Well, then, Rosie my love." He set her on her feet and gave her a playful smack on the bottom. "Whatever you've got cooking back there, bring us the best of it and tell 'em to warm up that tub!"

She laughed and flounced off toward the kitchens.

"No wonder Kari wants you kept at home!" Thero exclaimed under his breath.

Micum sipped his turab, smiling. "Time and place, my friend. All that dolly really wants is my silver."

"But what if she wants more?"

"Well, Seregil generally used to handle that end of things when the need arose. But you're welcome to step in, seeing as he's not here."

"I don't have the right sort of healing spells to risk it!"

"Don't be unkind. You don't know the life she's had, stuck in a place like this. She's probably somebody's grandmother by now, three or four times over. Now, as to why we're here, about to risk a dose of slop belly on the food?"

Thero palmed the tooth and closed his eyes. "He's close, but not in this tavern."

"Well, then, let's enjoy our dinner and this fine beer."

The turab was good, in fact, and so was the food, much to Thero's amazement. Razor clams boiled with wine and herbs was the specialty of the house, and the floor was strewn with the long, narrow shells. They were a rarity in Skala, and seldom seen this time of year.

Rose came back with a few hot, spiced bread rolls for them in a napkin. Thero was impressed until he tore one open and found a few weevils baked inside among the raisins. Micum ate his share with relish, though, picking out the bugs without a care.

"Now then, Rosie my love, I wonder if you know a man I'm looking for?" asked Micum, pulling the woman into his lap again.

"What you wanting a man for when you got me?" she teased, then nodded at Thero. "Or him? He's a bit on the stringy side, but I like his face. Does he always scowl like that?"

Micum laughed. "Most of the time, yes. And I'll see to you later, but this fellow I'm after owes me money and I've a mind to collect."

"Well, I know a lot of men," she drawled coyly.

Micum reached into his purse and held up another coin. "The whoreson's name is Notis."

"That one!" She laughed and shook her dark curls. "By the Sailor, he's a terror! Drinks himself silly, then pukes on the floor so he can drink some more. Wharit's thrown him out half a dozen times, but he's got the money to come back in when he sobers up."

"That's good news. I could use some of that good Plenimar coin in my pocket."

"Then you're out of luck, love," she told him, then burst out laughing. "For all his money is 'faie, stamped with the Virésse seal, every penny of it."

"Well now, I guess that spends just as good.

How's that tub coming along? And what do I have to do to get some soap with it?"

Rose was in good humor, it seemed, for all it cost was a kiss from Thero. She smelled of old beer and cooking smoke but he made a decent job of it and she pinched his cheek.

Micum gave him first go at the tub. It was splintery and in plain sight of the kitchen door, but he was anxious to show Micum he could act his part as well as the next man. He stripped off and climbed hastily into the tub while Micum sat on a barrel and smoked. As he soaped his hair, it occurred to him that he was being given a glimpse of the sort of life Micum and Seregil had shared all those years, out in the world, while his world had still extended little further than the Orëska gardens.

"I'm afraid I'm a poor substitute for him," Thero said, knowing Micum would know whom he meant.

Micum smiled around his pipe stem. "You're not so bad."

Pleased, Thero ducked his head and climbed out to dry himself with the threadbare towel Rose had left for them. As he reluctantly pulled his dirty clothes back on, Micum took his turn in the tub. As he stripped, Thero looked sidelong at the numerous scars that covered the man's body, including a thick rope of raised white flesh that wrapped around his chest to his hip. Seregil had many, too, and even Alec. He saw them as proof of the bond between the three—marks left by the lives they'd chosen.

Micum sank up to his chin in the water, pipe still clenched between his teeth. "That's a long face. What's the matter with you? I was only joking about Rose, you know."

Caught out, Thero smiled and waved aside his concern. "Just worried about them. I'll be happier when we find what we're looking for."

Notis did not make an appearance at the Serpent and Dragon that night, so Thero took the tooth in hand again and sighted for him along the dark, malodorous streets of the harbor front. They found him at last in a tavern on the far side, drinking with a handful of fellow Plenimarans and a couple of Zengat. None were dressed like soldiers, but they had that same hard, dangerous air about them, and they were all well armed. Among them was the man he'd seen. As he laughed with the man beside him, Thero saw the gap where he'd lost the tooth.

"Should we lure him outside?" he whispered to Micum. This place was even dirtier than the Serpent.

"No need," Micum assured him, and walked right over to them. Thero hung back, sure he was about to witness a knifing, but Micum said something that made them all laugh, and before Thero knew it, they were all drinking together.

Since Notis was already drunk, and Micum was liberal in standing more rounds for them, he had no trouble loosening the man's tongue. Micum started off arguing good-naturedly about horses with them, but somehow steered the conversation around to their trade.

Micum, whom Thero had never suspected of being such a consummate actor, pretended surprise when he heard what their business was. "What are you doing here, then? Aurënfaie don't deal in flesh."

"Shhhhh! We don't bring that here," Notis explained, leaning on Micum's shoulder. "We carry the poor buggers to the Riga markets, then take on cargo for here. You get the money here, get more flesh and round and round we go! The khirnari don't care, so long as we got no slaves aboard when we drop anchor here."

"Is that the best port for it? Riga?"

"Unless we got something real special. That we take to Benshâl. Good money in Riga, but best money in Benshâl. The Overlord? I hear he's got five hundred of the best in his private collection. And that's just the bedders. All the household slaves? They got to be perfect, too. No marks 'cept for the brands. Especially on the face."

"Not even what the clothes cover up?" asked Micum.

"Not even," Notis assured him.

"Do you get many of those?"

"No, damn the luck! We've not been up that way for months. Just come back from Riga, though." Notis slapped his purse down on the tabletop with a respectable jingle of coin.

"By the Flame, there must be good money in it," Micum exclaimed, slurring a little now himself. "How's a man get into that business, anyway?"

Eyes narrowed around the table at that. "You asking, Skala?"

"Do I sound like a Skalan to you?" Micum scoffed, offended. "I'm a northlander! No queens for me. No sir, I'm a free man, free to do as I please. And..." He paused and gave them a knowing wink. "Making money always pleases me. Only I'm wondering, if old Ulan knows the cargo you carry, why does he let your ships anywhere near his fai'thast, eh?"

A Zengat with a scar across the bridge of his nose leaned in and whispered, "That is because of the agreement."

"What agreement?" Thero asked, speaking up at last.

Notis and the others went silent and suddenly all eyes were on Thero, and not looking too friendly.

"That's a Skalan you're with," Notis growled.

"Him?" Micum jerked a thumb at Thero. "Don't mind him. I met him on the ship coming over and he's been buying the drinks. What do you say, Thorwin? You too proud to earn your living?"

It took Thero only a second to realize that he was Thorwin, and that a great deal rode on the proper response. "Since my father cast me out, I've made my own way just fine," he shot back, trying to match the coarse, off-hand way Micum had been speaking. "One country's silver spends the same as another's, in my experience."

The others stared at him a moment, then they all burst out laughing, and Micum with them.

Notis slapped Micum on the shoulder, rocking

on the bench. "You got you a fine companion, friend. He talks like a priest, all stiff like a dead fish." He stood and locked his arms at his sides, shuffling drunkenly from foot to foot, much to the amusement of his friends.

Why am I always compared to fish? Thero wondered, nonetheless relieved by this reaction.

"What sorts of things do you bring back over the water?" Micum asked, giving Thero a wink.

"Iron, copper, spirits mostly. This time we also bring back some 'faie."

"Aurënfaie?"

"Freed slaves. Bunch of rubbish, you ask me, all beaten down and branded. Better off throwing 'em into the sea. But we get paid by the head, so we took good care of them. Only lost one."

"You got paid to bring slaves out of Plenimar?" Micum shook his head. "I never heard of such a thing!"

"Ransom," the Zengat said, licking his lips. "Pays better than slaving sometimes. Trouble is, so many of the freed ones kill themselves before we can get them back."

"So that's the agreement?" Thero asked.

"Keep your voice down, fish priest!" the man hissed, looking around nervously. "You want to get us lynched? It's all—how do you say it?"

"Under the table," Notis explained with a wink. "No one in this port takes slaves from Virésse, and there's a good bounty for any brought home again. Been going on for years."

"Ulan í Sathil ransoms his people back?" Thero

whispered. "But if he knows they are being taken, why does he trade with you at all?"

"He only does business with those who bring him word of his people in Plenimar. And with the Zengati clans he's got treaties with."

"So you carried a load of that cargo recently?" asked Micum, filling Notis's mug again.

"Good raiding. Full load! And good ones, too."

"Except for those we had to leave behind..." the other Zengat muttered, and was elbowed into silence by one of the others.

"Lots of gold to go around this time," the scar-faced one said, grinning.

"Then you must have had a good time in Benshâl, I'd guess!" laughed Micum.

"Not Benshâl! Riga, I told you." Notis gave Micum a bleary grin. "I think you are drunk, friend. How 'bout you, fish priest?"

Thero did his best to smile, but in reality he wanted to throttle the bastard until he told them what had happened to their friends. But the pressure of Micum's knee against his own under the table made him hold his tongue.

"What was so special about this load?" Micum asked casually.

"Lots 'faie. Special ones, too," Notis whispered.

"But I thought those always went to Benshâl?" said Thero, casually as he could manage.

Notis was deep in his cups now. Leaning heavily across Micum, he whispered loudly, "Special raid, fish man, just for two. Killed a damn lot of others we could have sold, but orders are orders.

You see? Just the two, and no witnesses. Sent a *voron* to catch 'em, too."

A necromancer. That explained the damage to the swords.

"Who sent the voron?" Thero asked, gripping his wine cup tightly with both hands.

Notis shrugged. "Who cares? Our captain orders. We go. And then?" He patted his purse again.

"What was so special about them?" Micum demanded drunkenly. "Pretty ones? Big *trai*?" He raised his hands like he was cupping a pair of breasts.

Notis and the others laughed. "When you ever see big trai on a 'faie? Can't hardly tell the boys from the girls half the time!"

"Not that it much matters," one of the others said, giving Thero a leer that made his skin crawl.

"No, just a couple of poor bastards."

"The dark one was a *westerbok*," the unscarred Zengat opined solemnly.

"Oh, how do you know that?" one of the Plenimarans challenged.

"All my family great slavers, way back!" the Zengat bragged, poking the other man in the chest. "I can tell 'em *all* apart. Don't even need those head rags to tell. But the other one, he was different, a mongrel with yellow hair."

"Yellow hair, eh? That sells good?" asked Micum.

Notis shrugged. "To some, but the rich customers generally want 'em pure. This one didn't look like much, compared to your southern stock, but they kept him apart from the others and I seen the captain's own slaves goin' in to him."

"I told you, they was wizards!" a younger Plenimaran piped up. "Put the branks on 'em, didn't they? And the cuffs."

The Zengats both made some sort of hand sign, as if to ward off evil.

"How much did they fetch?" Micum asked.

"We unload 'em at the docks and that's the last we see of 'em." Notis grinned wider, showing the gap where his tooth had been knocked out. Thero hoped Alec had done that to him.

To Thero's dismay, the conversation turned to other things as Micum continued to buy round after round. And although he seemed to be drinking as much as the rest of them, when the last of the slavers fell asleep with their heads on the table, Micum sat back and said quietly, "Time we were moving on, Thorwin."

"What about them?" Thero whispered, gesturing around at the drunken slavers.

Micum shook his head. "Don't make a fuss. No sense getting noticed."

With a last glare at Notis and his compatriots, Thero followed Micum out into the dark street.

It was a cloudy night, with a cold breeze in off the sea. Thero shivered, feeling a little ill. He hadn't had enough of the strong turab to be drunk, really. *No,* he thought, *it's leaving those men alive that sickens me.*

"Where to now?" he asked.

"Well, as much as I hate to disappoint poor

Rosie, I think this would be a good time to take our leave. Unless you'd care to spend a night with her?"

"I think I'll take my chances in the woods."

They made their way back through the crooked streets, meeting no one but a few drunken sailors and a would-be footpad, who thought better of it when Micum showed his sword.

No one challenged them at the stables when they came for their horses. The tavern windows were dark now.

Thero drew a sigh of relief when they were finally away from the city and in the cover of the trees again. "So this is what you did, you and Seregil, when you were out on the road for Nysander?"

"In part."

"And the parts that gave you all those scars?"

"This was an easy night, Thero. You were quick-witted back there, by the way. Not bad, for a wet-behind-the-ears tower wizard."

Pleased, Thero took that for the compliment it was.

Silver Eyes

JUST BEFORE SUNRISE, Seregil and the others found shelter in the ruins of an abandoned stone barn. The house it had served had fallen into the foundation hole and there were no signs of life about the place, just ruined fences and a dry well.

The barn had been struck by lightning and half the roof had burned and fallen in. Rats and bats had taken over, and seemed none too pleased to entertain unexpected guests. A rodent half the size of Ruetha leaped from the shadows and snapped at the little bundle of food Alec had brought.

Ilar let out a startled cry and tried to run, but Seregil dragged him into the shadows by the back wall. "Behave yourself, or this can be your permanent resting place. It's your choice."

Ilar went sulky and made a great show of scraping the ground with his foot to clear away the various droppings before he sat down.

Alec kept the rhekaro with him as he and

Seregil made a survey of the place. A brightening sky showed through the large holes in the roof.

"Yhakobin is bound to come looking for us," Alec murmured, peering out through the broken doorway.

"Us, or you and that?" Seregil asked, pointing at the rhekaro. "Ilar told me it was you that he was after when we were ambushed. Because you're from the Hâzadriëlfaie line."

Alec nodded slowly. "He needed my kind of blood to make the rhekaro. He even tried to treat me well, sometimes, because of it."

"Only sometimes?"

"I didn't like him or the things he did to me."

"Like what?"

"No, nothing like that. It was just—Can we talk about this later? I'm so tired."

"Of course!" Seregil embraced him as best he could and felt Alec go limp against him for a moment, resting his head on Seregil's shoulder. It was the first proper embrace they'd been able to share, and he didn't want to let him go. "After the ambush, for the longest time, I was so afraid you might be dead."

Alec's arms tightened around him. "I thought the same, until I saw you on the deck of that ship at Riga. I knew then that I had to stay alive and find you again."

"I'm not sure who found who, in the end, but here we are." He kissed Alec and reluctantly released him.

Turning his attention to the landscape outside, he saw no sign of pursuit but doubted that would last. Who knew what sort of powers an alchemist had for finding lost slaves? Or the slave takers, for that matter.

Ilar was waiting sullenly for them, curled up in a ruined stall now and shivering in his stolen cloak.

Alec sat down some distance from him and fed the rhekaro again. Seregil made himself watch, figuring he might as well get used to it, though it still struck him as obscene.

Doing his best to hide his revulsion, he sat down beside Alec and opened the bundle. "Let's see what you stole for food. My belly thinks my throat's been cut."

The three of them ate sparingly, sharing a bit of bread around and paring hard cheese thin on slices of apples taken from the orchard the night before. As always, the rhekaro ate nothing and didn't seem interested in the water, either. According to Alec, the rhekaro had been given only a few drops of Alec's blood each morning to live on, and nothing more.

Seregil took the first watch, sitting in shadows of the barn door with his back to a beam and a good view of the western barrens. Alec stretched out beside him with his head on Seregil's thigh. Ilar remained in his corner, snoring softly.

The rhekaro seemed to have no more need of sleep than it did of food, but it curled up beside Alec, as if seeking the warmth of another body like a cat would. *Or a serpent,* Seregil thought, eyeing it warily as he stroked Alec's hair.

The rhekaro stared back at him. Those unnerving silver eyes weren't blank, but the kind of intelligence they might hold eluded him.

After a moment it turned away and looked down at Alec's sleeping form. Then it lay down beside him in a similar position, and closed its eyes.

It's trying to act like a real being, thought Seregil, surprised. He waited a few minutes, then shuffled his feet a little to make a noise. Those silvery eyes snapped open and it looked around, identifying the source. Seregil moved his feet again to show it. It stared at him for a moment, and Seregil felt the hair on the back of his neck prickling, strong as if there was lightning in the air. Apparently deciding that he was either no threat or very uninteresting, it returned to its semblance of sleep.

The light was stronger now, showing Seregil something he'd missed before; there was no mistaking the resemblance. Pale and unnatural as it was, the creature truly had Alec's face, or at least the face as it might have looked when Alec was a child. As he compared the two, he noticed something else. Alec looked different somehow, and it wasn't just from dust and exhaustion.

He looked more 'faie.

He shook his head. "What did they do to you, talí?"

Alec slept on, and Seregil returned his attention to the horizon as the day grew warmer, watching for dust rising against the sky. He wasn't looking forward to the conversation they were going to have when Alec woke up.

A few hours later Alec yawned and sat up. The rhekaro rose, too, and huddled close to Alec, as if it sensed what was coming. Behind them, Ilar was still sound asleep.

"Alec, you know we can't keep this creature," Seregil said, getting right to the point.

"What are you talking about? Of course we can!"

"Oh, yes. He won't raise any eyebrows when we get to Aurënen, with those looks, now will he?"

"Seregil—"

"Or in Rhíminee. What sort of explanation will we give there, eh? That he didn't get enough milk as a babe, or enough sun? Alec, I'm no wizard, but even I can feel a strangeness around this thing."

And there was that sudden stubborn set of the jaw again. "I don't know what we'll tell them, but we'll think of something. We always do! And he's not a 'thing.' His name is Sebrahn, I told you."

Seregil sighed. "This isn't some stray kitten, Alec. It's not even a child."

"Then what do you suggest? Just leaving him here to die?"

"Of course not. That would be cruel. I'll take care of it for you."

Alec sprang to his feet and put the rhekaro behind him. Then he did something he'd never done before: he drew his sword on Seregil. "You're not going to kill him!"

Seregil rose slowly and held his hands out by his sides, making no effort to protect himself, though his heart was hammering in his chest and he felt sick to his stomach. "You'd choose *that* over me? So all that's happened between us comes to no more than this?"

Alec lowered his sword at once, eyes brimming with tears. "No! I mean—Don't make me choose!"

"It's unnatural! For all we know, it's dangerous, too."

"Yhakobin said he could heal. He was making him for the Overlord, to cure his son. And he *is* alive, not just some—thing. He can learn. Yhakobin taught him to do simple tasks around the workshop. He understood me when I asked him to bring me things. Look, I'll show you!" He tapped the rhekaro on the shoulder and said, "Bring me the cheese."

It immediately went into the barn and returned with the scant remains of the cheese.

"What else does it—er, he know?" asked Seregil, surprised.

"I'm not sure, but I think if you show him something and name it, or how to do something, he remembers. You try."

"All right. Hey you, Sebrahn, bring me the bundle."

The rhekaro just stared at him.

Alec retrieved the bundle and put it in the rhekaro's hands. "Bundle." Then he carried it a few yards off and Seregil repeated the command. The rhekaro fetched it and brought it back to him, setting it at his feet.

Alec touched his chest. "Alec." He touched

Seregil's arm. "This is Seregil. Go to Seregil, Sebrahn."

The rhekaro stood and walked to Seregil.

"See? I told you, he has a mind. He learns."

"So it seems. Can he speak?"

"I've heard him cry out in pain, but never words."

Seregil tried again to imagine what it would be like, trying to sneak unobtrusively through a village or port with this thing in tow. "So, are you ready to tell me why you're so attached to him?"

"The alchemist *made* him from me."

"I guessed as much, when I saw you in that cellar."

"I don't remember you there. How often did he bring you?"

"Just once. Ilar was quite happy for me to see you like that."

"I'll bet. Anyway, that's why Sebrahn can only drink my blood, I think. He needs it to live."

Seregil reached out and cupped his hand under the rhekaro's nose and mouth. "No breath." He pressed his hand to its chest. "And no heartbeat, either."

Alec felt for himself. "Well, he acts like he's alive, so I guess he is."

"So, how was he made?"

"Well, from parts of me—my blood, piss, hair and—Well, other things like that. Yhakobin put it all in a sheep's stomach with some other things and buried it in that cellar."

"What other things?"

"Salt, quicksilver . . . That's all I remember."

"And you in that cage, your blood dripping down on it," Seregil murmured. "Is that why you look different?"

"You see it, too?" Alec touched his face self-consciously. "Yhakobin did something to me. He claimed it was some kind of purification, to get rid of my human blood. It took days, and when it was over, I looked like this."

"It suits you. It's just a bit startling, that's all. I didn't think something like that was possible."

"I hate it!" Alec hissed angrily. "It's like he took my father away from me."

"No, Alec, never think that. You'll always be his son." Seregil grinned and kissed him. "And the one I love. No doubts there."

"It might wear off. He had to do the purification again before he made the second rhekaro."

"Well, then, there you go. Don't worry about it." He stretched out on the ground with his head in Alec's lap. "Wake me when you get tired."

"Then you promise not to hurt him?"

Seregil looked up at Alec. "As long as he stays as he is, then he has nothing to fear from me. But Alec, if he turns dangerous—"

"He won't!"

Seregil caught his hand and held it firmly. "If he does, then you're going to have to make that choice, aren't you?"

"I will."

"And if it comes to a choice between that, and me?"

Alec raised their joined hands and pressed his

lips to the back of Seregil's. "You. But I won't let that happen."

Seregil closed his eyes and was glad to feel Alec's hand on his forehead. As he drifted off, however, he thought he felt cold silver eyes watching him, too.

Blood and flowers

IT WAS AFTERNOON when Seregil woke up to find his head pillowed on the bundle, with one of the musty cloaks draped over him. Alec sat a little way off, with his sword across his knees and the rhekaro beside him, staring over at Ilar, who was pacing at the back of the barn, trying to ignore Alec.

"Any sign of trouble?" asked Seregil.

"I'd have woken you."

Seregil sat up and stretched. "You should have woken me anyway. Do you want to sleep some more?"

"No, I'm fine. You'd better eat. There's not much left."

Seregil settled for a mouthful of tepid water. "We have to find more food, and fast. Maybe we can steal you a bow somewhere tonight."

"Do you really mean to walk all the way to the southern coast?" Ilar demanded. "It could be days, weeks even, for all you know!"

"It's not that far, a few days at most," Seregil told him, though he wasn't so sure.

Alec tugged at his braid. "This has gotten me into trouble a few times already. Guess we'd better cut it off. My knife is better for the job than yours."

Alec handed him the black-handled dagger and turned his back. Seregil gripped the braid at its base and brought the knife against it.

"What are you waiting for?" asked Alec.

Seregil lowered the blade, caught by the warm, familiar weight of the plait against his palm. "What's the point? Long or short, that hair will give you away. You might as well just cover it up for now. Cut some cloth off that sling of yours and make a head rag for yourself."

Alec gave him a quizzical look over one shoulder. "You're getting sentimental."

"Probably." He nodded at the rhekaro, whose hair fell well below its waist. "We'll have to cut his shorter, though. I don't think we can hide that much."

He turned to the rhekaro to find it staring at the knife, fear clear in those usually expressionless eyes. "What's wrong with him?"

Alec put a protective arm around its thin shoulders. "He doesn't like knives much. Yhakobin hurt him a lot and cut parts of him off."

"What parts?"

"Fingers. Skin."

Even Seregil felt a little sick at the thought. "Why?"

"I don't know. Here, let me do it. He trusts me."

Seregil handed him back the knife and watched

the rhekaro's normal blank expression return. "But he has all his fingers."

"I told you, things grow back. See?" He showed Seregil Sebrahn's right hand. Thin scars circled the base of three fingers, and there was another around its wrist. "That's where Yhakobin cut them off and they grew back. Drinking my blood helped him heal more quickly. The first one Yhakobin made . . ." He broke off and Seregil saw the shadow of something horrific in Alec's eyes. "Yhakobin butchered that one, then made me heal it, so he could do it again. He destroyed it, piece by piece, until it died."

Seregil touched the rhekaro's cool little hand with a bit more respect. "The bastard's no better than a necromancer."

"He's worse." Alec reached out and picked up a strand of the rhekaro's silvery hair, telling it quietly, "I'm going to cut your hair, but it won't hurt, I promise."

Seregil couldn't tell if it understood or not, but it didn't shrink away as Alec began carefully trimming its hair short above its shoulders. Handfuls of the silky stuff pooled on the ground around it. Seregil couldn't resist picking up a lock and running it between his fingers. It was very soft, like a real child's. It had its eyes closed now, and was almost smiling as Alec smoothed a gentle hand over its head.

"He really does like you," Seregil noted with a resigned sigh.

"How do you know it's a boy?" asked Ilar, coming closer. "It's not like it has anything between its legs."

"Neither do you!" Alec spat back.

"It doesn't?" asked Seregil.

Alec paused in his barbering. "Well, no, but he looks like me, so we might as well call him that as anything."

"Then how does he piss?"

"I don't think he needs to."

Seregil rested his face in his hands, trying again to imagine how they were going to manage.

Alec kept his gaze on his work, frowning. "No one's going to hurt him again. Besides, if Yhakobin wants him so badly, then he must be important, right?"

"To make some medicine."

"That didn't work," Ilar reminded them.

"I think we should take him to Thero and Magyana," said Alec. "Maybe they'll know what he is."

"I know a little," Ilar said, giving Alec an arch look. "More than you."

"Would you care to tell us?" Seregil replied evenly.

Ilar shrugged. "Ilban says there are many different kinds of rhekaro. The ones made from Hâzadriëlfaie blood are the rarest of all. According to the alchemists' histories, a perfect poison can be made of their blood, as well as an elixir of perfect healing, and that it possesses a power that can strike a thousand men dead on the spot when its master speaks the key."

Alec glared at him. "Liar! He couldn't even protect himself."

"As I said, this one turned out wrong, too," Ilar

replied. "Neither of them even had wings like they were supposed to. He blamed your mongrel blood."

Seregil struck Ilar across the mouth so fast the other man had no time to duck. "Shut your filthy mouth," he snarled as Ilar went sprawling.

"His words, not mine," Ilar whined, cupping his split lip. "Nothing he tried with it worked as it was supposed to. He tried making something from your blood, too, Seregil, but that didn't work properly, either. That's why he didn't free me, as he'd promised." He sat up and wrapped his arms around his knees. "I was so close!"

"At our expense." Seregil gathered the rhekaro's shorn hair and twisted it into a rope to go into the bundle. "What else did he tell you about it?"

"Not very much. But I did see something. I'll show you, if—"

Seregil arched an eyebrow. "If I promise not to kill you?"

"Both of you."

"Well, Alec? What do you say? He has been of some use."

"We could have gotten away without him," Alec muttered, trying to comb Sebrahn's ragged hair into some sort of order with his fingers. It stuck out in long, ragged tufts, but he looked slightly more like a normal child now. But only slightly.

"Maybe, but I think he's bought himself some time. So, Ilar, that's the best you'll get. What is it you have to show us?"

"I need some water, and that hog sticker of yours."

"You can have the water." Seregil pulled a cup

they'd stolen from the bundle and half filled it from their precious store.

"Now draw a drop of its blood and let it fall into the cup."

Seregil handed Alec his poniard. Alec pulled the rhekaro into his lap and took one of its hands between his. "Don't worry. It's just a little poke. Just one. Hold out your hand."

And it did, gaze fixed on Alec's hand. Alec carefully pricked the tip of one small finger. What oozed out was not blood, but something pale and viscous, like the jelly around frog's eggs in the spring. When it fell into the water, a flash of soft light spread, reminding Seregil of a firefly's glow. It quickly faded, and something dark formed and floated to the surface.

It was a flower, and looked for all the world like a tiny river lotus, except for the color. It was dark blue, almost black, and gave off a sweet, heavy fragrance.

"This is it?" Seregil asked, eyeing it closely.

"It's supposed to be white, according to the texts, but this rhekaro makes nothing but these blue ones. They're worthless," Ilar told him.

"I saw some of these in the workshop!" Alec exclaimed, reaching for it.

Seregil grabbed his wrist. "Be careful."

"He said it didn't work." But Alec used the tip of his knife to lift the blossom from the cup. Holding it out to the rhekaro, he said, "Sebrahn, can you show me?"

The rhekaro took it carefully in its cupped hands and looked around at the three of them for a moment. Then it moved toward Ilar, holding the flower up as if it wanted him to smell it. The man scrambled backward, face drawn with fear.

"So you're certain it doesn't work?" Seregil snatched the flower from the rhekaro's hand and leaped on Ilar, holding him down and mashing it against his lips.

Ilar clawed at his wrists and they grappled, rolling across the dirty floor. Alec jumped on Ilar's legs and helped wrestle him down. When Seregil looked for the flower, it was nowhere to be found.

"Where the hell—? Did you eat it?"

"Let me go! I had your word!" Ilar cried, still struggling weakly.

"We never gave you that, actually." Seregil grabbed Ilar's face and inspected his mouth closely. "Well, now, that's interesting. Let him up, Alec."

Ilar staggered up to his feet, outraged and panting. "You lied to me!"

"How does it feel?" Alec sneered.

"Better yet, how does your lip feel?" asked Seregil.

"My lip?" Ilar raised a trembling hand to his mouth. "What do you mean? Oh!"

The split was gone, the lip whole and pink under a smear of blood as if nothing had happened.

"No wonder Yhakobin didn't figure it out," Seregil murmured, grabbing Ilar again and holding him still while he ran a thumb over the healed place. "It does do something, just not what he wanted, apparently. Let's hear it for your 'mongrel' blood, talí."

He grinned at Alec, and for an instant something came to him along the talimenios bond: Alec was as surprised as he was, but there was something more, something Alec wasn't telling him.

Alec caught the look and made a discreet canting gesture in Ilar's direction: *Not in front of him.*

At the end of his patience, Seregil pulled Alec to his feet. "Come on. We need to talk. Ilar, you stay here."

As expected, Alec took the rhekaro by the hand and brought it along with them. Seregil led them outside.

"Well?"

Alec rested his hands on the rhekaro's shoulders. "The oracle at Sarikali said I'd father a child of no woman, right? And Illior knows, Sebrahn doesn't have a mother."

Seregil clenched his fists in frustration. "It's *not* a child!"

"He is to me, and he's mine."

For a moment Seregil was speechless. Then everything fell into place. "You think—? This— Alec, you're not serious?"

"I am, too! What else could it mean? Look at him!"

There was no mistaking the resemblance between them. Abhorrent as the thought was, Alec might actually be right.

"Tell me again how he was made. All of it."

Alec told him about the purifications in detail, and then, more haltingly, of the various bodily fluids that had been collected and how. When he got to the semen, he was blushing miserably.

"They drugged you for that, eh? Well, at least you dreamt of me," Seregil told him, ruffling his hair. "I'm surprised Yhakobin didn't order Ilar to get that from you . . ." The look on Alec's face told him he'd hit a mark. "That bastard!"

"Like I said, he tried, but I wouldn't."

Seregil gently clasped him by the back of the neck and rested his forehead against Alec's. "He can be very persuasive, can't he? Don't worry, I understand."

Sebrahn Stirs

THEY STAYED AT the barn until nightfall. By the time they set out again, striking south by the stars, the rhekaro's hair was halfway down its back again.

"I told you," said Alec, as he braided it and tucked it under the head rag he'd fashioned for it. He was wearing his, too, and Seregil decided that they didn't do much good. No one was going to mistake either of them—or him either, probably—for a Plenimaran, unless they tried dressing as women. And that wouldn't work, either. Even if they did manage to steal the proper clothing, none of them could pass as the male protector no proper Plenimaran woman would be without. Since there was no help for that, they'd just have to make do with trying to stay as far as possible from any locals.

Ilar was even more sullen now, opening his mouth only to complain. The others ignored him, scanning the moonlit landscape for signs of trouble.

The land grew drier and more desolate as they went and Seregil began to worry about his travel estimations. Their water was nearly gone and so was the food. It was colder tonight, with a hint of frost in the air. Walking kept them warm but left them thirsty. To spare Alec's strength, Seregil took turns carrying the rhekaro. It weighed very little and hung in its sling without wiggling or any sign of discomfort. Several times, though, Seregil felt it touching his hair with its cold little fingers. It was a disconcerting feeling, but it occurred to him that if the rhekaro could learn, then perhaps it could be curious, as well, and wondering at the fact that Seregil's hair was a different color than Alec's. He also noticed that whenever they stopped to rest, regardless of who had been carrying it, it always went to Alec's side.

A child of no woman, Seregil thought again. And the oracle claimed it was a blessing. His mind and heart both rebelled at such a thought; how could this unnatural thing be a blessing?

And yet, it had healed Ilar's lip.

The days grew steadily colder, and the wind never dropped. The further south Alec led them, the rougher the way became and he couldn't seem to find a way that was easier.

As far as the eye could see, the land fell steadily to the south. The ever-present wind cut deeply, sculpting the landscape into strange shapes and deep canyons they had to scramble around. It was slow going, and all of them suffered a fall or two. Alec found a small spring that night, but no food. When dawn came, they slept huddled in the shade of an outcropping, with Seregil and Alec trading short watches. Exhausted and a bit feverish, Ilar slept fitfully.

It was a miserable time, and made more so when Alec was forced to rely on Ilar for warmth while Seregil was walking about on watch. He wasn't certain which was worse: having to be so close to the man or seeing Seregil with him like that when Alec was on watch. It was some comfort that Seregil didn't appear to be enjoying the situation any more than he was, so Alec kept his bitter thoughts to himself, hating the whispers of jealousy at the back of his mind.

When it was his turn to rest, he had no choice but to sit close beside Ilar, with Sebrahn, who never showed any sign of being cold, on his lap. Unlike Ilar, the child gave off no more heat than a newt, but it was still good to have the weight of another body against his—one that he didn't detest, anyway.

"Keep still," he snarled as Ilar shifted around, trying to get comfortable on the stony ground.

"I'm helping you stay alive. If you were out here alone, you'd die."

"I've managed before," Alec muttered. "Don't talk to me."

"How long are you going to hate me?"

Alec rested his cheek against Sebrahn's cool hair. "Why shouldn't I?"

"I know how it all looks to you, the way things were at Yhakobin's, but what choice do you think I had? The man owned me, body and soul. My life was in his hands."

"And your comfort," Alec reminded him. "The way I heard it, you had an easy life there. If it wasn't for Seregil escaping, you'd still be there, wouldn't you, Ilban's pet slave?"

Ilar sighed. "You're right. I would be. But I don't hold that against Seregil. How could I, after what I did to him, and to you?" He gestured out at the barren, broken land around them. "If not for your mercy, I'd be dead or in the hands of another cruel master. If not for your forbearance, I wouldn't be sitting here now, a free man." He looked sidelong at Alec and smiled. "Well, almost free. Do you really think we'll get away?"

"We always do."

"I've heard a bit of your adventures. A kinsman of Vargûl Ashnazai is a good friend with Il—with Yhakobin. Is it true that you were the one who killed him?"

"Yes."

"How?"

"I *don't* want to talk about it."

"So you're a reluctant killer, too? Did Seregil teach you that as well?"

"We're not assassins, just nightrunners." Alec left unsaid the fact that before he'd taken up with Seregil, he'd never killed anyone.

"There's a difference?"

"For those who know," Alec replied, teeth

chattering in spite of the cloak he had pulled over him and Sebrahn.

Ilar shifted this way and that, then leaned closer, pressing against his side. Alec bristled at that, but there was no denying that it was warmer that way. He was too tired and too cold to argue the matter right now. His eyelids felt heavy as books.

Ilar was still talking softly when he fell asleep.

Seregil's eyes burned from staring into the distance. He longed for the cover of night and the feel of his feet eating up the distance that separated them from freedom with every pace.

The others were sheltered between two large boulders. As he passed, he heard the murmur of voices, and guessed that Alec was not enjoying the situation much. When he passed again later, however, he saw that he was fast asleep against Ilar's shoulder. The other man was awake, and nodded slightly, acknowledging Seregil's presence.

Seregil wasn't quite sure how to feel about that. But at least Alec wasn't going to die of a chill.

When his own watch ended and he woke them, Alec looked surprised and none too pleased at his own position. Standing up unsteadily with the rhekaro in his arms, he glared down at Ilar for a second, then walked stiffly away.

"You should leave Sebrahn with me," Seregil offered. "You're going to end up a hunchback, lugging it—him—around all the time."

"It doesn't bother me," Alec replied, preparing to nick another fingertip; they were all red and stippled with scabs now, except for his thumbs, and looked sore.

"I wonder if he could heal those for you?"

"It's nothing. I'm fine."

Seregil walked over to him. From here Ilar was hidden in the lee of the rocks. "Talí, talk to me."

Alec gave him a weary look. "I told you, I'm fine. I just wish we trusted Ilar enough for him to take a watch now and then. But I don't, and now you have to go sleep with him."

"I won't enjoy it, I promise."

"I know. Go on. You look like hell."

"So do you, love. Just keep thinking of the baths in Gedre. That's what keeps me going these days."

That actually won him a laugh. "I believe it. Micum always says you could go through fire and ice and shit without a complaint, but deny you a hot bath at the end of it, and—"

"Yes, yes, I know the rest." Seregil gave him a mock scowl and went to join Ilar.

That night's march was a bit better. They began to see a few big-eared rabbits, and some other small, furry nocturnal creature that would do in a pinch. Alec went off on his own, armed with nothing but a makeshift sling and a handful of pebbles, and came back with two conies and a long snake.

"That's a rock adder. Is it safe to eat?" Ilar asked, disgusted.

"So long as you chop off the first third or so, that gets rid of the poison sacs," Alec explained, doing exactly that and tossing the head away. "Do we dare make a fire?"

"My belly says yes," Seregil said.

Cobbling together a tiny fire from what brush there was, they cooked the meat and the coney livers until they were black on the outside, and mostly raw inside, but warmed through. When it was done, Seregil sliced it all up in three equal parts and doled out a few sips of water.

"Meat!" Alec laughed, ripping a mouthful off a leg bone with his teeth. "By the Four, Yhakobin was stingy with that. How about you?"

"My master was kinder," Seregil said with a smirk, plucking the tiny bones from a chunk of snake meat. "I got a bit now and then."

Ilar took a tentative bite of underdone rabbit. He gagged on it at once and spat it out.

"Don't go wasting that," Alec warned. "Those were hard to come by, and we may not get any more for a while."

"It's dreadful!"

"Better than starving, though," Seregil told him, chewing happily. He passed Ilar his portion of the coney liver. "Here, try this."

The man nibbled hesitantly at the dark morsel, then ate the rest. "That isn't quite as bad." He cast a longing glance at Alec's portion.

Alec popped his into his mouth and chewed loudly. "Mmmm. Delicious!"

When their scant meal was over Alec stamped out the fire and buried the remains of it and the bones. Then, still hungry and thirstier than ever, they continued on.

A few hours before dawn, Seregil was carrying Sebrahn when the rhekaro suddenly grew restless, squirming in his sling and clutching at Seregil's shoulders.

Seregil put him down, in no mood for any complications.

As soon as his feet touched the ground, Sebrahn clasped Alec's hand and tried to pull him in a more easterly direction, heedless of the stony ground on his bare feet. It was the first time Seregil had seen the rhekaro show this much initiative.

"What do you think he wants?" he asked, intrigued in spite of himself.

"I don't know. He's never done this before."

Seregil turned to Ilar. "Do you have any ideas about this?"

Ilar looked baffled, too. "No."

"Well then, I guess we'll have to follow him."

Set loose, Sebrahn tugged at Alec's arm like a dog on a leash and he led them down into a deep gully Alec had been trying to avoid. Tough little plants lined a dry creek bed at the bottom. Alec sniffed the air, then plucked a sprig and nibbled carefully at one thin leaf.

"I thought so! This is teawort. Chew it, and it will keep your mouth wet."

It tasted a bit like pine, a bit like rosemary, and made the spit well under their tongues, making the dry air easier to bear as they hoarded the last of their water.

But Sebrahn didn't let them stop for long.

Taking Alec's hand again, he continued on to where the gully let out onto a small valley.

"Well, look at that!" Seregil exclaimed. Less than a mile on, they saw the warm, square glow of firelight through a window.

As they came closer, they could make out the shape of a low stone cottage ringed with a stone enclosure. The wind carried the scent of water, and goats.

"How could he have known that was there?" wondered Alec.

Seregil gave the rhekaro a grudging smile. "I don't know. Maybe he's part divining rod."

They approached the place with caution, but all was silent.

"Doesn't anyone in Plenimar keep dogs?" whispered Alec.

"They're considered dirty creatures here, good only for coursing, and for fighting," Ilar explained.

"Fighting what?" asked Alec.

"Each other, or slaves."

"Let's hope they don't keep that kind here," said Seregil. "Ilar, keep quiet and follow our lead."

Skirting the house, they stole a few knobby turnips from a rocky garden patch and discovered a large, strong-smelling cheese in a covered bucket let down the well to stay cool. They pulled up the water bucket and drank thirstily, slaking their dry throats.

Alec wiped his mouth on his sleeve, then looked around in alarm. "Where's Sebrahn?"

The rhekaro had stayed right beside him, as always. Now he was nowhere to be seen.

"Shit!" Seregil pointed toward the house, where the front door now stood open, letting out a long bar of firelight. "Ilar, stay here. Alec, let's go fetch your—him."

They stole up to the open door and peered inside.

The house was a humble one, just a single room, with stretched skins on the walls and chunks of dried meat hung from the rafters. Apart from a few crude stools, there were no furnishings, and it appeared that the family had been asleep on pallets on the floor. Now a man and his wife and several small girls were sitting up among their blankets, staring in terror at Sebrahn.

The rhekaro was kneeling beside the only occupied pallet. His headcloth had come off and his long hair fell in tangled disarray down his back. The ruddy light of the fire made it look more blond than white and lent his face a little color, but there was no mistaking his strangeness. The man made a sign against evil with two fingers and muttered the word "*urgha*," thinking the rhekaro was a demon or ghost.

A gaunt young woman lay on the pallet in front of Sebrahn. Seregil could hear her labored breathing from here, and smell the sickly-sweet odor of diseased flesh.

As he and Alec watched, Sebrahn pulled the lower end of a tattered blanket away, exposing a foot that was dark and grossly swollen.

"He wants to heal her, like he did Ilar's lip," Alec whispered, moving for the door.

Seregil grabbed him by the arm and signed,

Stay here. Keep watch. I'll do the talking. Making sure his sleeves were well pulled down to hide the slave brand, he stepped inside, hands raised to show he meant no harm.

"Who are you?" the man demanded in thickly accented Plenimaran as his wife hastily turned away and covered her head with a shawl. He had the curly hair and swarthy skin that spoke of mixed blood, probably Zengati. The little girls had curly hair, too, but were fair-skinned.

"Just a wayfarer," Seregil replied, knowing his own Plenimaran spoke of western cities. "We were so glad to see your light. I'm sorry if my companion there has troubled you, but he's a healer."

"That pale little thing?" the man growled. "What does he care about my daughter? How did you come here?"

"We were lost, up in the highlands."

The man remained suspicious, but Seregil pressed on. "My little friend here smells disease and follows it like a hound." Actually, he suspected that wasn't much of a lie. "If you'll allow it, I think he can make her well."

The man started to object, but his wife muttered something low and urgent and he softened as he looked over at the dying girl. "Well, I don't suppose he could do her much harm as she is."

"What happened to her?"

"Rock adder bit her last night as she was bringing in the flock. She screamed most of the night, 'til she wore out. If your little fellow can help her, or give her an easy passing, you can ask of us what you will."

"I need a cup of water."

"She can't take none."

"I know, but he needs it for the healing."

One of the little girls hurried to dip a cracked bowl in a bucket. Seregil took it with a reassuring smile and set it down beside Sebrahn.

"Give me your hand," he whispered, drawing his poniard.

The rhekaro immediately shrank back from him, eyes fixed on the long pointed blade.

"What are you playing at?" the man demanded, reaching for a cudgel on the floor beside him.

Alec came in and went to Sebrahn. "Let me do it."

The woman peered at them from the folds of her shawl and let out a trembling cry. She uncovered her head and turned her face to the firelight.

"You're Aurënfaie," Seregil said, in that language. Worn and hollow-eyed from hard living, she still had the fine features of his kind. She also had a large bruise under one eye.

"I was," she whispered. "I thought you must be, and now I see the boy." She held out her right forearm, showing them an elaborate, flower-shaped brand mark there, as well as bruises left by rough, large fingers. "I'm a freedwoman. This is my man, Karstus. I'm Tiel. Please, can you really help my girl?"

"I hope so." Alec pricked the rhekaro's finger and let several drops fall into the bowl. Two dark blue flowers floated up. When Sebrahn placed them on the affected foot, they both disappeared as soon as they touched the hot, discolored flesh. He held his finger over the bowl again and made another. This one he placed on her mouth, where the same thing happened, but this time her eyes opened and she looked up at him in sleepy confusion. "Where's Mama?"

Her mother let out a happy sob and crawled over to take her daughter's hand.

But Sebrahn was still busy, making more flowers and putting them on the girl's foot and leg. A sweet fragrance filled the air as, one by one, they disappeared.

Ilar crept in and knelt just inside the door, making the husband a humble bow.

"How many of you are there?" Karstus growled, suspicious again.

"That's all of us," Seregil replied, shooting Ilar a dark look.

"Oh, look!" Tiel exclaimed, with no eyes for anyone but her daughter. The swelling was already noticeably lessened, and the angry red streaks that had extended up her shin were fading. "Oh, thank Aura."

"Don't cry, Mama. It doesn't hurt so much now," the girl said.

"By the Flame," her father grunted, gripping the cudgel in both hands now. "What sort of sorcery is this?"

"What's he saying? Why is he still angry?" Alec whispered.

"Stay calm," Seregil told him quietly. Then, to the man, "It's a healing, that's all. See? Your girl is better. She'll be up tending the goats for you before the next full moon."

"That may be, but I still don't like the look of your little one, there. I've never seen a natural child do such things, or look like that. He's a demon, sure enough. How do I know you're not a pack of necromancers, come for my soul?"

Seregil held up his hands in a gesture of peace. "No, we're not. I swear it by Sakor."

"What does it matter what they are? He healed our Saria!" his wife cried, clinging to her daughter's hand. The younger girls had retreated to a corner and were clinging to each other there, watching Seregil and their father with wide, frightened eyes.

"What now?" Alec murmured, staying close to Sebrahn; he didn't have to understand the words being spoken to tell that the situation was going sour.

"Let me handle it," Seregil muttered back in Skalan. "Master Karstus, we've done you a good turn tonight, and we ask nothing in return but a scrap of food and some directions. We're making for the coast."

The man's eyes narrowed. "So that's how it is, is it? If I was to look at your right arm, what would I see, eh?"

Seregil glanced at the bruised and fearful wife. "You were a slaver yourself?"

"Never!" Karstus pushed back his right sleeve and showed Seregil a large double brand, gone white with age. Then he shifted on his pallet and stuck out his left leg. It was just a stump. "I was born to slavery, me, and kept until I was no use anymore. I found my woman starving on the road after her kind master freed her and turned her out with nothing." He pushed himself up on his good leg with the help of the cudgel. "Do you think you're the first escaped slaves to break for the Strait?"

Seregil looked sharply over his shoulder at Ilar. "Did you know?"

"No, I swear it."

"For what that's worth," Alec muttered.

"How far is it to the coast?" Seregil asked the man.

"Two or three days, maybe."

"Any towns?"

"Just steadings like this one, far as I know. Goats are the only things that thrive out here. Goats and freedmen."

Seregil retrieved his bundle from Ilar and took out a few pieces of the silver jewelry he'd found in the attic, and one of the little gold lockets. "If slavers come by here, will this be enough to make certain you never saw us?"

"That sword of yours is enough," Karstus replied, scowling.

Seregil tossed the trinkets on the closest pallet. "For your girls, then. And any advice you'd give."

"Due south should bring you to the coast. There's a little port along there somewhere, called Vostaz. Slave takers'll be thickest there. South and west will get you to the ocean in three days or four, maybe. There are some fishing villages 'round there. If you're handy at stealing and sailing, you might get off. The takers'll be watching there, too, but there's less of 'em."

"Is there no better way?" Ilar demanded.

"Not for any purebloods like you two, or that yellow-haired boy. Or that." He made another sign at Sebrahn.

Seregil held out his branded arm. "Do you know anyone who can fix this?"

Karstus shook his head. "There ain't enough money in that pack of yours to buy that of anyone in this part of the world. We've seen too many drawn and quartered who tried."

His wife leaned close and whispered in his ear. He scowled at her, then shook his head. "Do what you will, woman!"

Tiel went to the makeshift kitchen at the back of the room and placed a loaf of coarse bread and some sausages into a clean rag.

Alec went to her and held out the cheese they'd stolen. "I'm sorry we took this without asking."

But she only raised an eyebrow at him, then cut half and added it to the bundle. Knotting it, she put it in Alec's hands. "We've enough to spare, brothers. Thank you for saving my daughter. I'll always be grateful, and so will she."

"What clan are you, sister?" asked Seregil.

"Akhendi."

"I know the khirnari there. Can I bring any word to your people?"

She gave him a sad smile and shook her head. "Tell them that Tiel ä Elasi is dead."

Her words haunted them as they set out again.

"They're so poor. I feel guilty, taking their food," Alec said, though the smoky aroma of the goat sausage in Seregil's bundle was already making all of them hungry.

"We gave them back their daughter," Seregil said with a shrug.

"And you think that will make any difference if the slave takers come pounding on their door?" Ilar scoffed. "There's always a bounty, you know, as well as swift retribution for those who aid runaways."

"Then it would be better for them to keep their mouths shut, wouldn't it?" said Alec.

Seregil looked over at Sebrahn, riding placidly on Alec's back again. "This rhekaro scared them both, even after he healed the girl, and he's too strange to forget. That might make it worth their while."

"You should have killed them, then," Ilar muttered.

"Aren't you the bloodthirsty one, these days?"

"Oh, how that wounds me, coming from you!"

"I only kill when I have to. I don't enjoy it." He gave Ilar a dark look. "Well, not usually. As for killing those poor starvelings, it's no different than stealing Yhakobin's horses."

"You could have burned the house."

"You want to go back and paint an arrow on the wall to make sure they know we came this way?" Alec snapped.

Ilar shut his mouth and kept his distance.

They hurried on, Alec leading them east to confound any trackers who talked to the goatherd. Suddenly Seregil—who'd been uncommonly quiet—reached out and ruffled Sebrahn's hair. "You surely aren't human or 'faie, but you're not just a thing, either, I guess."

"No, he's not," Ilar agreed, much to Alec's surprise. "As great an alchemist as Il—as Yhakobin is, I don't think he understood what he created."

Alec spared him a mocking grin. "Because of my mongrel blood."

"That may be exactly it," Seregil mused, still studying Sebrahn. "We don't know what a rhekaro is supposed to look like."

"I saw a few drawings in the old tomes Yhakobin used," Ilar told him. "They showed something with a human shape, apart from the wings."

"Well, that's something, I suppose. So, he has teeth but doesn't eat. He moves and bleeds whatever that white juice is but has no heart. He appears to have some sort of mind—"

"And he can feel pain," Alec reminded him. "But not cold."

"When Yhakobin finished with the first one he made . . ." Ilar began.

Alec stopped dead, a dangerous look in his eyes. "You were there? You helped butcher it?"

Seregil gripped Alec's arm, holding him back. "What did you see, Ilar?"

Ilar looked rather ill. "It didn't die easily. He had to keep cutting it up."

Alec sank to the ground and pulled Sebrahn into his arms, holding him tight.

"What did he find?" Seregil asked.

"Something like bones and organs, but they were all colorless, and he could not guess their function."

"I see." Seregil squeezed Alec's shoulder. "Let's keep going."

Alec settled Sebrahn in his sling again and took the lead without a word, but Seregil could feel the rage boiling in his lover's heart. It coursed along the talimenios bond like molten lead.

He had to keep cutting it up . . .

Seregil glanced over at Sebrahn and felt sick at the thought.

When they stopped in a dry gully, just before dawn, Seregil's thoughts had turned to other things.

They settled as comfortably as they could, sheltered by a few wind-twisted cedars that overhung the bank. Seregil sat down beside Sebrahn and stroked the rhekaro's hair. "You're a fine healer, little one, with those flowers of yours."

That got a wan smile from Alec. "He is, isn't he? Maybe if Yhakobin had figured that out, he wouldn't have hurt them so much."

"The fact that he didn't know makes me wonder what he was after." Seregil paused, working up the nerve to broach the idea that had come to him during the night's march. "Alec, I'm going to need your help with something. Is your knife still good and sharp?"

"Yes. Why?"

Seregil pushed back his right sleeve and ran a thumb over the slave mark.

"Oh, no! Are you insane?"

Seregil grinned. "Probably, but that's beside the point at the moment. I'm going to need your help."

"What are you talking about?" Ilar demanded.

"You said it yourself," Seregil replied. "These marks are nothing I want to wear for the rest of my life. And if we're caught with them here, then there's no talking our way out of anything."

"And I told you that the first thing the slave takers look for is a new wound where the brand should be."

Seregil nodded at Sebrahn. "But what if there isn't one to find?"

He unbuckled his belt and folded the end over, then clenched it between his front teeth. "That should do. Let's do the leg brand first, Alec. That's less likely to be noticed in passing, if this doesn't work."

"Why not try it on Ilar first?" asked Alec.

Ilar was halfway to his feet already, and looked ready to bolt.

"That's why," said Seregil. "He'll fight and scream and we could end up hamstringing him. And it can't be you, either. You're the only one Sebrahn listens to, and if he sees me come at you with a knife, he might not be very cooperative." He grinned and ruffled Alec's hair. "Don't worry, talí. I've been through worse."

True. But not for a long time.

It took a little more convincing, but finally he talked them both into it. Ilar stood with Sebrahn, holding the cup of water. Seregil stretched out in the dirt on his belly, clutching the folded belt. Alec knelt over him with the knife and pulled up his trouser leg to expose the brand.

He gripped Seregil's leg, and Seregil was glad

that hand was steady. "Be quick, Alec, and try not to cut too deep. Just the skin."

"I know."

Seregil put the folded leather between his teeth and bit down. He felt Alec pinch up the skin on the back of his calf, then bit down hard on the belt as Alec started cutting.

Seregil probably had been through worse, and Alec probably was working as quickly as he could, but it certainly didn't seem like it as white-hot pain shot up Seregil's leg. Having the brand flayed off hurt worse than having it burned on. Panting around the folded belt, he was only dimly aware when Alec stopped and said something to the others.

An agonizing moment later, hands gripped his calf and he snarled and jerked in their grip as something cold and wet touched his raw flesh.

"Lie still!" Alec ordered.

The cold sensation came back, but this time the pain subsided considerably. He tried to look over his shoulder, but Alec pushed him down again. "Stay still, please. It's going to take a few more."

After the second flower the pain was bearable. After the third he spit out the belt and buried his head in his folded arms, covered in cold sweat and overwhelmed by the heavy perfume of the healing flowers.

Alec used one more, and the last of the pain was gone. "It worked!"

Seregil rolled over and stuck out his arm. "Do the other."

"Maybe we should wait."

Seregil let out a shaky laugh. "If we do that, you'll have to run me down and catch me. Just do it!" He jammed the belt back in his mouth and locked his left arm across his eyes.

Either he had more feeling in the underside of his arm or Alec had to cut deeper. Seregil was fighting back wheezing little screams before Alec stopped and applied the flowers.

When it was over he let his left arm fall and lay staring up at the dawn sky, willing himself not to throw up.

Alec bent over him, concerned. "Does it still hurt?"

"No," Seregil gasped, "but that was less fun than I thought it would be."

Vomiting less imminent now, he sat up and examined his forearm. The brand was gone. The skin where it had been was smooth and thin, but whole. There was some lingering pain, actually, but nothing he couldn't stand. He looked up at the others. Alec was pale, and the fingers holding the knife were bloody but still steady. Ilar looked sick as he knelt beside Sebrahn with the cup. "Thank you. Everyone." He reached over and gave the rhekaro a shaky pat on the head. "Especially you!"

The rhekaro held out its right forefinger; a drop of his white blood had welled out from the little cut there.

Seregil smiled. "Yes. You made my pain go away. Thank you."

Alec managed a grin when he handed the bloody knife to Seregil. "My turn, if you're up to it.

Pinch up the skin and cut under it. You're less likely to cut into the meat that way."

Seregil shuddered as he handed Alec the belt. "I'm really glad you didn't say that while you were still cutting."

Alec shrugged, then put his hands on Sebrahn's shoulders. "Seregil is going to cut me now. That's all right. I'm letting him, and you'll make those flowers for me, too, won't you?"

The rhekaro gazed up at him, silent and emotionless as ever.

"All right." Alec stretched out on the ground between them and buried his face in his arms. His voice was muffled as he added, "I just hope you're as good as I am at skinning things."

Seregil's hand tightened around the black hilt. "Bite on the leather. I'll be as quick as I can."

Ilar gripped Alec's calf at the ankle and just below the knee, his face inches from Seregil's. Their eyes met, and Seregil was surprised at the encouragement he saw there as Ilar murmured, "Don't make him wait."

Seregil pinched up the smooth golden skin around Alec's brand. The hard muscle underneath was lean and corded. Seregil took a deep breath, then sliced away the brand in one go, leaving a raw oval of exposed flesh. He sat back on his heels and watched as Sebrahn placed a large dark flower on the bleeding wound. It disappeared, just as he'd seen at the goatherd's cottage. The rhekaro made three more, and when the last had done its work and the wound was closed, Alec let out a choked moan and rolled over, still clutching the belt between his teeth. Tears of pain welled in his eyes as he stuck out his arm and gave Seregil an imploring look that said *hurry*.

Seregil quickly sliced out the second brand and helped Sebrahn place the flowers. When that wound was healed he grabbed Alec's hand in both of his, heedless of the blood. "Better?"

Alec spit out the gnawed belt and closed his eyes. "You're right," he whispered. "That wasn't much fun."

Sebrahn curled up next to him with his head on Alec's chest. Alec stroked his hair. "You did a good job."

Seregil looked over at Ilar, and saw him swallow hard. He was terrified. "I could hide if the slave takers come."

"We can't risk that. If we're caught with a marked slave, Alec and I are just as dead as if we'd stayed branded. It doesn't take long, and the flowers take away the pain very quickly."

Ilar nodded slowly, though he was trembling badly. "I'm not as brave as you two. You'd better hold me down. Seregil, will you do the cutting?"

"All right. Lie down."

Ilar was already whimpering as Alec lay down across him, pinning Ilar's leg with both hands. Seregil braced one knee on the back of Ilar's calf and went to work.

Ilar screamed around the belt but didn't struggle very much as Seregil sliced off the branded skin. Sebrahn placed the flowers as before, but

Seregil noticed that they were smaller now, and it took more of them to heal the wound.

When that was over, Alec got off Ilar. "Turn over."

"I can't! No more!" Ilar whimpered.

"Yes, you can." Alec roughly flipped Ilar over and flattened himself across the sobbing man to grip his arm.

Ilar did struggle this time, making it harder for Seregil to make a single clean cut. His fingers were slippery with blood and he got only half the brand, and managed to slice his own thumb, too.

"Stop moving, damn it! You're only making it worse."

Ilar froze, trying to choke back his sobs.

"Cover his eyes, Alec." Seregil got the rest of the brand off and sat back to let Sebrahn do his healing work.

Despite the healing, Ilar was a sobbing wreck. Seregil patted his shoulder awkwardly. "That's enough, now. Come on. Get up."

Seregil tried to pull him up, but Ilar's legs wouldn't hold him and Seregil ended up on the ground again with Ilar halfway in his lap, clutching Seregil's coat in both hands. Seregil had little choice but to hold him until he calmed down. He could feel the raised ridges of old scars under his hands, through the back of Ilar's thin robe. Past suffering had made Seregil stronger, and Alec, too. It had broken Ilar.

"You're getting blood all over him."

Seregil looked up to find Alec cradling Sebrahn in his arms. He was watching Ilar with a mix of pity and disgust. But when he looked up at Seregil, he caught a flash of resentment there, too.

They sat like that for a long time as the sun came up, each of them holding another in their arms.

CHAPTER 43

Divisions

ALEC HAD NO idea what the date was, but the wind grew sharper every day and smelled of winter. At night the ground under their feet sparkled with frost.

With careful rationing, and a bit of luck he had hunting, they managed to make Tiel's food last two nights, but the cold was rapidly becoming more of a danger. When they had to rest there was nothing to do but huddle even closer together than before, trying to keep the heat in each other's bodies.

Three days out from the goatherd's cottage not only were they still not in sight of the ocean, but it began to rain. By dawn it was coming down so hard that he and Seregil gave up on keeping watch and joined Ilar in the scant shelter of a ruined cottage they'd come across.

"At least water won't be a problem today," Seregil joked through chattering teeth.

When they moved on that night, they were still

hungry and filthy, but little rills flowed in the formerly dry gullies, enough to keep the water skin filled.

Since healing the girl, Sebrahn had returned to his usual silent, passive state, showing no interest in diverging from each night's chosen march. Hungry most of the time himself, Alec fed him several times a day, and the rhekaro seemed content with the extra feedings. He nestled close to Alec when he slept, but he always did that, anyway.

Looking into those pale eyes as he washed Sebrahn's face or cut his hair, however, Alec was convinced that he saw more intelligence there each day. The way the rhekaro sensed the sick girl and insisted on finding her was proof enough of that. And Seregil had begun to soften towards him, too, much to Alec's relief.

The only signs of habitation they saw over the next two nights were a few herders' huts. They stopped just long enough to take what little food they could steal, careful not to show themselves to the householders.

The subject of getting rid of either Ilar or Sebrahn had died somewhere along the road. Seregil had to admit that he'd had the easier choice. At first he'd made an effort to refer to the rhekaro as "him" and "Sebrahn" for Alec's sake. Since that night at the goatherd's cottage, he couldn't help but begin to think of him as a real being. Silent and strange as he was, Sebrahn had somehow known of the girl's distress and acted to help her. The sight of him drinking Alec's blood, and the touch of his cold little fingers were still a little unnerving, though.

Alec and Ilar also seemed to have established a truce of sorts, enough at least they could sleep next to each other without a fight, but that was about as far as it went. Seregil had never seen Alec hold a grudge like this; he'd always been the more forgiving one, and it made Seregil wonder if there was something Alec hadn't told him about his time with Ilar in the alchemist's house.

Less clear were Seregil's feelings toward Ilar. He still had every reason to hate the man, and years of a bitterly nursed grudge on top of that, yet whenever he looked at Ilar, all he could see were the scars and the beaten look in his eyes. This wasn't the man he remembered.

Days ago, when they'd first had to huddle together while Alec was on watch, Ilar had been quiet and nervous. But as the days went on, he began to talk of Aurënen and the past, like he had when Seregil had been playing the dutiful slave. Now he asked for news of people he remembered, and recalled friends they'd shared. Grudgingly at first, Seregil found himself having real conversations with Ilar. If it had been anyone but Ilar, it would have been rather pleasant. The fact that Alec had nothing good to say to the man during their marches, but could sleep next to him in the daylight, made Seregil wonder if he was softening toward Ilar, too. When he tried to broach the subject in a rare moment of privacy, however, Alec just stared at him.

"I use him for warmth, like a campfire. Nothing

else." He gave Seregil an oddly appraising look. "What about you?"

"The same," Seregil replied, but in the back of his mind, a little doubt niggled. Alec saw through him in an instant. "I can't explain it, talí. I don't want him. I don't *like* him! I just can't seem to hate him anymore. As soon as we get away from Plenimar we'll send him on his way, I promise."

"Just like that?"

"Yes. Just like that."

Alec let it drop, but only after giving Seregil a skeptical look that cut him to the heart.

By the time the first hint of dawn showed that morning, Alec could tell by the scent on the breeze that they were finally nearing the ocean. He waited until the sky brightened along the horizon, then pointed off to the southwest. "There it is. The Strait!"

Between the still-dark land and the golden lip of the horizon, a dark strip of ocean curved into the hazy distance. Beyond that, out of sight, lay Aurënen, and safety.

"I don't believe it!" whispered Ilar. "We might actually make it."

Seregil gave him a crooked grin. "Two nights. Three at most. I hope you have a good stomach for sailing, my friend."

Friend? Alec's own grin died—not for all the days Ilar had slept beside Seregil, or for his betrayal of Alec in Yhakobin's house. No, it was the way

Seregil had called Ilar "friend." It sounded almost like he meant it.

"Come on!" Seregil urged, not noticing.

They came across a rutted dirt track leading south and gave it a wide berth. They skirted a small hamlet, too, and finally took refuge in a lonely copse of trees next to a stream. It was less than ideal, but the sun was up and they couldn't risk being caught out in the open.

There was plenty of dry wood lying around, and after some consultation, he and Seregil decided to risk a small fire. The three of them breakfasted on boiled water and a few slices of raw turnip. It wasn't very filling but the heat felt good in their bellies. They kept the rest of their scant provisions—a few more turnips, two wizened apples, and some cooked meat from the skinny coney Alec had killed two days earlier—in the rag sack, hoping to eke them out one more day.

He and Seregil took turns on watch through the day. It was a sheltered spot and the sun had come out at last, so Ilar was left to sleep by himself again.

Seregil was on watch late that afternoon, burning wood ticks from his arms and legs with the hot tip of a stick, when Ilar woke and scratched glumly at his own dirty clothing and hair. Moving carefully past Alec, who was still asleep with Sebrahn, he walked over to Seregil and whispered, "You'll have to show me how to do that. I itch all over. I have to piss, too. May I have some privacy?"

Ilar always went off by himself, and in the dark, too, to attend to bodily functions. Seregil was about to object, then thought of the gelding scars Ilar had shown him. "Go on, but stay inside the trees."

Ilar stepped behind a large trunk and a moment later Seregil caught sight of a bare, bent knee sticking out from behind it.

Of course, he has to squat. He looked away, more affected by the sight than he thought possible. He remembered that body the way it had been, strong and whole and pressed close to his . . .

Seregil threw his stick into the fire and went to make a circuit of their little hiding place, looking for any signs of life and trying not to think about the man.

Ilar, however, followed him. "I'm hungry."

"We'll eat when Alec wakes up. Have all the water you want. The stream is good."

Ilar drank deeply and capped the skin. Then he turned and looked back to where Alec lay asleep on the ground. "So that's what you can love, eh? Can't say I blame you. He has a kind heart."

"Not for those who betray him," Seregil retorted softly.

"I'm sorry about that. What choice do you think I had? Ilban ordered it and I had to obey."

"Stop calling him that! You're free now. Aurënfaie don't have masters."

Ilar's soft laugh was bitter. "Can either of us call himself that anymore?"

"That's the blood that runs in our veins, no matter what anyone says, or does to us."

"I see. Well, I'll try to take your advice, until someone sees me naked. I'll be quite the darling of the baths, won't I?"

"Self-pity is not a very productive emotion, you know. Or an attractive one."

"Forgive me, Ilban," Ilar returned with heavy sarcasm.

Seregil bit back a snide remark, not wanting to wake Alec. Even asleep, the younger man had dark rings of exhaustion under his eyes. He lay curled on his side with his head on the bundle, with Sebrahn nestled against his chest as always.

"I wanted to die when I was first exiled, but I was too young and scared to carry through," Seregil admitted softly. "But after that passed, even with all the shame—Despite what you may think, going to Idrilain's court in disgrace wasn't pleasant. Everyone knew why I was there, and what I'd done. But a wise friend told me that if you act like a whipped dog, that's how people treat you, and that I'd better learn to hold my head up if I wanted anyone's respect ever again."

"That's easily said." Ilar turned away and stared out at the sinking sun. "I'm so dirty." Seregil thought he was talking of his spirit before he added, "The sound of that stream is driving me mad. Please, can I go and wash?"

Seregil hesitated, tempted by the idea himself. They hadn't seen or heard anyone all day, and just down the hill from where they sat, the stream curved in among the trees. The sun was nearly down and stars were already showing through the branches overhead. "All right. We'll keep watch for each other."

Seregil went first. Leaving his sword within easy reach, he stripped off his coat and squatted on the muddy bank, trying to wash away the sweat and stink. He glanced down at his right arm where the brand had been, glad not to go the rest of his life with that kind of reminder in plain sight. Bad enough that he'd let himself and Alec be taken like that; he felt most guilty at how long it had taken him to get loose again.

Long enough for that thing *to be made. And he loves it, too, as if it really were his child.* Seregil bent to rinse his hair in the current, thinking again of the oracle's prophecy. If this wasn't the fulfillment of it, then it was damn close.

The cold water felt wonderful against his sweaty scalp. He stayed there a moment, then sat up and shook his head like a dog, scattering droplets in all directions.

"Now I'm wet, too."

Seregil looked back over his shoulder and was startled to see Ilar standing close beside him. *He is a 'faie, after all*, he thought, but still disliked having the man creep up on him like that.

Ilar wiped his face on his sleeve, leaving a streak of wet dust on his cheek. "That much less I need to wash, eh, Haba?"

"Don't call me that," Seregil snapped, more out of habit than any real anger.

"I'm sorry. I've always thought of you that way."

"Well, don't," Seregil growled, going back to his washing.

"I wish Alec could forgive me. I really do like him, you know. It wasn't easy, lying to him like that, but I had no choice."

"So you keep saying." Seregil snorted as he washed his face.

A light touch on his shoulder startled him. He slapped Ilar's hand away and stood up, water running down his chest to soak the front of his trousers. "Damn you! What do you want from me?"

Ilar stepped closer. "Your forgiveness, Seregil. I don't understand. You saved my life, but you still treat me like a plague rat. Why didn't you kill me or leave me when you had the chance?"

"I've been asking myself that a lot."

Ilar smoothed a hand down the front of his dirty robe. "You didn't know, did you, what had really become of me? You thought I was wandering around free, just like you."

And there it was again, thought Seregil, that little fish hook tug in his heart. Ilar held his gaze as he undid the ties at the neck of his robe and pulled it off over his head, baring his devastated body—the scars, the stripes, and the terrible emptiness between his legs.

When Ilar reached for his shoulder this time, Seregil just stood there, looking into those sad hazel eyes, and seeing the depth of pain there.

"Haba," Ilar whispered, leaning closer. "Can't we call the tally even? We ruined each other's lives, and now we've saved them. Without me, how would you have gotten them both away?"

"I'd have managed!" But Seregil couldn't help wondering how. Ilar's hand slid to the back of his neck and he could not for the life of him understand why he was allowing it. Ilar suddenly bent closer, bringing his lips close enough for Seregil to taste the man's breath.

Seregil jerked back. "What the hell—?"

Before they could discuss the matter, Alec burst from the trees and flung himself at Ilar, tumbling them both into the stream with a mighty splash.

Seregil stood dumbstruck, watching them flailing at each other with knees and fists. *He almost kissed me. I almost let him!*

Alec quickly got the upper hand and was holding Ilar's head under the water. Seregil waded in and dragged him off, pulling him to his feet. They were both soaked now.

Alec whipped around and punched Seregil squarely in the jaw, knocking him on his ass in the shallows. He was livid.

"Is that how it is?" he shouted, fists balled, body tensed for attack. "Is that why you dragged him along?"

Seregil stared up at him. The whole side of his face throbbed and his mouth was full of blood. "Of course not!"

"I saw you! Him—naked. Kissing you!"

"He did not!" The accusation stung, and pain was giving way to anger. "And what about you? I saw you in the garden with him, more than once! He held you."

"I told you, he tried to seduce me, but *I* didn't let him!"

"Neither did I!"

"Oh, so he was just getting something out of your eye for you?"

"For fuck's sake, Alec!" He looked over at Ilar, who was still sitting in the water where he'd fallen. Water streamed down his face, and blood, too. Ilar was beaten, miserable, helpless. Pitiable.

Seregil staggered to his feet. "Hit me again. Harder."

"What?"

"Please, talí. Once more."

Alec gave him another doubtful look, and then slapped him, hard.

Ilar staggered up, looking at them like they'd both gone mad, then edged around them to grab up his discarded robe. "I didn't mean any harm, Alec," he mumbled, trembling.

"The hell you didn't! You've been trying to cozy up to him from the start." He turned accusing eyes on Seregil. "Did you let him?"

Alec might just as well have hit him again. Seregil yanked on his discarded coat and stalked back up the hill to their camp, not trusting himself to answer. He wasn't sure whom he was most angry with.

Probably himself.

Alec leveled the point of his sword at Ilar's throat. "First me at the house, and now this? Leave him alone, damn you!"

"Please don't! You promised," Ilar begged, as his legs gave out under him.

"Don't tempt me." Disgusted, Alec sheathed his sword. "You put a slave collar on him, but he saved you anyway. Why are you making trouble now?"

Ilar hugged his knees to his chest, rocking back and forth a little. Eyes downcast, he whispered, "I wasn't always like this. All these years of being one master's possession after another... I can't expect you to understand, or him. I was just 'Khenir' for so long."

"Yhakobin didn't give you that name?"

"Of course not. When the slavers asked me what my name was, I just said the first one that came into my head, so as not to shame my clan any more than I already had."

As much as he hated to admit it, Alec suspected Ilar was telling him at least a partial truth. "How did you become a slave in the first place?"

"When I failed, all those years ago, Ulan í Sathil had to make certain that the truth of his role in all that never came out. So he had me caught and sold."

Alec snorted. "Because the Aurënfaie don't like to kill each other?"

"Scoff all you like. He couldn't very well declare teth'sag on my clan and me. And he couldn't risk the Haman claiming their right to it, in case I talked. If he'd had me killed, it would have been murder and set his clan at odds with mine and their allies." He was shivering harder now. "Besides, this is more of a punishment, isn't it?"

"And you wanted to punish Seregil, too."

"When I overheard one of Ilban's visitors speak of you and Seregil a few years ago, something happened..." He paused, gaze fixed on his muddy feet. "Some part of me came back to life. I wanted revenge. I couldn't think of anything else. And Ilban trusted me enough to look into the matter, once he heard the claims about your mixed blood." He looked up, a bit of spirit coming back into his eyes. "Seregil is right when he says that all that's happened to you was my doing, but he bears some of the responsibility."

"Don't start that again. I don't believe you and I don't care."

Ilar stood up slowly and pulled on his discarded cloak. "What's stopping you from killing me now?"

Because I wouldn't let Seregil do it, and now he won't let me, Alec thought, resigned.

Ilar pressed his hand to his heart and gave him a small bow. "Whatever your reason, I thank you. If you only knew what it was like, seeing him again... But I'll take more care around him, I swear!"

"You'd better."

Seregil had found Sebrahn squatting in the dappled shade under a gnarled tree. His back was to Seregil but he turned as soon as he heard him approaching, long silvery hair swinging around his shoulders. Seregil had given up cutting it as often. It was too disconcerting to see it grow back.

Distracted by the hair, it took Seregil a moment to notice that Sebrahn held a cup in both hands.

The rhekaro rose and offered it to him. A large blue lotus filled the cup. "What's that for?"

Sebrahn pointed at Seregil's bruised face. "Oh that? It's—"

There was a deep gash in Sebrahn's forearm. The strange pale blood was still flowing, and a trail of dark spots in the dust led back to the open bundle, and the knife beside it.

"How did you know?" Seregil muttered. "And what have you done to yourself? I don't need that."

He scooped the wet flower from the cup and pressed it to Sebrahn's wound. It evaporated like a mist between his fingers, but the gash remained open and bleeding.

"You can't heal yourself?" Seregil's hands were covered in that strange blood now. It was cool and slick and unpleasant on his skin, yet he couldn't help feeling pity for the rhekaro. What sort of life was Sebrahn supposed to have, made as he was?

The rhekaro walked unsteadily back toward the fallen cup, perhaps intending to make another healing flower for Seregil, but he wobbled and fell before he could reach it.

"Alec, come quick!" Seregil shouted, forgetting caution for a dangerous moment. Going to Sebrahn, he tried to staunch the wound with a rag from the bundle. Sebrahn was limp and slumped over on his side, eyes half-closed.

"What is it?" Alec asked, dashing through the trees toward him, sword drawn.

Seregil gathered the little body into his arms. "He's hurt himself. I think he needs you."

Alec knelt and examined the wound. "He did this himself?"

"Alec, I wouldn't..."

Alec gave him a brief smile. "I know that. I just didn't think he could—never mind. Give me that knife, quick."

Alec sliced his own finger deeply and let his blood flow between Sebrahn's parted lips.

For a long moment nothing happened. Red blood trickled from the slack mouth, streaking the pale chin, which looked even whiter than normal. Then those pale lashes fluttered and the tip of a grey tongue appeared, lapping like a kitten at the blood.

"Watch his arm," Alec told him.

As Seregil watched, the skin closed itself, sealing into a thin white scar like the ones on Sebrahn's fingers and wrist.

The rhekaro's eyes were open now, and he was sucking harder at Alec's finger.

"Maybe you should give him extra. He fainted, or something, just from what little blood he lost."

"We don't know what a lot or a little is to him." Alec cradled Sebrahn's head in one hand. "Poor little thing. Maybe I've been starving him."

This time Alec let Sebrahn drink as long as he wanted. He'd always felt a strange pull inside when he fed him, but it was much stronger now, like when Yhakobin had Alec feed the first rhekaro after one of the alchemist's crueler explorations. He was shivering by the time Seregil reached over and pulled Alec's hand away.

"No more, talí. You've gone pale, yourself."

"I feel a little shaky," he admitted. "But look!"

For the first time, the rhekaro's face and the quick of his nails showed the faintest tinge of pink. His eyes were darker silver now, too, almost the color of steel.

Seregil cupped Alec's chin and inspected him closely. "You look different, too. More like your old self."

"It's like he's pulling the Hâzadriëlfaie out of me," Alec whispered, hugging himself and shivering harder.

Seregil fetched the water skin and made Alec drink, then sat behind him and pulled Alec against his chest to warm him. Sebrahn climbed into Alec's lap and cuddled against him.

Alec hugged the rhekaro close. "He doesn't feel quite so cold now."

Seregil wound a strand of silvery hair around one finger. "I wish you could talk, little one. There's more to you than meets the eye, and I'd be a lot happier if I knew what it was."

"Maybe there's more Ilar hasn't told us," said Alec.

"Maybe." Seregil rested his unbruised cheek against the side of Alec's head.

He relaxed back against him, glad for a moment of peace. Any anger he'd felt toward Seregil was gone. They were all in a miserable situation.

"What was all that shouting?"

"I just told Ilar to stay away from you."

"You threatened him."

"I just told him to leave you alone."

"Good."

Alec turned to look at him. "You really mean that?"

"Ah, Alec."

"I wasn't the one calling him 'friend.'"

"I loved him once. You know that. And then I hated him."

"And now you pity him."

"I wish I didn't. But I swear to you, talí, you have no reason to be jealous."

"I'm not jealous of him!"

Seregil smiled sadly. "Just as I'm not jealous of Sebrahn?"

"You don't—Wait, where is Ilar?"

"I'm here." The man joined them and crouched beside the fire, chaffing his hands over the flames.

"I heard what you said before," he told them dully. "I've told you everything I know about the rhekaro. I don't care if you believe me or not. It's the truth. What reason would I have to lie now? You were right, Alec. It's only because of you two I'm alive, and I'm grateful for that. Just take me out of this cursed country. After that, I'll fend for myself."

Alec watched him closely through this little speech, alert for any false notes. But all he saw in Ilar's red-rimmed eyes was resignation, and—when he spoke of going off on his own—fear.

By sundown everyone was warm, dry, and somewhat rested. Alec had managed to sleep again with

Sebrahn safely beside him. He woke smiling from a dream of Seregil's long fingers caressing the nape of his neck, but the moment didn't last. Ilar had interrupted them before they could really settle anything between them and now Seregil sat on the far side of the fire, looking sad. He looked away quickly when he realized Alec was awake.

Miserable, Alec sat up to feed Sebrahn. "Do you think we can reach the coast tonight?"

"If not tonight, then tomorrow for certain," Seregil said as he parceled out the last of the rabbit meat and an apple for each of them.

Alec ate his portion very slowly, aware of the silence underlying the words. He wanted to grab Seregil, tell him he understood that all Seregil felt for Ilar was pity, but the words backed up in his throat as Alec pictured the two of them there by the stream.

He *did* trust Seregil! So why couldn't he let go of this?

"Maybe I can find us some rabbits here. It's better country for it," he offered, hoping to get a response, but his talimenios just stared into the fire, as if he knew Alec's thoughts.

"Better that than snake," Ilar remarked with a weak smile.

"Too cold for snakes now," Seregil told him, rising to his feet. "We're more likely to find a village, or at least a decent farm. Hunger always sharpens my thievery skills."

As soon as it was dark, they cleaned up their camp, then took off their boots and walked down the streambed as far as they could bear, feet going numb in the icy water.

When Seregil judged they'd gone far enough to confuse the trail, they struck north and east for a while to finish the job. It lost them miles and time, but hopefully any pursuers wouldn't come looking in this direction.

As the night dragged on, Seregil's silence continued. His past had come between them again like an unwelcome shadow and now he was a dark, driven shape in the dark beside Alec and the bond was silent.

They stopped a few times to rest and feed Sebrahn. Perhaps the rhekaro picked up on the tension between them, for as soon as he was let out of his sling, he settled close against Alec's side and wouldn't be moved. When Seregil offered to carry him, he clung to Alec like a squirrel.

Before Alec could say anything, Seregil turned and strode off again, setting a brisk pace.

Almost as if he's trying to run away from something, Alec reflected sadly. And knowing Seregil as he did, he probably was, if only from his own feelings.

The Parting

SEREGIL DIDN'T MEAN to shut Alec out; he just didn't know what to say.

As the night waned, the way grew more barren rather than less, with no signs of habitation, and everyone's concentration was taken up with not breaking an ankle or falling into a hole. By dawn their food was gone, and the water skin was just half-full. Alec took his hunting sling and left an unwilling Sebrahn with the others.

Hunkered down in a dry gully, Seregil settled with his back to a rock—well away from Ilar, even though Alec wasn't there to see—and regarded the restless rhekaro with some concern. "I thought we were beginning to get along, you and I?"

Sebrahn squatted where Alec had left him, eyeing them both with apparent wariness.

"He's very attached to Alec, isn't he?" Ilar remarked. "How are you going to manage, back in Skala?"

"I have no idea."

"Perhaps he could be of some use to your queen?"

Not in the mood for conversation, particularly that one, he tried to ignore the man, but it seemed Ilar needed to talk.

"You and Alec... Are you still angry with each other?"

Seregil rested his head against the rock behind him. "I'm not mad at him. He's young. It's hard for him, thinking of me having others before him. Especially you."

"I could talk to him."

"Don't."

"Then you should."

Seregil gave him a meaningful glare. "Keep on like that and I'll drop a rock on your head while you sleep."

After that, Ilar kept his thoughts to himself.

When Alec returned empty-handed, they set off again, looking for better cover. There weren't even rocks large enough to shelter under, much less trees.

"No wonder the Plenimarans are always trying to take someone else's land," Alec muttered, shading his eyes as he scanned the distance.

"I hear it's like this all the way—"

"Oh hell!" Alec was staring hard at something in the distance ahead of them.

There, not a mile away, a long plume of dust traced a trajectory in their direction, straight as a bowshot. Seregil had been expecting this for so long, it was almost a relief. "Could be nothing, just traders or something. All the same—*run!*"

"Run where?" Ilar cried.

Seregil knew there was no point in going back the way they'd come, so he struck out west. "Just keep going. Maybe we'll find something."

But they didn't and now they could make out the shapes of horses, coming on at a gallop, and hear the distant baying of hounds.

Seregil cocked his head, listening. "I guess they do keep dogs, after all."

"Bad luck . . . to kill . . . a dog," Ilar panted.

"I'll risk it. Sounds like they've got a scent."

"It took them long enough," Alec muttered, holding Sebrahn's legs to keep the rhekaro from falling out of the sling as he ran.

They ran for all they were worth, but it was no use. Within minutes, Seregil looked back over his shoulder and saw a pack of riders following the hounds and heard the sound of a hunting horn.

"We might as well save our strength," said Alec, stopping to watch their pursuers.

"What are you saying?" Ilar quavered. "If they catch us . . ."

Seregil cast a longing look south. In the distance, the dark blue ocean mocked him, hopelessly beyond reach. He could even make out the tiny white specks of sails on the water.

"Alec . . ." This was no time for long speeches and explanations. He grabbed Alec and kissed him; their cracked lips tasted of dust and salt. Sebrahn, still in his sling, touched Seregil's cheek with his cold little fingers, almost as if he could feel the sorrow between them.

Alec buried a hand in Seregil's hair and rested his forehead against his. "I'm sorry."

"Nothing to be sorry for. No one is taking us." Seregil drew his sword. "Give Ilar your knife. We stand and fight."

Alec tried to hand Ilar his knife, but the man backed away.

"No!" The color had drained from Ilar's face, and Seregil recognized the same look of terror and despair he'd seen in Rhania's face, just before she drove a knife into her own heart. Before Seregil could stop him, Ilar turned and ran, away from the oncoming riders and away from them.

"Let him go," said Alec, though Seregil had made no move to follow. "He won't be any help."

"I suppose not."

Alec put Sebrahn down and stepped in front of him. "Stay there." The rhekaro whimpered and clutched at the back of his coat.

"I think you were right, about the oracle and all," Seregil said, shaking his head.

"Thanks for that, talí."

"Better late than never, I guess."

The dogs reached them first, six huge mastiffs. Their hackles were up and their heads low.

"Do the dog thing," Alec muttered.

Seregil fixed as many of them with his gaze as he could and performed the spell. "Soora thalassi!"

Two of the dogs relaxed, tongues out and tails wagging.

Seregil quickly did it again, and a third time, then sent them running north.

That was certainly going to help, but as the riders

closed in on them, Seregil counted at least twenty men, with Yhakobin in the lead. At least half of them were archers. "I sure miss that bow of yours right now."

"Me, too. I could have pared down the numbers." Alec paused. "It's me he wants, and Sebrahn."

"Don't even think it. If we go down, we go down together."

Alec grinned bravely, but his eyes were sad. "Kari always said you'd get me killed. At least we can find the Gate together."

"We're not dead yet."

Yhakobin and his men reined in a few dozen yards off and fanned out to surround them.

"Master, Khenir is getting away," one of them said to Yhakobin. Ilar was already far off, and dwindling from sight.

"I'll attend to him later." The alchemist rested his gloved hands on the pommel of his saddle and raised an eyebrow at Seregil. "You've taken what belongs to me."

Seregil raised the tip of his sword, deadly calm now. "I could say the same."

"Say what you like. You'll be dog's meat soon." Turning his attention to Alec, he said, "You have stolen from me, too, Alec, and run away, but I am prepared to be somewhat merciful. Drop your sword and bring the rhekaro to me."

"Kiss my ass, *Ilban*!"

Yhakobin smiled. "I believe those were the first words you spoke to me. I promise you, you'll regret them." He raised his hand. The two archers beside him raised their bows and took aim.

At Seregil.

Things went very clear and shining, the way they often did in a crisis. Seregil could see the sharp edges of the steel broadheads, and count the vanes on the shafts. He could hear the creak of the bowstrings and there was no time to run...

Something struck him from the side, hard, and he fell. He'd been hit by an arrow before; it didn't feel like this. Before he could figure it out, however, Alec came down on top of him, knocking the wind out of him.

Seregil pushed at him, trying to get up, but he didn't move. "Alec?"

He was far too limp, and too silent. Seregil pushed himself up on his elbows. Alec lay faceup, arms still thrown wide to protect Seregil, with two arrows protruding from his chest—one near his heart, the other just below his throat.

Mortal wounds.

A faint gurgling sound came from his lips as blood welled there and ran down his chin. His eyes were open and already fixed, reflecting the lowering grey sky.

He was dying.

Alec was dying, and not even Sebrahn could help him now.

With a ragged scream of pure rage, Seregil scrambled to his feet, gripped his sword in both bloody hands, and ran to meet his own death.

Kari was lifting the lid from a kettle when a terrible chill rolled over her. She dropped the lid with a clatter and sank down on the settle.

"What's wrong?" Illia cried, kneeling beside her and wrapping her arms around her mother to keep her from falling. "Are you sick?"

"No," Kari said faintly, pressing a hand to her brow. It was wet with cold sweat that hadn't been there a moment before. "I don't know. A goose must have stepped on my grave—" She'd meant it lightly, but suddenly she was clutching her daughter to her breast and sobbing. "Oh my heart! Something... Where are the children? Are they safe?"

"They're in the yard, Mama. Please, don't cry! They're safe, I promise. There, you can see them through the doorway."

Gherin and Luthas heard the commotion and ran to her, terrified.

"Mama, what is it?" Gherin wailed, burying his face in her skirts.

Kari gathered both little boys into her arms with Illia, but the grief was just as strong. *Oh blessed Dalna, please! Not when he's so far from home!*

In the deepest recesses of the caverns beneath the Temple at Sarikali, the Dragon Oracle laughed.

Beyond the peaks called Ravensfell by the Tír, a dark-eyed half-breed woke in her hut with tears on her cheeks.

The Plenimaran coastline was a dark line on the horizon sight. Micum was too restless to sit still now, and divided his time between pacing the deck and standing watch at the forward rail. It seemed that no matter how the hours passed, the land remained as far away as ever. Their captain promised that he'd have them ashore somewhere near Riga by midnight, but the winds were changing and Micum could tell that he and the mate were worried.

And once we get there, where to start? Micum wondered, admitting to himself at last what he could never say to Thero.

Just then the wind went colder and the hair stood up on the back of his neck. Turning slowly, he gripped the rail in one hand to keep from staggering. "Oh Illior, no!"

Chilled and discouraged, Thero had retired to their cabin to rest. Despite all his assurances to Micum, he knew it might be impossible to find them, even if they were able to get ashore. Every sighting had failed. It was as if Alec was veiled from sight. And Illior only knew what their reception at Riga would be, even with the Gedre traders to vouch for them.

Lying on the narrow bunk, he threw an arm across his eyes, hating this feeling of helplessness. He could only imagine Micum's agony; the look of disappointment in his eyes, every time Thero failed with his magic, haunted him. To lose Seregil and Alec like this, never knowing what had become of them . . .

To fail them like this!

He sat up, blinking away tears. *I can't give up. I won't!*

Composing himself cross-legged on the bunk, he closed his eyes and brought his hands up in the figure of seeing as he threw his mind's eye once more into flight toward Riga.

Give me some sign. Anything. Lightbearer, I beg you, guide my eye!

He held the spell until his head throbbed and his breath gave out, and then broke it, gasping, to find blood streaming from his nose in twin rivulets. That had never happened before. He must be more exhausted than he thought. In fact, he was shaking badly and felt chilled to the bone. And when had the sun gone down? The room was so dim, and so cold!

Thero...

Startled, Thero looked around the little cabin. There was nowhere for anyone to hide, yet the faint, tremulous whisper seemed to come from all around him.

Thero, help...

"Who are you?" he whispered.

Thero, can you hear...

He knew that voice. Thero pressed his palms together, opening his mind's eye again, but this time within the confines of the cabin.

It was a strong spell for such a small space. Every detail of the tiny room appeared with razor-edged clarity behind his closed lids, and there in front of him stood Alec.

Thero had seen only a few ghosts in his life, and never one so clearly. No shredding, rippling shade, this. Alec seemed almost as solid as life, except for the fact that Thero could see the faint outline of the door through him, and the edge of the window. He was dressed in strange clothing, and his chest was soaked with blood. His lips were moving, but Thero couldn't hear him now.

"Alec!" Thero's voice broke but the spell held. "Please, let me hear you!"

Alec faded almost out of sight, but his voice returned. *Help him! Save Seregil and the child.*

"Child? Where are they? Can you show me?"

Show you! Alec reached out and clutched Thero's spirit by the hand in a crushing grip and suddenly they were flying, the sea and sky a blur around them, then the land under them. Not Riga. No, someplace miles to the east and south.

I was looking in the wrong place all along!

. . . hurry!

Thero could see the coastline from here and far below, a few tiny specks of riders hemming something in.

No, someone.

He could see Alec on the ground now, pitifully splayed in death, with arrows in his body. He saw Seregil running, sword in hand, at more men than he could hope to bring down alone. And someone else, a blur of white, so indistinct, yet the sight of it sent a shudder through Thero's very soul.

What is that? Even from here I can feel it!

Alec's shade looked at him with such sad eyes, then he was falling, falling—

"Thero, look at me!"

Thero opened his eyes to find himself sprawled

on the cabin floor with blood running down the back of his throat from the nosebleed. Micum was crouched over him.

"Alec!" There was no sign of the shade now. The deathly chill was gone and sunlight was streaming in through the window.

"You saw him, too?" Micum was looking panicked now, something Thero had never seen before.

"I know where they are!" Thero told him, and burst into tears.

"You fool!" Yhakobin shouted, not at Seregil but at the slave takers. "Kill him! Kill him now, but don't touch the rhekaro or I'll have your skins!"

Seregil felt the arrows that struck his thigh and shoulder with no more concern than if they'd been gnat bites. His throat hurt, too, and perhaps he was screaming. Some part of his mind was aware of other shafts hissing around him, and the shouts of the men dismounting to stop him, but his vision had narrowed to one long dark tunnel and at the end of it all he could see was Yhakobin, sitting his horse with one hand raised as if to fend off the certain death bearing down on him.

Two swordsmen dismounted to block his headlong rush. Seregil sliced the head off the first one with a single swing and plunged his poniard into the chest of the other. Not caring if he was dead or not, Seregil trampled him underfoot and kept on running.

The alchemist tried to rein his mount aside, but Seregil sprang at him, dragging him from his horse.

Throwing Yhakobin to the ground, Seregil hacked off one upraised hand, then plunged the point of his sword into the man's belly and yanked it hard, spilling his guts on the ground in his fury. He could see the man's mouth open, and guessed that he was screaming, but all he could hear now was a single clear, ringing note, too pure and piercing to come from a living throat.

He turned slowly, still caught in a nightmare. The rhekaro was standing over Alec's body, his mouth stretched in a perfect O. The sound was coming from him, and mingling with it were the screams of the slave takers and the cries of the horses as they reared and bucked.

As Seregil watched, the remaining riders fell from their saddles, screaming and bleeding from their eyes and ears and noses. One by one they went still and silent, and only when the last one was dead did the rhekaro's deadly song die away.

When it was done, Sebrahn collapsed across Alec's chest, and that pale grey little tongue flickered out, lapping at the blood on Alec's throat.

"Get away from him!" Seregil screamed. He staggered back to them, wrenching the arrows from his flesh as he went. "Can't you just leave him alone? Go suck the blood from your maker, you monster!"

Sebrahn looked up at him and Seregil saw that there were tears streaming down the rhekaro's cheeks. Seregil pushed him aside. Falling to his knees, he dragged Alec's limp body into his arms and felt frantically at Alec's throat and wrists.

But there was no pulse, or breath. Those

beloved eyes had the fixed glaze Seregil had seen too often in the faces of the dead. "No! Oh Illior, no, please! Alec!"

He shook him, and chafed his blood-soaked chest, knowing that it was useless, but unable to give up yet.

Sebrahn pulled at Seregil's shoulder and he shoved the rhekaro away. Choking back a sob, he pulled the arrows from Alec's chest. When Seregil pressed his hand to the wounds, bright blood oozed up between his fingers, but it was no longer flowing.

Only then did he notice the hot blood soaking the leg of his own trousers, and feel the pulsing wound on his inner thigh. *Ah then, they've finished me off after all. Small mercy.*

Burying his face in Alec's tangled, dirty hair, he broke down completely, not caring that they were in the open, or about the carnage Sebrahn had wrought. He could feel his own strength slipping away, and welcomed it. He'd have sat there with Alec like that until they were both food for the crows, if that damn creature hadn't kept tugging at his shoulder. Seregil tried to push him off, but Sebrahn simply wouldn't let him be.

"What?" Seregil demanded, wearily raising his head. Sebrahn was still crying, and holding something out in both bloodstained little hands, something he wanted Seregil to see.

It was another of those flowers, but this one was pure white with a golden center, and as clean as if it had just been plucked from a pure lake.

"I don't want your healing," Seregil growled, slapping it away.

Sebrahn shoved him back with surprising force and dragged Alec from Seregil's lap onto the ground between them. His silvery eyes burned with an inner light, and his tears glowed. Those pale lips moved, forcing out a hoarse whisper. "Ah-lek."

Growing weaker by the moment, Seregil watched as Sebrahn leaned over Alec and let his tears fall on the wounds. Everywhere a tear met blood, a white lotus sprang up, one after the other until Alec's chest was covered in them, like a pall. Then Sebrahn threw his head back and sang again.

Seregil thought that he would die then, like the others had, but he didn't. Instead, the piercing sound went on and on, until Seregil could feel the vibration of it in his bones and skull. One by one, the white flowers turned to light and sank into Alec's lifeless form. When the last of them disappeared, a tremendous shudder went through the body and Alec coughed.

"Alec?" Seregil gathered him into his arms again as best he could, and held him while Alec coughed and gagged, bringing up long black clots of congealed blood. When he was done he went limp in Seregil's arms and stared up uncomprehendingly at him. The death glaze was gone; those eyes were clear and blue and filled with consternation.

"I—" he wheezed, fighting for breath. "I—"

"It's all right!" Seregil was laughing and crying now, on the verge of hysteria. "You were right. Oh

Illior, you were right! He saved you. Your 'child of no woman.' You were right all along!"

But Alec clutched Seregil's arm, and shook his head. "I—I chose—*you*."

"Yes, you did!" Seregil bent to kiss those bloody lips, but a grey mist came between them and the world slid away. He smiled as he went, though, taking the sight of Alec's face with him into the darkness.

Sorrowful Journey

THE GEDRE SHIP slipped into a remote southern in-let under the cover of night. Once again, Micum and the wizard slipped ashore unnoticed, this time with heavy hearts.

They brought along packhorses, and rode until dawn, guided by the stars and the vision Thero had been given by Alec's ghost. This country was only sparsely habited, and they steered clear of the few villages and steadings they did see.

Micum prayed to the Four for Alec's shade to visit them again, but Thero could not seem to summon him, though he tried several times as they stopped to rest the horses. There'd been no sign of Seregil's ghost, either, despite the dire vision. Micum clung grimly to the hope that he'd somehow survived. Seregil always had, after all, no matter how bad things got.

The sun rose over a lonely, arid landscape like nothing Micum had ever seen. It was a dead land, with nothing green in it. He could taste dust on the breeze, and the cold wind carried scents that reminded him of temple incense. Far in the distance, the rising sun cast deep shadows across flat-topped cliffs. Apart from a few sluggish snakes, there seemed to be no life here at all.

At midmorning, Thero reined in abruptly. "I have to do another sighting. Nothing looks the same." He dismounted and sat cross-legged in the dirt with his crystal wand between his hands. "Put your hands on my shoulders. I need your strength."

Micum did as he asked and felt a strange sensation pass through him when Thero raised the wand and pressed it to his own forehead. After a moment, however, the wizard got to his feet.

Micum thought he saw the glimmer of tears in the man's eyes. "What is it?"

"Almost there. That way." Thero pointed a little east of the way they'd been going.

"What did you see?"

Thero wouldn't look at him as he climbed back into the saddle. "Nothing good."

They finished their journey in silence. Every so often Micum would feel that strange tingle again, and Thero would point this way or that, correcting their course. Never once did he give any sign that he'd seen them alive, and never once did Micum ask.

And so it was, when the sun was high and the bare white ground gave back the glare of it through the dust, that they made out the first dark specks circling in the sky ahead. Micum knew what they were.

"Thero—"

"I see," came the weary reply.

As one they kicked their sweating horses into a final gallop and closed the distance. Cresting a slight rise, Micum could see vultures on the ground, shifting and flapping in a huge circle around something there, feeding.

He rode at them, yelling to drive the carrion eaters off. They spread their black wings and retreated a little, screeching at him.

There were bodies sprawled on the ground, at least a score. Some had their eyes pecked out already, and others had their guts spilled and torn. All had short black hair and beards, and Plenimaran clothing.

At least you took some of the bastards with you, Micum thought numbly, gentling his horse when she went skittish at the smell. He dismounted and limped forward, scattering more of the birds away from more and more bodies.

The Plenimarans lay scattered in a wide circle. At its center, Seregil and Alec lay side by side, hands clasped between them even in death. A child sat slumped at their feet. Her long fair hair looked white in the midday glare. She was dressed in rags, and beside her lay an empty water skin. She had a dented metal cup cradled in her hands and that was empty, too.

"The child," Thero whispered. "Alec said there was a child, but that's not what that is!"

Micum ignored him, and the child. As he approached his friends' bodies, tears slid unnoticed down his cheeks.

They were gaunt and hollow-eyed. Dried black blood covered them both, skin and clothing alike, and the white dust had settled over them in a thin pall. Their hair was dull with it and their lips were dry and cracked. And yet they looked so peaceful, as if they'd fallen asleep together.

Thero sank down beside Alec and covered his eyes. Micum dropped to his knees beside Seregil and took his hand. It was cold.

"Oh, my friend!" Micum began the grim business of looking for wounds. Lifting away the bloody coat, he found more blood on Seregil's chest, but no sign of an open wound. As he moved to turn him, he was amazed to feel the flesh beneath his hand move. Looking up, he found Seregil's eyes open a little, clear and grey and calm.

Micum was so startled he almost dropped him.

"Ah, here you are," Seregil whispered, and those cracked lips tilted slightly into the old grin. "Alec said you'd come."

"Alec?"

"Oh Illior, he's alive, too!" Thero pressed two fingers gently to Alec's throat, then unslung his water skin and wet Alec's parched lips as Micum did the same for Seregil. "But how? I saw his ghost!"

Seregil swallowed a few drops from the water skin, then raised one finger slightly, pointing to the child. "He did it. Sebrahn." His eyelids closed again, but he was still breathing. And smiling.

Micum glanced up at the child again. It still looked like a girl to him, with all that hair. His eyes were closed and he hadn't moved, but Micum could see the long tracks of dried tears on the boy's pale dusty cheeks. Micum reached out to see if he was breathing, but Thero grabbed his hand. "Don't! That's no child. Can't you see?"

"See what?"

The child opened his eyes and Micum saw that they were the color of steel. "What is it?"

"I don't know." Thero was squinting now, as if the child was giving off a bright light that Micum couldn't see. "It has human form, but there's something else showing just around the edges—And magic! It's like a storm in him, but muted."

Sebrahn, as it was called, whimpered and crawled slowly past Thero to stroke Alec's hair. The wizard scuttled back away from it, wide-eyed.

Micum didn't doubt Thero was seeing something he wasn't, but his heart went out to the child-like thing all the same. That was, until it lifted Alec's left hand to his mouth and licked weakly at the dry blood there.

"Bilairy's Balls!"

"It's all right," Seregil rasped as his eyes fluttered open again. "He's starving. Eats..."

"Blood," Thero finished for him, looking appalled.

"Alec's. Just a little," Seregil whispered as his eyes slid shut again and his voice failed. "Please, help him. Saved us. Save him..."

"You can't be serious," gasped Thero.

"You heard him," Micum said. "He's in no shape to explain." He took out his knife and pulled Alec's hand from Sebrahn's grip. The child was surprisingly strong, but gave up with another pitiful little whimper when Micum gently insisted.

"Look at that." Micum showed the wizard the tips of Alec's fingers, all stippled with small scabs. "I guess that's how they do it." He nicked the least damaged finger and Sebrahn lunged forward, grabbing Alec's hand and sucking frantically on Alec's finger.

Micum watched in mixed wonder and revulsion. "I don't suppose you could get word to Magyana to send us one of those translocations of hers? I don't know what Seregil meant when he said this little mite saved them, but it can't be much help to them anymore. We have to get them somewhere safe, and quickly."

"Translocations don't work that way, and even if they did, the shock of the magic would surely kill Seregil, weak as he is, and probably Alec, as well."

Micum looked around, trying to ignore the loud sucking noises. "There's no shelter in sight. We'll have to make do with the tarp for tonight. Can you do more of that healing on them?"

"I can, but I don't know how much good it will do. They need a drysian."

"Do what you can. And give them more water. The child, too."

Micum left him to it and led the packhorses away from the carnage. Not far on he found a dry gully deep enough to hide the horses. He used the tarp they'd brought to make a small lean-to, spread the bedrolls, and rode back for the others.

He found Thero still bent over their friends. The strange child hadn't moved.

Thero had their dirty coats open and was inspecting their chests. "Look here!" he exclaimed, pointing to what was obviously a freshly healed arrow wound on Alec's chest. "Seregil claimed this happened yesterday."

"But that would have gone right through his heart, and a lung, too."

"I know. Seregil has a similar scar here under his shoulder, and one that went into the large artery in his thigh."

"We call that a 'man killer.' How in Bilairy's name did they survive, half-starved as they are, much less heal?"

"Seregil kept insisting that this—creature did it, though I can't get enough sense out of him to know how, and it seems to be mute."

"Never mind. All that matters is getting them to shelter."

Handling the wounded men as carefully as they could manage, they slung them each over a saddle. They had some trouble with Sebrahn when they went to move Alec. The child clung to him and hissed at Micum when he tried to pull him away. In the end, Thero had to hold him back until Micum could get Alec on the horse, then lift the struggling, spitting child up onto the horse behind him. Once there, still gripping the battered cup in one hand, he clutched the back of Alec's coat with the other.

"It's all right, little one," Micum soothed, patting the child's skinny leg. "You stay with him and we'll be safe soon."

"I'm telling you, that's no child," Thero warned.

"You heard what Seregil said. That's enough for me."

They led the horses toward the camp Micum

had set up, going slowly so as not to jostle their friends too much. Even so, halfway there the child began to whimper and squirm. Then Seregil began to moan and struggle weakly.

Micum pressed a hand firmly between his shoulders. "We're almost there. Just a little further."

Seregil's face was turned away, but Micum heard him gasp out, "So—undignified!"

"He's bleeding again!" Thero pointed out. "It's his leg."

Looking back, Micum saw bright red splashes in the dust. He halted the horse and walked around to the other side. Seregil's left thigh was soaked. Feeling carefully, he found the wound, then took off his belt and tightened it above the wound. "We'd better hurry."

"Yes. Alec is bleeding a little from the mouth."

The child grew more and more frantic as they went on, until Micum finally had to pull him off and carry him. He weighed almost nothing, but struggled all the way, reaching out for Alec and crying out softly.

At the tent, he scrabbled about underfoot until Micum and Thero had the wounded men settled on the bedrolls they'd brought. Seregil was unconscious, and Alec was in agony, coughing up bloody foam.

Micum put the child aside as gently as he could, but he persisted, tugging Micum's water skin from his shoulder. Squatting between Seregil and Alec, he filled his dented cup, then held out one little hand.

"What is he doing?" wondered Micum.

"Cut his finger," Alec wheezed. "Now!"

Despite his doubts, Micum did as he asked. As he and Thero watched, the child held his cut finger over the cup and something far too pale to be blood dripped into the water. There was a faint flash of light, and then a beautiful, dark blue flower appeared. Sebrahn scooped it out and put it on Seregil's wound. It melted from sight, leaving a pleasant scent behind.

Micum reached down and felt the wound. "It's closed up again."

The child made another flower and placed it on Alec's chest wound. Alec was still coughing blood, but he managed to get his breath long enough to gasp out, "That's how—Flowers—heal."

They watched in awe as Sebrahn repeated the procedure several times and laid more flowers across Alec's chest and Seregil's leg.

After a moment Seregil came around. " 'lec!"

Micum clasped his hand. "It's all right. He's right here beside you. You're both safe."

Alec took Seregil's other hand. "Told you. They found us."

Micum carefully undressed both of them and checked for more wounds. The one on the inside of Seregil's thigh was closed, but the skin there looked fragile and thin. The arrow wounds on Alec's chest and throat had healed more completely, but the breath still rattled a little in his throat and bloody foam seeped from the corner of his mouth.

Micum covered them both warmly and drew Thero outside.

"What do you think?"

The wizard shook his head slowly, looking a bit dazed. "I don't know what to think. I've never seen anything like that."

"But the child did heal them. He saved their lives."

"Yes." Yet Thero looked less than pleased. "I suppose we'll have to stay here until they're stronger."

"And pray no one else comes looking for them."

"I can hide us. I'll obscure this whole gully if need be."

"We should send word to Magyana and Korathan."

"I did, while you were away setting this up. She advised me not to contact the prince yet. She thinks it would be dangerous to bring that—" He pointed into the lean-to, where Sebrahn was still crouched over the sleeping men, cup clasped in his pale little hands. "To bring him to Skala until we know more about what it is. And most especially not to the Orëska House. Every wizard in the place would feel it, as soon as it got anywhere near them, and word of it would soon reach Phoria."

"You're saying we should keep this from the queen?"

"She's no friend to wizards, or to magic. I don't know what she'd do with this thing. However, I'm more concerned with what it might do. You saw those men back there. All dead, and not a mark on them. Can you imagine if this creature felt threatened in the heart of the city? No, we can't risk it. Magyana will meet us in Gedre. The khirnari has offered us temporary sanctuary if Seregil can give his word that it poses no danger."

Micum shook his head. "We both saw how this little fellow can heal. He saved their lives again right in front of us. But how could it kill all those men? It couldn't protect itself!"

"Do you have a better explanation?"

"I haven't looked yet, have I?" He went to his horse and struggled up into the saddle. "Keep a sharp eye out, and send me one of those little lights if you see anyone coming. I won't be long."

Micum's idea of not being gone long was different than Thero's. He was about to send a sighting out for him when Micum rode back into camp, looking grim.

"What did you find?" Thero asked, helping him down from the horse.

Micum sat on a large stone and stared down at his hands; they were smeared with dark blood. "There are thirty-one men lying dead back there, and all but three don't have a scratch on them, except that they'd bled from their eyes and ears."

"And the other three?"

"One decapitated. One stabbed through the heart. The third one gutted and hacked to pieces."

"In that vision with Alec, I saw Seregil running at the riders with a sword. I was sure I was seeing his death."

"It should have been. But I'd say he managed to kill those three. They were close together, and the gutted one was dressed like a noble. Seregil must have cut the other two down to get to him. But the others? Seregil didn't do that, and neither did Alec."

"Then you agree that whatever this thing is it's dangerous."

"But it didn't hurt us, not even when we pulled it away from Alec," Micum pointed out.

They both turned and looked into the shelter, where the strange pale creature was curled up between the two men now, its silvery hair spread across both their chests.

Micum sighed and shook his head. "What have you two gotten yourselves into this time?"

CHAPTER 46

At Bay

THERO SAT WITH the two wounded men that night, while Micum kept watch at the head of the gully. He'd cast a sheltering spell on the little tent to keep the wind and cold out. The heat of their bodies made it comfortable inside, and Thero was dozing when Alec started awake. Looking around in alarm, he found Seregil first and reached across Sebrahn to stroke his talimenios's sleeping face.

"He's healing," Thero assured him quietly.

Alec stared up at him. "I thought it was a dream, seeing you on that ship."

"No dream. You came to me and I saw you. It was you who guided us here." A sudden tightness in his throat made the wizard pause a moment. "I thought you were dead, Alec. I thought I was seeing your ghost. What happened?"

"Yhakobin came after us with the slave takers. There were archers. They were aiming at Seregil."

He broke off, and Thero saw his hand tighten around Seregil's. "Are you sure he's all right?"

"Yes. This odd little friend of yours is quite the healer."

"The flowers. I was hit, and when I came around, he was putting them on Seregil."

"He must have done quite a bit of that before we reached you, and he's done it a few more times since."

Alec let out a long, wheezing sigh of relief that turned into a ragged cough. "I really thought we were for the Gate this time," he whispered when he got his breath back. "Where are we?"

"Still in Plenimar, not far from where you and Seregil were—attacked. Can you tell me any more about how you ended up in Plenimar in the first place?"

"Ambushed by slavers on the road—somewhere." Alec closed his eyes.

"We tracked you that far. And then they took you to Riga and sold you, right?"

"To an alchemist. Yhakobin." His eyes stayed shut, but his breathing grew shallow and quick as more memories came to him. "Gave Seregil—to Ilar. I didn't know—didn't know who Ilar was— Thought he was friend—"

"Stop, Alec. Get your breath!" Thero urged, pressing a hand to Alec's brow with a small spell to calm him, then to his chest to heal what he could. When Alec's breathing grew easier, he asked, "Who is Ilar?"

Alec shook his head. "Long story. Ask Seregil, if he'll tell you."

"All right. What about this creature?"

Alec frowned up at him. "Sebrahn. He's named Sebrahn." He coughed again and Thero helped him take a sip from the water skin. "He's my child . . . of no woman. 'kobin made him."

"That's enough, Alec. Stop now."

But Alec was still struggling to talk through the coughing fit. "A rhekaro—Mine! He can heal."

"So I've seen," Thero murmured, adding a bit to the spell to quiet him.

"He can do more than that," Seregil rasped, opening his eyes. "You were dead, Alec. He brought you back."

Alec looked over at him, then up at Thero again. "That's impossible. I was just hurt. Right?"

"I know what death looks like. I know what a dead body feels like . . ." Seregil's voice cracked. "Alec, you died. You saved my life doing it, and you *died*!"

"I'm afraid that's probably true, Alec," Thero told him.

"It is." Seregil wiped his eyes on one bare arm. "They killed Alec. I killed Yhakobin. His archers shot me. Then Sebrahn, he—He *sang*."

"Sang?" Alec touched the sleeping creature's shoulder. "I don't remember."

Seregil let out a ragged laugh. "You were still dead then. He killed the rest of them with his song. Then he spoke your name, Alec, and he brought you back with his tears."

"Yhakobin used my tears—to make him."

Thero patted his shoulder. "That's enough for

now. Sleep, both of you. I'd like to examine the rhekaro."

Alec's eyes flew open and he clutched at Thero's arm. "Don't you hurt him!"

"I won't, I promise." Thero held out his hand to the creature and forced a smile. "Just come out by the fire, won't you, so I can have a better look?"

Sebrahn looked to Alec, who gave Thero another warning look, then nodded. "It's all right, Sebrahn. Go with Thero."

Only then did the rhekaro let Thero lead him out into the firelight. As soon as Thero stopped, Sebrahn hunkered down and stared back into the lean-to where Alec lay.

Thero sat down beside him, letting himself feel the weird energy coming off the rhekaro like heat. It was obvious that the others did not see what Thero saw when they looked at this created thing. They all spoke of a child and seemed to think he was helpless and fragile.

But Thero saw the jagged aura of scintillating white light that surrounded that little body. It shifted and danced like winter sky fire, as if it was trying to take on some larger shape. Hesitant to attempt any direct magic, Thero closed his eyes and did a sighting instead, but the image remained the same.

Despite everything he'd seen so far, however, he sensed no evil in it, or any immediate threat. The energy that surrounded it was strong, but at the same time felt somehow empty. If he hadn't seen the splayed, lifeless corpses still lying out there on the plain, he'd have guessed that Sebrahn was harmless. Seregil spoke of a song, but Thero doubted that's what it had really been.

He sat quietly with the creature until the rhekaro grew used to him and studied him in return. It was unnerving, having those strange eyes watching him so intently. There was some degree of intelligence there, but it was nothing human or 'faie.

He heard the crunch of footsteps nearby, and the rattle of falling pebbles.

"Hello in the camp," Micum called softly, letting Thero know it was him. He sat down by the fire and looked at the two of them. "How are you getting along?"

"Fine, so far. Now that you're here, though, I want to try something. Pour a cup of water, would you? Set it down where Sebrahn can reach it."

When Micum had done so, Thero stuck a finger into the fire and pressed it briefly against a hot coal.

Micum grabbed his wrist and yanked his hand away from the fire. "What are you doing?"

"It's all right." Gritting his teeth against the pain, Thero held the blistered finger out for Sebrahn to see. "Will you heal me?"

The rhekaro looked around, then picked up a small sharp stone and used it to cut the end of its forefinger. A drop of white blood oozed out and fell into the cup, making another dark flower. He scooped it out and pressed it to Thero's burn. As soon as it touched him, the wizard felt a wonderful coolness. The magical flower disappeared like mist against his skin, leaving that same sweet fragrance on the air. The burn was completely healed, except for a bit of shiny skin where it had been. Thero inspected it closely. "Amazing. And Seregil claims he brought Alec back from the dead with his tears."

"Do you believe him?"

Thero gazed at the rhekaro, watching the nimbus of light around it shift and swirl. "Yes, I do."

Micum lifted the rhekaro into his lap and wrapped a clean bit of rag around its cut finger. "Thank you, little one, whatever you are, for helping my friends."

Sebrahn gazed up into Micum's face for a moment, then curled up against his broad chest and closed its silver eyes. Micum cradled it gently, stroking its long hair as if it was one of his own children.

Thero stared into the fire for a long time, absently rubbing a thumb over the healed burn.

Micum and Thero kept watch by turns over the next two days and watched their friends grow stronger faster than they had any business doing. Alec fed the rhekaro several times a day, and now and then it would insist on making another of its flowers for him or Seregil.

During that time Micum had the story from both of them, and more than once, trying to piece together the series of events.

"So because you've got the northern 'faie blood in you, you were the only one this alchemist could use to make these rhekaro things?" asked Micum.

"That's what Yhakobin said," Alec replied, huddled in his blankets by the fire wtih Seregil.

"Ilar told me the same," Seregil told them.

"And what about him? It sounds like he had a hand in all this, too, but I've never heard you speak of anyone by that name before."

"I don't speak of him," Seregil muttered, looking away.

Alec caught Micum's eye and shook his head slightly.

Now that they were stronger and alert, Thero told them what they'd learned in Virésse of Ulan í Sathil's role in their kidnapping.

"Not Phoria?" asked Seregil, looking more disappointed than surprised.

"So it would seem."

"Well, I don't suppose he has any great love for me, considering. And he knows that since I've been cut off from my own people, they have no standing to take revenge against him for it. How much did you tell my sister, Thero?"

"Only that you and Alec have been found, and that you're safe."

Seregil glanced around the gully and gave him a wry look. "I don't call this safe. Yhakobin is an important man, and claimed he was making the rhekaros for the Overlord himself. Sooner or later, someone else is going to come looking for us."

Unfortunately, Seregil was soon proven right.

Thero was at the edge of the gully the following morning, watching the vultures circle, when he caught the distant jingle of harness and the muffled thud of galloping hooves. He sent out a wizard eye and discovered twoscore or more riders coming from the north, making straight for where they lay hidden. As they came closer, he saw for certain that they were soldiers, and that several men dressed in black were leading them. One of them drew Thero's attention more than the others; even through the spell he could feel the cold, nasty energy of a necromancer.

He hurried back to the lean-to and smothered their small cooking fire with a spell.

"What's going on?" asked Micum. Seregil crawled to the front of the lean-to, poniard in hand.

"Soldiers," Thero told them.

"How many?"

"Too many." Thero drew his wand and reinforced the obscuration spell he'd woven over the gully. To anyone outside it would look like level ground. "We should be safe unless someone accidentally falls down here." *Or unless their necromancer notices my magic,* he thought, but chose not to worry the others for now. Seregil probably knew, anyway.

Alec joined Seregil at the mouth of the tent, one arm around Sebrahn, the other hand grasping his black dagger.

"Neither of you is strong enough to fight yet," Micum warned.

"We're not going to just sit here and let them take us," Seregil replied. His eyes and Alec's were haunted and dark with purpose.

"No one's taking you," Micum promised. "Stay here and save your strength until it's needed."

"Wait!" Alec pushed the rhekaro forward. "Go with them, Sebrahn. Protect my friends."

The rhekaro went at once to Micum's side.

"I'll take all the help I can get," Micum said, shouldering his bow and taking Sebrahn's little hand in his.

Thero followed Micum back to the lip of the gully and watched the search begin.

"They have a necromancer with them."

"I'd be more surprised if they didn't."

Some men dismounted to inspect what remained of the corpses while others, trackers most likely, fanned out in all directions. Micum had covered their tracks, but they still held their breath as several men started in their direction.

Micum reached for his quiver, but Thero stopped him. Then, forking two fingers at the men, he whispered a spell. A moment later, they wandered off in the opposite direction.

"What did you do?" whispered Micum.

"Just planted a thought or two. They'll report that there's nothing of interest in this direction."

The ruse seemed to have done the trick, until a darkly clad figure broke from the group and strode in their direction, accompanied by several swordsmen. It was the necromancer, and he knew they were there. Thero could feel the man's mocking gaze on him already. "It's the rhekaro. It's like a beacon to him! My magic can't hide it. Stay down."

Thero stood and cupped his hand in front of him. He spoke the spell for thunder and released it, feeling the magic leave his body in a great rush as a shock wave made the air in front of him ripple like water.

The spell struck down the swordsmen, but the necromancer was still standing, coat whipping around his legs.

"Orëska!" he called out. "Is that the best you have for me?"

Micum drew his bow and let fly. The arrow sped true, but shattered before it could find its mark.

"Save those for the soldiers. This one's too powerful," Thero snapped. He took a deep breath and summoned a fire spell. This one took an even greater toll; he would not be able to keep this up much longer, but he didn't have much choice at this point. At his command, a wall of fire roared out, scorching a broad swath of ground as it went. This one was more far-reaching and was greeted with screams of pain and the terrified cries of horses.

But still more men came on, and the necromancer with them, flicking tongues of flame from his fingertips. He was close enough for Thero to see that he was grinning as he pointed a hand at the ground beside him.

A huge, dark, misshapen form rose from the blackened earth, like a waking nightmare. It had the body of a huge boar, but a man's face with jutting tusks, twisted in agony.

"What in Bilairy's name is that?" gasped Micum.

"I have no idea, but it's bad," Thero whispered,

terrified. Behind the necromancer, more armed men ran forward over the bodies of their fallen comrades.

"I make that about forty men," Seregil gasped, one arm around Alec as they staggered up to join them, still clutching their knives. "I say we split 'em, and leave the ugly pig for Thero."

Micum caught them as Seregil stumbled. "You damn fools!"

Alec sank to his knees, one hand pressed to his chest, but grinning. "Might as well die here as there."

"Suit yourselves." Micum drew his bow again and concentrated on bringing down as many soldiers as he could. Their archers were shooting back now.

The necromancer gave some command and the nightmarish creature bore down on them.

"Tell me you can stop that," Seregil demanded.

Thero raised both hands, clutching his wand, and shouted the strongest protection spell he knew. Throwing out every last ounce of power he possessed, he imagined a limitless stone wall and projected it at the creature.

It didn't even slow down. Leaping into the air, it came down on them like a storm, knocking Micum and Thero backward down the gully. As Thero threw up his arms, trying to ward off the fetid darkness closing in around him, he caught a flash of white against the sky overhead, and suddenly the air was filled with a single crystal note. It made his skull throb and his teeth ache, but he hardly noticed as he watched the monster halt, then throw back its hideous head and dissolve in a cloud of stench and flies.

Micum was on his feet again, bleeding from several wounds and shouting something that Thero could not hear over the continuous deafening sound. He was pointing up at the edge of the gully.

Seregil and Alec lay sprawled halfway down the slope, bodies tumbled together by the force of the monster's charge. But Sebrahn stood facing the enemy for them, singing that one clear note as his silver-white hair coiled wildly about his head.

Micum grabbed Thero by the shoulder and together they scrambled up to help the others. The rhekaro's song ended just as they reached Seregil and silence covered them like snow.

Micum dropped to his knees beside their comrades, but Thero took Alec's fallen dagger and climbed up to see what Sebrahn had done.

Every man lay dead, and foremost among them was the necromancer. Thero approached him slowly to make sure.

The man lay on his back, wide-open eyes reflecting the vultures that were already heading this way. Blood had burst from his ears, nose, eyes, and mouth, just as Micum had described. Thero nudged him with his foot, but the body was limp and empty, its power gone.

Satisfied, he went back to the others. Seregil was leaning against Micum's shoulder. Alec sat holding the rhekaro. It lay limply in his arms with its eyes shut. Its skin had gone from pale to grey, and it had a frail, starved look about it. Its closed eyes were deeply sunk in their sockets, and its arms and legs looked thinner than ever. Thero could hardly see the aura that had been so strong before.

"He used himself up." Alec pricked his finger and let a few drops fall between the rhekaro's lips, then gave Seregil a worried look when it didn't respond.

"Is he dead?" asked Micum.

"Hard to tell," Seregil murmured.

"It's not," Thero said. The little edge of light around the rhekaro grew brighter as it fed on Alec's blood.

Seregil turned and surveyed the scattered dead. "They didn't know."

"Know what?"

"What Sebrahn can do. Not any of them. Yhakobin would never have charged blindly at us the way he did if he'd suspected what might happen, or this necromancer, either. They knew we had him, but they didn't fear him."

Alec let out a small sigh of relief as Sebrahn stirred. "Yhakobin kept saying the ones he made were failures."

"There are others?" asked Thero.

"One, and he destroyed it, trying to figure it out. He was looking for something else. Ilar said something about a poison, but he was probably lying."

And there was that name again. "What else did he say, about it being wrong?" asked Thero.

Alec though a moment, stroking Sebrahn's wan cheek with his thumb as the thing continued to feed. "When the first one was made, Yhakobin was concerned that it didn't have wings."

"Wings?"

"Never mind that," said Seregil. "Two groups have found us, so there's no reason to think there won't be others. We need to get to that boat of yours, and fast."

"I can ride," said Alec, though he was still the weaker of the two.

Thero looked back at the fallen soldiers again, then down at the exhausted creature curled in Alec's lap. "We couldn't hold off another attack like that one."

"Then come on!" Seregil struggled up to his feet and clutched at Micum's shoulder to steady himself. "Someone tie me onto a horse."

Sanctuary

THEY WAITED UNTIL nightfall to leave the gully. A cold half-moon silvered the scudding clouds and made the frosty ground sparkle.

Seregil hadn't been joking about being tied to his horse. His wounds and Alec's were healing, thanks to Sebrahn, but the flesh was still fragile. He still tired quickly, but Alec was critically weak, and rode double with Micum, tied in place against the man's back. Sebrahn hung in his sling on Thero's back. The rhekaro had not woken up since the battle, though he had taken nourishment several times in his sleep.

They reached the desolate bay just before dawn as rain rolled in off the water. Thero had sent word ahead to the captain, and they found a pair of lookouts from the Gedre ship waiting for them in the bushes above the shingle.

When everyone was safely aboard at last, Seregil finally collapsed, and woke up sometime later, tucked into a narrow bunk in a small cabin.

Another bunk was built into the opposite wall and he could just make out Alec's pale braid and a long hank of Sebrahn's silvery hair above the blankets.

Every joint and muscle protested as Seregil went to them and slipped in behind Alec, wrapping an arm around both of them.

Alec gave him a sleepy smile over his shoulder. "There you are, talí."

"Here I am, talí. You do know that Sebrahn is going to have to learn to sleep in a bed of his own?"

Alec wasn't amused. "I'm worried about him. He's so still."

"He's made from magic, Alec, and he's used a lot of it, helping us."

"You think he can use himself up?"

"I don't know. He probably just needs more rest."

Alec found Seregil's hand and grasped it tightly. "You're really all right with me keeping him?"

Seregil kissed the back of Alec's head, glad that the thick braid had been spared after all. "I owe him my life, and yours. Whatever he really is, he stays with us. You have my word."

He listened as Alec's breath slowly evened out, but found he wasn't sleepy anymore. He stayed where he was, thankful that they were finally safe enough for him to savor the feeling of Alec's body, whole and alive, pressed close to his. His hand rested on Sebrahn's shoulder. The rhekaro's skin felt colder than usual, and had since it faced down the demon creature.

After a little while, however, Sebrahn sat up, the blanket slipping from his narrow shoulders. The bones of his chest and shoulders stood out in harsh relief under his white skin. He regarded Seregil for a long moment, then touched Alec's cheek and whispered in his faint, scratchy little voice, "Ah-lek."

"He's sleeping," Seregil whispered.

"Sleeeee-ping."

"Yes, that's right." Seregil blinked up at him, wondering if it was only his imagination that Sebrahn looked somehow more real, more 'faie.

They reached Gedre without incident other than bad weather. Sebrahn did not speak again, not even to Alec.

As they sailed into port in the rain, Seregil was glad to see Magyana and his sisters, Adzriel and Mydri, waiting there with the khirnari to meet them.

"Oh my dear boys!" Adzriel exclaimed, kissing first Seregil, then Alec. "And you, as well." She smiled at Thero and Micum. "You have the thanks of my clan for bringing them back. Come, let's get you in out of the weather."

Alec was still a little unsteady, so it was Micum who carried Sebrahn off the ship, closely muffled in a cloak.

Seregil stayed close to Alec. Thero and Magyana hung back, talking quietly.

Riagil had sent a carriage for them and soon had them all safely behind closed doors in the clan house.

Thero nodded to Alec. "It's time to show them."

As Alec unwrapped Sebrahn and smoothed his tousled hair, Magyana said nothing but regarded the rhekaro for a long time in silence.

"He can heal?" she asked at last.

Alec filled a cup with water and showed her the trick. She lifted the blue flower from the water and smelled it, then set it aside without comment. Taking the rhekaro's hand in hers, she stroked the hair back from his face.

"Well?" he demanded, unnerved by her silence.

"In all my travels, I've never encountered such a thing," she replied. Rising, she left the room, gesturing for Thero to come with her.

Thero followed her into the next room and closed the door. She cast a seal on it, ensuring that they would not be overheard.

"What do you see when you look at it?" she asked.

"I see an aura of light, and the hint of another form."

Magyana nodded, pressing her folded hands under her chin and closing her eyes.

"What do you see?" Thero asked, as the surge of her power filled the room.

Without opening her eyes, she replied softly, "I don't understand how it is possible, but I see a dragon."

Epilogue

WINTER CAME EARLY this year, before the end of Erasin. Looking out from the shelter of the domed *colos* on the roof of the clan house, Seneth ä Matriel Danata Hâzadriël admired the way the moonlight glistened on the new fallen snow. From here she could see the entire valley below, her beautiful fai'thast, and the warm glimmer of lights in the villages and steadings. Her lands stretched from the head of the long valley to the gleaming peaks of the Ravensfell Pass far to the south. Here and there, in the highlands above, distant fires marked the villages of their neighbors, the Retha'noi.

How long had it been, since she'd slept a whole night through? Weeks, it seemed. Night after night she woke from a sound sleep, feeling like she'd forgotten something very important. She usually ended up here, while the household slumbered below.

Tonight she found her gaze straying to the Pass

again. Twin watch fires burned there, steady and bright, but the sight gave her little comfort.

Just then Uri knocked at the doorframe behind her. "Khirnari, you have a visitor."

"At this hour?" She turned and found her old friend, the seer Belan ä Talia, standing just behind the servant, and with her a stooped little Retha'noi man. Seneth did not know him, but recognized the witch marks that covered his face and neck under his wild grey curls. The shoulders of their cloaks were dusted with snow, and the hems heavy with little ice balls. Both of them were shivering.

"My friends, come warm yourselves!" Seneth urged them downstairs to the great hearth in the hall. "Uri, fetch shawls and hot mead for our guests."

"Thank you, Khirnari," the Retha'noi said as he warmed his bony little hands over the flames. More witch marks, the gift of the Retha'noi mother goddess, covered them and what she could see of his arms. She'd never seen so many on one witch, and wondered how she'd never met him before.

Uri hurried back with one of the young cousins of the house, carrying the shawls and steaming cups. Seneth wrapped both her guests up snugly on the bench closest to the hearth.

Belan wrapped her hands gratefully around the mug of honey wine. "I would not have disturbed you at such an hour, Khirnari, but I've had strange dreams lately, and tonight this witch man, Turmay, came to me with the same vision." She paused, and Seneth saw that her hands were shaking. "I believe a white child has been made in the south."

For a long moment Seneth could only stare at her friend; this was the last thing she'd ever expected to hear.

"And so I saw," Turmay said, nodding emphatically. "It meant nothing to me, but the Mother guided me to friend Belan."

"What did you see?" Seneth asked.

"A child that is not a child, Khirnari. One with a dragon in its eyes."

Seneth clasped her hands together in her lap. "How? How did this happen?"

Belan looked away uneasily. "I can think of only one possibility, Khirnari."

Seneth closed her eyes as old pain gripped her heart. Twenty years had passed since Ireya ä Shaar's name had been spoken aloud in this valley. She could not bring herself to say it now. "It isn't possible! The blood was mixed in half parts."

"But I believe something has happened," Belan told her. "What shall we do, Khirnari?"

Seneth gathered her will and hardened her heart. "The *Ebrados* must hunt again."

About the Author

LYNN FLEWELLING'S ONGOING Nightrunner series and her Tamír Triad have received worldwide acclaim and are, at last count, in print in thirteen countries.

Peripatetic Maine natives that they are, she and the love of her life, Dr. Doug, have currently come to rest in Redlands, California, where they have developed a deep appreciation for palm trees, feral parrots, earthquake monitoring, and going to the mailbox barefoot in February. When not slaving over a hot computer, she can be found at her Live Journal, and at the Flewelling Yahoo! Group. In addition to sundry ramblings, she frequently posts updates, cruelly teasing snippets of works in progress, and answers to readers' questions about the books, including how to pronounce those words she makes up.

Website: www.sff.net/people/Lynn.Flewelling
Live Journal: otterdance.livejournal.com

Fans of Alec and Seregil fear not!
Your favorite nightrunners will return
for a thrilling, all-new adventure in

The White Road

LYNN FLEWELLING

NOT EVEN THE best nightrunners can escape
the past.

Unwilling to abandon the mysterious and enigmatic Sebrahn—Alec's unnatural child of no
mother—Seregil and Alec have no choice but to go in
search of the only people who might know the true
meaning of its existence: the Hâzadriëlfaie. Bad
enough is the Hâzad's reputation for killing outsiders—including Alec's father. But even worse, enemies from all quarters are intent on not only taking
Sebrahn for their own ends, but reclaiming the only
source of creation for more: Alec.

Seregil, the self-professed disbeliever in fate,
now finds himself and his small band of friends in-
exorably bound by the echoes of their collective
pasts as they are forced to choose between loyalty
and conscience, peril and peace, and perhaps even
between mercy and murder. . . .

Coming in Summer 2009
from Bantam Spectra.